"GIRLS *like me,*" *said Diana,* "*are out of luck when it comes to marriage. We haven't got homes and money and dads to mix up cocktails, or mothers to buy us pretty clothes. Sometimes I think I'd marry any-one just to* live."

THEN, quite suddenly, there were three men in Diana's life. Solid, red-headed Peter who was studying law and wor-shiped Diana across her grandmother's boarding-house table. Neal with his careless charm who had played *Young Woodley* in stock and had Hollywood ambitions. And Bruce, wealthy, cos-mopolitan—the perfect gentleman.

One of them held her heart, all of them helped her to happiness. *Three Men and Diana* is one of Kathleen Norris's most human stories.

Three Men and Diana

THREE MEN AND DIANA

BY
KATHLEEN NORRIS

PALO ALTO EDITION

New York
P. F. COLLIER & SON CORPORATION
BY SPECIAL ARRANGEMENT WITH
DOUBLEDAY, DORAN & COMPANY, INC.
GARDEN CITY, NEW YORK

Three Men and Diana

CHAPTER I

"HO! I'M GOING to be a politician better'n Henry Gates ever was!" Peter Platt chanted, hanging upside down on the backyard fence.

Diana Carmichael and Emma Mae Tauber looked at him in strong distaste. He was a noisy big boy from across town; he had burst in upon their Saturday morning play of "Flower Ladies" without invitation. Why didn't he go away and play with the other big boys?

"I'm going to be in a candy store," Emma Mae could not resist telling him primly.

"I'm—I'm—I'm—now——" Diana stammered. She was only five; Emma Mae was a year older, and Peter unbelievably old. But she had to tell him. "I'm—I'm—I'm going to have a velvet dress—and it'll be black, and I'm going to come downstairs with—with—with—now—pearls on!"

"Who ever did?" Peter demanded, red-cheeked from his exertions, facing her challengingly.

"I don't know. I'm *going* to!" Suddenly Diana thought that they were laughing at her; that she had made herself ridiculous. She began to scream heartbrokenly; she stumbled, screaming, toward the kitchen and her grandmother's arms.

Emma's grandmother took boarders, and Diana's grandmother kept a lodging house. There was a great difference and distinction here, and Emma was made proud by it, and Diana correspondingly humble.

Both houses were down at the end of Mason Avenue, where the town trailed out into empty lots, and railway fences, and the willows and mallows and shabby old thin oaks that fringed the deep dry creekbed. Emma's grandmother's house faced west, and so got the rising sun in the high-priced back bedrooms, and had a cool afternoon kitchen. The forlorn remains of a once elegant garden surrounded it; it had rose bushes and pampas grass, brick walks bordered with old stout and porter bottles, and even a latticed arbor harshly embraced by woodeny old grapevines. The house had a name, too, a name that was dimly painted in chipped and fading letters over the round wooden top of the gate: "Arbor Villa."

Emma's name was Emma Mae Tauber, and her grandmother was old Mrs. Pawsey. Diana's name was Diana Chamberlain Carmichael, and her grandmother was old Mrs. Chamberlain. The two little girls had been neighbors and playmates ever since they could remember anything definite at all, but Emma's vague earlier impressions were of a back parlor in Brooklyn, with folding doors, and Di had hazy and evasive memories of a ship's deck, and a white coat, and seams of soft black tar that could be poked with a small finger.

The Pawsey house was no credit to the flourishing and pretty town of Bayhead, but at least it preserved something of dignity and pretense in its decay; it held itself erect, like some shabby old polite relative at a rich door; its patchy lawns were occasionally raked; its window curtains were occasionally changed.

But the Chamberlain house had sunk beyond all such niceties. It had no shame left. Dingy, peeling, unpainted, with boards gone from its chipped steps, and poles missing from its front porch railing, it sagged into an open confession of poverty and neglect.

At its windows, between draggled soft mud-colored lace curtains, feeble, hand-lettered signs flourished, grew flyspecked, and fell into drunken attitudes; were gone. "Cas-

sidy, Modes," "Piano," "School of Latin Languages," all
had their moment, all disappeared. "Rooms without Board"
was always there, and there had been a brief exciting era
when the front parlor windows had shown a placard with a
stretched human palm outlined upon it in red and green,
with stars and crescents and scorpions for a border. This was
the invitation "Oracula the Mage" sent forth to the world
to have character read, destiny unrolled, the future opened
like a book, lost fortunes restored, and prosperity assured.

Oracula, clad in a red robe, with a turban wound about
her greasy curls, had lurked behind the sign and the dirty
curtains, but Diana saw her every morning in the kitchen, by
a special dispensation from Gram, brewing her coffee in a
tin pot, doubling up her soft roll to dip it in the said coffee,
glancing interestedly at the headlines of Mr. Larks's paper
that was always courteously left by the little undertaker's
assistant for Gram to read, and muttering, "Ain't it the
truth?" to pretty nearly everything that was said. So Oracula
held neither mystery nor charm for Diana.

After Oracula left, crying about unpaid rent, and fatter
and more untidy than ever, the Coggleses took the front
parlor and backed the old iron double bed with the dingy
brass balls on the corners right against the folding doors.
The Coggleses and Amy and Pauli slept in the big bed, and
Rudolph and Leontine slept on the lounge. The baby had a
washbasket to herself.

This arrangement made the back parlor, where Diana and
her grandmother slept, rather dark and gloomy; Oracula,
perhaps in return for the breakfast-cooking privileges, perhaps in anticipation of the fact that she was not going to
pay any rent at all, had left the folding doors sociably open.
And before that Diana and Gram had occupied both rooms.
But now they needed the two dollars weekly that the Coggleses paid.

The seven Coggleses lived mysteriously in the front parlor

for a long time. All the years when Diana was eleven, and twelve, and thirteen, and fourteen, they were there; Evelyn, the new baby, was born there. Mrs. Coggles was a lean, quick, painfully eager little woman who would put down the nursing baby and hurry to help Gram with grocery packages, or take the broom from Papa's hand when he started to sweep down the front steps. She wanted to be friendly, to be of use, but she was so thin, so tired, so burdened that she had little time or strength to spare. Gram often generously urged her to cook in the kitchen; feeding seven— feeding eight—she ought to have more hot food. But Mrs. Coggles rarely accepted the offer; no one knew what the Coggleses ate. Sometimes Mr. Coggles brought home food in a paper bag; there was never any garbage left from which its nature might be judged. The little Coggleses,—all small in build, with white flax hair and frightened sea-blue eyes,— were always as hungry as little cats; everyone in the house knew they didn't have enough to eat. But when Diana Carmichael shrieked to all and sundry that the ice cream cart was down the street, and went speeding forth with streaming tawny hair to secure a "comb," the young Coggleses proudly withdrew into the one dim, dark-papered room that was their home; they didn't want any ice cream, sank you, they always had ice cream evvy day.

The back parlor had one angled window, looking darkly out on the dank neglected shrubbery that had once been roses, lemon verbena, and evergreen hedge, and that was now only a dry half-dead tangle of growth, and upon the flat gray side of the "Eureka Garage," which had been closed for years. Dust and spider webs within made into mirrors such windows of the Eureka Garage as were not broken; nailed against its empty door was an old sign: "This desirable corner to lease or for sale." But everyone knew that Leoni had built his garage without the proper municipal credentials, and that whoever bought or leased the desirable corner would have to begin operations by tearing down the garage building.

Empty, illicit, useless, it still shut out from Diana Carmichael's dreary bedroom every possible glint of sunshine, and most of the daylight as well. Diana, at ten, had spiritedly suggested to her grandmother that they turn the kitchen, cold and forlorn and grim as it was, into their bedroom and make the back parlor the kitchen. But Gram only looked puzzled at this; who ever in this world ever heard of folks sleepin' in their kitchen?

Behind the back parlor was a big closet with a window, where Papa's narrow cot was shoved up against a sink, under shelves; Diana's and Gram's clothes hung in here, above a dusty rabble of old boots and rubbers on the floor. Pop smoked in bed and reached up to put his cigar stubs on the dry sink, and Diana, making his bed the next morning, daintily scraped them onto a piece of newspaper and carried them away.

The kitchen came next, a big gaunt room with three high windows. It faced northwest and never had any morning sun or winter sun. It had sun only in the burning summer afternoons, when nobody wanted sun anywhere. There was a rusty old stove in one corner with a three-burner gas stove on top. Gas was supplied through a meter in the basement, and Diana had to creep down there, every day or two, and put a quarter of a dollar into the meter. The signal for this was the flickering and waning of the flame in the stove burners under the kettle or frying pan; sometimes one of the lodgers gave her the quarter, but almost always it was Gram who opened her flat pocketbook with spotted old lean fingers and handed out the silver.

The cellar was unfloored; broken utensils and rubbish had been flung on the rough hummocky earth; the place smelled sourly of cats and ashes. It was lighted by two dim, dirty, quarter-windows level with the earth. Diana hated to go down there and had once asked the gas man if she could not reach the meter in some way from the front of the house, as he did when he read it once a month, under the street steps. But the gas man had merely said, "Listen, you be a good girl and I'll take you to dinner some day if you don't tell my wife!" and there had been no change.

She and her father and grandmother cooked their meals in the kitchen, occasionally hindered or helped by various lodgers. Gram disliked having them ask this favor, but she did occasionally concede it, when they were nice and steady pay, or if there was sickness or a bottle baby. Sometimes a new lodger was surprisingly, refreshingly brisk about it: "Here, dear, run down and put this quarter in the meter, for pity's sake, and ask your Gram where we can get cream in this God-forsaken place!" and then Diana flew about happily, assisting this prosperity and assurance eagerly, glad somebody in this world wasn't counting and grudging pennies. But as a rule such lodgers did not remain long with Gram; they found rooms elsewhere in a little while, rooms with an alcove to herself for Ethyl, and even perhaps a combined bathroom and kitchen.

Most of Gram's lodgers were old persons, thin, shriveled little old women subsisting somehow on pittances as shriveled and thin as themselves. Diana came to know their apologetic little coughs on rent days, their eager, feeble laughter at any humorous opening her grandmother gave them, their pathetic little journeys to the offices of busy men whose grandfathers had once owed their grandfathers seven dollars, their confidence that the garnet brooch or the second American edition of Dickens was worth untold money.

"If I get my seventeen dollars on Uncle George's policy——" the cracked, explanatory voices said appealingly. "If my niece sends me five dollars for my birthday like she usually does——"

Otherwise, Gram's tenants were young workingmen; mys-

terious lodgers who came and went in a general flurry of
unmade beds, dirty clothes lying on dirty floors, and smells
of cigars and cheap whiskey in cheap bare rooms. Sometimes
they stayed a month, sometimes three; Gram, who got two
dollars a week for most of the rooms, did not like transients.
"Some of you boys must have been born in railway stations!"
she would say good-naturedly when they made too short a
stay.

Gram liked them all, and they liked her, but almost before
she knew anything else Diana knew that Gram did not like
Papa,—despised him, indeed, although she never said so, to
Diana at least. And Gram hated Mr. Coggles for a "Socialist
Turk." He was not a Turk, of course; he was as innocently
blond and small as his children, but all Socialists were Turks
to Gram. And that was one thing she had against Papa: he
loved to talk about capitalists and trusts and the people's
rights and the people's money.

"Rights!" Gram would say, dealing vigorously as she
talked with the end of the loaf, the skimpy cut of butter,
the stained sugar in the blue china bowl, the blue milk in
the bottle. "I'd like to rights some people into paying their
bills,—I'd like to rights 'em into getting a job, now and
then!"

But this was manifestly unfair, for Papa did have jobs
now and then. Once he had a job taking the census, and
could walk into anyone's house and ask questions; "yes, and
they have to answer 'em, too!" Diana exulted to Emma Mae
Tauber. Then he had another job as watchman on the new
post office when it was being built, and twice he got jobs
at the dog races. Papa knew everyone at the race track, for
Diana once went with him to see the swift slender hounds
run, in the bright afternoon sunlight, between the whitewashed fences, and to hear the band, and watch the crowds
and the blowing flags, and have her hot dog and her ice
cream and her pop bottle with the rest. She liked the flatter-

ing fact that these men knew her father; their good-natured voices, "Hello, Doc; that your kid? Hello, Carmichael,—hello there, Doc!"

"Why do they call you 'Doc,' Papa?" her patient little voice persisted on the way home in a crowded trolley car. "Why did that fat man sucking the pencil call you 'Doc'?"

She got no answer. Something had silenced her father, driven him into himself; he was brooding. "Damn that damn' tout!" he muttered more than once, sullenly, under his breath. "That's all he is—a damn' tout!"

Afterward in the home kitchen there was an icy opening between Gram and Pop. Gram began by saying, "I thought you were to get ten dollars, Mr. Carmichael?" Pop muttered something like "What of it?"

"This of it," Gram persisted, in a high, strained tone. But Diana heard no more. Her throat was suddenly hot and her stomach deathly cold, her mouth was filled with water, and her forehead beaded with sweat. The hot dog, the pop, the cone claimed their dreadful hour; Diana rushed for the open—the woodshed—the shelter of the old mallow bushes at the edge of the arroyo in the backyard.

This arroyo made the rear premises fascinating to Diana and Emma Mae and all the other children of Mason Avenue's most forlorn block, without in the least enhancing, for Gram's comfort, the real value of the lot. Far at the back, beyond a string of empty sheds and broken fences, the old deep waterway cut across the yard; it had long been dry and choked with a light growth of willow and mallow and milk weeds and tar weed and Queen Anne's lace. Beyond it were the backs of the houses of Niggertown, Bayhead's poorest quarter, peopled with an impoverished and constantly changing population of colored families, Mexicans, Italians, Irish, always noisy and crowded and shabby, with mud-crusted old open cars parked at bare open kitchen doorways, and dogs lying about like flies in the springtime sun.

And between Gram's boundary and the beginnings of Niggertown was the dump, going down right into the creek-bed and over and among the mallow and willow bushes and the tar weeds. Carts came to the dump every day, and cans and ashes rolled like a slow cascade down the banks; sometimes big rusty bedsprings slithered to the very bottom of the arroyo, or a washboiler, with holes in its thin bottom, went down with a spring. But most of the rubbish dribbled lazily over the brink and descended in little trickles; a can still wearing the picture of a bright tomato turning and turning here, a sticky bottle clanking, then silent, and clanking again there.

Diana and Emma Mae and certain other girls and certain boys used to scramble lithely over the dump in small childhood and secure all the bottles, and wash them in one of Gram's sheds, and sell them shrilly and shrewdly to the rags-bottles-sacks man. They then raced to the grocery, where candy was cheaper than at the candy store, and bought a pound of "broken mixed" for fifteen cents. And over the grimy bits of taffy, caramel, hard sugar peppermints, odds and ends of lemon and butterscotch and chocolate suckers, handled and divided into complete grayness and stickiness by their hard little hands, they squabbled happily for the remainder of the afternoon.

CHAPTER II

DIANA's grandmother had brought to her sixties one remaining passion and one remaining hope. They were solely concerned, they were centered in, Diana. She would have died at any moment since the child's birth to serve Diana; she had in living no other object than Diana's welfare.

Back of the ashes and the dump, the fortune tellers and the big sweaty lodgers, the dirty curtains, the bleak halls that smelled of carbolic acid and whiskey and boiling cabbage, Gram had memories. She never spoke of them; they seemed no longer to be a part of her, but they were there.

They encompassed vague, long-ago summer Sundays, and herself, Addie D'Arcy, and Sis' Maggie Lou, in white tarlatans, and a green lawn stretching to a scallop-topped pole fence with a white creamy La Marque rose burgeoning along it. Sis' Maggie Lou singing "Bright things can never die, e'en though they fade," and all of them laughing over "Just Before the Battle, Mother" and "Titwillow." Joe Brownlow putting the letters down at Addie's hem and saying "There's a male at your feet, Addie." How they had laughed!

There had been a dance at old Mare Island, and a yellow parasol with the sunshine pouring lavender light through its taut silk, and Belle's new friend, Lieutenant Chamberlain. Miss D'Arcy, this is Beauregard Chamberlain; how do you do?

Oh, picketed garden of roses, and summer sun shedding lavender blots through a parasol upon the spread white tarlatan! And Aunt Mary Lee calling everyone in to a lunch of soda crackers and cold beef and cherry pie!

After that there had been a carriage wedding, more roses for Miss Adelaide D'Arcy, Mr. Beauregard Chamberlain. And then a bride in the Palace Hotel, down in the city, laughing fondly at all the torn tickets found in his darling coat pocket.

"Why, Beau, do you go to horse races?"

"Haven't you evah been to a horse race, deah?"

"Nevah in mah life."

"Well, then, we'll go tom'ow."

And to the race they and the yellow parasol had gone, and what fun it had been to win! Of course one couldn't always win, and of course,—but of co'se, Beau dearest, it was only sensible not to miss a day, for that might be the lucky day! They were going to have a deah little baby; they needed money.

After a while Beau had resigned from the army,—no money in it, he had told Addie. She didn't suspect for years that he had been asked to resign. She had gone on dancing and singing and trusting him, and presently they had moved to a boarding house, and little Adelaide had been born, and there had been no money,—and Beauregard junior had been born. And then Beau had disappeared,—poor Beau, he was so proud!—and Addie had wept away her beauty and had taken over the boarding house when old Mrs. Pendleton Ralston had died.

Little Adelaide, the precious daughter, had always been a joy. But young Beau had been what his mother called a "trarl" from his very babyhood. His father had turned up again; Beau senior was the type of husband who would always reappear at unfortunate moments; he had needed money, and after a while young Beau had begun to need it, too.

Mrs. Chamberlain, grim and enduring, and pretty little Adelaide, round-eyed and scared, had supported the men bravely. The older woman, for pride's sake, had paid their gambling debts, their racing debts. Her boundless charity had found excuses for them; "the saloon keepers had drugged them," they were both lovely when they were "themselves," she and Adelaide had to be "very good" to them. She had seen her best patrons leave, her house go down and down, she had never complained. The older Beau had sued her for his imaginary share in her property; she had never blamed him. She had blamed the "crooked lawyer" he had employed. Her thin, nervous hands had opened her purse again and again. "Will this be enough? It's all I happen to have today."

She had had Adelaide, gay and sweet and dancing; she would live on for Adelaide. Adelaide and her mother had left San Francisco, had gone to Bayhead, the sleepy, oak-shaded little college town that lay thirty miles south of the city, down the Peninsula. They had opened another boarding house there, and for a while it had been a happy time for both mother and daughter, with nice boys of Southern families drawn to the house and falling in love with Adelaide.

Beau senior had died; Adelaide Chamberlain had been a widow. But Beau junior had lived and had presently been brought home, late one night, by a man named Frank Carmichael.

Old Mrs. Carmichael, philosophical and resigned enough in her recollections so far, always felt her soul shrivel away from the memory of that fatal night. The sudden lights, the familiar sight of poor Beau, collapsed and unconscious, the handsome dark young fellow helping him, and Adelaide, delicate and eager and grateful, at twenty-seven, thanking Mr.—Mr. Carmichael?—for his kindness to her poor brother. . . .

It had all been the work of only a moment. Adelaide, tired and indignant, awakened from sleep, had been saying "It's only someone bringing Beau home!" at one minute; in the next she had been glowing, shy-eyed, ecstatic. There had been no room for protest, for fight. She and Frank had met with the rush of falling planets. They had been married just six weeks later.

Old Mrs. Chamberlain would not think about those days. She blamed herself bitterly for not having known at once, from the beginning, that any friend of Beau's, met at the races, lucky at the races, was no match for her pearl of girls. Oh, he had been handsome and dashing, and the nicest set had taken him up enthusiastically enough, as they always took up any new man for a while, but that had not been enough—that had not been nearly enough! There were so many better young men about; men who were serious, successful doctors and lawyers and business figures in the business world of the city now. Any one of them would have been better for Adelaide, would have appreciated her, guarded her, made her happy.

He—Frank Carmichael—had done none of these. He had broken her heart, that's what *he* had done! No money, no home, no position from the very first, and Addie coming back to her mother, pale and patient in ten short months, with her lovely figure twisted all out of shape, and her purse empty, and her quiet, dignified story that Frank had "had to go to Kentucky."

Addie had been two years in her grave, and the gold-headed Diana was toddling about Grandma's kitchen, jabbering and singing to herself, when her father came back. He had been a member of Mrs. Chamberlain's establishment at intervals ever since.

CHAPTER III

ONCE, when Diana was ten, her grandmother bought her for twenty cents a school sweater coat at the Children's Convalescent Home Annual Rummage Sale. It was a smart garment, dark blue, with a belt and pockets, and it was almost new. Diana went to public school, but she passed the aristocratic gates of the Rutherford Private School on her way, and on the third afternoon of her proud possession of the blue sweater some of the girls of about her own grade, the upper seventh, and of about her own age were standing there.

They laughed and whispered together when they saw Diana coming along, and somehow, although she had no warning, she felt a little cold and a little sick when she heard their laughter. She walked along steadily, but her vision was blurred and her hands were wet.

Presently she heard it, louder and louder, in their rising voices, "Doesn't go to Rutherford but wears a Rutherford sweater! Doesn't go to Rutherford but wears a Rutherford sweater!"

Diana's heart came into her mouth; she felt the sick terror and fear of the hunted. She walked along.

"Look!" said a big twelve-year-old named Consuelo Newbegin. She sprang to Diana's side, and Diana began to cry and said, "You leave me alone!" "Look, there's my 'nitials still in the coat!" Consuelo called, twisting the collar of Diana's sweater open, and showing the neat monogram, "C. S. N." "Consuelo Smith Newbegin!" shrilled the owner

14

of the title triumphantly. "She bord it at a rummige sale,—
she bord it at a rummige sale!"

"You oughtn't to wear a Rutherford coat, little girl," said
another little girl severely. Diana knew her; she was
Minna Porter. She was Judge Porter's granddaughter.
"Those coats b'long to Rutherford," Minna went on, "and
girls that don't go to Rutherford have no business to wear
them."

Diana, crying, trying to dry her eyes on her cuff, had
jerked away. Now she began to run, weeping the heartbroken
tears of childhood, breaking into loud sobs as she reached
her grandmother's kitchen and her grandmother's arms.

They were always there, ready, tender, comforting. Her
grandmother gave her bread and apple sauce and analyzed
the situation for her sensibly. And Diana, her face washed,
and her hair spatted back with water, and her fury cooling,
ate her bread, drank her milk, gulped her stammered words.

"Those little girls are very rude and naughty," said Gram,
patiently. "But that doesn't matter to *you*. You're Diana
Chamberlain Carmichael; you don't have to do anything rude
because *they* do."

"But I didn't, Gram!"

"No, but it would be rude to me, and silly, too, for you not
to wear that nice coat. Consuelo's mother bought it in one
store for her, and I bought it in another for you; there's no
difference.

"You've got your own way to make, Di," her grandmother said then, and said often afterward, as the years
went by. "But if you've got character, and courage, and
patience, you'll go a lot further than the Newbegin girl and
the Porter girls!"

Diana doubted it. But she did her best and graduated with
great glory from the eighth grade, entered high school with
honors, and left Emma Mae far behind her.

Not only because Emma Mae was stupid and Diana was

smart. But because Emma Mae, at a precocious fourteen, went frankly boy-crazy, and worried and rather disgusted Diana by her incessant flirting and smiling, her rouging and powdering, her murmurs of kissing and petting. This was a hidden world to Diana, and she looked about for companions to take Emma Mae's place.

Oddly, excitingly, she met them in the Rutherford girls, and found, as she told her grandmother eagerly, that they were not snobs at all; they were terribly nice girls, almost all of them. Connie Newbegin and Elinor and Patsy Palmer came to the high school dances, and once Joan Rowley herself and her brother from Yale came; Diana met all the girls' brothers there, and through the brothers met the sisters, and so some of the happiest friendships imaginable began.

The Rutherford girls were generously concerned that she should take her last two high school years at Rutherford, and Diana hinted it more than once to her grandmother. Gram was unresponsive, although she seemed troubled, and was absent-minded for a day or two. Then a miracle happened, and Miss Benchley of Rutherford sent for Diana, and suggested that, as Diana in the public high school had been distinguished by extraordinary honors in both French and algebra, she attend Rutherford in return for certain hours in coaching the boarders in those studies.

So Diana became a Rutherford girl and perhaps the happiest of all the two hundred. She loved the beautiful school; the brick building and the oaks, the mellow sunshine on green lawns, the blazing flower borders, the cool deep rooms.

Proud and slim and tall at fifteen, she took her position boldly; she was there helping Mademoiselle with the French, and Miss Foulks with mathematics. It was Miss Benchley's generosity. And the girls adored slim, proud, beautiful Di Carmichael for her poverty and her pride. She went to their homes in the afternoons; they had crackers and milk and cake and whatever else they could filch from the big iceboxes, and consumed their feasts in big clean pantries where shining plates and glasses lined the walls and shining faucets dripped into empty white sinks.

Diana caught awed glimpses of the glory and luxury of their homes; enormous dim dining rooms, great stairways, rooms lined with books, rooms where maids were sewing. Then she walked back from Chelsea Crescent or Newbegin Park, and across College Avenue, and down Lincoln Street as far as the awnings and racket and smells of the free market, and so on into Mason Avenue and home. She saw nothing amiss; her first Rutherford year knew no clouds.

When she was almost seventeen Miss Benchley talked to her seriously one day about college. Diana surely wanted to go on with her studies, and Rutherford would recommend her strongly to the board, if she would work to gain the required credits in her last high school year. Diana saw stars; the world was all stars when she walked home that day, and she could hardly keep her feet on the sidewalk. College! Why, even Elinor wasn't sure of making the requirements. And she, Diana Carmichael, could do it easily,—*easily!*

Bayhead was a college town, and all the girls there hoped to get into Lucas Memorial University. But they were handicapped by sex, for the Lucas regulations admitted only four hundred girls—only about sixty women to the freshman class—while keeping their male enrollment close to three thousand. It was not fair, of course, but it made it all the more thrilling for the girls who did get in, and it was accolade to Diana Carmichael to hear, through the all-powerful Miss Benchley herself, that she had a chance. The granddaughter of a Mason Avenue lodging-house keeper, and she had a chance!

It was beginning somehow to be dreadful, and it was becoming steadily more and more dreadful, to go from the ordered beauty of Rutherford to the yard, the kitchen, the dinginess and dreariness of home. Diana never brought her friends home; it was tacitly understood that that was not feasible. Even if Elinor or Joan offered her a lift in the car, she managed to spare herself and them the embarrassment of the contrast. At those times Di would ask them to drop her at the market or the library; "I've got a couple of errands for Gram."

But when she walked home alone there would be no evasion. She must turn the shabbiest corner of the market, —the corner where men were dumping decayed vegetables and empty crates,—and cross the wretched broken end of Lincoln Street, where the beginnings of Niggertown cut in, and go down Mason Avenue past the poor little houses that said "Rooms" and "Meals" and "Garage for rent" and "Housekeeping Apts.," and past the dry neglected gardens and broken fences and gaping doorways, and so to poor Leoni's empty garage, and up over a bulge in the sidewalk where the flagging was worn and broken, and along the dry, flattened grass to Gram's gate,—only there was no gate,— and around the corner of the house, and into the kitchen door.

But Diana saw nothing of all this on that great day two months before her seventeenth birthday, when Miss Benchley first talked to her of college. Filled with excitement and hope, she rushed into the house to find her grandmother stemming strawberries on a hot May afternoon. The broken window shades had been drawn at the western windows, but the kitchen was hot, and the merciless light battered at the crevices and streamed in bars thick with motes to the worn, oily boards of the floor.

"Oh, good, strawberries!" Diana said, with her own friendly smile for the three forlorn old women who were keeping her grandmother company. Mrs. Petrie, Miss Corrigan, Miss Gooey. The Coggles children were swarming in the backyard, ducking their tow heads at the old pump; three quite big boys were sitting in the shade of the oak, idly talking.

"Gram, I've just been talking to Miss Benchley!"

"Get yourself a saucer, Di, if you want some of these now."

"No, I'll wait for dinner. It's all I want for dinner, too. It's too hot to eat!"

"I don't believe you'd have it any hotter than this in the East," Miss Gooey observed. Miss Gooey was responsible for the card that said simply "Violin" from the upper front bay window. She had thin, nervous, very clean hands and bore herself with a certain professional dignity.

"I don't know's you would," Mrs. Petrie, who had never been further east than Stockton, agreed. She fanned her creased, fat, shining face with a newspaper. Her chocolate percale wrapper, sagging open, showed a bagging full throat.

"Gram, Miss Benchley says she thinks I could make Lucas!"

"Why, for pity's sake, Diana!"

"She said so."

"Yes, but my gracious! That's more than she's promised lots of those girls who've been going to Rutherford since dear knows when——"

"I know. But I'm an A scholar, Gram!" Diana laughed triumphantly, her spread hands and dancing eyes apologizing for the boast even while she made it.

"Well, you don't tell me, Diana," her grandmother said slowly. She stopped hulling the strawberries.

"College!" the girl sang rather than said.

"What possesses you you want to go to college?" old Miss Corrigan asked harshly. "They'll take your religion away from you, that's what they'll do. My sister's boy went,— nothing'd do but Royal made college. He hasn't amounted to a row of stringbeans ever since!"

Diana laughed delightedly. She knew Miss Corrigan had

a stomach ulcer; she was always cranky because she was always hungry; no matter what she ate she suffered agonies afterward. Now she looked darkly at the red berries.

"If I touched them berries I'd all but have a convulsion," she said.

"No, but Gram, what do you know?" Diana, stealing a small round red fruit, biting it in half, looking at the bite, and finishing it with one more clip of big white teeth, asked in an undertone.

"College, you mean?"

"Because listen, I could walk. It isn't fifteen minutes. And I'd know a lot of the freshman class next year."

"College!" Mrs. Chamberlain repeated thoughtfully.

She carried the berries away; came back with a gray damp rag and wiped the table. It was her dining as well as her work table. It was covered with worn red oilcloth, patterned in black-and-white worms; upon it always stood the sugar bowl, the spoon glass, the salt and pepper shakers in an old revolving caster. Now, with the damp rag, Gram wiped all of these, wiped the tablecloth where they had been standing, replaced them.

"Just bein' able to walk there isn't all there is to college, Di."

Diana felt a first shock. Her tone fell a little.

"I know, Gram. But *college!* I've always wanted to go."

"Well, we'll have to see."

"It means a profession, Gram, instead of just a job!"

"I know, dear. And I'd be glad enough as far as that goes."

"It goes all the way!" Diana exulted, catching her around the lean bowed old shoulders, kissing her joyously. "I'm going to be a college woman!"

"I remember when my Grandmother Willis came over to tell my mother she'd give me two terms at Jarvis Musical," Miss Gooey observed, in a frail, bloodless, sympathetic voice.

Her faded, bulging gray eyes filled with smiling tears. "Well, was I a happy girl!"

Diana, glancing at her, felt for a second time a little chill ripple over her. Miss Gooey was so old, so gentle and feeble and poor and unsuccessful; one wouldn't want to follow Miss Gooey's footsteps,—down from youth and Jarvis Musical Academy, through the years of pupils and lessons and timid recitals in parlors, down—down—down to Mason Avenue, and the upper front room at Mrs. Chamberlain's.

After their supper of bread and tea and strawberries Diana and Gram went out on the front steps and sat there in the cool. Diana was silent for sheer hope and happiness, and lost in dreams. She would be a college girl, coming and going as all the girls did, with books and dates and plans filling every day to the brim . . .

Gram was rather silent, too. The Coggleses were out in the front yard; Mr. Coggles had moved a chair out there for his wife and the baby. The little Coggleses were all very quiet and obedient when their father was around; he whipped them at the slightest hint of insubordination or quarreling. He had only to ask, "What did I hear you say, Pauli?" to have Pauli burst into terrified tears in anticipation of punishment before the poor draggled little blonde girl could even speak. Among their six, the Coggleses had only one boy; Diana thought they spoiled him, and were far gentler with him than with the girls.

Tonight Mrs. Coggles was sitting as still as a statue; she was like a creature stricken to stone by the burden and heat of the day. The child in her arms was motionless, but the father was smoking a pipe and occasionally conversing with little Mr. Larks, the undertaker's assistant, who was smoking, too, and seated on an upturned box.

Across the-street at Mrs. Pawsey's various persons were also sitting on the steps; they had turned on the house radio for the Amos an' Andy period, and the hoarse low voices of the actors were pouring out into the heavy dusk. Emma Mae, Diana noticed, was not there; she was probably at the movie with one of her boy friends. Diana had not been intimate with Emma Mae since her terms at Rutherford had begun, and tonight, with the glory of a college career so close to her, she felt superior to Emma Mae. She had left most of her childhood chums far behind her already; it would not take her long completely to outdistance the granddaughter of the house of Pawsey.

"I believe I'm ambitious, Gram."

"Well, it's a good thing to be, Di,—in a way."

The street lights shone down brightly on the trampled grass of Gram's front yard and the humped sidewalk before Leoni's garage. The little flax-headed Coggleses gathered about a moth that had fallen wingless to the path; his velvet body flopped and struggled wildly beneath their sea-blue, curious eyes. In the western sky, beyond the dump and the railroad, red color still shone in a great dim fan against the gathering dark. Diana stretched her lithe young body on the steps, yawned. There was no one to whom she could talk exactly as she wanted to talk. She wanted somebody young in whom to confide, with whom to share her excited thoughts, tonight.

"Di," said Frances Sellers, a tall, deep-voiced girl from the house beyond Emma Mae's, "how about coming uptown and having a milk shake at Sticky's?"

"Oh, I don't think so," Diana answered promptly, instinctively.

"Oh, come on!"

"Oh, I don't think I will tonight, Frankie. I'm awfully tired."

"I offen wonder where you get all your money for sodas, Frances," Miss Corrigan, sitting up on the porch in the dark, said sourly.

"Lissen, it isn't my money, it's somebody else's money!"

Frances said, with her loud laugh. "There's always some freshie glad to pay for it, isn't there, Di?"

"Don't you go!" breathed Gram, pushing her foot against Diana's hip, as Diana sat on the step below her, close to her knee.

Diana knew she would not go with Frankie to enter the bright big candy shop, where the fans were buzzing, and look about for hospitable young men. She marveled that she had ever done it; realized suddenly how far she had advanced in fineness,—the real Rutherford fineness,—since she had gone uptown on a hot summer night a year ago with Frankie.

She had not really liked the adventure, exciting though it had been. There had been two young sailors there in the candy store, nice rosy boys in their blue jackets and round white caps, and they had instantly made friends with her and with Frankie. They were lonely; they had come down to have dinner with an aunt, and the dinner being all over, and conversation being exhausted by half-past eight, they had drifted uptown, as the girls had, for possible amusement and companionship.

They all had had ice cream and had sat at one of the wet-topped sticky tables enjoying it and one another. But to Diana at least the occasion had been fraught with uneasiness and a sort of vague shame; these were nice boys, of course, and she was a nice girl, and Frankie was a pretty nice girl, but—but somehow she had been very glad when they all turned down dark Lincoln Street, and she could murmur bashful good-nights, and escape. Diana remembered looking out across the street later and seeing that Frankie still had the two sailors engaged in laughing conversation at her gate. It had made her very thankful somehow to be safe in the dim odorous comfort of the back parlor, with the bed-lounge drawn out and the gas lighted.

And remembering it all, she knew that she would not go

uptown with Frankie tonight, or any other night, ever again. It cost her nothing to let Frankie discontentedly depart without her.

Presently Emma Mae and two tall, ungainly boys came across the street, through the hot shadows and the bright shafts of light, and sat with Di on the steps for a few minutes. The boys were restless and muttered, between deep awkward bursts of laughter, of "the flickers" and "Sticky's." They wanted to "boom."

"Come on, less get going!" one of them kept saying. The other, or Emma Mae, returned punctually, "Less not and say we did!" and there was laughter.

Diana joined in all this to a certain extent. But in her heart the magic word "college!" was singing like the clapper of a bell, and her thoughts were trying to fight free to a vision of a slender girl in a—a brown tweed suit with a little soft brown tweed hat, coming and going among the arcades and quadrangles of beautiful Lucas University, meeting men,— big brown athletic college men, not uneducated raw boys like these of Emma Mae's,—and having them talk football and junior prom and chem lab with her! The warm spring night seemed to quiver with beauty, promise, youth, joy.

"Di, I want to say that you seem to be real sensible sometimes," her grandmother said, when Emma Mae and the boys had gone away.

"What was sensible then, Gram?"

"Your tellin' them you wouldn't go uptown."

"Oh, that!" Diana's voice was amused, happy. She went off into a dream.

"And sendin' that Frankie about her business, too. I don't trust that girl."

"Oh, *that!*" Diana murmured dreamily again. "I'm wondering if there's any chance of college, Gram," she confessed presently.

There was a silence.

"Oh, that's it?" her grandmother said, after the pause.

"Miss Benchley was so wonderful today, Gram. She said, 'Diana, you could do great things with yourself, dear, if you would. You could be almost anything,—a teacher, a director, a lawyer, even. We want Rutherford to be very proud of you!'"

"Well, Diana," the patient voice behind her said thoughtfully, "you've got good blood."

"I'll work so hard, Gram!"

"I'd like you to have one year of college, first."

"Oh, but I *mean* at college!" The girl's slender body turned in the shadows, and her grandmother could see a surprised flash in her eyes.

"Well," said Adelaide Chamberlain, after another little pause, "you've got your senior year at Rutherford first. We'll see what happens then."

Diana looked keenly at her face; she could make nothing of her grandmother's expression, in the gloom; she turned back to her dreams. The dreams came to be more and more absorbing and her actual waking life more and more of a dream.

CHAPTER IV

"WHAT are you going to do, Di?" Joan Rowley asked.

"To do?" Diana stopped in her swift addressing of envelopes and sat back, smiling. Joan was school president, this senior year, as anyone might have predicted she would be, even from the hour that little smiling Joan had entered the lowest kindergarten class at Rutherford, thirteen years before. But close after Joan, as star of the May Festival, as an A scholar, as leader in dramatics, came Diana Chamberlain Carmichael, of Mason Avenue.

"Yes. I mean—with yourself, Di."

"After college? There's four years of that, you know."

"Of course I know. That is, if you take it all."

"Oh, but why not take it all?"

Diana's splendid eyes were opened to their widest in surprise. Joan laughed.

"Well, I mean to take it all," she said.

"Oh, but so do I."

"I didn't know."

Diana did not stop to analyze it, but she felt somehow a trifle uncomfortable that Joan should imply that she would not stick to college,—if that was what Joan *had* implied. What else could she have implied? Joan didn't talk idly or do anything that was not admirable; she was the most wonderful girl in Rutherford, or in any school. She could very probably go to any one of the Eastern colleges if she liked: Smith, Vassar, Bryn Mawr. Diana idolized Joan; everything that Joan did was perfect in Diana's eyes. She was almost a year younger than Joan, but even the explanation

of Joan's being a whole year late in graduating was thrilling; "there was my year out, in Switzerland, for my French."

So of course Joan spoke perfect French, although Diana
usually got higher marks for grammar and composition.

Joan at eighteen was small, compact, extremely pretty in
a dark clear winning fashion; dark eyes smiling, exquisitely
carved mouth speaking precisely and prettily, rich soft hair
trimly bound. At Rutherford all the girls wore costumes
alike: plain blue jackets, blouses of white, pleated skirts of
white or olive green, olive green coats. Only their silk ties
showed their class rating, and the seniors monopolized a
brilliant vermilion that set off the green and white beautifully. Diana, long-legged and shabby and tawny-headed at
seventeen, was like a tousled puppy circling about Joan's trim
Persian-kitten neatness.

"What are *you* going to do, Joan, when you graduate?"

"Oh, Lucas, of course!"

"But I mean after college?"

Joan mused, and Diana prompted:

"Have a coming-out party?"

"Oh, horrors, no!" Joan protested, raising clear-penciled
brows. "I'd hate it. I don't like—" the girl went on con-
scientiously—"I don't *like* the idea of being a butterfly. Besides, I'll be twenty-one when I graduate, Di; too old for a
début!"

"Is it?" Di asked, wrinkling her nose.

"You know it is!"

"I don't," Di reminded her, smiling, "know anything
about it!"

"Well, it is," Joan said, after a glance.

"You'll marry, Joan."

"No," Joan answered quickly, with another of her earnest
looks, "I won't. I don't believe I'll ever marry, Di."

"Joan, they'll all be after you! Look at them already."

The other girl shrugged this off.

"College boys!" she said. "No, I think my ideals of marriage are too high, Di. I really do. It wouldn't be a question of—of falling in love——"

"Oh, no!" Diana agreed quickly in the pause. "It wouldn't be a question of falling in love!"

"It would be a question—" Joan glanced about the deserted office at Rutherford, where she and Di were addressing announcements for the Christmas Masque—"It would be a question of ideals, Di," she said, very low.

"I know," Di agreed in the same tone.

"I don't say this to everyone. I don't say it to my own mother!" Joan confessed. "But marriage is sacred to me."

"I know."

"But I shall find my work!" Joan said, with an uplifted look.

"Of course you will!" At such moments as this Diana fairly adored Joan.

Joan stretched a brown slim hand, as smooth as satin, and laid it on Diana's hand.

"And you must find yours," she said seriously.

"Oh, I will!" Again Diana was just a trifle uncomfortable under the smiling, the loving, reminder. There was something about all this that she did not quite understand. Joan sometimes moved into an exalted air whereto Diana could not follow. "My problem——" she blurted out suddenly, and was still, her face flushed.

"I know it's hard, Di!" Joan said, in quick sympathy.

"Well, it is hard," Di admitted, with a little vexed laugh. "You know how we live—where we live! My grandmother and I share a room on the ground floor. She's been an angel to me all my life,—I've no mother, you know."

"I know your parents are dead, of course."

Diana let the sentence stand; it was as if she had not heard it. This was flagrant disloyalty to Papa, but it was the better way.

"Poverty isn't disgraceful, Di," Joan's sweet young earnest voice said prettily.

"No. But—but it does make difficulties!"

"You mean," Joan began, her own face reddening, "about making Lucas?"

"Oh, no, not that. My grandmother's tremendously proud to think that I can—that I *may* do that. But it's—oh, everything!"

"I do think at least I'd try for a room of my own!" Joan said in her reasonable, bright helpful way.

Diana was thinking. The big mansard-roofed front room at Gram's was never rented; it was not even completely plastered or furnished. But it was high and airy, and a girl with paint and burlap and ruffled calicoes might do wonders there. At Rutherford they were always doing charming inexpensive things in the decorative art department; shellacking benches and stenciling on linen. Miss Benchley prided herself on her practical domestic courses.

At the first opportunity she spoke to Gram about it. But Gram gently, regretfully, refused.

"I couldn't climb all those stairs, Diana."

"But Gram, you wouldn't have to! I mean, just for *me*."

"I couldn't let you sleep up there alone,—not with so many men coming and going in the house. It isn't wired for lights, anyway, Di, and there's no water on that floor."

The dream died; the light went out of Diana's face. Her big "studio" room, with burlap on the walls and checked red calico at the windows, faded away into nothingness. She could not have her books and her writing table, her wide couch and reading lamp up there in heavenly solitude and peace at the end of her busy college days. She had no writing table, no lamp, no couch, no burlap, to begin with. She must go on sleeping with Gram on the folding couch in the back parlor and doing her studying in the kitchen after the dishes were washed at night.

Up to Christmas of her senior year at Rutherford everything was somehow inspiring, splendid, amusing. But after Christmas, as June drew nearer and nearer, with commencement and commencement frocks and flowers to think about, life became increasingly perplexing.

The contrast between her friends' lives and her own, their homes and hers, fretted her more and more. It had not troubled her at all, at first; it had been glory enough to know Joan and Patsy and Connie, to go to Rutherford at all, and wear the white middy and the pleated green skirt. But now she could not forget it.

Joan and Elinor and Connie had their own luxurious rooms in their own homes, of course; their own bathrooms, big closets where all their frocks and blouses and coats were neatly ranged on hangers; their shoes alined in little slanted frames below. From their talk Diana had glimpses of big bath towels, scented soaps, fragrant toilet waters; clothes that went regularly to tailors and cleaners. There were Japanese butlers, finger bowls, candles, flowers. All the girls took these things for granted, as they did the smart little open cars in which they raced about the tree-shaded streets of Bayhead and the horses they rode at the club on Saturday mornings.

Diana must do without all this. Her struggles to keep her tawny thick soft hair brushed, her school clothes in order, her hands nice were unaided. At Gram's house even a bath was a matter of chance; a good many persons used the two bathrooms; in the hours Diana could be at home she did not always find one free. If she did, there was always the important question of hot water.

To balance all this she had only her own will. Diana drank eagerly from the sources of knowledge and culture at Rutherford, and she knew that she could conquer the world, if she would. The will to believe, the will to do, the will to dare. She searched for their beginnings in her own character; they must be there, she would put them there.

"Diana Carmichael," said Miss Fotterel to Miss Benchley, "is changing. You see it, of course?"

"My dear Alma," Miss Benchley returned gently, "am I not here to see how the girls develop?"

"Well, of course!" Miss Fotterel hastened to concede. "But I think I have never seen any girl grasp—pick up— assimilate things as rapidly as Diana. The way she dresses her hair, now, her speech, her hands,—everything. She seems to me,—I realize her unfortunate background, of course,— but she really does seem to me to be one of our finest girls."

"I think she is,—you remember that I always have thought so. And if she passes the Wellesley and the Smith examinations," Miss Benchley said complacently, "it qualifies Rutherford, and that is what I have had in mind all along."

"Poor child, I don't suppose she could afford to go to either?"

"I don't know that she can afford to go to Lucas,—even living at home. But Diana," the head mistress said, "has character. She has ambition. She should go a long way."

"Poor child, I often wonder if she realizes how handicapped she is."

"I don't believe she does. She always seems in the highest spirits, and very natural and simple with the other girls. If I could," added Miss Benchley, "I'd help her in some way."

"Dear Miss Benchley, as if you *didn't* help her!" murmured the lion's jackal.

Miss Benchley liked praise, but she liked to deserve it, too. She sent for Diana, when Liberty Somers left for an Eastern school, and gave Diana the white blouses and pleated skirts Libby had left behind her. She recommended Diana to Mrs. Sturgess when Benita needed coaching in arithmetic, and Mrs. Sturgess gladly paid Diana for helping Benita.

But even with these helps commencement loomed menacingly. The dress, the shoes, the flowers for which a two-dollar charge was made in pale blue ink on every girl's bill, —these were bad enough. But besides there was the year book,—three dollars a copy. Diana's picture was all through it, with the dramatic group, the dance group, the senior officers group, the basketball group, and finally, or rather to begin with, as class president, yell leader, and chairman of the school board of governors. She must have a year book! Some of the girls' fathers were giving liberal donations to the year book, but possibly there would be an assessment all round the graduating class to pay for it. And whence would that come?

More, this class always made a gift to the school,—a map, a globe, a set of books, a fountain or chair, and made a lesser gift to Miss Benchley, of money, at commencement. Miss Benchley, in her speech of acceptance, usually gave the money to the Convalescent Home, but once she had asked the girls' "permission" to donate it to the fire sufferers of Clay Park.

Then there were presents for fellow graduates, and for loved teachers. These were small,—handkerchiefs, compacts, books; the girls agreed that one dollar apiece, or two at most, and no more, should be spent on these gifts. But the graduating class alone numbered more than thirty, and there was a staff of twenty teachers at Rutherford.

"Gram, you're coming to see me graduate?"

"Not until June!"

"No, and this is only March," Diana laughed.

"Yes, I guess I'll have to get there to see you graduate."

"What would you do if you didn't make Lucas, Diana?" her grandmother presently asked her.

"Oh, but I will. You don't know quite *how* you know," Diana said confidently, "but you do!"

"But supposin' you didn't, dear?"

"What would I do? I'd cry all night!"

"Well, you'll cry overnight about something before you get through!" Mrs. Chamberlain said. Diana laughed again.

But she was not happy; underneath all the thrill of last months at the beloved school she felt constant uneasiness. If someone would give her a hundred dollars! If she could be *sure* of having the right shoes and the right dress!

CHAPTER V

THE SPRING rushed on. Easter was past, and the girls of
Rutherford settled down to weeks of stern studying; nobody
wanted to flunk, and everybody was in imminent danger of
it. Diana had to practise for the May Festival, when the two
hundred girls of the school as fairies, Indians, sibyls, cory-
phæi, gypsies, would all dance on the green. Diana was
leader; she danced with the others, and alone; she carried
the responsibility, and she loved it. She had a dress as the
Queen of the Gypsies, and another as the Queen of the
Woodsprites; they cost very little—they were made by
the girls themselves during the long spring afternoons.

Her father had not been at home for several weeks; she
could not help wondering and hoping sometimes that he
would return with good news; a job, money, prospects. It
seemed improbable, but Diana was naturally optimistic, and
she included him in her dreams.

However, some five or six weeks before graduation, he
returned with an unusually depressing story; there was no
work anywhere; the race track to which he had gone seeking employment had been closed, and his traveling bag, with
all its contents, had been stolen.

"It's the capitalist theory, my dear," he said to Diana, sitting on the front steps in the warm gloom of an April night.

"That's right, too!" agreed Ernest Coggles. A newcomer,
the red-headed clerk from the drugstore, rolled over on the
grass and listened to them. His name, Diana knew, was
Peter,—Peter Something-or-other; a nice boy, but not exciting.

"But what *is* the capitalist theory, Papa?"

"The theory is," the last speaker put in swiftly, "that if some man was rich enough to buy up all the bread, and charge us five dollars a loaf for it, we'd all starve to death!"

"The theory is that if men got jobs, and worked six days a week, women could take a day off now and then!" May Rogers said.

Miss Rogers worked in the Bayhead Hardware Store and lived with her sister, Beet, in what had once been the library, dining room, and servant's bedroom of the Chamberlain house. These rooms matched the front and back parlors and the kitchen where Diana and her grandmother and the Coggleses were established, and completed, with the square wide entrance hall and the back passage, what had originally been a spacious lower floor. The Rogerses kept their bare apartment very clean and managed to pay their bills; they worked day and night; Beet taught the upper sixth at the Horace Mann and had a political economy class in night school; May reported at the hardware store every morning at eight and walked slowly home at half-past five.

The Rogers girls were respectively aged forty-seven and forty-nine. Beet was the younger, and deferred respectfully to May in most things, but May considered her sister a prodigy of intelligence. Both women were lean, spotted, graying, with clean nervous hard-worked hands and big teeth. They were cheerful and spirited, laughing a great deal when they talked, exposing stretches of gum, congratulating themselves upon their maiden state.

Years before they had had a hard-drinking father, a hard-drinking brother, and a paralyzed and semi-idiotic mother. All these burdens kindly Time had lifted; the Rogerses were saving money now and were going to have a cottage at Carmel some day. They worked grimly, tirelessly, for that halcyon hour. Phil and Pa and poor Ma had used the best years of their lives; but there was a golden sunset left, and they kept their faces turned toward it.

In summer they went for two weeks to Carmel and looked at little unpainted three-room shacks,—a nice backyard to this one, and an adorable breakfast ingle to that. Imagine, for thirteen hundred! They noted with excited approval the previous tenant's little devices. "Look, May, she's got a lot of blue china in here!" "Look, Beet, if this isn't cute,—the firewood in this Chinese chest!"

Both May and Beet were devoted to Diana, whom they had watched like two admiring aunts from babyhood, and they held Diana's grandmother in real affection and esteem. But for Frank Carmichael they had nothing but suspicious and scornful looks, and they openly sneered at Ernest Coggles.

"He'd much better get steady work and feed those children!" May would say sternly. "What does he know about Rockefeller and Morgan and such men!"

Beet was not as talkative as May. But tonight, in answer to Ernest Coggles's outburst, she observed dryly:

"Political economy says differently."

"Oh, is that so?" Ernest asked quickly.

"You'd ought to study it, Mr. Coggles."

"I don't have to study it! In my country," said Ernest Coggles, "the children know more than the professors know here! What do they know? Nothing! We need a revolution in this country, and by God, we're going yet to get it!"

"If you know that," May Rogers, stirred to anger at any hint of challenge to Beet, observed neatly, "it's a wonder you wouldn't go in and get some sleep!"

"We won't ever have a revolution," Frank Carmichael said, in his amused lazy voice. The red-headed boy from the drugstore laughed but did not speak.

"Don't you think so, Papa?" Diana asked anxiously. She

was not pleased with the idea of a revolution in her college years.

"No-o-o!" He was so sure of it, she felt sure of it, too. "The big fellers will continue to get everything there is in it, and we others will continue to take it on the chin!" he said, good-humoredly, and that made Diana feel uneasy again.

Papa was black of hair and eyes, and almost of skin, too; he had been handsome once; now he was a little fat and careless in dress, often saving collars by wearing a loose soft silk handkerchief about his neck, and saving soap by not shaving regularly. Diana was as tall as he, at seventeen, but with a smooth ivory skin and thick tawny hair of blonde red; her blue eyes were lashed with black, and she had a wide firm mouth always ready to laugh and show big square even teeth. They had no features in common, but sometimes her expression was like his, and her voice often had the rich, amused, indulgent Celtic notes that were characteristic of his.

She listened for the most part with indifference tonight. If she could somehow manage her graduation with decency and dignity, there could be ten revolutions for all Diana cared. The men were ranging in their semi-argumentative talk toward Cæsar and paternal government, the red-headed soda clerk was asleep on the grass when she went in to bed, and she heard May Rogers say sharply of some boasted leader, "The way he treated women was enough for me!"

Diana paused at the door of the big front parlor, where all the Coggleses lived. The room was filled with small sodden blonde figures in every stage of undressing and washing. Mrs. Coggles sat on a backless chair at the washstand, the baby nursing as best she could in a hit-or-miss fashion, dodging under the thin quick arms. The pitcher, nicked and with a broken handle, stood upon the floor; the basin was half full of water coated with a gray scum. In turn the meek little tow-headed girls came to stand before their mother, who plunged at them with a dripping gray rag, wiped their faces as if she were trying to wipe away the features completely, and hooked bony fingers into their delicate ears. Afterward, flinging down the rag and snatching up a comb, she dipped it in the gray scum and dashed it through the pale-gold locks. Tears of bitter agony streamed from the eyes of Amy, Pauli, Tina, Thelma, in turn. Only Hilda, expertly nursing and bobbing her ten-months-old head about with agility, escaped combing. Her head was bald.

Amy had to comb Rudy's hair, because he would not come to his mother when, exhausted, sweating, brushing back her own slipping locks with a wet hand, she called him. The room was in tremendous confusion, for the little beds and big were all opened, and small garments were laid in heaps everywhere, but there was little noise. The young Coggleses did not make any noise. Hot lights streamed down upon them, and their fair hair stuck to their tender little blonde brows. They ran about diligently; they sat down with their knees higher than their heads, unlacing shoes, they shoved and bumped and urged one another into activity. Only Rudy was unmanageable and backed away into corners when Amy went after him with the rag and the comb.

Mr. Coggles came in to stand beside Diana and said, "It's a nice place to have to bring up fine and intelligent children, ain't it?"

"She hurt me!" Rudy sobbed, of the comb.

"Amy, what'd you hurt your brother for?"

"I din!" Amy whispered, terrified, beginning to cry.

Her father had sat down. Now without leaving his seat he stretched out his arm to reach a bureau drawer. He took out a belt.

"You come here, Amy," he said. "You got to learn not to hurt Rudy!"

Amy began to sob loudly; all the other children were deathly still now, busily doing whatever duty lay nearest, and doing it with speed. Diana went away; she hated to see him whip the children, and when times were bad and the weather hot he found reasons for doing so almost every night. Before she slept tonight she heard Pauli's shrill protest in turn: "I din, Papa!" and later a medley of wild sobs and protests came from the younger girls. She heard the father's voice, "Yes, and you go to sleep, Rudy, or you'll get a taste of that!" But that was as far as Rudy's punishment went, then or ever.

Diana lay awake for a long time in the spring night. She thought of the dim old noisy house, stretching above and about her, shabby and bare, and filled with lights and bodies and thin mattresses and lifeless blankets. She thought of her father, talking socialism with Mr. Coggles on the bare strip that had once been garden, and of the red-headed clerk who always studied on his night off, and of the weeping, hot, wakeful little Coggleses in their beds. She thought of her grandmother, and the kitchen, and the bread in the bread box for breakfast, and the old blackened coffee pot. Somehow they were all like a solid weight upon her.

In no way could she ever be like Joan or Patsy. Not in her home, or the persons in that home, or the way she lived or dressed or spoke, or in the clothes she wore and the food she ate. Diana might as well give up any dream of the airy gracious beauty in which Joan lived; the big rooms and the flowers, the shadowy doorways and awnings, the pleasant servant voices and the assured air that such an environment bred. Joan was so sure of herself,—the way her skirts hung, the pronunciation of this word or that, the things a girl might do and might not do!

And Diana was so wretchedly, miserably unsure of herself, in every possible way!

Her father, sitting out there in the warm spring night, with that idiot Ernest Coggles and the red-headed boy from the drugstore, was no help to her. She loved him,—she supposed she loved him,—because he was her father, but he was chiefly associated in her thoughts with the memory of years of excuses, idling, sums borrowed from Gram, cigar stubs in the little pantry bedroom. Papa never had gotten anywhere, somehow; Diana suspected that he never would.

Her only other asset was Gram; hard-working, hard-fingered, burdened Gram could do no more for her than she was doing.

And all the rest was poverty, shabbiness, roomers, unpaid bills, quarreling voices, drafty bare halls, and the smells of boiling onions and dust and soapy water.

Diana sighed; turned restlessly in the dark. Her dress, her flowers, her little presents for her fellow members in the graduating class,—it all meant money—money—money, and where was she to get money?

"Take a job!" said the red-headed clerk from the soda fountain at Meigs's Drugstore.

"How can I, finishing school?"

"Well, I'm in coll, you know."

"Yes, but I don't see how you do it, and study, too."

"Oh, I only have three nine-o'clocks," Peter Platt reminded her.

Diana looked at him thoughtfully. He was a square, stocky, clumsy boy, with red hair on his hands and curling thickly over a bullet head. His nose turned up squarely; his jaw was wide and hard, and he liked to talk what Diana secretly considered a sort of half-baked socialism. His people lived over by the packing plant, beyond the College Avenue Bridge; now they had all climbed into the disreputable car and were driving to Montana to see their "folks," and Peter was temporarily lodging with Gram.

Peter got his breakfast at the house, he and Diana sharing the casual meal in the big bare kitchen; Diana refilling the coffee pot, Peter clumsy with the toast. Working as hard as he did, he had no time for exercise or play; his skin was unhealthily pale, and he was too heavy.

"Coffee, and nothing but white bread,—that's what he lives on,—and sodas and sandwiches at the fountain!" Diana thought, looking at him. She was beginning to be interested in balanced diets, as illustrated by Miss Benchley's lunches. She felt sorry for Peter, somehow, and presently agreed to go to the "flickers" with him on his free night. He rarely went; it excited him very obviously to have her promise to go, and he talked eagerly of it for two days.

Then she had to telephone him at the drugstore and break the engagement. Diana was excited herself now. Joan had asked her, for the first time, to spend the night at the Rowley house! Joan, in her own fascinating and careless way, had explained that Mother had a date, and Duncan was away; "it'll be just *us!*"

No formidable grown-ups; Diana would have chosen it to be just that way. She rushed home at lunchtime for her things; her blue silk Sunday dress was her best; her pajamas were thin and faded and had been much washed,—no matter, she was going to stay at Joan's house! Gram would not let her take either at the moment. No, she would "rub out" the pajamas and take the spots out of the dress and press it. She had nothing else to do. And she would leave them with the suitcase at Rutherford that afternoon.

"You oughtn't," Diana protested, troubled, in the midday heat.

"I won't mind one bit!"

"But I oughtn't let you." However, Diana did let her, and went confidently for the suitcase to Rutherford's office in the afternoon. There it was with its contents nicely packed with tissue paper; it was thrilling to have Joan catch it up gayly and throw it ínto the big Rowley car and say to the driver, "We have to stop at Meigs', George."

At Meigs's, Joan bought some sort of powder to put on

roses, and Diana bought toothpaste and a little nail file.
Also they had sodas, as the Rutherford girls loved to do,
at the counter, and Diana was embarrassed because she felt
that she would like to introduce Joan to the red-faced Peter
Platt and yet did not quite dare. Suppose nice girls didn't
introduce soda-fountain boys to their friends?

Peter did not wait on them, but he kept going to and fro
behind the counter, mixing malted milks and dropping
scoops of ice cream into tall glasses; Diana could have
attracted his eye quickly enough if she had been sure it was
correct. But even when he spoke to her, she did not introduce him to Joan.

"So we don't go to the flickers tonight?" he said, split-
ting a banana for a sundae.

"I'm going to be away tonight." Diana felt confused and
ashamed; she did not enjoy her soda, and breathed easier
when she and Joan were back in the car again. "He's a boy
that lives at my grandmother's," she explained then.

"Who, the perspiry boy who got his thumb in the ice
cream?"

"That's Peter Platt." Diana had to laugh at the descrip-
tion, but she felt a little ashamed of both herself and Peter.
It was some minutes after they had left the drugstore that
she remembered that she had intended to see Mr. Meigs
himself and ask him for a summer position there. It would
justify her in being a little reckless about graduation ex-
penses to have a job and a salary definitely ahead. She could
ask Gram to "loan" her money then.

CHAPTER VI

SHE HAD BEEN in the Rowley house before, but only down-stairs. Her heart was beating hard with excitement and pleasure when they went through the big central hallway, and past the palms and mirrors and the deep seats with carved dark high backs, and mounted the curved stairs. The mansion was stately and old-fashioned and dark, with an elegant clumsy dignity and security in its heavy fireplaces, rich rugs, books, statuary, oil paintings. It was sure of itself, as all the Rowleys in everything they did and had and said were sure of themselves. Diana breathed hard.

Flitting lightly upstairs, with all her usual simplicity and easiness, Joan preceded her guest to her own room,—an enormous room. It was incredible that just one slim girl should have this luxury of space to herself; windows look-ing down on trees, twin beds exquisitely complete with pink cretonne covers and fat pink comforters; Joan's new desk, with Joan's new feather pen, and blotting pad, and mono-grammed writing paper, all neatly awaiting Joan's pleasure.

And the bathroom with the fat towels and the deep tub and the canary to whom Joan talked and chirruped, and the overpowering sense of order and bigness and beauty on all sides! Diana accepted it all shyly. Pride kept her from too obvious surprise, too obvious admiration. But her breath was short, and she felt excited; it was not easy to talk.

"Let's take our baths later, when we're going to bed," Joan suggested gayly. "There's nobody here but us,—at least Mother and Dad are going up to a dinner, and I think my brother Duncan has a date."

Diana agreed that they might take their baths later, and wandered out to the porch,—really the top of some downstairs room,—floored with thick tarred canvas, high up among the trees.

"Joan, this is lovely! Do you study out here?"

"Oh, no, too lazy to move out! Come on and see Mother."

This might be a little formidable, but again Diana followed in proud silence, and they went into Mrs. Rowley's room.

"That you, Joan? Who's with you?"

"Diana Carmichael, Mother." Somehow it sounded very pretty in Joan's pretty voice.

"Oh, hello, Diana." Mrs. Rowley was lying down; magazines had coasted from her couch to the floor; she stretched a soft ringed hand to Diana. "Did you have something to eat, girls?"

"We had sodas at Meigs'. We're going down now to see what we can find."

This room made even Joan's look bare; it was incredibly beautiful. The walls were cream and the rich brocade curtains at the windows a metallic blue; the rug over Mrs. Rowley's knees was blue, too, with lines of bright crimson, and the great dim four-poster bed gave back the same note of crimson and cream and blue. All the books were handsome; the lamps were handsome; every conceivable luxury was in sight,—a dressing table flounced demurely in taffeta; mirrors, clear crystal bowls of flowers, delicately curtained French windows opening upon an awninged upper balcony that showed a bright balustrade of tiled flower boxes. It was incredible that so much splendor could exist unsuspected in quiet Bayhead, hidden away in deep gardens and behind high hedges and brick walls. Something starved, eager, in Diana's very soul fed upon it, drank it with insatiable delight.

Like a creature in an enchantment she followed Joan downstairs and through a dark dining room where silver flashed subduedly on the long carved sideboard, and afternoon light struck in thin bright lines through drawn curtains at high windows. They went into a large white pantry, where Joan did casual amazing things in opening jars of jam and peanut butter; slashing into cake; pouring milk.

"We've got a regular machine for making milkshakes here; my brother makes 'em all the time. But Hong gets mad at me!"

Milkshakes in one's own house! The thought was dazzling. It was all dazzling. Diana could hardly study, when they settled down to study, because of the confusion and excitement in her soul.

"Is this the library?"

"No, this is a kind of study,—workroom, I guess. The boys used to have their lessons here. Dad doesn't like me to go into the library because he says we get butter on his special editions." Joan laughed. "I never do," she said, "but I guess Duncan used to,—and my cousin Bruce before he went to Harvard. But anyway, I don't mind studying here, do you? I like this room,—when the windows are open. We could study up in my room, if you'd rather."

She bit into a sandwich, not expecting a reply. Of course Di wouldn't rather. Di was in a state of dazed acceptance and enjoyment; she would object to nothing.

"Are you the youngest, Joan?"

"My sister Marjorie was younger," Joan said seriously. "She was backed into by the chauffeur when she was six. That was nine years ago, but my mother never will get over it."

"Wasn't that awful?" Di's eyes were wide.

"Awful! They said Mother simply went from one faint to another,—well, Marjorie really was beautiful, and she was smart, too." Joan finished her milk, bit into a slice of chocolate cake. "She was going to Rand Phillips' birthday party," she went on. "She was all dressed up in a hand-made batiste dress Mother had brought her from Paris; I couldn't go because I had poison oak. Marge ran out to the back of the house, and she must have thought she'd get in the car in the garage, with the man, you know. And he backed out, fast—— I heard them all screaming and yelling——"

Both girls were silent for a while.

"You're an only child, aren't you, Di?"

"Yes, I never had a sister or brother."

"And your father and mother dead?"

It was easy to be honest, here in this beautiful place, with Joan's friendship so pleasant and heartening.

"My mother is. But my father's living."

"Your *father* is?"

"Oh, yes."

"I didn't know that!"

"He comes and goes. Usually his business keeps him going about."

"I didn't know that!"

"He's here now," Di observed, in a hesitant voice. There seemed little to add to the statement. Joan was still amazed.

"I thought your father was dead!"

"No, he's living."

"What's his profession, Di?"

"Papa isn't a professional man," Di explained, with all a daughter's gallant generosity. "He's had—*theatrical* interests," she went on a little painstakingly, "but just now he has—he has—*agencies*."

Joan looked up quickly, keenly, from her book; looked down again. Both their faces were a little red.

"I like you, Di!" Joan said, somewhat confusedly. "I love—I love your loyalty!"

"I'm glad," Diana could only answer, clearing her throat. But somehow Joan's voice and her words had made her feel that it was romantic, it was heroic, to have a father of whom one might not be proud, and she was comforted.

"But your father's a *Republican?*" Joan asked anxiously, in the silence.

"Oh, yes!" Diana assured her, feeling anything but sure herself.

"My father says that the whole country would be ruined," Joan said seriously, "if the Republicans didn't get in."

Vague memories of enthusiastic mention of the Democratic candidate, and even of the Socialist candidate, kept Diana silent, but she felt an immense respect for Joan and her intelligence.

"One knows this," Joan went on, "that in my father's business it would spell ruin!"

The graceful phrasing of this, the casual use of the third person, thrilled Joan's listener. After a pause Diana asked respectfully,

"Your father's in the hardware business, isn't he, Joan?"

"Wholesale," Joan answered, a little surprised. "I thought you knew. And then of course he has 'Hearitall.'"

"That's the radio?"

"He owns the patent," Joan answered, and Diana realized afresh what a wonderful family the family of Rowley was.

"There's a little trouble now," Joan presently went on, "about the five-and-ten stores. They're undermining everything and selling things for nothing! It makes Dad terribly mad, and he and Mr. Palmer are always talking about it. Dad says if he has to go to Sacramento himself he'll have to stop it; he says lots of the little dealers look to Rowley & Palmer to protect them."

This impressed Diana afresh with Joan's intelligence and with the importance of the Rowley family. But then everything did that.

After they had finished their lessons,—Joan's only a little less clean and correct and well done than Diana's,—they

walked about the place. It was very large; it was as large,
Diana thought, as two square blocks, but as it lay at the
top of Crescent Avenue, at the end of Newbegin Park, with
the pleasant oak-strewn meadows and the beginnings of
farms and foothills back of it, it was hard to estimate exactly
what its proportions were. It was all heavily cultivated, too,
and planted; poplars and willows and the tall shafts of
cypress were in among the natural growth of the oaks, and
there seemed to be any number of gardens. There was a
tennis court, and there were berry vines, and rose gardens,
and arbors and latticed summerhouses buried in banksia and
La Marque rose vines.

Far at the back were fences and stables, all painted clean
white, white chickens in white runways, lengths of clean
paddock where young horses stood with their heads on each
other's neck symmetrically, looking over the fence.

Then there were clean Guernsey cows in a long clean
milking shed; "Dad's blue-ribbon heifers!" Joan said of them
amusedly, and there was a peacock, walking rapidly away
from the girls, and more than one dog; Duncan's fawn-
colored bulldog, slavering ecstatically when Joan scratched
his head, a thin wire-hair mother dog and an alert puppy;
a gentle old spaniel with dangling silky ears.

Grapevines were just coming into full fresh leaf on
frames; cherries were ripening on trees, and several great
towering fig trees, like lofty tents of foliage, shaded the
side yard. Sunshine came slanting down on whitewashed
walls, and grass, and blooms, and fences; everything was
raked and orderly and spacious and,—to Diana, at least,—
of bewildering charm. Oh, what a home to call one's own,
what a place to come back to after school! So comfortable
and homely and pleasant, and yet so elegant and impressive,
too. One could not hate Joan, one could not even be jealous
of her; she was too sweet, too unspoiled. But what a place
to live in!

Coming about the side of the house again, they could look down on the roofs of Bayhead, smothered in the round tops of oaks, and see the little cars twinkling like beetles as they wheeled about the college gateway beyond. The stately Moorish towers and arcades of Lucas were lost in a soft haze of sunset; fog was blanketing the mountain range toward the north; in a few moments the sun would slip from sight, and the air grow chill, and the hills turn a cold purple, but this was the last exquisite glance from the departing day, and everything at Holly Oaks was transfigured in warmth and sweetness and beauty. Bees were tearing by on their way homeward; gnats spun in the light, and the two Persian kittens moved stiff-legged on the grass with side-wise rushes that all but capsized them.

The girls stopped at the old sundial, and Joan scraped from its face a light strewing of leaves.

> "Through the sunne and through the showr,
> Fate do move to fynde hys hour,"

she read.

Diana was speechless. She had never seen a sundial; she had supposed only queens and kings had sundials.

"Ten minutes of six," Joan said. "Let's go in and see if we can—— Oh, hello, Bruce! Di, this is my cousin Bruce Palmer!"

A young man had come up behind them on the terrace; he stood there looking at them unsmilingly. Joan kissed him, jerking his dark head down with her slender arms, perhaps not sorry to have Diana see with what a handsome cousin she might take liberties; he endured her embrace good-naturedly.

"Be calm, my poor girl," he said. "Restrain yourself! I'll hear your case presently—presently."

"Diana," Joan said, flushed and breathless, altogether a most charming and unusual Joan, "this is Bruce."

"Diana." Bruce acknowledged the name. He looked at Diana. And Diana stood there, in the full flood of the sunset light, and looked at him.

He had been playing golf with his uncle; he looked flushed and happy, his brown throat was bare, and he wore a brown sweater with a band of cream color around the bottom, and brown knickers, and big square brown shoes. His dark hair was in some disorder; he had a nice brown face and a friendly hand grip. But it was the look in his eyes that rendered Diana speechless; perhaps she was a little tired, too; certainly she was excited and confused; his smiling, appraising, kindly look somehow made her want to cry.

Tired, disheveled, yet there was a vitality, a something young and hard and brown and eager about him that stirred her to her soul. Bruce Palmer—Bruce Palmer—the name rang in her heart like the tolling of a bell. Something happened to her, there in the sunset garden by the sundial, that all the years of her life were not to undo; upon her always would be the stamp of this insufferably exquisite moment, when she stood, in her blue silk gown, by the sundial, and Bruce Palmer looked at her. Diana at the moment could sense only that she loved him instantly, completely; she surrendered everything that was herself,—everything that she might ever be,—to his keeping in that first minute.

"What are you two wenches doing?" Bruce said, lingering.

"Oh, nothing," Joan said. "We've been wandering around."

"I thought that Newbegin infant was coming."

"No," Joan said. "Diana."

"Well," he presently began, "I've got to change. I cleaned up Uncle Will and took five dollars away from him."

"Oh," Joan commented delightedly, "was he mad?"

"Sizzling."

"The way we treat my *father!*" Joan said, in an undertone to Diana. Her little laugh added, "Aren't we a crazy family? We're always like this!"

"What are you girls doing tonight?"

"You're taking us to a movie," Joan answered promptly.

"No such luck! I'm going to the Kents' shindig."

"Oh, Burlingame?" Joan said, still exploiting the marvelous big cousin.

"Hillsborough. And I've got to get going!" He went away toward the house, turned at the first of the brick steps up from the terrace, called back. "Diana *what?*"

"What-t-t?" Joan called. He repeated the two words, and she laughed and Diana laughed. "Carmichael!" Joan shouted, and Bruce, just before disappearing, said, "I get it!"

"He and Aunt Emily are staying here tonight," Joan explained, when he was gone. "Isn't he a dear? I'm so fond of him! He's just like a wonderful big brother."

Diana said nothing. Before dinner she and Joan went down to one of the many sitting rooms, and joined Joan's brother Duncan and Mr. and Mrs. Rowley and the imposing Mrs. Palmer,—a big woman, with a high bust and big teeth, and a horse's white-rimmed suspicious eye. Diana hardly dared raise her voice in this august gathering; she did not think Mrs. Palmer's manner very friendly.

Bruce, very stunning in his evening clothes, came in to say good-night, with his big coat on his arm and his gloves and his silk hat in his hand.

"Good-night, everyone," he said. "Good-night, Diana!" Diana could make no sign, no sound in answer; she smiled a strained smile, wondered whether he saw her confusion. All the grown-ups began to gather up wraps and bags; they were going to a dinner. Mrs. Palmer, magnificent in a fur-edged wrap, put a big hand on Diana's shoulder as she passed the girls on her way out.

"I want to talk to you," she said abruptly. "Come see me."

Diana's heart soared.

"This—this week?"

"Any time. Telephone first!" Mrs. Palmer gathered up her wrap and went on her way. Joan and Diana and Duncan, a nice, negligible boy of twenty, sat down to dinner together.

In the beautiful dining room three places were perfectly appointed; soup spoons, salad forks in heavy silver, napkins heavy and square, crystal glasses. There were pink flowers in an ornate silver vase and pink candles. Saunders passed the crackers, the celery, the black olives. Marie brought the cups of soup. There was a roast, jelly, vegetables. Afterward a salad, with more jelly, and cheese. Afterward éclairs, which Duncan wolfed ravenously. Joan did not want any black coffee; Diana did not want any coffee.

They went upstairs, considering Duncan's rather ungracious offer to take them to "the flickers." But they had seen the Bayhead picture, and the chance of anything good being in Mountain View or San José was vague.

"Find out what's in San José, Dunk," Joan said. But Duncan only growled, "Oh, find out yourself!"

In the end a boy telephoned him, and he laughed a great deal at the telephone, and hung up to observe briefly that he was "going out with Bud." Then Connie telephoned Joan, and they had an interminable talk, in which Joan evidently had something to explain, for she kept saying in pleasant impatience, "Don't be so silly, Connie. That wasn't it at all. Well, I can't,—now. No, I can't. Well, there's a reason."

Diana did not pay much attention. She could hear Joan's voice, and some of her words, but they did not matter,— nothing mattered. Even the dinner had not impressed her especially; she had been hardly conscious of all its beauty and state.

She had wandered out to the terrace, and sat there in a

long, low basket chair, her feet up, a comfortable great
pillow pulled under her shoulders. Moonlight streamed down
upon her and upon the sundial, twenty feet away. It sent
a slender blot of shadow onto the tiles of the terrace. Diana
lay wrapped in a sort of floating ecstasy; she wanted to be
alone, to think, and yet she liked to have Joan come out and
interrupt her thoughts, just for the delight of returning to
them again.

Bruce,—and Bruce,—and Bruce. There was living in the
world this dark-haired man, in golf clothes, in evening dress,
assured, handsome, careless.

Shudders of joy went over her. She did not think; she
felt.

"Connie's a very dear little person," Joan said, coming
out to the terrace, dropping into the chair beside Diana, "but
how she does like to manage her friends!"

She mused. Diana's thoughts were far away, loosened to
some enchanted ether where soul, body, and spirit seemed
to be floating together.

"Jealous!" Joan said under her breath, with a laugh.

Diana brought herself back to earth with an agony of
effort.

"Jealous," she murmured. The word meant nothing.

"It's too silly!" Joan laughed gently. Diana turned in her
chair, brought her eyes to the shimmering pale blot in the
moon shadows that was Joan, struggled to respond.

"Why—" she began mildly. The words seemed to choke
·her; there was a dry pain in her breast—"why should Consuelo be jealous?" she managed to say.

"Oh, your being here!" Joan supplied lightly.

"Oh, silly," Diana murmured. Oh, Bruce, Bruce, Bruce,
abstracted, handsome and trim and hurried, in evening
black! Oh, voice that had said "Diana what?" so carelessly,
so laughingly and good-naturedly, on the dial terrace!

She looked off at the dial; at its blot of shadow on the

lawn. Surges of emotion rose in her like tidal waves, swelled, inundated her, ebbed slowly. And no sooner was the richness of the moment gone than it began to rise again, inevitably, deliciously, and again she was caught in its inexorable dizzy rapture.

"Diana, this is a dull evening for you," Joan presently observed.

"Dull? I'm just *loving* it!"

"Well, it *is* restful. I like good movies," Joan expanded, "but just to go to a movie, good or bad, I think is silly!"

"I don't go very often," Diana said, with effort.

There was a long silence. The two girls were motionless in the warm spring night, while the moon climbed steadily over a dark blue sky thickset with stars.

"Bruce didn't want to go tonight," Joan began, after a while, in her amused, indulgent voice.

"Didn't?"

"No. He gets himself all dated up, and then he hates it."

"Does he—does he go back to Harvard?"

"Oh, no. He's graduated! He had to take two extra terms to finish up. But he actually graduated with his class last June."

"And is he going to be here, in Bayhead, now?"

"Well, we don't know. Bruce," Joan said, lowering her tone, glancing cautiously back toward the dimly lighted windows of the house as she spoke, "is just over a—a terrible affair, you know."

"At college?"

"Well, he was at college, but it had nothing to do with college. He—" Joan jerked her long chair a little nearer to Diana's chair in the shadows—"he fell in love with a perfectly terrible woman," she added.

"Oh?"

"Now don't ever breathe that I told you this, Di!"

"I won't, of course."

"Because, honestly, he'd never forgive me. It was really terrible. Aunt Emily nearly died over it, and Uncle Chase went East and talked to Bruce, and all that!"

"Goodness!"

"She was a Broadway chorus girl, and she was mixed up in that Steelman scandal."

"Goodness!" Diana could only breathe again.

"Imagine it. Bruce! You see, they wanted to get her out of the way, and she slipped away to Cambridge, and stayed with a woman who pretended to be her sister, and changed her name. Bruce met her,—how on earth was *he* to imagine anything wrong? They fell *madly* in love with each other. He wrote Aunt Emily about it,—oh, last Christmas,—and she just thought it was an ordinary nice girl, you know, one of Bruce's crushes. And all the time it was this Lily Brugière."

"I remember that name, but I don't remember the case."

"My dear, this girl,—with practically nothing on,—ran around an apartment house screaming that a man,—a very rich man, too,—had killed himself."

"Oh, horror!" Diana murmured.

"Horror, I should say so. And this is the girl," Joan ended dramatically, "who has to come up to Harvard and carry on with Bruce!"

"Well, but was she—I mean did she do it? Were the police after her?"

"No, she was just a witness. She just got out of the way."

"Did he—" Diana asked rather timidly, after a pause— "did he take it hard?"

"Well, it almost killed him, of course," Joan answered readily; "but he knew it was—simply—out of the question! He told my uncle he wanted to have one talk with her, and I guess they settled it all then. Anyway, in April, when Aunt Emily was on there, she—this girl—was playing again, and Aunt Emily asked Bruce if he would like to see the show, and he sort of yawned and said he would, and then said he wouldn't; anyway, they didn't go."

"I wonder," Di began dreamily, "if he still loves her."

"Oh, no, he's all over it. But it certainly," Joan said earnestly,—"it certainly has made an older man of Bruce. Mother sees it; we all do. I don't think he'll ever marry now."

"Does he—does he talk about it?"

"Oh, heavens, no! Not to anyone. He shuts up like a clam if you even mention the stage, or murders, or anything."

Diana added this one more romantic fact to her dream of Bruce. Long after Joan was asleep in the beautiful pink bedroom that night, she lay awake, comfortable, happy, sleepless, and thought of that last talk Bruce had had with Lily, when, completely disillusioned, his idyll of a first love shattered, he had gone to her, stern and young and handsome, to say "good-bye."

CHAPTER VII

OH, IT was hard to walk home from school the next afternoon with her suitcase, feeling that the whole wonderful experience of spending the night at Joan's house was over!

Over with no pleasant result, too,—no "We'll do this again next week," from Joan, no "We'll see you soon again, Diana," from Joan's mother.

No. Joan's mother had been asleep when the girls had breakfasted and started for school in the big car; Bruce had not come home at all. Everything had been flat, stale, depressing.

School had gone badly, too. That is, Diana had stupidly invited mortification in French class, and of course Mademoiselle had leaped gladly into the breach. Diana had been dreamily looking down at her written exercises when Mademoiselle had asked her first question, and had answered it automatically, rather under the impression that nobody else was prepared, anyway. And it had been intended for Patsy.

This had been embarrassing enough without the further humiliation of having actually missed a question, later on, when it was asked, and having had recourse to the vague usual senior murmur, "Was that in our lesson?"

Of course it had been in the lesson. Minna Porter had answered it sharply and correctly.

Joan and Connie had evidently made it up, whatever their difference had been. They were together all through the recreation period, and Connie carried Joan off for lunch. Diana usually brought her lunch, for Rutherford was eleven long blocks away from home; but of late Miss Benchley had asked her to sit with the smallest girls at noon and encourage their first shy efforts at French conversation, so she had her hot good lunch now with the rest.

She did not happen to see Joan or Patsy after school. Elinor always stayed for gym, and Connie had coaching in geometry. Today Diana walked home alone with her books and suitcase.

It was very hot; a sultry spring day. Bayhead smelled like a hothouse; lilacs and roses and low garden flowers scented the still moist air. Suddenly Diana felt tired and jaded; her head ached, she wanted to cry.

Newspapers had blown across the front yard; yesterday's hot sun had burned them yellow. A flock of little Coggleses, fluffing in the dust like chickens, were under the backyard willow. The kitchen door sagged open; nobody was in sight.

Diana went on into the back parlor; threw down her suitcase and books. She tossed off her hat, pushed the hair back from her wet forehead. Her heart was lead.

Back in the kitchen again she buttered herself a large cold biscuit, selected prunes from a bowl, and filled the saucer up with their pale thin juice. She sat down to the feast at the kitchen table, but for a while she did not eat. She remained motionless; staring into space.

Joan and Patsy would be at the Palmer house now; it was quite a new house, Spanish colonial in type, with cloisters and a patio. They would lounge in basket chairs, drinking ginger ale and nibbling cookies. There were no lessons tonight, tomorrow was Saturday, they would ask each other if they were going riding tomorrow. A cook there, and another cook in Joan's house, would be getting ready a delicious meal; neat little maids in caps would be setting the candlesticks on the dinner table, arranging flowers. On all sides would be peace and order and spacious beauty.

On all sides of Diana were the distempered dirty walls

of the kitchen; the windows with their dangling strips of lifeless gray net curtains; the chipped and grease-darkened floor. A worn linoleum rug was at the sink. The table wore an oilcloth cover and was always embellished with the sugar bowl, the spoon cup, the salt and pepper shakers. The gas stove was dark from years of service; its door had lost all vitality, and it fell forward heavily when anyone opened the oven; its rings were an unhealthy red from rust and wear. On it stood the kettle with a cork cleverly substituted for the missing knob of the cover. Beyond the stove the pantry door was open; Diana's gaze found the familiar battered bowls and pans, and she smelled the stale scent of spices and rotting apples, mice and old wood.

Her grandmother came in, with her face dark and wet from the heat. She had been shopping, and lowered from a cramped arm the various paper bags she carried.

"Asparagus, six pounds for two bits," she panted, accepting Diana's kiss. "I said to him, 'That's 'most as cheap as carrots!' Well, did you have a good time?"

Diana reported everything with false animation and enthusiasm; Joan was such a darling, and their place was simply marvelous! She followed her grandmother into their dark room.

"I believe I'll lie down for a few minutes and put those things away later. Di, did you see the shoes at Philliber's?"

"No, and there was a sale today, wasn't there? Some of us said last week we'd be there, and then I forgot."

Mrs. Chamberlain, relaxed against her sodden pillow, with her shabby old feet among Diana's books, stretched her lean hand for her purse. She extracted a five-dollar bill.

"They're selling those sandals at four sixty-nine," she said. "I got this money for you at the bank, and you walk right over and get your graduation shoes. You'll wear 'em all summer.—My gracious, it feels good to lie down for a minute!"

"Gram, stay there. I'll get supper, and I'll be right back and clear up!" But Di had snatched her hat again. Anything to get out into College Avenue in the late afternoon; see who was there, perhaps join the crowd at Sticky's! She could not stay home, and think of Bruce, and feed only with dreams and hopes the gnawing need to see him—hear his voice—again.

Uptown, next to Philliber's Shoe Store, was the "Nosegay." The "Nosegay" was a smart little flower shop, which several gentlewomen were running for the Junior League. Joan went in there sometimes and helped them sell things; lots of the Junior League girls did. Their window today had Sicilian jars in it, and a long-legged Negro doll, and only one great burst of banksia roses as flowers.

Diana, in no hurry, was struck with a sudden inspiration as she passed it; she turned back.

There had been talk of Mrs. Rowley's birthday at the Rowley house. Sunday would be Mother's birthday. Why not send her a little birthday reminder in the shape of a nosegay, and also as an acknowledgment of her hospitality? Diana's blood began to dance, and her eyes sparkled. She went into the "Nosegay."

Five minutes later she was out in College Avenue again, feeling a little flat. The potted pink rose was handsome; but already Diana had an uneasy sense that it might be too handsome. She had written on the card: *"With wishes for a happy birthday and thanks for a wonderful visit, lovingly, Diana,"* and now that began to seem a little extreme, too. She wished she had left out the "lovingly."

No shoes, now, but she could wear her old ones,—have them cleaned by the colored man in the Medico-Dental Building doorway.

"That's all right!" she said to herself aloud, walking home excited and confused. "Oh, well, what of it?" she asked the unanswering air almost roughly. "She'll have lots of flowers, she won't pay any attention to my card, she'll just think it was a nice thing to do! I wish I'd sent her just a few marigolds or something, but——oh, what of it!"

Her face was red; and it reddened every time she thought of the pot of roses during the evening. She could not go back to last night's thoughts of Bruce; the charm was broken tonight, the spell was over.

She must deceive her grandmother, too; tell her the shoes were "coming." Diana thought of the lean old hand reaching for the five-dollar bill, and her soul was sick within her. Before ever the asparagus and the meat cakes and the dough-nuts for dinner were on the table her whole spirit was in a blaze of shamed protest against what she had done; she could not bear the thought of it. Sending a rich woman like Mrs. Rowley, who lived in a very garden of flowers, a four-dollar rosebush!

Diana lay awake again that night, but tonight there were no moon-washed dreams; she was writhing in an agony of shame. They would know that she did not know how to do graceful social things, they would laugh at her!

At about three o'clock, lying very still because to turn or twist would disturb the slumbering grandmother beside her, Diana made up her mind. She would run away from it all; Bayhead, Rutherford, the Rowleys, Mason Avenue, everything! Defiantly, desperately planning the details of her escape, at last she fell asleep.

But the next day she remembered that Mrs. Palmer had said that she wanted to see her. That was surely an excuse to telephone,——that meant something. Perhaps it meant help. "Diana, I've been watching you; of course I hear of you in school through Patsy and Joan. Now if two hundred dollars would help you——"

Or perhaps it would be: "Diana, we want someone to be with Patsy and Noni this summer, to help them with their school work. Mr. Palmer and I were wondering if you could come with us to the Lake and just keep them in touch?"

No, she would not run away until she had at least responded to Mrs. Palmer's invitation. There must be some reason for it, and it was probably a nice reason. Diana had completely recovered her equanimity when she started off for school. Not that she exactly liked to remember having sent Mrs. Rowley the flowers yesterday, and not that it was exactly pleasant to see Joan and Connie so cozily intimate, but it was a singing June morning, all lilac fragrance and scented new grass; there were pools of delicious green shadow under the blossoming hawthorn trees; pink and white, pink and white, that went up and down the pleasant morning streets.

"Your mother said she wanted to see me," she said to Patsy.

"Oh, did she?" said Patsy, with a vague look. "Oh, yes."

Diana put off her appointment with Mrs. Palmer as long as she dared. It was a definite tie with the girls of the nicest set, and when it was over perhaps she would have no other. And it was a definite hope of something that might be important, that might lead to great things. She must not hurry it.

On the following Monday afternoon she walked after school to the Palmer house; a little tired, a little flushed after the school day, and ready for any adventure. Commencement was only ten days ahead now, and there was a thrilling sense of acceleration and excitement in the atmosphere of Rutherford. Diana had gotten yards of organdie, and Emma Mae's aunt, Lil Pawsey, was making it up, for three dollars. Miss Beattie had asked Diana to help her with the school bills, at sixty cents an hour, and that would mean at least ten dollars. Altogether, Diana Carmichael, walking toward the Palmer house, felt pleased with herself and with the June world; she thought Bayhead was lovely,—probably the loveliest college town in the world, with its gardens all in fresh bloom, and the sun slanting down in floods of light through the oaks and the pepper trees.

All the homes up in Newbegin Park were new and hand-some; most of them of the Spanish colonial type, with tiled roofs, balconies, shuttered windows, fountains in flowering patios. The Palmer house was the finest of all; Diana, wait-ing in a basket chair, in the sunshine by the fountain, thought that it must be like a corner of old Spain. An old iron bell had rung clankingly to announce her; the fountain was splashing punctually,—higher, lower, higher again, a fine tower of glittering water,—and doves were walking on the roof.

After a while, when Diana had fallen into a sort of wak-ing daydream, Mrs. Palmer came down. High-busted, high-colored, with a high, harsh voice, she first showed Diana a letter she had just received; one that had obviously pleased her. It was from some extremely exclusive society in an Eastern city; The American Society of the Descendants of the English Nobility. Mrs. Palmer had been accepted for membership, the letter said, although,—Mrs. Palmer ex-plained in her sharp, insistent accents,—although Mr. Palmer could not be admitted. "And possibly Noni and Patsy will not be admitted, on his account!"

But this was all in an aside. Presently she put the letter away and began to talk to Diana.

CHAPTER VIII

TEN DAYS LATER, their arms full of roses, their young slender bodies clad in virginal white, the sun shining down upon them, the organ's solemn strains filtering through the warm June air, the world all laughter, tears, congratulations, Miss Benchley's twenty-third class graduated.

Noticeable for beauty and for honors, even among so many who were pretty and were praised, was Diana Carmichael. The medals, the ribbons, were half hers. For good citizenship, for excellence in French, for general scholarship, as class president, as school leader, as chairman of the school board, for work in dramatics and basketball she was summoned again and again to the platform that was bowered in masses of acacia and spiked with blue delphinium and garlanded in roses: "Miss Diana Carmichael!"

For a while the packed mothers and fathers and sisters and aunts, and the raw, handsome college boys from Lucas clapped enthusiastically. Then they began to laugh when Diana's name was called, and finally it was laughter and clapping mixed, and even—especially where darling grim old Gram, in her wilted voile, was concerned, and where May and Beet Rogers were concerned—it was tears.

Serious in her fresh white organdie scallops, the roses on her slender arm, her blue eyes dark with excitement beneath the shining wavy cap of her bright hair, she came and went. Diana's breast, lifted and rounded under the white organdie, was crossed with ribbons, glittering with medals. And all the time the loved walls of beautiful Rutherford encompassed her; the lawn and the quad and the library, the

silences and the green shadows, the paths and stairways she
had loved so long. And all the time the organ played softly,
and the packed audience and the rows of white-clad girls
rustled and were still, and birds sang and flashed beyond
the open windows, in the high branches of Rutherford's
famous oaks. And all the time she knew her heart was
broken.

"We have one girl who has qualified for Vassar, Smith,
Bryn Mawr, *and* Lucas," said Miss Benchley's pleasantly
modulated voice. "Rutherford is proud of her! Miss Diana
Carmichael."

And then there was a burst of applause such as perhaps
the old chapel had never heard before. Afterward everyone
seemed to take it for granted that Diana was going to Lucas.
Joan had been accepted for Lucas, as a matter of course; the
amazing thing was that Connie Newbegin had also gotten
in with conditions.

"So you three girls will go right on together!" the con-
gratulatory voices said, when the graduates were all out on
the lawn, having their pictures taken, circling about radiantly among families and friends.

Diana said little to this. She was pale, after the excitement
of commencement, and she kept close to the rather ungainly
shabby bulk of her grandmother. Miss Benchley and all the
teachers were charming to Mrs. Chamberlain; most of the
mothers knew her and were cordial. As for Di, they were
all kissing her, running across the lawn after her, tearful
over the farewells. School days were over; Di and Minna
and Elinor and Joan would know Rutherford's happy ways
no more!

"Hello, Diana!" Bruce Palmer said. She lifted her head
in surprise; color flooded her cheeks, and she smiled gravely.

"Oh, how do you do!"

"You were the whole show, weren't you?" the young man
asked.

"Oh," she indicated medals, ribbons, diploma,—"oh, *that*," Diana said, carelessly. "I didn't see you," she went on.

They stood in a stretch of mellow shadow; the June midday was hot and still. Suddenly Diana was very happy.

"I was at the back, standing."

"Oh. I didn't see you. Perhaps," the girl confessed smilingly—"perhaps I was too fussed to see anyone."

"I should think you might have been!"

"There isn't," she said demurely, "the competition you might expect."

Bruce laughed suddenly.

"I suppose not! And now," he went on—"now it's Lucas, is it?"

Diana looked at him bravely.

"No, I'm not going to college," she said.

"Not? I thought pretty nearly every college in the place wanted you?"

"I can't afford it," Diana said simply.

"Oh, listen——" he protested, embarrassed.

"By some miracle, by October, I *might!*" the girl went on, cheerfully. It wouldn't do, reflected Diana, to let him think she was appealing for sympathy. But now, she said, "Monday I begin in the Bayview Hardware Store."

"You do not!"

"I assure you I do!"

"Listen, you've not got a job in the hardware store!"

"But I tell you I *have*."

"Oh, listen, that's a funny break!" Bruce said.

"Why is it a funny break?"

"Why, here's the catch," the man answered, grinning down at her in the way that made her heart stop beating, and race, and stop again, "I'm going to work for them in July!"

"Not the Bayhead Hardware Store?"

"Yep. My father's part owner, you know. They carry all

our stuff. I'm starting in there, after the family moves up
to the Lake."

Life suddenly soared, began to sing. Diana's expression
·did not change; she kept her eyes fixed speculatively upon
his face.

"Seriously?" she asked.

"You bet your life seriously! My father wants me to go
in with him next year, and he thinks this is the way to
begin. What do you know about both of us going into the
same place! Mother," he interrupted himself, catching at
Mrs. Palmer's stout, lace-covered arm, "come over here and
hear this!"

Mrs. Palmer wheeled about; she was largely built, much
too stout. The freckles on her thick fair skin showed through
her lace gown and on her fat full neck. She wore a lace hat;
spatters of sunlight came through it and lay on her powdered puffed cheeks and large pale mouth. She said im-
posingly:

"I must congratulate you upon all your honors, Diana."

Diana glanced at her absently; glanced away.

"Come with me, Bruce, I have to speak to Miss White!"
she said. "I beg your pardon, Mrs. Palmer, I didn't hear
you."

"I wanted to congratulate you on your—your distinc-
tions," Mrs. Palmer repeated. But the hard red color had
come up into her pale face. Diana looked at her for a second
unsmilingly.

"Oh, thank you," she said vaguely. "Can you come with
me, Bruce?"

"It's the best thing I do!" Bruce assured her enthusiastically.

Mrs. Palmer watched them with narrowed eyes as they
went away across the grass.

An hour later, having a scrappy lunch with Gram in the
kitchen at home, Diana suddenly began to laugh. Her grand-

mother looked at her in great satisfaction. It had been an emotional morning; it had been natural to expect that the fairest, the cleverest, the most popular of the girls might long to go on with the others, into college days—into young ladyhood. Mrs. Chamberlain had feared the parting hours for Diana at Rutherford; she was not reconciled yet to the girl's plan of going to work.

Now to find her happy, laughing, laying her fair head down on the kitchen table to laugh, was reassuring. Diana was back in an old home apron; she was going to clean the kitchen thoroughly after lunch. Then she was going to press her dark blue silk, and wash all her collars and cuffs, to be ready for work Monday morning.

"They're nothing but a pack of cards!" she said.

"Who, Di?"

"Oh, these people! These small-towners, with their American Society of the Descendants of the English Nobility!"

"I never heard of that society," Mrs. Chamberlain said mildly. She loved her tea, even on such a hot afternoon. She liked her quiet kitchen, and especially she loved the company of the slim girl in the old blue-checked apron.

"I'll teach her a lesson!" Di said, resuming her meal.

"Teach who?"

"Bruce Palmer's mother."

"I didn't see her this morning. She must have been there."

"She was there." Diana looked into space for a moment, her fine mouth quivering with mirth. "I rather think I'm going to have some fun with that old girl!" she said, half aloud.

Her grandmother looked up curiously. But Diana was evidently talking to herself.

CHAPTER IX

ONE LUNCHTIME Diana and Margaret Hyde were talking about boys. It was a rainy November day; the store had been dark from the opening hour, and lights had been lighted. There was little business today, for tomorrow was Thanksgiving, and everyone in Bayhead who needed knives or plates had long ago selected them; sheets of driving rain had been sweeping up College Avenue for hours; there were no women and children downtown.

Often on pleasant days at noon, or a few minutes after half-past three or half-past four, Rutherford girls, in their white middy blouses and pleated dark green skirts, would come wandering past the front windows; they would be downtown buying tennis shoes and gym shoes, bérets and scarfs and socks, chocolate malted milk at Sticky's, and caramel corn at the odorous little shop on the corner. They rarely came in to the hardware store, but Diana never missed seeing them as they went up or down the street. Sometimes she saw Patsy or Joan, too; flying by in a stripped little open car with a sweatered big college boy at the wheel. Now and then she would meet them, and they were always sweet, always looked delighted and happy, and exclaimed "Diana!" as if they had been hoping for days to encounter her. But there was no intimacy between them now.

May Rogers was still a faithful plodding clerk at the hardware store, but Diana's friendship and interest had gone more naturally in her very earliest days there to Margaret Hyde. Margaret was the cashier; hers was a much more important position than that of Diana, who was merely a saleswoman, but she had been kindly and helpful with Diana, when Diana had first come in, shy and strange, two years ago, and now the girls were fast friends.

They lunched every day in the storeroom above and behind the shop. A mezzanine gallery ran about three sides of the hardware store; the door into the storeroom opened from the mezzanine gallery at the back. On one side of the gallery there were certain bulky housekeeping things that would have taken too much room on the floor; waste baskets and wash baskets, brooms, ice-cream freezers, garbage cans, wash boilers, iceboxes, meat safes. On the other side of the gallery were correspondingly clumsy articles from the hardware side of the shop: ropes, sprayers, stepladders, tool boxes, coasters, incubators, sets of pails.

To gain the storeroom the girls went through a sort of alley made of lawn mowers, vacuum cleaners, and other long-handled ware, and opened an inconspicuous narrow door without molding or frame set lightly in a light partition. Beyond was a large room somewhat blocked by crates and by the big pigeonholes against the west wall where packages and boxes of tacks and small nails, brads and staples and spools of copper and steel wire were ranged. New stock always came in here and was assorted and distributed; sometimes it was white-enameled tin cups, sometimes flashlights or pocket knives, sometimes books of trout flies, or fish baskets, or tennis rackets.

In the clear space there was a large table, and against the back windows another. There was a door giving upon a roomy upper porch, with steps down to the littered backyard. There was a view of other disorderly backyards; that of the music store always had an empty piano box or two awaiting use; that of the delicatessen shop, barrels of empty tins piled up for removal. Beyond was the side wall of the "New York Frocke Shoppe," known to all the Rutherford girls as the "Frocky," and above it, with much Spanish garnishing in the way of striped awnings, creamy plaster, grilles and tiling, the Art Gift House, the "Gingham Tea Shop," the "Coin de Chine" and the Peltrie Sisters' photograph gallery. Sometimes the activities of these places diverted Diana and Margaret as they sat at lunch, but today streaming rain blurred and veiled them all, and wind blew the awnings and the oak leaves drearily to and fro. Nobody was doing any business today.

Diana and Margaret sat at the little wall table where there was a gas ring on a rubber tube, and a hinged old box, that had once sheltered assorted scissors, to hold their knives and forks. Above, there was a small wooden cabinet on the wall. Someone had long ago experimented with the cabinet in trying enamel paints; streaks of rose and blue, green and egg-yellow still decorated its sides. Beside the table, on the wall, were several big black hooks, where the girls hung their coats and hats, and beyond these, jutting out into the porch, upon which it also opened for the convenience of the men downstairs, was a primitive lavatory, with assorted bits of odd plumbing set about in a large square space, and a small rippled mirror above a glass table with a deep crack through it.

Diana, with deep paper cuffs pinned to her sleeves to protect her gown, and a limp black silesia apron tied about her waist, was making toast. Margaret on her feet had measured the tea leaves and filled up the pot. Now she stood looking down into it doubtfully.

"That's the last," she said. "I think it's going to be kind of weak.—Don't you worry, Di," she added, reverting to an interrupted conversation, "you'll like boys all right when you're older, and they'll like you."

"I'm nearly twenty."

"Ha!" Margaret said. "I'm twenty-four."

"Well, and you've had Len for years!"

"We've only been engaged for three," Margaret offered.

She said it reluctantly. She hated it to be three years since she and Len had found each other, hated to feel that those first dreams of theirs had had to wait so long. Three years, —and it might be another three before they could marry! "And of course," she added delicately, "we—while they need me at home, and while his mother is alive,—we really aren't —planning."

"Well, he's a *beau*," Diana reminded her forcefully, "he's *something*."

Margaret laughed her sudden laugh that was like a chime of reluctant bells; it was always as if it were forced from her against her will. Margaret, although the daughter of a postman, although a resident of the slovenly region beyond Diana's house known as "The Gully," just on the edge of Niggertown, was herself somehow fine,—gentle, courageous, self-controlled.

"I'll say he's something!" she agreed.

"Well, I didn't mean that, exactly," Diana hastened to say.

"As far as beaus go, you could have Peter Platt tomorrow, Di."

"Now that's exactly *it*, Margaret. I couldn't!"

"I know he likes you," Margaret said, without conviction. "That is, I know he *likes* you," she added.

Di, her steaming cup unnoted beside her, her elbows on the table and her chin cupped in her hands, stared unsmilingly into space.

"Well, I don't know why he wouldn't *like* me," she offered moderately. "Good heavens, we know each other well enough! But it's something more than that that you've got to have before you can say a man is your beau," she went on.

"Encourage him!" Margaret suggested boldly.

"Who? Peter Platt?"

"Well,—don't act as if you didn't understand, Di. Of course Peter Platt!"

Rain streamed down the windowpanes; the shaken branches of the oaks spattered against the Gingham Tea Shop, and the Corner of China, and the photograph gallery. In the girls' lunchroom the air was cool and vague, but the steaming teapot and the little gas ring were helping to soften the cold.

"I want to tell you something about Peter Platt, Margaret. He lives at our house now, you know,—his family has moved away. And he studies law in the kitchen evenings, because there isn't any light on the top floor. And I want to tell you something about him. He never takes the slightest interest in me,—in that way, I mean. He tells me what he's doing, and I listen, and then he asks me what I'm doing, and he listens, and all the while there isn't any—fire in it, excitement, mushing, petting, whatever you want to call it!"

"But you don't want that, Di?"

"No. But I don't—I wonder if I can express this?" mused Diana, interrupting herself. "I don't know why," she recommenced,—"why he doesn't *want* to mush and to pet—those are disgusting words!" she broke off, "but you know what I mean. Peter'll carry on with other girls,—he had a great crush on Linda Volkmann, he was crazy about her. And before that he liked some red-headed girl from Mountain View who used to come into Sticky's for ice cream,—I never knew her name, and I don't think he did, but he'd come home all excited. 'My darling little red-head with the Chinese eyes was in today!' I got sick of that red-head with the Chinese eyes!"

"He may not feel that sort of thing because *you* don't, Di!"

"Well, then, why don't I?" Di demanded, looking with bright hard blue eyes at the other girl, her chin up. "Is there something the matter with *me?*"

"You're nineteen!" Margaret reminded her, smiling.

"Yes, my dear, and some day I'll be twenty-three, and then twenty-eight, and then thirty-nine."

"Oh, you'll be married long before that!" Margaret, with the instinctive feeling of the engaged girl that no state other than marriage could possibly be happy, said hearteningly.

"I don't see how, exactly. There are hundreds of boys at Lucas College, but they never see me. I haven't any place to invite them, I can't give suppers,—I've never in my life asked a boy to come to Gram's."

"Mother says that if a girl shuts herself up in a bandbox the right man will find her somehow."

"Oh, come now, Margaret. Look at the Peltries and the Canns, and Lucy Rhodes and Judy Coombs! No fine man hunted them down, in the post office and the telephone office! Look at Beet and May Rogers!"

"Well, maybe they didn't want to marry."

"Nonsense! Everyone wants to marry."

"I don't believe Beet Rogers ever did."

"Well, you ought to hear her talk, then. There was a sergeant in the army, 'way back in the Spanish War, when she was eighteen, and to hear her talk you'd think they were Aucassin and Nicolette!

"No," Di went on decidedly, as Margaret, finishing her tea, and looking at Di over the cup with her round gray eyes, was silent,—"no, it's something in me. Or something *not* in me!"

She fell brooding, staring into space somberly.

"Some women," she went on, "just naturally have whatever it is that attracts men. Some haven't. I haven't."

"You're one of the prettiest girls in Bayhead!" Margaret stated positively.

"I'm not. And if I were, beauty has nothing to do with it."

"Well," Margaret insisted, after a pause, "I believe you could wind Peter Platt around your finger tomorrow if you'd give him a chance."

"I know different. When I'm with him I simply—can't let go," Diana argued.

"You don't want to, idiot."

"I don't want to—well, go the limit," Diana agreed quickly. "Of course not! But I would like to—to get him excited about me, to have him saying silly things—and incoherent——"

"Oh, shut up!" said Margaret laughing, her face red.

"Well, you know what I mean."

"I know. But you're too fine for that sort of stuff, Di. You're above it. After all, you're a Rutherford girl. You're waiting for the—the real thing, before you let yourself go, and Peter isn't it."

"And the Rogerses and the Peltries and Lucy and Judy are all waiting, too! No, Margaret, I'll tell you what it is," Diana said, forcefully, "there are certain girls like me who are out of luck when it comes to marriage. We're working, to begin with, which isn't the most romantic situation in the world; we haven't got homes and money and dads to mix up cocktails, and mothers to buy us pretty clothes. No, I'll plug along here for about six more years like May, and then they'll offer me your job, and I'll be so pleased!"

There were angry tears in her eyes; her voice broke off short. Margaret dared not speak.

"Sometimes," Di said darkly, in a voice that was thickened by tears, "sometimes I think I'd marry anyone just to—just to *live!* Sometimes I think I'd just as soon go bad. Look at the fun Frankie Sellers has; she's out every night."

"She certainly is," Margaret conceded dryly, and Diana laughed.

"She and Emma Mae Tauber don't seem to worry about lacking—well, sex appeal," Diana persisted, a little ashamed of herself.

"Diana," Margaret began, after an interval in which both girls had cleared away expertly the last signs of the luncheon and had moved into the dressing room for a general scrubbing and combing and powdering, "do you ever hear from Bruce Palmer?"

Diana, her fresh skin emerging apricot-colored from the towel, her bright hair disordered, looked quickly at her companion.

"Never," she said briefly. Yet Margaret was shrewd enough to know that she was not sorry to be asked the question.

"Where is he?"

"Sweden."

"Funny!" Margaret mused.

"His mother managed that," Diana said, running a wet comb through the wavy red-gold of her hair. "She rushed him to Washington; she managed it somehow. His uncle has a lot of influence there; they all have. They made him a sort of secretary to the minister. I hope," she added a little viciously, as the comb jerked on a tangle,—"I hope he likes it!"

Margaret knew all this, but the subject was inexhaustibly fascinating.

" 'Member the day she came in, and you and he were back in the kitchen furnishings, talking?"

"He was only here three weeks," Diana mused, unpinning the disfiguring paper cuffs slowly, as she spoke. "If he'd been here another three weeks, I think it might all have been different."

"He was crazy about you."

"In his way maybe he was. But what break," Diana asked, looking out at the rain and the blown oaks, her thoughts far away,—"what break did I get? She was on the job like lightning,—his mother. She wasn't well; Brucie had to go with her to Washington. And then, when they were there, she talked diplomacy to him; she wanted her boy to do something worth while in the world. They knew

Mr. Pope, our minister to Sweden,—the whole thing worked like a charm!"

"If you saw him again, Di, do you think it would all come back?"

"My feeling for him? I don't know."

"She was afraid of you."

"His mother? She hated me. And I," Diana said darkly, —"I hate her!"

"Oh, no, you don't, you simp."

Diana laughed, suddenly herself again.

"Well, maybe I don't. Big fat freckled snob, why should I hate her? I told you about the day she sent for me and told me I couldn't afford to go to college, and that my grandmother was trying to borrow money to let me go,—sat back and enjoyed telling me what she thought of me for wanting to do what the Newbegin Park girls did!"

"I know!" Margaret, who knew the story, said sympathetically.

"Well, since that day I've thought that if ever—if *ever* I could get even with her—— Yes, Mr. Carkey!"

The last ejaculation was elicited by a shout from below. A lady wanted a washing machine demonstrated. What the hell were the girls doing up there—taking baths?

Laughing, tying on their aprons, Diana and Margaret fled precipitately down the narrow stairs, reëntered the store, hastily resumed their duties. Rain was still pouring down; the day was black, but the shop was lighted brightly in spots, and there were dangling lights waiting everywhere, so that the lawn mowers or the paint shelves or the fishing rods might be displayed at any moment.

The floors of the Bayhead Hardware Store, between the counters and the heaped and ranged merchandise, were oiled darkly; even in summer it was usually cool in here, and smelled not unpleasantly of varnish and machine oil and tar paper. The shop was really two large shops, and had

deeply indented windows on the street, almost like a theater
foyer; Diana often had to arrange one quarter of the window display, setting out green glasses, pink-and-white plates,
guest-room sets of tumbler and carafe. There were constant
sales in the china department. The obnoxious Mr. Morey,
imported from Chicago to add efficiency and pep and
modernity to the old-fashioned methods of the manager, old
Wat Eisenmann, was despised by them all; but he did seem
to know how to bring in customers, and spur their interest,
and even make them buy when they came in.

Today he had a washing machine churning steadily in
Diana's window, the clean suds frothing and foaming against
the sides of the glass tank, and the life-sized cardboard lady
who stood behind it beaming radiantly at her friends out
there in rainy College Avenue, and saying enthusiastically:
"Why, it's just fun to get through my wash with the
Homesmith!"

Inside the door there was another cardboard lady; this one
with her arm on an electric refrigerator. Beside her stood
her proud young husband; a golden-haired girl of five and a
handsome manly boy of eight were sharing his satisfaction.
"This is a birthday present with a future and a past!" the
happy wife and mother was exclaiming. "Now try to get me
out of my kitchen!"

Delighted cardboard folk were everywhere. A cardboard
boy on the knife counter was shouting, "Gee, Dad, what a
knife!" A cardboard householder was pouring a flood of
electric light into a burglar's face and sternly telling the
invader: "I wouldn't feel safe without my Flasholite!" Back
of the glass counter a stout, comfortable cardboard house-
keeper, holding forth a tray of ruby-clear jelly glasses,
advised younger women confidentially: "No mold gets in
under Perry's patent Jellclere tops, girls!"

Besides Margaret, the cashier, and Diana, who was the
only other young woman clerk, there were in the shop some

half-dozen men and boys, and in the houseware department there were Miss Rogers, Mrs. Race, and Mrs. Olsen. May was past fifty, and old Mrs. Olsen almost seventy. Mrs. Olsen was a faded little Norwegian, frightened, hard-working, her hands rough and hard, her voice a nervous whisper. Mrs. Race was ample, friendly, her white hair nicely piled, her big figure quite adept as it negotiated the narrow aisles, stooped to reach for bowls under the counter, stretched up to grasp the coffee pots on the high shelves. She was the president of the local chapter of the W. C. T. U. and went home, two short blocks, every noon to lunch with a model widowed daughter and exemplary grandchildren. Everything about her was exemplary—the kindly way she talked about her neighbors and paid her bills; the budget on which she and Ellowese and the children lived; her grandson's conduct and honors in the Scouts. It was perhaps natural that at nineteen Diana should despise Mrs. Race, pity her, and sometimes secretly make fun of her.

She herself, Diana Carmichael, was the only woman employed by the hardware firm who had any ambition or ever made plans for the future. If Margaret had any plans, they included Len, and a cottage out toward California Avenue, and babies. The older women had no plans; they merely had jobs, and they clung to them with pathetic tenacity. When Mr. Morey, the new assistant manager and efficiency expert, had suggested that they might dispense with the services of May Rogers, not only Diana, but Margaret and some of the boys, and all of May's group, had indignantly canvassed the town, working up sales for May, who had triumphantly weathered the storm and was now more secure, in her humble dim salesmanship of tumblers and egg beaters and shelf paper, than ever.

Diana had outstripped them all before she had been more than a few months with the Bayhead Hardware Company. Good-naturedly, easily, she had risen to be the firm's most

trusted woman clerk, and even to hold her own with the men.
She was pretty, alert, interested; she had liked making sales
and writing out bills in her fine, square little handwriting;
she had worked hard. While Margaret had been telephoning
her lover and growing dreamy and abstracted over memories
and visions, Diana had been briskly absorbed in her job.

In the beginning, poor little lovesick fool of almost-
eighteen that she had been, it had been all for Bruce Palmer's
admiration and notice, she told herself now. Diana had taken
her position in late June; Bruce had come in in mid-July. The
next few weeks had been for her a time of fluttered excitement when she would not have changed places even with
Joan, or with anybody else. Still in her pleated dark green
skirt and white blouse, she had loved the excitement and
novelty of the store and the continual daily thrill of seeing
Bruce there.

Joan and Patsy and Connie had naturally come into the
shop on all sorts of pretenses and occasions then; they were
all keenly interested in Bruce, and Diana more than once
had thought that they would have liked her legitimate excuse
for being there in his company. She had had constant need
to consult him: "Mr. Palmer, Mr. Eisenmann wanted to see
you. . . . Mr. Palmer, did you sell that green standard
lamp?"

Twice Bruce had taken her home in his car,—yes, to the
disreputable end of Mason Avenue. And he had brought her
candy and chocolate bars and caramel corn in his careless
magnificent way, and twice had telephoned in the evening for
breath-taking suggestions,—the movies, and Sticky's afterward——!

They had talked, she and Bruce, of college and polo and
his car and his duck club. Diana had asked him everything
she knew he wanted to be asked, had listened in absorbed
attention when he answered her. It had been to Diana that he
had first confided in September the news that meant for her

the end of their companionship. The family was home again from the Lake; the dream was over. He would not need amusement in the evening now; everyone was home, the Newbegins and the Porters and the Rowleys. And he might be leaving the shop; his mother might be "obliged" to go to Washington, and she was trying to talk him into considering the diplomatic service there. Diana's heart had sunk— sunk.

Patsy and Connie had gone away to school; Joan had entered Lucas so pleasantly, so easily! There had been regular supper parties at the Rowleys' for Joan's new college crowd; sorority girls, handsome big boys who rooted at football games in thin sweaters and heavy corduroy trousers. Joan had been lovelier than ever,—rosy, dark, glowing in new furs, happy, and when Connie and Elinor had come home from Eastern schools for Christmas, the social columns of the San Francisco newspapers had taken note of the fact, under the heading: "Bayhead Sub-Debs Return for Holidays."

They all had lived in a world that was not Diana's world. It was for her to sell electric iceboxes to happy young husbands, and waffle irons and toasters and radios, in cardboard boxes papered in holly and ribbons, for Christmas presents.

If she had cried herself to sleep sometimes, nobody knew it. If she had suffered, she had kept her head high. She had been Wat Eisenmann's best salesman,—not that it mattered. At eighteen it meant little to her that she could surpass her companions,—homely, short-haired May, with the nervous manner and the smile that showed her gums; little old obsequious Mrs. Olsen; bland big plain Mrs. Race, whose one interest in life outside of her model family was the Woman's Christian Temperance Union. These always did their humble best; Diana's careless second best was better. But after a while she stopped trying even for that. Life was too dull to have anything matter much.

Men did not pay much attention to girls who worked in hardware stores. Diana had discovered this for herself, as the weeks went by and were months, and she was eighteen —nineteen—nearly twenty. It was all very well to be helpful and neat and prompt and sweet-tempered and respectable, but it got one nowhere. You could just work on like a mole in the earth, and the other girls had all the fun.

She might have had some fun with these other girls,— with girls like Frankie and Emma Mae,—if it had not been for those years at Rutherford. In those years she had been the equal—no, the superior—of Joan and Patsy and Con. She could not forget it. She could not run about with all sorts of men, all sorts of girls, to all sorts of places. It coarsened them; it would coarsen her. She had no inclination toward that sort of thing.

But life certainly was not making fineness and culture easy for her, she would think bitterly, in moods of young rebellion and heartache. To be so cut away from her old associates, so poor; to share with Gram a dreary big front parlor for a bedroom, and have to mount a flight of dim, odorous stairs to reach the nearest bathroom; to know that that bathroom was also used by casual lodgers,—all this hurt her pride, held her down, discouraged her.

However, there had been some changes at Gram's house. The Coggleses had moved away shortly after Rudy had been killed by a truck in Lincoln Street much more than a year ago. May Rogers's aunt in Connecticut had died and left her nine hundred dollars one midsummer when the Rogers girls had been renting for their vacation the actual Carmel cottage they had instantly bought with the windfall; and Peter Platt had come to live at Gram's. Sixteen months ago Diana and her grandmother had moved into the empty front parlor where the Coggleses had been hived, mating and bearing and living and dying for several years, and Peter Platt had been installed in their old room, once the mansion's back parlor.

They had scoured and scraped and papered their new quarters and opened the old fireplace, it is true; they had taken away the scarred table where Mrs. Coggles had heated so many baby bottles, so many kettles of water with which to wipe the small blonde frightened faces of her daughters. But Diana's dream of turning the back parlor into a sort of study and making the pantry where her father slept into a bathroom was not destined to come true. No, Gram could not afford that. Peter would pay four dollars a week for his room; and Gram had bills to consider.

There was not much use in struggling to improve her environment anyway, Diana thought. Mason Avenue, backed by the Gully and Niggertown, walled by the empty and dilapidated Eureka Garage, facing Mrs. Pawsey's forlorn "Arbor Villa," and its embellishment of signs: "Rooms," "Board," "Modes," "Violin," "Apartment To Let," was not hopeful material.

CHAPTER X

RAIN and rain and rain. Diana, on a wet afternoon like this, had time to think of matters at home, and of what she felt were lost youth, lost hopes, lost years. She looked out of the windows of the Bayhead Hardware Store and saw the rain dancing in wild drops on the empty sidewalks and running like thick milky coffee in the gutters. She had been less than eighteen when she had come into this store, and she was nearly twenty now. She wondered if she would still be here at twenty-five, at thirty.

Going to Margaret's little cage with a customer who wanted a check cashed, she asked, "How on earth are we going to get home?"

"Oh," Margaret said, "Len just telephoned. He's got the truck, and he'll come for us."

"Oh, good!" Diana said, delivering package and change carelessly. She did not see the annoyed look the customer gave her as she walked away. Half an hour later she and Margaret scrambled to the high driver's seat beside Len, after a dash through flying drops; the truck skidded and slipped on the wet streets, and presently set her down at her own door. "Len, you are a darling!" she said. But thin, shabby, absorbed Len rarely paid any attention to her. There was but one woman in the world for Len. Sometimes he would say, almost sourly, "Sure, I'm wonderful!" and Margaret would look quickly at Diana, afraid that he might have hurt her feelings.

Tonight he said nothing. Diana ran up the peeled and

shabby steps of her grandmother's house through the rain and disappeared into the dusky, unlighted bare hallway.

The usual rainy-day smell of dampness, dust, plaster, boiling vegetables assailed her. Today it must be beets; the strong earthy odor pervaded the house. Diana turned left into the big front parlor bedroom; it was dim, orderly; it breathed an air of emptiness, moisture, the odor of a kerosene stove.

Her wet clothing hung on hangers, her soaked hat stuffed with a crumpled newspaper, Diana yawned wearily as she slipped into a kitchen cotton and ran a comb through her hair. Oh, dear——

She went through the hall, glanced into the pantry where her father's narrow bed stood beneath the empty old shelves, beside the unused sink. Everything was chilly, ugly, shadowy today.

In the kitchen it was better, much better. The big range was fired, because Bluebell, Mrs. Chamberlain's big colored woman from Niggertown, had been washing and cleaning all day long and had left beside the violently boiling beets upon the stove a pot roast smothered in carrots and onions and turnips, and a yellow bowl covered with a napkin, in which salt-rising dough was forming into a smooth mold. There was a homy warmth about the kitchen in the rainy late afternoon, with the lights lighted, and the deepening dark and wetness assaulting the high windows; there was a pleasant sense of security and calm.

Diana's grandmother was busy with the making of a pudding at the table.

"I haven't made my apple, suet, and cornmeal pudding for I don't know when, Di."

"Is that what you're at?"

Di sat down and reached for a peeled quarter of apple. She gnawed upon it idly, relaxing in her chair, watching her grandmother like a child.

"Want me to butter your mold?"

"It's buttered, Di."

"How long does it bake?"

"You're hungry, you poor child, you. It doesn't bake but an hour. The meal's all cooked."

"What's happened today?"

Mrs. Chamberlain removed her thoughts from the pudding with a start.

"Well, I don't know why I didn't tell you. Ella Corrigan went to the hospital today."

"Did?"

Diana's fair forehead wrinkled. "Oh, that's too bad!" she said. "Was it bad?"

"No, she seemed real calm. She said she was glad to go."

The girl at the table, nibbling her apple, reflected upon the other woman's face. Ella would never return from the hospital; it was the end of the road for her. Pain and drugs and sleep, and drowsy farewells now. Ella,—gone in the rain——

"Then your front room's empty?"

"No. I declare there does seem to be a Providence in these things," Mrs. Chamberlain said, carrying the pudding dish across the big room to the oven. "I went to the door with Ella, and I told her I'd get up somehow to the hospital and see her tomorrow, if the rain stopped. And while I stood there I thought I'd put out my sign, so I took it out of the hatrack drawer and hung it up,—'twas raining, so I didn't believe anyone would come in, but it wasn't half an hour— Bluebell was working up there—before this lady and gentleman came in,—Tressady,—that's the name. Hasn't he got it written there,—Neal Tressady?"

"Neal Tressady! It sounds like an actor . . . Hollywood."

"Well, he has been in the pictures, and on the stage, too. They seem to be real well fixed."

"A retired old actor?" Diana mused. "Well, we've had everything else, haven't we?"

"He isn't old, Di. Twenty-six or -eight, maybe. He's her son."

"Oh-h-h."

"They want the big room, and then he'd have Louis Hall's old room, right next it. I'd have to do considerable cleaning, and I said I'd paper some."

"And that'd fill the whole house, wouldn't it?"

"I was thinking that. I don't know," Mrs. Chamberlain said, sitting down at the table again with the yellow bowl in her lap, and beginning to tear off spongy bits of dough and mold them into balls. "I don't know how 'tis I'm so fortunate. Mrs. Pawsey is having a real hard time over at the Villa."

"But what of these Tressadys, Gram? Are they coming?"

"They were going over to Mrs. Robbins, but I don't believe she has any room, either. She liked the big room, because it has the big closet with the window in it. She can get her breakfast, and she says she likes a cup of tea about four o'clock,—she's been in England, it seems."

"Where would she have her meals, Gram?"

"Oh, I forgot to tell you that. She's a sort of partner of Kate Witherspoon, over at the Virginia Tea Shop. That's one reason she likes our neighborhood. He was going to come back this afternoon and let me know if they found anything else, but maybe—" Mrs. Chamberlain glanced at the gray deluge that was pouring down the window panes— "maybe the rain's kept him away," she said.

"They've probably found something else!"

Diana's grandmother was placing the neat little rolls of dough in a buttered baking pan to rise. Her old fingers worked expertly; she presently used two fingertips to butter the tops of the little white lumps.

"Peter's coming to dinner, Di."

"Peter is?"

"He phoned. Seems Phil wants to go somewhere tonight, and Peter said he'd take the late shift."

"Three then." But Diana made no move to clear or set the table. Plenty of time. The vociferous alarm clock on the sink shelf said seven minutes to six; the pudding would not be done until quarter to seven.

"Quiet in the store today?"

"Dead." Diana remembered suddenly the officiousness of Mr. Morey, and her eyes narrowed. But it was not until Peter had come in, spattered and breathless, that she mentioned the matter.

Then, when they three were enjoying the pot roast, the beets, the fluffy rolls, she said idly:

"You should have heard little sneezy Morey today."

Peter looked at her expectantly. He was wolfing his food, for before he took the nine-o'clock shift he intended to go to a political meeting downtown. Peter was public-spirited, not to say socialistic in his tendencies, and never missed an opportunity to listen to fiery campaign arguments, or indeed, if encouraged, to leap to his feet in public denunciation or defense of them.

"What'd Morey say?"

"Oh, he said he was disappointed in me, and that I was not showing the true coöperative spirit that made the Bayhead Hardware Store unlike any other on the Peninsula, and so on!"

Di spoke on the tone of a yawn, shrugged.

"Ha!" Peter ejaculated, interested. "What joo say?"

"I looked at my nails."

"What's this meeting tonight, Peter?"

"For Rocket. We're trying to get Torrey out. He's a crook. Why don't you come, Di? It's keen; you'd love it."

"Not in this rain!" Diana took small interest in public affairs. She sighed, rested her elbows on the table; won-

dered what Joan and Patsy were doing. The storm rattled
the windows.

Peter attacked his pudding enthusiastically. There was an
interruption. A young man, with a handsome face and dark
curly hair dashed with rain, opened the door from the inner
hall and smiled into the kitchen.

"I rang twice, and then, as the door was open, I walked
in!"

"Well, for mercy's sake, Mr.—Mr. Tressady!" Gram
stammered, flustered.

Neal Tressady. He came in, was introduced, and drew up
a chair to the table. He shook back his hair and sent his
engaging eager glance from face to face.

"I was sort of afraid you'd be at dinner, but I couldn't
come any other time."

He and Diana looked at each other, and she saw in his
eyes that odd kindling and darkening that she had seen in
other men's eyes in the first minute of meeting. She was a
woman, beautiful and twenty, with slim hands and ivory
skin, with her fair hair pressed by her own fingers into a
cap of ripples and waves about her proud young head, her
heavy eyelashes only half raised, and her mouth puckered
into only half a smile, as she watched him.

Peter faded from the scene, bent upon his patriotic
errand; Gram went to answer a telephone; Diana and Neal
were left alone.

They sat on at the disordered table, talking. He had de-
clined pudding, but was enjoying tea and rolls. He told her
almost immediately that his real name was George Neal, but
that he had taken one of the names in his mother's family
upon becoming an actor.

He had acted in a great many plays, and knew a great
many players. Some of the famous folk of Hollywood were
"Nancy" and "Joan," "Ben" and "Wally," to him. He had
been many places,—born in Turkey twenty-nine years ago,

his father, a consul, had dragged him and his mother from one place to another all through his childhood.

"Bess got tired of it. Bess is my mother. She's the most wonderful woman alive. I'm crazy about my mother!"

"I'm hoping to meet her."

"That's right, you didn't meet her. She's terribly cute. I call her 'Bess,' or 'Chérie.' I've never called her 'Mother.' She was only nineteen when I was born,—she doesn't weigh a hundred pounds."

He told her that his mother had been living apart from his father since he himself had been twelve years old. He and she were chums, and all his friends adored Bess, or Chérie. She often was taken for his sister.

"Kate Witherspoon's a great friend of hers; they're crazy about each other. I've always called her 'Aunt Kate,' see? She lived with us in Culver City, and she came up here two years ago and opened the Virginia. She's made a great go of it, see? So now she wants my mother to be with her and open one of those giftie shoppies, see?"

He was so eager, so friendly and confidential and entertaining that Diana was immediately transported into her most sparkling mood. Her blue eyes danced with mischief and amusement as she talked to him, or rather listened, and led him to talk.

When her grandmother came back and began, in the desultory yet interruptive fashion Diana so often found annoying, to clear the table, Neal jumped up and lent her expert assistance. He asked for an apron, and Diana laughed as she tied it about his bigness and straightness and broadness. He was something more than six feet in height, three inches at least taller than Peter, and had an athlete's slim-waisted, broad-shouldered figure.

"Bess and I used to do all our own work," he explained, wiping dishes rapidly. "We had a top floor in an old building on Washington Square South, New York,—you know New York?"

"Not yet!" Diana said, but in a tone that indicated that New York and adventure were only around the corner.

"Well, we had a great little place there. And all the crowd would come in Sunday afternoons, and Chérie'd send 'em after rye bread and Swiss cheese——"

It sounded such fun! This crazy boy was probably drawing a pretty long bow half the time, but what fun he was, with his quick, animated speech, and his illustrative gestures, like a stage Frenchman,—and his "despising" this, and "all but going off into a coma" at that!

"I was so mad about this Russian woman, mind you, that I wanted to kill myself!"

"But you said her son was your age?"

"Vanni. He *was*."

"Then you were simply crazy."

"But I *tell* you I'm crazy. Anyway," Neal said to Mrs. Chamberlain, "I've got her jealous, haven't I?"

He made them laugh again, when, having finished the dishes, and the swabbing of the sink, and the disposal of the last crumb, he asked in a businesslike way, "Here, haven't we any Koralax? Can't get old sinkboards clean without Koralax!"

Afterward he said, "I parked in the street. Have you got an old hat that the rain couldn't hurt? Let's boom somewhere."

"This child's much too tired to go out," Gram protested, alarmed.

"Listen, Mrs. Chamberlain, here's all we'll do. We'll take a look at the movies, here and in Redwood City, and if we don't like 'em we'll go over to Chloë's and have a sandwich. How's that?"

"Chloë's is all right."

"Sure it's all right. There's dancing, and the radio, and broiled chickens; that's all safe, isn't it?"

"How do you know about Chloë's?" Diana asked.

"I went to Lucas College, you know, for half a year."

"You *did!*"

"Sure. Six years ago. I lived at the Fraternity House."

"You did! And where was your mother?"

"She was with Aunt Kate in Culver City. My mother, you know, married again about seven years ago. I think she did it to give me a home. But it didn't—" said Neal, with his brilliant smile,—"it didn't—*take*. She beat it after a year. But meanwhile I'd held the old boy up for my first year in college. Go get your hat and coat!"

Diana, excited, happy, forgetting all her woes, flew to obey. Gram quietly telephoned Kate Witherspoon.

CHAPTER XI

NEAL'S MOTHER, duly moving into the big upstairs front room a few days later, proved to be a pretty, youthful little person, whose life had held one event and one only—the coming of Neal. Her boy was her world. His babyhood, his childhood, his brilliant young manhood, what Hollywood thought of him, what all his teachers and friends always had thought of him, these formed the theme of her inexhaustible discourse. That sometimes they were taken for sister and brother, or man and wife, was a source of almost tearful pleasure to her.

Neal was charming with his mother, just sufficiently disrespectful, just sufficiently tender. He made fun of her sentimentalism, jerked her about, kissed her, bullied her.

"Isn't she a sap?" he asked Diana, over her small proud head. But when he and Diana were alone he made it more loving, "Haven't I got some mother?"

The Tressadys had a piano, which was somehow got upstairs, and on which Neal played charmingly. He was not a musician,—he did not pretend to be,—but he could accompany himself when he sang certain songs, unusual songs. "Absent," and "Cargoes," and a Jacobin Scotch song, "Son of Mine." Diana never tired of them, or of watching the splendid body on the piano bench, the dark rich hair, the moving hands. Often he wore white silk shirts, without tie or vest or collar; she thought him the handsomest creature she had ever seen.

Almost every afternoon now she went up to Mrs. Tressady's room, and they had tea together, Neal's mother and she. Sometimes he was there, sometimes not. Often he came in when they had almost finished, and teased his mother's cat with bits of cooky, or drank cups of hot water. Tea fattened him, he said, and he had to think of his public.

"There must be four or five persons who remember me in *Young Woodley,* Diana. For their sake I will be true!"

He had played *Young Woodley* in stock in Cincinnati. Irvin Watts, the dramatic director of Lucas Memorial College, had no sooner heard of Neal's presence in Bayhead than he planned a presentation of the English college play for Lucas, so Neal had to be away for rehearsals. Also he wrote a Christmas article about the Bayhead university, and other universities, and, to Diana's amazement, actually sold it for one hundred dollars. But then he could do anything!

Mrs. Tressady had made her room quite lovely with hangings, pillows, lamps, books. She liked things to be pretty about her, she said; she had had to pitch her camp in some funny places since she had run off, like the bad little thing of seventeen that she was, with Neal's father, and yet she had always tried to make every one of them homelike and comfy.

Her tea set was on a low table, with a spirit lamp, a cracker jar, and little fringed napkins. She missed,—oh, she did terribly miss,—a fireplace; she always had had a fireplace. But never mind, it was a lovely old room, and they weren't going to stop being happy just because they didn't have a fire!

She liked Diana, and Diana liked her. They talked together most happily, the little faded lady sitting back in her high chair behind the teapot, the girl glowing and absorbed at her knee. Sometimes Diana tried to retail to her grandmother some of the things that Mrs. Tressady told her; descriptions of social triumphs, of Neal's little-boy days, of frocks, compliments, of the glories of the Rightwells. Mrs.

Tressady had been a Rightwell. But Gram, as a usual thing, was not interested.

To Diana the glowing, comfortable room upstairs, with the loving little aristocratic woman in it, and the laughing, impudent, clever boy, was like a miracle in the drabness of Mason Avenue. She could not believe that one house could at once hold rooms as drear as the Rogers girls' shabby suite and an apartment as wonderfully transformed as the Tressadys'.

Neal had a motorcar, "The Road Louse,"—a disreputable affair, but yet it moved. He was presently to return in it to Hollywood, where all sorts of "propositions" awaited him. He sometimes discussed these with Diana; Bert Somebody wanted him to do this, and Bill Somebody Else wanted him to do that,—they'd have to come through if they wanted him.

"Because look," he might say to her moodily, "listen. I've got about six more years when I can do juveniles,—that's all. I've got to get something good."

"But Neal, you can do lots of other things besides act!"

"Yes, but I want to act."

"I know."

He fascinated her without in the least dazzling her. Diana had never known persons just like the Tressadys; Bohemians, gypsies, and yet with the old silver and the old daguerreotypes and the fine names behind them, and so much that was pretty, amusing, affectionate, exciting, in their way of living. Life took on exciting contours when Neal was anywhere about; he was in many ways a boy, he was completely natural, spontaneous, often ridiculous, and yet he did manage to pack more laughter, music, nonsense, argument, thrill into every hour than most of Bayhead folk experienced in a month. His talk was interpolated with French words, German phrases, odd bits of philosophy that could not but impress Diana's youth and ardor and hunger for life.

She and he became warmly friendly, and the new element in her days made every other element tolerable.

Even Peter Platt succumbed to Neal's careless charm. He told Diana that sure, he liked Neal. Peter and Diana went to see *Young Woodley* in Lucas Auditorium in Thanksgiving week, and afterward they went behind the scenes and found Neal surrounded by friends, hot, wet with perspiration, excited, his eyebrows darkly marked, his eyes shadowed in blue, his upper lip beaded. He laughed excitedly at Diana's praise and, putting his big arms about her, kissed her, a distinction that made everyone laugh, and Diana, flushed and happy, feel that somehow she was living at last.

Neal made one feel that way,—but Diana wished, somehow, that it wasn't Neal who did it. Despite all the excitement and all the laughter, she wished that Neal weren't quite —*quite* what he was. It was all pleasant and novel and thrilling enough, but Diana felt uneasily that it was largely on the surface, frothy and frivolous and shallow.

Neal did not drink and he did not smoke; that was to his credit with Gram, at least. Diana did not feel very strongly about either habit, but she was glad to count these as two points in his favor. But he was disgracefully procrastinating and lazy; he would come cheerfully down to the kitchen in a handsome dressing gown and slippers at eleven o'clock on Sunday mornings; Diana suspected he was just as late straight through the week, although she was not there to see it then. He never answered letters until too late; it drove her frantic to realize that opportunities of all sorts were eternally slipping by him unimproved.

Peter worked harder than ever on Sundays; Sunday was the big day at the soda fountain, and Peter was on duty from noon until midnight. Diana, however amused she might be by Neal's absurdities, yet somehow could not be proud of him, when Peter, shaved and clean and businesslike, came

out to the kitchen for a late breakfast, and found Neal
enthusiastically making a sponge cake. His grandmother
had taught him how to make sponge cake; it was no good at
all unless you could turn the whipped whites of the eggs
upside down in the bowl without spilling them, he said.

He went to Los Angeles about a "proposition," flying
there to save time after the period when saving time might
have had any effect was past. He went to San Francisco
about another proposition, and played there in stock for one
week, as an Indian prince, looking so stunning in his turban,
white European clothes, and red sash that Diana did not
wonder girls sent him mash letters. A hundred dollars for
one week's work, and twenty mash letters besides; it was
not surprising that Neal did not find the idea of an office
job very thrilling!

By the time the Tressadys had been two weeks at the
Chamberlain house he was desperately in love with Diana.
Reluctantly, she had to admit to herself that she was not in
love with him. But nevertheless it was gratifying to know
that he was there.

CHAPTER XII

JUST BEFORE CHRISTMAS Miss Adler came into the Bayhead Hardware Store as a holiday extra. Five clerks were added to the regular staff for the rush; by December first the shop was crowded every day, and lamps, china, radios, ice-boxes, toasters, skates, and knives were being bought in scores, marked for delivery Christmas Eve, wrapped as gifts, put into the "Hold" bins to wait for the twenty-fourth.

May Rogers, nervous, veiny-handed old Mrs. Olsen, Mrs. Race, bland and kindly, with her white ribbon always in view, were kept flying. Diana was everywhere, and Margaret worked swiftly and steadily with bills and silver in the cashier's cage. But it was soon to be seen that Miss Adler, affectionately known to a large circle of friends and relatives as "Jackie," was outstriving the best of them. Diana did not like her.

Jackie Adler made much of the obnoxious Morey, for one thing. She listened to him, quoted him, obeyed him enthusiastically. She talked with him humbly, as a disciple with a master; might she try to sell off that extra stock of flower-pot jars on a table by the door? Had he noted that every one of those lamps he had gotten in San Francisco had sold right away?

Officiously, Jackie always appeared to be right in Diana's way. No matter what she did she found Jackie there first, opening packages, storing stock, marking prices. Jackie always had Mr. Morey's authority; old Mr. Eisenmann was not important nowadays, and the new efficiency expert was all-powerful. Eventually there was some question of the saleswomen using the old stockroom for a lunch and rest

room. Jackie had brightly suggested its use as a toy sales-
room.

May lunched with her sister at school two blocks away;
Mrs. Olsen ran all the way home to cook lunch for her
grandchildren; Mrs. Race walked majestically to the noontime table of her impeccable family group. But these three
shared with Margaret and Diana their consternation when
their lunchroom was taken away.

"The tendency is for you young girls to spend too much
time up there, beautifying!" the odious Morey explained
with a wink to Diana, when she protested.

"How do you mean, 'beautifying'?" Diana asked coldly.

"Well, maybe you're not beautifying. Maybe you're
settling the affairs of state," the manager amended it good-
naturedly. He was never so agreeable as when he was being
devilish, Margaret and Diana agreed.

The battle raged to and fro in the hardware store. Christmas was past, and the first weeks of the New Year, when
practically every Christmas gift was credited or exchanged,
went by, and still Jackie remained complacently in the employ of the Bayhead Hardware Store and assisted the
admiring Morey, and still everything she did was as inevitably right as everything Diana did was wrong. In
mid-January, when Diana was half kneeling to arrange a
tower of trays that had cascaded to the dark oiled floor,
Mr. Morey, passing, asked to speak to her for a moment.
They stepped to the comparative privacy of the office.

"Miss Carmichael," said Mr. Morey, "I thought I'd like
to tell you before discussing it with the other young ladies.
We are making some changes in here; as you know, my one
object is the welfare of the shop, and what I feel I owe to my
employers. I'm an employee with the rest; that's all. I was
telling the boys this morning that it's as much up to me as to
anyone else to make good.

"We hope very much to have you back with us some day.

But for the present we must make some changes,—dispense with your services,—for the present, that is. When things pick up, you may be very sure that we'll let you know. Meanwhile I have made a different distribution of work, I'm dividing yours between Miss Rogers and Mrs. Race. Miss Adler feels that she can take on Mrs. Olsen's department,— perhaps she can't. Perhaps we'll have to try some other arrangement——"

There was a great deal more, but Diana did not hear it. She was concerned only with the desperate need of not showing him the shock and amazement that were shaking her to the soul. Fired! Fired from this little one-horse hardware store. It was not thinkable! She felt sick with anger, her mouth was filled with salt water and her hands were cold, but she could remain outwardly calm—she *must*——

"You mean from the first, Mr. Morey?"

"I thought from Saturday."

Saturday would be the sixteenth. Two weeks' salary less. Diana walked away from him and over to Margaret's cage.

"I'm fired," she said, with a shaky little laugh. Margaret's conscious eyes met hers; Margaret knew.

They went to lunch at Sticky's and told Peter, and his indignation and their own made them all feel better. Diana kept repeating that she did not care about herself, but when she thought that that rotten Adler had gotten poor Mrs. Olsen out, too, it made her mad. She told the family about it at dinner that night; Mrs. Tressady had persuaded Gram to give her and Neal dinners,—breakfast was late, luncheon neither one ate, dinner was the only meal they needed, and the Virginia had been closed for repairs.

So there were four of them at dinner in the big kitchen. Neal helped cook it with his own amazing expertness and minimized the calamity in his own convincing way.

"What of it? You weren't going to stay in a hardware store much longer, Di!"

"No-o-o. Of course not!"

"Twenty a week after three years! A three-dollar raise in three years!"

"They only pay Margaret twenty-five."

"It's silly! I'm glad you're out."

"But it's that snake Jackie that makes me mad."

"Oh, forget her!"

"Mrs. Morey coming in today and making a fuss about her! She brought her some violets."

"In six months," Neal assured her roundly, "you'll forget the whole bally thing! That isn't life; that's marking time!"

And when they were alone together he expanded it.

"You're so exquisite, Butterfly; you're so different! How *could* a bonehead like Morey do anything but hate you!"

This was consoling. And it was restful not to have to hurry on Monday to see other clerks moving along Mason Avenue, and be idle and at ease; to loiter over coffee and toast with Neal, who was very bright and amusing, and full of preposterous suggestions for a new start.

Also, prettily dressed, it was fun to walk with him into College Avenue, feeling so oddly free with the clocks showing half-past eleven, and to have him buy her a brass idol and a china bowl in the Japanese store, and caramel corn at the corner. They looked at fresh rolls in the Women's Exchange, loitered past the banks and the real estate offices, studied the photographs of suburban homes for sale, and the shoes in Philliber's.

"Let's just get on the trolley, Di, and see where it goes. I've never really known. And my car's laid up today."

"Oh, let's!" Di told herself that she was tired of struggling; much better to do things Neal's way and let the idle, happy current of life carry one along in its flood. Ride aimlessly on a trolley, come aimlessly back to buy a ten-cent book in the second-hand bookstore, buy cookies for dinner, and lie down and read for two hours before it was time to prepare it. She had not tried to lose her position, she was more than willing to help Gram and carry her share of the load, but if things turned out this way, then it was just silly to wonder and worry; Neal didn't worry, and he had a lot more fun than Peter did.

The evening paper, twisted into a projectile, was always flung on the garden earth. Diana, returning from her happy truant afternoon with Neal, picked it up and carried it into the house. Neal was going to practise; she was going to lie down. But she would be up for tea with his mother at five.

Mrs. Tressady had by this time perceived clearly how the wind was blowing, but her own enthusiastic fondness for Diana had preceded Neal's, and she rejoiced that she and her adored boy shared this wonderful thing, like so many others. Diana was "our girl," "our marvelous Papillon," and "you Delicious!"

"But of course he's head over heels, poor infant," said Bess Tressady. Diana laughed. "But he *is,* you bad girl," the mother persisted.

"Good for him," said Diana, a little off the solid earth.

"Good perhaps ten years ago, but Neal's twenty-nine now. That isn't puppy love."

"He's so enthusiastic," Diana murmured, a little embarrassed by the almost tragic intensity of the other's tone, "that I imagine he is always finding—ideals."

"No, he isn't, Di," his mother answered at once, seriously.

Diana refilled her teacup. What did Mrs. Tressady expect her to say or do? Obviously, until Neal declared himself formally, there was nothing for her to say, and he would hardly do that until he had a job. She felt suddenly silly, and as if she were playing a part; as if they were all playing parts.

He came into the dim twilight room that was scented with

tea and violets, while they talked of him, and when he saw Diana, although he had left her only an hour or two before, she saw his expression change. He settled down on a hassock at her knee, taking possession of her hand, not saying anything. She felt his lips against her fingers, and in spite of herself her blood began to warm and her heart to beat with slow, heavy strokes.

"You're here!" his mother said.

"Bread and butter?" Diana asked, bending with the plate so that he could reach it. He immediately doubled up a sandwich, finished it in two bites.

"Di tell you what we did today?"

"She was telling me. Riding to the end of a car line, and walking in a graveyard!"

"It was fun!" Diana said youthfully. But she felt her tone a little artificial. She could not make it come real, somehow, the lovely room, and the lamp, the tea kettle and the lump sugar; the little loving purring woman so insistent on romance; the big man, conquered, quiet, at her knee.

"It was the happiest day of my life," Neal observed unemotionally. Again Diana felt her blood quicken. "You're so matchless!" he said in a whisper, when his mother had bustled to the adjoining hall for more water. "I'm simply —simply dotty about you!"

Diana went down to tea a little dazed. How could Neal, and how could his mother, go so far and no further? Yet he had not a job, and had not any money; she knew that. They did pay their bills, the Tressadys, but irregularly and tardily. Mrs. Tressady would give Gram ten dollars with an appealing look. "Now, where does that leave us?"

Gram kept accounts strictly; often the Tressadys' payments left them still considerably in her debt. Neal had meals with Gram and Diana; breakfasts were thirty-five cents, dinners fifty. Even if he helped with dishes or made sponge cake there must be a charge. There were telephone charges; San

Francisco, Menlo, once even Los Angeles. There was a check that Gram had cashed.

Once Gram, to Diana's embarrassment, presented the Tressadys with a bill; it came to something close to a hundred dollars, and Diana, anxiously watching her grandmother write it out with a steel pen and a bottle of ink, murmured that it might be made a *little* less.

"Why?" Gram asked brusquely. "It's all out of my pocket."

Diana subsided. It was with tremendous surprise as well as relief that she heard, that afternoon, that it had been paid in full, and that Mrs. Tressady had presented Gram with a little pot of begonias to seal the bargain.

"I don't think she liked it, either!" Gram observed. Diana shriveled.

"Don't?" she asked fearfully. And that afternoon she did not quite dare to go up to tea, for fear that Mrs. Tressady might be resentful of Gram's rapacity.

But presently Neal came bounding down for her, and a laughing, deprecatory allusion to her grandmother's "tremendous business capacity" was the only allusion his mother made to the recent unpleasantness.

"Which silly folk like you and Neal and I don't know anything about!" she said.

"Why was he named 'Neal,' Mrs. Tressady?"

"Oh, come, it was going to be 'Chérie,' wasn't it?"

Diana flushed. Somehow, although she admired and loved Mrs. Tressady, she did not quite want to call her "Chérie." It seemed like a yielding, a letting herself down into the too sweet, too soft, too languorous atmosphere of her room.

"Chérie, then," she smiled awkwardly.

"Why did I name him George? Neal was his last name, you know. But I've told you that?"

No, she hadn't told Di that. So, quite happily and eagerly and substantially, she told it, and Neal sat quiet at Diana's knee, now and then pressing the fingers of her hand against his hard young cheek, now and then turning about to look up at her and smile.

It grew quite dark in the room, and Diana knew that she ought to be downstairs helping with dinner preparations. But it was so easy, so pleasant to sit on here in the dusk, with the smell of oolong and violets dying on the air, and Mrs. Tressady telling of her uncle, Judge Rightwill, and her husband, George Neal, and how, when little Geordie had decided upon a professional career—he was not more than twelve, and it was not flattery to say that Goldmark had said that he was really the most beautiful boy that this manager, Goldmark, had ever seen——

"I think you will have to be kind to this boy of mine, Madame Butterfly," Mrs. Tressady presently said. Again Diana laughed uneasily; again she could find no words with which to reply.

Afterward, when she went downstairs, she felt a little silly. Baked potatoes, and frizzled ham, and jelly doughnuts were somehow not the food of romance; Diana went about getting dinner soberly, wondering how it would all turn out; whether Neal would get over his crush, what was the next step. . . .

Presently he came down, once again making her feel conscious and happy and proud and ashamed all at once. He drew her into the dark laundry; whispered feverishly.

"Diana, I'm in agony. Tell me honestly,—did Chérie make you mad?"

"Make me mad?" She echoed the question innocently, in surprise. In the shaft of faint light from the kitchen her dark eyes glittered blue, her hair stood about her head in a dim aureole.

"Yes,—I mean, you know how she feels about me!"

"No," Diana said in an amused sweet voice, knowing the

effect her eyes, and her hair, and the scent of her, and the touch of her, were having upon him.

"If ever you were angry at me——!" he said.

"Of course I'll be angry at you, lots of times."

"No, don't joke about it. I'd kill myself!"

"Well, don't kill yourself yet; I'm not angry!"

"Oh, please," he whispered, "please let me kiss you!"

Again Diana laughed, caught tight in the circle of his big arms.

"I *thought* you did that sort of thing," she murmured.

A moment later she was back in the kitchen, a little disheveled and breathless, but all the prettier for it. Neal helped her with her preparations, getting in between her and the sink, between her and the table, obliging her, with a look of infinite patience and gentleness, to go around him.

"Come into the laundry a minute, I want to speak to you."

"I *will* not!"

"Oh, come on."

"Oh, nonsense!"

She put the baked potatoes, in the blue vegetable dish, on the table. They sat down, and her grandmother told them of Miss Corrigan's release from a world that had meant only privation and pain for her for sixty-one years, and that Ernest Coggles was seriously ill.

"With those five little girls!" Diana lamented.

"Six,—she's got a new one, two months old."

"Girl?"

"Girl."

"I wonder he didn't brain her with an ax," Diana said. "They have five, and their only boy was killed here in Lincoln Street last year," she explained to Neal. "Five little towheaded girls—six now. Amy, Pauli, Tina, Thelma, Hilda,——"

"They sound like a string of Pullman cars," Neal observed.

"What'd she name this one, Gram?"

"She told me, and I've forgotten. Oh,—Ernestine. That was it."

"And he's sick?"

"He's had some sort of stomach operation."

"Let's hope he dies!" Diana said cheerfully.

But she was a little shocked when he did die, a day or two later; Neal drove her and her grandmother down to the Coggleses' strawberry farm for the funeral. It was a cold winter day, with an iron sky, and the wind buffeting at bare trees and frosted manure piles and heaps of dead corn stalks. On the flat base of the Santa Clara valley the poor little farms were spread; fifty-acre farms, ten-acre farms, patches of flat earth shut in between the mountain chains that were not large enough to be called farms at all. The shedlike houses, tenanted by Japanese, Mexicans, Chinese, by the poorest class of Italians and Spanish, were unpainted; broken machinery and farm rubbish surrounded them.

The Coggleses, their small noses pink with colds, their flaxen heads still wet from brushing and combing, were huddled in one of the meanest of the sheds. Mrs. Coggles was nursing the baby in the one large room the shanty contained; a few feet away from Ernestine Lily's bobbing silver-yellow head lay her father, looking menacing and angry and insignificant even in death. Neighbors were buttering fresh bread for the little girls, who ate it ravenously. An official from the State Board of Pensions was there, among the milling group of sympathizers; the widow was answering his questions patiently, hopelessly. The one note of life in the group was Aunt Hilda, large, shabby, bracing, from Stockton. She would take Amy and Hilda; she would not take Pauli, because Pauli always cried all night if away from her mother. Aunt Hilda had tried her before.

Gram decided to stay and cook them a supper; they were all going to the graveyard seven miles away in an open grocery delivery wagon. Even the baby, whose face was blistered from constant violent nose-wiping, would go; rags of sweaters and small coats were being unearthed from a heap in the corner. Diana and Neal left the scene at this point and drove back to prosperous Bayhead, with its ordered gardens and magnificent oaks, its handsome houses approached by curving drives, through imposing hedges and gates.

"Do you suppose they've all slept in the room with the late lamented since Tuesday?"

Diana gave a forlorn laugh.

"Oh, horrors, I suppose so!"

"My country, 'tis of thee!" Neal hummed.

"Their country, you mean; they're not Americans. Or at least——" Diana interrupted herself, was silent a moment. Then, "That's the Palmer house," she said.

"They built that only a couple of years ago, didn't they?"

"About five; the old place burned down. Drive round it, Neal!"

They were on top of the hill at Newbegin Park; they drove slowly about the high wall, the glimpsed arches and Spanish tiling of the Palmer house, and Diana's heart remembered it all, as seen from the bedrooms of the Rowley house, next door; remembered her talk in the patio with Bruce Palmer's mother, just before graduation.

"That's the Rowley house, the old one, next door. I like it better than all the new ones."

"Diana——" Neal had stopped the car; they were facing away across Bayhead, whose trees, spreading oak and tall eucalyptus, curved over the roofs of the comfortable houses. Cold afternoon sunlight flooded it all; down by the railway tracks a train fussed on an embanked siding, throwing up white puffs of smoke into the air. Long after they saw the smoke Diana and Neal could hear the measured "chuff-chuff-chuff."

"Diana," Neal began again, "I want to talk about you and me."

She shifted her smiling blue eyes to meet his.

"What about you and me?"

"Oh, you know," he said. "I love you."

Her demure little hand, in its warm shabby glove, touched his.

"I'm glad."

"No, you're not glad! You don't care a scrap."

"Oh, but I do, Neal."

"No, you don't. And I love you so much!"

"No, do you really?" Her dazzling, amused gaze was close to his own ardent one.

"Diana, you do care a little?"

"I care a great deal. I really do! But—but is there anything else to say, now?"

"I got my father's pistol out last night."

A pause.

"That was an edifying thing for you to do," Diana then said equably. "Did you tell your mother?"

"You're right," Neal said quickly. "I was showing off. No, of course I didn't let Chérie know. But I am miserable. I am *miserable!*"

"Miserable? When we're having such fun?"

"But Di, I don't want you to look at anyone else, I don't want you to talk to anyone else! I'm sick over the whole thing."

They were squared about on the front seat; Di, gloved and warmly coated, a rough little hat pulled down almost to her dark eyebrows, laughed at him teasingly.

"Don't be sick over me."

"I am. I want you all for myself. Damn that damn' silly ass Platt!" Neal growled.

"Peter?"

"He's crazy about you!"

"*Peter?*"

"And you know it!"

"He's kept it a profound secret, if he is."

"Well," Neal muttered stubbornly, "he is."

Diana glowed, dimpled.

"Is *zat* so?"

"Oh, Di, I love you so!" Neal pleaded.

She sobered a little, touched his hand again with a charming little gesture of confidence and affection.

"And I say I'm glad you do."

"You do like me better than fat Peter, with his red hair, don't you?"

"Aren't you mean to Peter?"

"No, I'm not mean to Peter. That's Bruce Palmer, now, isn't it?"

The second phrase followed the first without emphasis. Diana whirled about; the blood receded from her heart.

"I used to go to school with him," Neal said. "Sure that's Bruce."

Tall and slender, belted into a heavy coat, gloved hands plunged into his pockets after he had closed the handsome iron gate behind him, Bruce Palmer was walking slowly toward them.

The high clean winds that were sweeping the wintry world seemed suddenly to be singing, and the air swam with crystal motes. Diana swallowed with a suddenly dry throat and, as the man in the big overcoat came near, said his name confidently:

"Bruce!"

He turned, smiled vaguely; his face brightened suddenly, and he came quickly to the car.

"Well, Diana!"

"I didn't know you were home."

"I got home yesterday."

The two men looked at each other, and Neal said in an unfriendly tone:

"Hello, Bruce."

"Why, hello, hello, Neal! I didn't recognize you at first. By George, it must be years!" Bruce said. He returned to Diana, leaning on the door of the car, so that their faces were only a few inches apart. "You look *marvelous!*" he said, in a low tone.

"I must. We've just been to a funeral, and we stopped to take a look at the view."

"You weren't going in to see Mother?"

"Oh, no."

"Well, but isn't it nice to see you!" He was really pleased; Diana's heart sang. "I was just going over to the New-begins to play bridge," he said. "About the best thing you can do on a Sunday afternoon."

"I thought it was always golf on Sundays?"

"Well, it was. We were playing all morning."

"And how long will you be here, Bruce?" Her eyes were devouring him; the exquisite color of April fluctuated in her cheeks.

"Two weeks."

"And then back?"

"Then back,—but not to Sweden. I think to Berne."

"Germany?"

"Switzerland."

"Oh, Switzerland, of course. And shall you like that?"

"It will be a great opportunity." He was gravely handsome as he said it. She remembered the finely modeled mouth, the fine serious glance of his eyes.

"But your mother, doesn't she mind?"

"The three years rather frightened her, at first." He had changed, he was a man, and a fascinating man, now. Somehow an aura of travel, of culture, of cosmopolitanism hung about him.

"Three years!"

"I think so."

"Oh, but that's a long time!" she protested.

"I think my mother may bring the girls over in June. I saw Joan with them in New York, by the way!"

"Yes, she's taking her junior year there."

When he went on his way, with his good-bye, he said:

"I'll see you soon, Diana."

"Oh, I hope so!" She was dazzled, dreamy, when she and Neal turned to drive home. Presently, through the roseate clouds that enveloped her, she perceived that Neal was in a bad mood. He would hardly speak.

When they reached the house he followed her into the kitchen; stood by the door.

"I'm so sorry I've been *annoying* you, Di," he said stiffly.

"Oh, don't be silly!" She was feeling the reaction from too great emotion; this theatricalism really did annoy her.

"I'm perfectly aware that I'm silly."

"Well, you are." She pursued it grudgingly. "What's the matter?"

"Simply that I realize that—I'm in the way."

"How in the way?"

"That you can dispense with my friendship in future."

"I certainly can, if you're going to be so ridiculous!" Diana sputtered, nervous and tired.

"Thank you!" Neal gasped, in the tone of a man stricken mortally. She did not turn when she heard the kitchen door close behind him.

He did not appear for dinner, nor did she go to his mother's room for the usual teatime chat. It was next morning that Diana knew for the first time that he had gone to Los Angeles; his long letter was awaiting her in the kitchen.

"I have been walking for hours, I'm going mad, I guess," the letter began without preamble. *"I know what I've done, —all men do it; they kill the thing they love, and I've killed*

what you could *give me, Di. I wasn't satisfied, ass, ass, ass that I am!*

"Oh, my darling,—for you must let me call you that this once, and then I won't any more,—I knew it, when I saw you with him, when I saw the expression of your face! That's why you've never even seen me, Di, never been anything but so heavenly kind——

"Chérie understands, of course; you knew that she would. She told me it had to be work—work—my only salvation.

"Di, that moment in the laundry, last week, when you let me kiss you,—don't be angry at me for reminding you, it was such a heavenly thing to do,—it meant so little to you, so much to me! It was the happiest moment of my whole life.

"My eyes are full of tears, dear, but they're tears of happiness, tears of gratitude to God that He ever let me know you. Forgive me for boring you, for hurting you, for being so stupid and so selfish. I am selfish, Di, I'm jealous; you've called me both those things, you know, but it's only because I want so much to have you all for myself. I'm going away now,—you'll not see me again.

"Some day you'll be proud of me; some day you'll give me just one other hour of yourself; we two, alone together, as we've been in the exquisite last month sometimes,—and that will pay me for the agony now."

It was signed, "your Neal."

Di read it more than once, put it away in her upper bureau drawer. She felt a little stunned.

After a while she tried her coffee; tried a tasteless piece of toast. She had no appetite. Her grandmother had gone to market, in mid-morning the house was very still. Diana took the letter out, when she went into her bedroom, and read it again.

When her bed was made, and the lower floor in order, she heated a cup of coffee, made fresh toast, cut an orange in half, and carried a breakfast tray upstairs to Mrs. Tressady,

just as Neal so often did. Her heart beat fast as she tapped
on the door with a corner of the tray; she was a little constrained, a little pale, as she entered the room.

Mrs. Tressady began to cry a little when she saw her.
Then she very sensibly and with much appreciation attacked
the tray, and Diana sat on the foot of the bed, and they
talked together.

"Poor Neal! You had his letter?"

"Yes. He must have shoved it under the door last night."

"Last night! He was walking almost all night, alone in the
dark, poor boy. He was writing when I woke up, about
three."

"Three!"

"Yes. Isn't it too bad, Diana?"

Diana looked embarrassment, compunction. It couldn't
be that Neal, the carefree and casual and independent, really
was suffering about all this! Yesterday all noise and gayety
and assurance, and today gone,—gone away because he could
not be near her and not have her.

But it was all so absurd, she told herself half angrily, half
impatiently, as the day wore on. They could not be married,
without any money, any job, any prospects, even if she did
love Neal,—which she didn't. Or if she did love him, it was
in an impersonal sort of sisterly way.

It was a relief to have him gone, and yet she missed him.
She walked over to the hardware store, at noon, and she and
Margaret went to lunch together at the cafeteria.

"I telephoned you," Margaret said, "because I have some
news for you. Bruce Palmer was in this shop this morning."

"Bruce Palmer!"

"Yes. Did you know he was back?"

"Yes. I saw him yesterday."

"I knew it!" Margaret exclaimed triumphantly. "I *knew*
he came into the store to see you!"

"What makes you think so?"

"Just the way he drifted about. Di, isn't he stunning?"

"Yes, he is. Stunning."

"I think he's the handsomest man I ever saw."

"He's terribly handsome."

"He's stunning. Well," Margaret conceded, upon thought, "maybe he isn't as stunning as Neal Tressady."

"Neal's gone to Los Angeles."

"Has? When was this?"

"This morning."

"Train?"

"No. Driving."

"What for?"

"Well, I suppose he hopes to get a job."

A silence. Then Margaret said shrewdly:

"Di, is he in love with you?"

Diana had always thought it would be thrilling to be able to say "yes" to this question, no matter of whom it was asked. But somehow now it felt flat, and she a little ashamed.

"Well, yes, in a way."

" 'In a way!' Has he told you?"

"Oh, yes."

"Di, when?"

"Oh, always,—right along." Diana laughed, her face very red. "He—yes, right along," she said.

"Well, and aren't you thrilled?"

"I suppose I ought to be."

"He's the best-looking thing ever."

"Do you think so, Margaret?" All this was delightfully flattering, even if it was only about Neal. After all, he was twenty-nine; after all, he was handsome and clever and he might at any moment get a job in the movies . . .

They went out into cold, wintry College Avenue, she and Margaret, and there was Bruce Palmer, coming up the street in his belted big overcoat and gloves. Diana did not think about Neal again that day.

CHAPTER XIII

BRUCE TOOK HER to the Hotel Mark Hopkins in San Francisco for dinner, and afterward they danced. Some college men he knew were there, and Rosalie Parker, who had graduated from Rutherford when Diana had. Diana and Rosalie had never known each other very well, but tonight they liked each other; Rosalie proved to be rather shy, unsure of herself, glad of another girl to support her; there was a dazzling superfluity of men.

Diana was all in white. Her white coat with the white fur collar had cost nineteen dollars, but it looked stunning, with lovely glowing orchids pinned against it. Her head was bare, her white silk frock very simple, but infinitely becoming. Her blue eyes welled liquid lights, like sapphires, there was a blur of happy rose color on her cheeks.

Oh, this was living—living—living. It was so good to be happy, to be young, to be pretty, to be dancing with the man she loved! And how she loved him, when the delicious music began, and the lights were lowered; he kept his firm arm about her, and she could touch his cheek with her soft hair. "Bruce Palmer took me to the Mark!" her thoughts kept repeating triumphantly.

The men were not formally dressed for this mid-week dance; the girls no more formally dressed than Diana. It was all perfect,—everything was perfect. Kenneth Jerome, one of the young men from the University of California, to whom Bruce introduced her, kept saying to her as they danced, "But where have I been all your life?" They all made her feel not only that they liked her, but that they admired her, that she was something like a discovery.

Bruce was magnificent, sure of himself, pleasant, at ease, expert in ordering their supper, in selecting the table he wanted, quietly, positively, easily the gentleman. Polished, —that was the word! He smiled his own charming half-smile, that had a note of gravity in it, when she questioned him.

"Important? No, I don't think my work is important, Diana. I know Mr. Cooper depends on me a good deal,— asked for me to go to Berne, if he is transferred there, and that's complimentary, I suppose."

"And you've been to Paris?"

"We all go to Paris for vacations. But I'd been there as a kid, for a year. Yes, I love Paris."

"And you speak French?"

"Pretty well. *And* German," he smiled, *"and* Spanish."

"But then, Bruce——" Very lovely and earnest in her blonde whiteness, she leaned on the table with her elbows, cupped her chin in her hands. "But Bruce, then does that mean that you'll live *always* on the other side?"

"Looks like it."

After a while she tried another tack.

"You must meet lots of fascinating girls."

"Not so many. But Sir Charles Topper, who's the English minister, has a nice kid, and Mr. Cooper's daughter, Harriet Cooper, is a stunner."

"Pretty?"

"Yes,—that. But *class*. A real little aristocrat. She was brought up in Europe, principally. Her grandfather was Judge Fanning. It's a Washington family."

Diana had a moment of vision, "Harriet Fanning Cooper dies suddenly in Berne, Switzerland," and indulged it, while her soft, shining eyes never left Bruce's face. She was living in a dream, and Harriet's removal was part of the dream.

Or no, she thought, lying tucked up warm and wide awake in bed that night, Harriet need not die. Harriet could marry some member of the diplomatic staff, too, and she and Diana, the two young American wives, could be friends. Berne, Switzerland——

"Dearest Gram, we left Paris yesterday, and now I am really writing you from Berne, Switzerland——

"Mrs. Adelaide D'Arcy Chamberlain announces the marriage of her granddaughter, Diana, to Mr. Lloyd Bruce Palmer——"

Dreams, dreams,—but of what deliciously substantial stuff they could be made, nowadays, with Bruce at home and telephoning her nearly every day and making some thrilling plan for nearly every night! His mother and father were alone at home, except for him; Patsy and Elinor were away at college in the East, and Mrs. Palmer was not well; there was a trained nurse installed at the Palmers'. So Bruce was free, and he seemed to have no plans for his freedom that Diana could not share.

He was very generous, and he had plenty of money. Diana always wore violets, orchids, now; the thick sweet scent of gardenias pervaded Gram's bedroom. Bruce might treat her as if she were a little sister, but it was a well-beloved little sister.

The time of his departure drew near; her heart fretted her for his definite plea, his definite promise. He liked her so much, indeed he loved her, but he did not say what she wanted him to say, what her whole soul was sick to hear. There was no familiarity in his manner; Bruce was no amateur lover, always maneuvering for a chance for stolen kisses, hand-squeezing, liberties. He was above all that; she knew he was. His affectionate glance, his concern for her comfort, her happiness, his evident liking for her company above any other that Bayhead offered, were proof of his feeling,—a thousand times more proof than Diana ever would have dared demand. But the terrible twenty-eighth drew near; he was going away on the twenty-eighth, and still he offered her only kindliness, interest, companionship.

It was so much; one word would have made it enough! Well, Diana told herself, glowing under his friendship, basking in the new happiness that flooded her world, he would say that word. She must believe that he would.

She heard nothing of Neal; she saw his mother only rarely. The Virginia Tea Shop had reopened, and Mrs. Tressady spent most of her time there with her old friend. Not having a job to make her get up promptly in the mornings, and being away with Bruce almost every evening, Diana did not even see Peter Platt often. Sometimes she and Bruce went into the drugstore for sodas, but their plans usually took them to more pretentious places.

One day, quite without self-consciousness, Di went with him into the hardware store. She had almost forgotten Jackie Adler; it was odd to see Jackie, in the familiar striped silk dress, still busy with window cards and glass sales, and to speak to Mrs. Olsen and Mrs. Race. There was a man in Margaret's cage now; Margaret had married her Len; principally, Diana gathered, for the privilege of nursing his cranky old mother, cooking for the whole family, and doing the housework in the dreary O'Connor home.

Diana, talking to Jackie, was interrupted by Bruce. She turned happily; there were violets on her shoulder, her gloves were white,—and no one but she could catch the faint scent of benzine they exhaled.

"What is it, Bruce?"

"I can't get it. They haven't got it. But there are pen-knives here. Need a penknife?"

"I believe I do." She leaned over the case; studied them. Bruce did not even have to give his name here; Rowley and

Palmer were part owners of the shop. He just slipped the penknife into Diana's bag, and nodded to Jimmy Tomkins, who nodded back. All right, of course, Mr. Palmer!

The day before he went away they went to lunch at the Fairmont Hotel, leaving Bruce's car parked in the street and Diana's old coat tossed carelessly into the car. And when they came out the coat was gone!

She could not quite believe it; there, with the doorman so near, and so many persons coming and going. But the fact was the fact; the doorman very apologetic; he was sorry, Mr. Palmer.

Diana only laughed; it was an old coat, and she did not care one bit! But she grew more serious when Bruce insisted that he replace it.

"Nonsense!" she said uncomfortably. "I wouldn't *think* of letting you!"

But in the end she did, and he bought her a delicious great soft woolly garment of dark brown, with a lynx collar in gold and brown stripes, and bought her a brown hat, too. He would not let her look at the price tags, but she told him joyfully that she could guess what they were.

And that was the last happy hour. For when they were driving down to Bayhead that same afternoon he reminded her that today must be good-bye; he must spend tonight with his mother, and he and his father left for New York in the morning.

"In the *morning?*"

"Yes. We go to Portland, Seattle, first. By air, you know."

She was stunned; silenced. After a while, when he was still rambling along comfortably about the sensations of air trips, she said slowly, thickly:

"Then I don't see you again?"

"Not—no. Not this visit."

She had been counting on tonight, their last night, praying that it might have been the beginning of a new order.

All her thoughts had been concentrating upon what he would suggest for tonight; what he would say when he saw her tonight. Now—now there was to be no tonight. Her mouth was dry, and she felt weak and vague, in the rich softness of the new coat, felt as if she might be fainting.

"Is your mother—is your mother better?"

"Much. Downstairs for the first time tonight. The Newbegins and the Rowleys and the Stokeses will come over for dinner,—it'll be a great send-off. I'd rather," Bruce ended smilingly, as he turned the car into disreputable Mason Avenue, "I'd a hundred times rather slip off with you for a movie, and eat some chow mein afterward."

Diana, sitting beside him in the now stopped car, could not speak.

"Well, we've had some fun," he said. "And I fooled you on the coat, didn't I?"

Her dulled eyes hardly brightened; her lips twitched in a shadow of a smile.

"It wasn't lost?"

"No. But I wanted to make you a little present!"

He looked at her, and Diana looked back at him. She felt the burning unwelcome color flood her face, felt her throat thicken and her lips tremble. There was no help for it. She swayed toward him.

"Why, Di—" the man said pitifully, "why, you poor little thing! Do you mind so much my going away?"

"Don't—don't go away," she said thickly.

He did not answer. Instead he put one big overcoated arm about her, along the back of the seat, and fumbled with his free hand for his handkerchief. With the great soft crumpled yard of it he dried her eyes, laughing at her.

"Why, Di, you little goose, you, is this being a sport?"

"I *can't* be a sport!"

There was a pause. Held close against him, she looked at him defiantly, with tear-reddened eyes.

"Oh, but look here, Di dear, I never saw this coming on! You don't mean—why, but I've thought of you as if you were Patsy or Elinor. You can't have——— You poor little sap!"

"I don't want you to go away," she whispered, her cheeks wet.

"But you knew I had to go away."

"I know———" she said unsteadily, and stopped.

"I never dreamed of this!" Bruce muttered, thinking aloud.

"I know. I feel so ashamed! But I can't—can't help it."

"Nothing to be ashamed about." He knit his brows. "How old are you, Di?"

"Nine—nineteen." She caught her breath childishly, almost on a hiccough, and he laughed.

"Why, you're only a baby! You've got to be sensible. Will you be sensible?"

She could not rally to the tone of affectionate laughter. She drew another deep breath.

"I don't know."

"Well, but don't you see that otherwise you spoil it,— the beautiful time we've been having together? You don't want to do that? I never dreamed———"

Silence. Her smoldering blue eyes were looking at him from between soaked lashes. She did not smile.

"And look here, you'll make me feel awfully badly if I think I've hurt you. You don't want to do that? I'm just a big brother who's given you a nice time,—and a new coat, too, and you're getting tears on the cuffs———"

She laughed brokenly, her heart far from laughter.

"That's better." Bruce's tone throughout had been low, coaxing, lovingly reproachful. "Why, I'd never forgive myself if I'd made you unhappy," he said. "I never dreamed it. I never dreamed that you were getting a little too fond of me,—getting notions into your little head!"

She loved him so, every inch of him; the big arm about her, the brown handsome face so serious, with its anxious affectionate eyes and the troubled lines of his forehead, the low voice. It was an agony of ecstasy to be scolded by him, to feel herself mastered, shamed, yielding under his persuasive low tones.

"I'm as sorry as you are to break it all up," he was saying. "Will you believe that? And the first thing you know I'll be home again, and we'll have another party. This time we really *will* take our lunch over to Halfmoon Bay, shall we? And we'll have more violets."

Still not trusting herself to speak, she made no answer, only continuing to look at him with her rain-washed blue eyes.

"And some day you'll laugh about this."

At this she shook her head.

"Don't think so? Ah, but I do. Look, now, I've got to get home; it's six o'clock. So I'm going to say good-bye just as if we were going to see each other tomorrow——"

She got out of the car; raised heavy eyes painfully smiling held her trembling mouth firm.

"Good-bye——" she said inaudibly.

"Good-bye, Diana, for a while anyway." He leaned over sideways, the car purring under him, his right hand on the gear shift. "Forgive me?" he asked, smiling.

Then he was on his way, and Diana was walking into the dreary house,—the house that smelled of yellow soap and carbolic acid and boiling onions,—tears raining down her cheeks.

A sort of distraction immediately seized upon her, and she felt that she would go out of her senses. Her face burned, her mouth was dry, her thoughts were in complete confusion. Unconscious of what she did, she hung up the new hat and coat in the dim odorous closet across the hall; changed her dress. Dinner was cooking when she went wearily to the kitchen, but the kitchen was empty; her grand-mother had perhaps taken the pan to the fence, to get milk from the Klopsch family. Diana began to pace the floor.

"People don't die of this, you fool—you fool!" she whispered. "Oh, my God, he's gone. Bruce. Bruce. People don't die of this!"

What had she expected, what hoped? She did not know. Certainly not this, not this. He had been so kind, so gentle, so sorry. So sorry for her! She could not breathe; she could not endure the agony of it.

That night, after a pretense of making a dinner, she slipped out saying that she must go to the library, to change her book. Instead she walked eagerly, feverishly, up to New-begin Park, and stood for a long while at the gate of the Palmer house, looking in.

It was brightly lighted; she saw the Rowleys arrive and drive in. They did not see her in the shadows; when the party had assembled she went in at the gate, moved nearer and nearer the house. She went through the iron side gate, her heart beating fast, the thought of retreat always upper-most in her mind.

The dining room was level with the ground, with two great grilled windows that came down to the floor. They were uncurtained; they gave upon a flagged terrace sur-rounded by flowers and shrubs and leading to the back lawn. There were no neighbors so situated that their curiosity could penetrate the deep back garden that protected the Palmer house.

But Diana could look straight in through the plate glass and the twisted ribbons of ironwork to the long dining room and find the table bright with flowers and with lighted candles that struck sparks from the silver and crystal. Except for the candles the room was dark, but evidently a big fire was lighted; she knew the chimney must stand between the two windows; she could see the red light flickering in the dark shining floor and in the glass that twinkled in the patio window opposite. The whole scene,—dim great paintings of flowers and fruit, creamy distempered walls, handwrought peasantlike wall brackets for the unlighted lamps,—was perfect in its simplicity, its glowing, colorful beauty.

The dinner party began to drift into the room, laughing and talking; Diana saw Bruce, and her heart stood still. He was with Marian Stokes,—young Mrs. Paul Stokes, who was Mrs. Newbegin's sister. In his impeccable evening dress he looked handsomer than she had ever seen him before.

The butler walked straight toward the window outside of which she was crouching,—ten feet of dark terrace was between them, but his direct approach, his curious look, filled Diana with terror. She turned and slipped away into the blackness of the night; down the side road, past the tennis court that was swimming in white moonlight, and so to the street again.

Here she waited, panting. She wanted to go back and see more; she did not dare. Painted upon her inner vision was the picture of Bruce, handsome, smiling, secure in all that beauty and fragrance and light. He had helped his mother to her place, turned to Marian to say something smilingly——

Diana was consumed with the varied emotions that tore at her like teeth. Not knowing what she did, she walked and walked aimlessly, always with the need to see him again in mind; her hope always breaking against the misery of the knowledge that he was going away tomorrow, and that she could not hear his voice tonight. He was there,—so near, in that candle-lighted place,—and he was talking to other women; he was no longer hers.

After a while she went home and, white and abstracted under her grandmother's anxious questions, went to bed. But in the morning she was up early, trying to drink her coffee in the sunshiny kitchen, with her ears eager for interruption; the telephone, the telegraph boy, the sound of a familiar car horn in the street.

There was no interruption. Her breakfast finished, she loitered restlessly about the house; sometimes fitfully busy with bed-making, dishes, the familiar routine; sometimes standing idle, dreaming, staring dully ahead of her.

Ten o'clock. Eleven o'clock. If they were going to fly at noon from the Alameda field, they could not be much later than this. Diana took a sudden resolve, went to the telephone, called the Palmer house.

She felt nervous, gay, confident. Why *shouldn't* she telephone Bruce Palmer, or any other man she knew, if she felt like it? There was nothing to prevent her telephoning——

She sat long at the telephone after she had had her answer, rubbing her thumb idly over the black shiny rubber of the receiver. The response had come in a maid's impassive voice:

"Mr. Palmer and Mr. Bruce left about an hour ago. Was there any message?" No. No message now.

Moments went by. The clock in the kitchen ticked, and water dripped in the sink. The morning air, pouring in at the open window of the back hall, close to the telephone table, was fresh and vital. Diana could hear the cheerful sounds of Saturday morning over in the Gully and Niggertown, where children raced and screamed, dogs barked, muddy, collapsing open cars honked and rattled. They were all alive. But it seemed to Diana that she never could move again, that life had stopped short. Everything was over.

After a while, dazedly, she began to move through the strange garish day. There was nothing to do, nothing to hope, nothing to plan. Her heart felt as if it were bleeding; now and then she pressed her hand against it, as if to ease an actual pain.

Everything said "Bruce" to her. The clothes she had worn so happily yesterday, the telephone bells, the familiar

corners and turnings of Bayhead's streets, when she walked
aimlessly through them in mid-morning trying to tire herself, to distract herself, to forget, were all so many re-
minders of him.

It was no use. She could not bear it! She was suffocating.
Somehow the days followed one another, but there was no
relief. Diana ate fitfully; she could not sleep. The unsub-
stantial dream that had been her friendship with Bruce, the
few scant days,—less than a fortnight in all, of heaven,—
had taken away all relish for life.

She began to go up to Mrs. Tressady's room for afternoon talks again; between the somber, brooding girl and
the fluttering little affectionate woman there developed,
without any real basis of friendship, a comforting intimacy.
Bessie Tressady told Diana of her youth, her courtship, her
feelings as a bride, hour by hour, minute indeed by minute,
of the long day in the hospital when Neal had been born.

Diana listened moodily. After a while, reluctantly, irre-
sistibly, she made her own confidences. She had met all the
rich girls of Bayhead at school. They had had everything,
she nothing; she didn't mind that. She had qualified for four
colleges, for all that she had attempted,—no matter. Gram
couldn't afford to send her to college, and she had gone to
work in the Bayhead Hardware Store.

But then she had met this man; just a school friend's
brother,—not out of her reach, if she had been given a
chance. But she had not been given a chance.

His mother had whisked him out of Diana's zone fast
enough; put him by some sleight-of-hand influence in Washington into the diplomatic service. And then he had come
out of the romantic European background back into Diana's
life again; that was what was so unfair! She had not followed him up; she had not wanted him. He had found
her again.

"You don't mean, darling girl, that if it hadn't been for

this—this Lochinvar—that Neal might have had a chance?"

Diana's somber eyes did not brighten; she faintly shook her head. No, she hadn't meant exactly that——

She spent hours, almost silent, in Mrs. Tressady's pleasant room, looking at the photographs of Neal that all but papered the walls, the rugs and hangings and pillows. Forever afterward the scent of oolong tea would be associated in her mind with the memory of this room, in the languid dull February afternoons, when Bruce had gone away.

One night, desperate with hunger and restlessness, she suggested to Peter Platt that they spend his free evening "doing something." Peter, bull-necked and red-headed and absorbed in his law book, looked up in alarm.

"Gosh, no, I can't. I've got to see Mr. Curley."

Di felt she hated him; hated herself for wasting any time on him.

"Who's Mr. Curley?"

"This feller in Sacramento. I may be taken into their firm," Peter said.

"As president?"

"No. But you know I finished my work here at Christmas. So now I've been just waiting—but, gee! I'd love to take you somewhere some other time, if you'd go, Diana."

"Oh, don't bother!" she said coldly. A few days later Peter actually did get his position with a firm of lawyers in Sacramento, and went away, as Neal had, and Bruce had.

Diana was somewhat scornfully touched by his delight in his "chance." A hundred dollars a month in a lawyer's office,—but then of course Peter had never had much leisure, thrill, beauty in his life, and he was correspondingly easy to please. His bag, which she and her grandmother packed for him, his new freedom from the soda counter, his trip to the state capital all excited Peter.

"Gee, I will be right up there in the know of everything!" he exulted.

"In the know of California politics," Diana amended it, with a little twist to her lip.

Before he went he talked to her one night; it happened to be a bad night, when her heart was like a great aching lump, sore in her breast, and her mind and soul were so weary with the constant hammering need of Bruce that she hardly heard what he said.

"I know I don't count one-two-three with you, Diana, but I sort of wanted to say that—well, I guess you know how it is. I guess you know that I—I haven't butted in because— well, there's usually someone else ahead of me."

He was muttering along; she looked at him, faintly frowning.

"Oh, thank you, Peter," she said with a little effort. "But I——" Tears filled her eyes. "I don't think I ever will get married," she ended thickly.

"Well, that's all right," Peter assured her bravely.

"I hope you'll always be lucky, Peter, and that everything will come out all right!"

"I certainly am lucky enough now," he said, brightening. "Going to Sacramento and everything!"

Sacramento! Her dream was of Berne, Switzerland. She could have screamed at his stupid complacency.

At his suggestion she took his place at the soda fountain, but the experiment lasted for only two unsatisfactory weeks. Diana could not put her heart into it, she hated it. It was a satisfaction to her mind, if not to her pride, when the manager told her kindly that they would have to have a man for that post; the work was too hard for any girl. After that Diana went into San Francisco and applied for work at the great hardware house of Rowley & Palmer, in Front Street. The nice woman in the office marked "Employment" assured her that she would keep Diana in mind.

Then she was ill. It was almost a pleasure to be really sick, with a throat and a temperature, and nothing to do

but lie still in the back room that was once more turned
into a bedroom, and sleep, and wake, and sleep again. Diana
was only vaguely conscious that Margaret was there a good
deal, and her father, and always Gram; it made her cry to
see Gram's anxious face.

Her head hurt, her throat hurt, and she was horribly,
achingly weak. She did not want especially to get well, but
presently she was getting well,—lazily, luxuriously, with a
good deal of feeble laughter and a good many times of weak
tears.

They moved her out to the sunshiny kitchen, when she
was able to move, and she sat bowed in the April sunshine,
reading, and lay back, with her gold ruffled hair against a
pillow, when someone came in to talk to her,—Gram, Mrs.
Tressady, Margaret, Beet and May. Finally she was well
enough to trail her way, in her thick silk Chinese wrapper,
up to Mrs. Tressady's room, and they had tea and talk
again.

Diana felt washed clean; made anew. After all the pain
and the weariness worse than pain, she felt life creeping
back into her veins. The fever, the excitement, the hopes
and despairs of the weeks past seemed like a long-ago, half-
forgotten dream; she let it all drift away from her. The
present moment was enough.

One heavenly April afternoon, when the sun was shining
after days of hard rain, she was up in Mrs. Tressady's
room. They had been idly chatting for a while; now both
women were silent, the older busy with spirit lamp and tea
tray, and Diana established in a pillowed chair, dreaming,
half smiling, wholly lost in her own thoughts.

There was a stir on the stair outside, and quite suddenly,
without warning, Neal was with them. Neal, very handsome
in new clothes, bringing, as always, life and animation to
whatever he did and said. He kissed his mother, came over
and quite simply kissed Diana,—going down on one knee

to bring his face nearer hers, holding her frailness and whiteness and beauty steady with a big arm, as she bent forward and drooped her smiling blue eyes, her soft cheek, the brushed gold of her cloudy hair against his temple.

He said nothing; she saw the expression on his face as he got to his feet, and went over to his favorite hassock close to his mother's knee, and fell into the charming, amusing, desultory talk for which at least one of these women had hungered for weeks.

It was all a little forced; Diana knew why. When he looked at her she knew why he could not speak quite naturally, why his hand trembled on the cup when he passed her her tea; why he lost the thread of what he was saying now and then.

It was wonderful that he should care so much. Marriage was always happier for the woman if the man were the one to care more. Marriage with Neal would mean an escape forever from detestable, petty, petty, cruel Bayhead, with its officious Jackie Adlers and its supercilious Joans and Patsies. At least one would be married, at least one would not stagnate here forever, like the Rogerses——

In the dusk, when he and his mother had talked themselves silent, he went to the piano and sang "Cargoes," and "The Heavens Are Blue," and "Son of Mine." And Diana, watching him, felt glad that he was young and handsome and devoted and fascinating, and said to herself that it would be folly to try to escape her fate.

CHAPTER XIV

PART of her convalescence was spent at Carmel. Neal had taken a little cottage there for six weeks, and on a perfect April day he drove his mother and Diana from Bayhead right to the door of the new home.

For two perfect hours they rambled comfortably in the old car between blossoming orchards and roadsides deep in buttercups, new grass, flaming poppies. The sky was clear blue, set toward the south with galleons of dazzling white; the sun shone warmly down upon a shining and rain-washed world.

After the Los Gatos turn the road went winding over the hills, dipped deep into fragrant redwood canyons almost too dense to let the sunshine through, mounted to the sandy cliffs above Santa Cruz, and swept down again to the cliff farms. The sea was calm and blue beneath them; a line of lazy breakers creamed on the long strand. Diana drank deep breaths of the scented, salty air, and her color came back, and her eyes danced in their old way.

The cabin consisted of two low brown rooms, with a small brown bathroom, and a garden full of disorderly sweet flowers run almost wild. It had a deep sleeping porch; a side porch over the sea was fitted up for a dining room, and below the side porch was a shabby brick terrace shut in from the road with pepper and laurustinus bushes. Everything was simple, charming. Two music teachers, women, owned the place; they had named it "Old Maids' Paradise."

Diana at least thought it Paradise. She was still weak, but not so tired when they arrived but that she could absorb every detail: the blue cotton Japanese curtains, the Quimper platters and bowls, the quality of the classic little books aligned above the couch where she rested, the niceness, the simplicity of every inch of the little domain.

And the first meal was perfect, too; indeed all their meals were. Neal loved to cook, and there was always hilarity and conversation in the kitchen that was a part of the big main room. He made not only sponge cakes but chicken curries and marvelous salads; his coffee was a triumph, and one day he and Diana made hot biscuit from a book, and the two grew weak with laughter as they worked together.

He had brought several hundred dollars back with him from the south; he had been lucky. A four weeks' engagement in a picture, though bringing him no fame,—for after this period the whole thing had been scrapped,—had netted him a little bank account. And he had been lucky at the races at Tia Juana. In July he was to go back for another "try-out," and all his friends down there told him he would surely get into the business firmly now.

Late in June he and Diana were married. She told him the whole truth honestly, as far as she knew it; told him that she loved Bruce,—or thought she did——

" 'Thought' is right!" Neal scoffed good-naturedly. "Why, you hadn't seen him for years, and now you've only seen him a dozen times. You'll forget him."

"I only wanted you to know, Neal." She was very beautiful in these days; there was a spiritualized quality about her thinner face, her deeper eyes.

"Know that you'd had a crush on another man? Well, you wait until you've been married to me three months and you'll know what love *is*."

"I like you so—so horribly, Neal, that I wouldn't want to risk it by—by marrying you, and then not liking you so well."

"Oh, forget it!"

"I wish I knew just what all the kinds of liking mean."

"You like to kiss me, don't you? That's enough. That's all that counts. We'll get married as soon as we go home."

"Oh, give me time to think!"

The Carmel idyll was only too short; they were back in Bayhead. The newspaper had published the engagement, and everything was more dreamlike than before. Margaret came across the arroyo to talk interestedly to Diana about it.

"Don't you feel *thrilled?*"

"I would, if I could feel at all."

"Oh, I know!" Margaret agreed eagerly. "I know just how you feel. Sort of dreamy and unreal somehow, and as if it were all happening to someone else."

"Exactly! You felt that, too?" Diana was glad. To herself she said, "I *must* love Neal. For certainly Margaret was gaga about Len! Margaret," she went on aloud, after thought, "is it fun to be married?"

"Fun!" Margaret echoed, with a shocked look. "My gracious! It's—*terrific!*"

Both girls laughed suddenly, their faces red. Then Diana resumed:

"No, but you know what I mean. Is it fun to be 'Mrs. Somebody,' and not to go to the store any more, and all that?"

"Not so much as you think," Margaret answered seriously.

"How do you mean?"

"Well, you see, you're another person, Di, and what you feel now may not be in the least what that other person will feel."

"You mean because your name is changed, and you don't live at home any more?"

"Oh, heavens, no, that's nothing, all that," Margaret said scornfully. "No, I mean, thinking about him, you know, and whether he'll like things you do, and being sort of—sort of excited and happy all the time, or else terribly blue——"

"Blue? What about?"

"I don't know," Margaret answered, tears in her smiling eyes. "But—I don't know,—when I think of Mother, and everything, I get—well, not often! And it's sort of silly!"

"Margaret, if you weren't married now, would you marry right over again?"

"If it was Len, I would," Margaret said, in a hesitant way that surprised Diana. "Len's—marvelous," his young wife went on loyally. "But—but I tell you it is terrific, Diana, and it's months—months before you get to feel—like yourself, as if you belonged to yourself. There's always that —that feeling that someone else is right in everything with you,—you light a light at night, and you say 'Oh, excuse me, dear, I didn't mean to wake you up, but I thought I'd read for a while.' Or you leave him a note, 'I'm so sorry, I'll be delayed at the dentist's.' Or if he doesn't like beets,— Len doesn't,—you just don't have beets. And then Len's a Republican, you know, and Papa is just a raving Democrat, and I have to say I'm a Republican, too,—at least I won't be anything against Len,—and it makes everything so mixed up. Grace Leonard, for instance, I've always liked her,— kind of. I mean, she was in the store before she was married, and we were good friends. Well, she came in one day, when we hadn't been married very long, and she stayed and stayed, and finally Len's mother asked her to dinner,—I wish she hadn't,—and Grace acted so silly, telling Len how she adored me, and how we used to talk all night when we stayed at each other's houses,—I don't know, it made me feel so silly!"

"She always was a sap."

"She always was kind of that way,—sentimental. But you haven't any idea how different it is when a man's listening in and hating it."

"Do you and Len fight?"

"Oh, *no!*"

"But you used to, when you were engaged."

"Oh, well——" Margaret shrugged, laughing and flushing. "Well, we don't now," she said. "There's a kind of—of *sacredness* in the way you feel toward each other; it would kill me to fight with Len now."

"Would you feel badly if you knew you were going to have a baby, Margaret?"

Margaret looked at her steadily.

"Awfully."

Diana was conscious of a sense of shock.

"Oh, but Margaret, you've always been so nutty about babies."

"Ah, well, but that's a very different thing, too, Di, once you're married. You see, before that you just think of them as sweet; 'Oh, the dear little thing!' and all that. But afterward you think, 'Great heavens, what would I do!' I've got my hands full now," Margaret said seriously, "getting breakfast, getting lunch, always afraid I'll forget to turn out the gas oven or empty the pan under the icebox, and if I had to add on bottles and cribs and didies and 'getting him out in the sun every day,'—I tell you, it wouldn't be any joke."

Diana laughed.

"It's something you think about and worry about all the time!" the young wife said. "It's not so funny!"

"I'll bet I have one first!" Diana predicted gayly. "I'm determined to, because Neal says he'll hand it over instantly to Father Haley."

"He doesn't like children?" Margaret asked, alarmed.

"He says he hates 'em! But it's only because he's jealous of anything that comes between him and me."

"Di, I'd think twice before I married a jealous man."

But the one thing Diana could not do, would not do, in these days was think. She knew that under the surface of all this laughter and planning there was something about which she did not quite dare think; she sensed it in her grandmother's silences more even than in the few cryptic things she said.

"I guess you've got to get your experience the way most of us do, Diana. There wasn't anything in my marriage, or in your mother's, to keep you back now."

"You mean you think I ought to be kept back, Gram?"

"No, I don't say that, dear,—exactly."

"Don't you like Neal? You know you like him!"

"I don't dislike him. I don't feel that I could say to you that you'd ever be sorry; I don't know. Nobody knows about a marriage. Only,—when you come back, one of these days, you won't be the girl you are now. And you aren't but twenty, Di, that's what makes me feel sort of—sorry."

No, she could not think that out. She must ride over it; ride straight to the day when the beds were taken down, and the rooms cleared for masses of spring flowers, and when she was in her new brown suit, with her brown hat,—all dressed for her wedding. The great fur-collared brown coat Bruce had given her was waiting to be put with her bag into Neal's car; he had had the "Road Louse" put in order for the trip; they were going to drive down to Hollywood for their honeymoon.

Just at the end, when the Rogerses were crying, and Margaret, very pale and smiling, was holding tight to Len's hand, and Emma Mae Tauber, squeezed into an entirely inappropriate light blue satin dress, was being very sportive with rice and slippers, Diana had a moment of panic. All the past seemed to hover here at the end of Mason Avenue; the hot days of long-ago springs when she had dawdled home with her books, had been sent for bread, had dreamed at the end of the kitchen table while Gram made cocoa. The Coggleses, swarming like pink worms in their hot apartment, Oracula the Mage, pitiful little Miss Gooey, and Mrs.

Petrie; Mr. Larks talking socialism,—it frightened her to let them all go. No more friendship with Rutherford girls, in their pleated skirts and white blouses, no dreams of more lasting friendships with Joan and Connie and Elinor. It was all over.

The last kiss was for Gram; the band of new gold on her slender hand, she got into the car beside Neal. "Make this quick, darling!"

They were gone. They were moving along Lincoln Avenue, they had turned into College. Bayhead's southern developments,—new plastered Spanish houses, colonial houses, English houses in half-timber,—faded away. Mayfield, Mountain View, San José went by, all lovely in new green and hawthorn blossoms; they had taken the Gilroy road, they were really married, they were on their way.

"Tell me just one thing," Neal said. "Do we ever have to see those O'Connors again?"

"Margaret and Len?" She was surprised; turned her face toward him. "Didn't you like them?"

"I can't stand them."

"Oh, Neal, I didn't know that!"

"I hate women who cry."

Diana spoke slowly in a subdued voice:

"She's very fond of me."

"Oh, that was all right," he said good-naturedly. "You see," Neal went on, laughing a little, "I'm a freak. You've married a complete freak. I'm never going to like anyone you like, or be able to stand anybody butting in on us or trying to take you away from me."

"But Margaret—good gracious, Neal, that would be the last thing she ever would think of!"

"Oh, don't you fool yourself. She hates me; I could see it in her eye."

"Oh, *Neal!*" Diana said, laughing helplessly at his absurdity.

She was always laughing at him, his young and pretty wife, as they went gypsying on their way southward and finally found themselves in a microscopic cottage in a "court" in Los Angeles: "La Doradoita."

The big sprawling southern city, with its ramified trolley lines, its endless long flat streets that petered out into open fields and oil wells, was filled with these little courts. They were made by turning two building lots into one and facing six or eight little cottages upon a strip of central lawn. Lanes went behind the tiny dwellings for motors and delivery trucks; each cottage in "La Doradoita" group at least had a fair-sized living room, a tiny kitchen with a windowed ingle for meals, and a bath. A double bed, based on a revolving door, was hidden behind panels in the main room; it was a big, secure bed, comfortable enough, and behind it, when it had revolved majestically into use, was a deep closet with hooks, a chest of drawers.

Neal and Diana delighted in their first home, for which they paid fifteen dollars a week. They were a mile from the heart of the city, but trolleys kept spinning by, and there were splendid shops strewn all along the highways; the dazzling banks of fruits and flowers enchanted Diana. For ten cents she could bring home enough delphiniums or roses, stocks or marigolds, to decorate entirely her modest domain. Oranges at two dozen for five cents and cherries for five cents a pound made her budget worries light; she and Neal reveled in their freedom and their love.

They loved each other gloriously, completely, without limitations. If Diana had had her uneasy moments, just before their marriage and on their very wedding trip, they were gone before she had been long a wife. She gave herself to the business of love whole-heartedly, as she did everything, and in her joy in him, and in being his, she never told herself that he was different from the man she had thought she was marrying, that marriage itself was different from her dream of marriage. Perhaps she did not realize herself that she had shifted him from the position of the husband who was to protect her to the child she must protect. He was delightful, amusing, passionately devoted,—but lovably, surprisingly, only a boy, a spoiled boy, sometimes a jealous boy.

No matter. Their youth rushed together like a clean, strong rushing river; they were exquisitely, excitedly happy in their absurd little domicile, from the moment when Diana reproachfully awakened the great, sleepy, protesting fellow in the morning until she crept into his arms to sleep at night.

They could share every moment of the novelty and fun; that was one great advantage. Bernstein, who was their great hope in moviedom, had told Neal that there would be "nothing doing" in the way of an engagement for a month at least, perhaps not until September. The young Tressadys could take a holiday with easy consciences.

So they dawdled in the hot mornings, laughing over their coffee and fruit, teasing each other, stopping all along the way for kisses, for idle quarter-hours when Diana would sit on Neal's knees and he would lock his arms about her, their cheeks together, and when neither one would speak or move. "Our chimpanzee act," she called it.

Afterward it was delightful to walk out together, staying on the shady side of the wide streets, looking all about them with inexhaustible interest. They went to the big movie studios, and although most of them were empty and quiet in the year's hottest month, Diana at least found them fascinating; she hardly dared breathe, she could not speak, when she and Neal were permitted to explore the wide level stretches where bits of medieval castle, ghetto streets, New England villages were jumbled together in wild confusion. Rotting plasterboard prison cells and collapsing palace walls of painted flimsy wood jutted upon Venetian canals where gondolas disintegrated on stagnant waters in the hot California sunshine.

Inside the tremendous sheds the "stages" were even more thrilling. Boudoirs, dining halls, shabby bedrooms, palatial bedrooms, scraps of curved colonial stairway and vistas of Chinese opium dens—were set about at all angles; to walk about an enormous scaffolding or high partition meant to come upon some unexpected and convincing bit of scenery. Inside, too, the great arteries that fed the lights lay like masses of coiled snakes; when a scene was being "shot," armies of sweating men moved them about; they trailed their serpent lengths from platforms and ladders. The blinding lights poured down, hissed, flickered; the weary players, perspiring in beads through their paint, sat about idly, awaiting the pleasure of the lights, the scenery man, the director and assistant director, the quiet woman who checked the script. All these consulted endlessly in the hot shadowy space between the tangle of screens and walls and scaffolds; the musicians practised quietly, the fringe of assistants, onlookers, supers shifted to and fro in the background, the star sat retouching her lips, eyeing herself in a palm mirror, talking languidly, in a bored voice.

Going away, after a while,—and no mere spectators were ever made very welcome,—Neal and Diana would drive out to one of the beaches,—Santa Monica, Venice, Malibou,— and swim, and eat enormous balls of molasses-taffy popcorn, and lie on the sand murmuring, murmuring.

Then home in the streaming late afternoon sunshine, with a stop for peaches or blackberries, or great bronzed split apricots, and a few rolls, and frankfurters, and cream cheese and butter. And if the little house were hot and dry-smelling, they might pack their supper and be off to the beaches again.

Before Diana had been long in Hollywood she had "tests" ·made in one of the studios. Krellin, a casting director, was a friend of Neal, and he suggested it. Thrilled, she posed for the big camera, walked toward a table, sat down at it, held a telephone conversation, leaned back to call a message to someone in the next room.

Later in the same day she and Neal and Krellin saw the pictures unroll in one of the show rooms; even Diana had to laugh at them, though she secretly thought her fair hair came out well; Krellin's one comment was, "Well, we'll try that again some day. We can do a lot better than that! She's got something, and she ought to be using it."

With the cooler weather the movie world came back to town, and Diana met some strange folks: men and women who had had their little day of success and popularity, and who had been long forgotten; men and women who never would have it.

She and Neal went to parties, and the talk was all of the film world; there was nothing else. Everyone had influence, everyone had hope; everyone had had encouragement. It was not that they were pathetic in failure, nor that they were quite truthful in asserting that many of the studios were working only half-force; it was not that many of these persons had been refused employment again and again. But it was the fact that there were so many of them that discouraged Diana; hundreds, thousands, chattering of the new pictures, the new successes, the directors, managers, stars,— of the only life they knew.

They went the rounds continually; they seized any chance. They groveled, toadied, bribed, lied, fought for an opening. Even the successes, the stars that shone high up above the head of this feverish swarm, were running the same desperate race with time and luck and the fickle favor of a capricious public. Even the most eminent of them was being destroyed, and knew himself or herself being destroyed, in the fierce heat and contest of the game. The story of the studios was one of quarrels, misunderstandings, reproaches, anger, bitter resentment. Diana could at once despise them and long with a jealous heart to be one of them.

"It's an unhealthy atmosphere," she said.

"You said it."

"I mean,—it's all rush and struggle to do something, and when you do it, it's nothing. Look at the old pictures,—the ones we were all crazy about five years ago. They cost millions, and they aren't worth showing now, not the very best of them."

"Five years! A picture's old when it's five months old."

"And a star lasts only about five years."

"They don't average that. I could name you forty that were getting their thousand a month five years ago and that nobody knows are alive now."

"Then what's the fascination, Neal?"

"Oh, well,—I feel it. You feel it, too, don't you?"

"Well, I do," Diana confessed. "It's the money, I suppose."

"No, it isn't the money. Most of 'em come out without any money. They don't know what to do with it when they get it!"

"Well, if we get hold of any money, we'll keep it."

"We'll go down to Agua Caliente some day and double what we've got."

Diana innocently thought that this would be a good idea. But the races and the roulette wheel instead drained away an alarming amount of what money they had left. The races were fun, but it made her a little uneasy to see the desperate concentration with which Neal watched the spinning wheel at the green table later on. He seemed not to know what he was doing, as he whipped out his pocketbook and tossed the precious green bills across to the croupier; his fingers, jerking the chips from number to number, had a dreadful certainty and accuracy. The long-handled rake came smoothly forth; Neal had hardly time to ascertain that he had lost again before the chips were gone, dragged away in a sea of chips.

Quite suddenly it was all over; Diana, not gambling, and watching in a sort of uncomfortable dream, saw him get to his feet.

"Come on!" he said briefly. She dared not ask him, as they walked out into the clear moonlight and got into the waiting car, how much he had lost. They stopped at some roadside place where he drank a great deal; for the rest of the long way home Diana drove the car, and Neal slept heavily against her shoulder.

Much of what she saw and heard shocked her as the weeks went on; Diana never found the woman with whom she wanted to establish a real friendship. Things that Bayhead did not do were commonplace occurrences here; things that Bayhead never discussed, topics of daily conversation.

"It isn't so much that I didn't know about it," she protested to Neal, when he laughed at her, "but it's the *way* it's talked about, or rather isn't talked about. They just take it for granted that every girl is living with someone, and that half of them all are abnormal——"

"Oh, well, it's true!" Neal would say on a yawn.

"It sickens me. I used to think those subjects were thrilling, if ever Joan and Patsy and I talked about them,—not that any of us knew anything. But now it—it kind of sickens me."

The southern climate was too languid and warm for her; she felt enervated, sleepy, most of the time. Quite suddenly, without warning, Diana realized that her marriage had been a mistake, that she was fighting a losing fight.

A mistake as far as her own interior happiness was concerned, that is. She could still go on gallantly, indeed she would still go on gallantly,—picking strawberries, heating rolls, brewing coffee, sleeping with Neal's big arm about her. But somehow the glamour, the excitement was gone; he was just a man, she just a woman, there seemed to be no special reason for their being together.

Perhaps the discovery was made the more quickly because there was always a strain in dealing with Neal in any way. He was very simply and naturally and cheerfully the center of his own universe, everything revolved about him. He was sure that if his voice could be heard by the right managers he would be a great night-club success; he was sure that just ahead of him was a day when he would be a movie star, —perhaps the greatest of all the stars. He told Diana what other women had told him of his looks, and that he had to keep his body in perfect shape. "Damn' funny thing, Di, I've got what they call the ideal measurements!"

Wanting to do a thing was enough to make it a sacred obligation to do it, with Neal. If he "felt like" going to see a movie, taking a Turkish bath, not getting up in the morning, that was enough. It was always, "I'm going to," or "I'm not going to"; he never consulted Diana, or anything else but his own supreme whim.

Being Neal, he somehow made all this seem at least partially excusable and even likable. When he had his way he was happy; there was no such thing as his not having his way, and so he was happy most of the time. "Sure," and "Nix," were his comment upon any suggestion from Diana, and she came to realize that there was no appeal.

She could give in to him of course, endlessly, endlessly, and often what he wanted to do was what she also would have selected. But it was oddly tiresome to have to place another person's desires always, *always* before her own. Diana sometimes wondered what she had had to worry about before she had had Neal. Girlhood responsibilities faded away into nothingness; the only reality in life was to have a big man always lounging about somewhere in the picture; to have to consider his likes and dislikes for the whole day and for all the days.

"Neal, Betty and Phil telephoned and asked us if we wanted to go swimming at the club this afternoon."

"Well, phone and call it off, will you?"

"Oh, I think they're kind of counting on us, Neal."

"Well, they can stop counting. I don't want to go."

A pause.

"What *do* you want to do, Neal?"

"I don't know yet. Let me have my breakfast in peace, there's a good kid. I don't know what I want to do, but I know I don't want to go anywhere with Phil and Betty."

He disliked all men who were handsome and all women who did not specially admire him. He was quite simple about it. One of his favorite diversions was to be photographed in various classic poses; almost nude, as a Greek wrestler, in magnificent oriental robes, in Spanish attire with bells on his round hat and a muleta in his hands.

"Does Krutz want you in the *Julius Cæsar* thing?"

"He'd be lucky to get me."

Neal presently won a small part in a screen version of *Quo Vadis*. In the part of an old teacher of wrestling he did well, and the opportunity was regarded as a good opening wedge for others. During the weeks when the few scenes in which he played were being taken and retaken, Diana often met him in the studio for lunch; they would nod happily to the various men and women who came in in costume and make-up to sit at the long counter in the cafeteria, and order sandwiches and coffee.

"What are all the Arabs for, Neal?"

"They're using the *Garden of Allah* sets for a picture called *When the Sphinx Was New*."

"What a title!"

"I know. That's just the working title."

"They'll probably call it *Sex Among the Pyramids*."

She despised it all now, and yet from the bottom of her twenty-year-old heart she envied the girls who came and went securely, the big stars, who were idolized, spoiled, enriched, famous. Everyone who could manage to get into the studio wanted to see them. "Is that Meta Brooks? Is that honestly Orville Orville? Is that his dressing room?—Look, girls, that's his dressing room."

These great folk, furred in white, glittering with diamonds, sometimes came to the night clubs, and danced, and were bored, and went away. They hurried through the crowds honestly enough; it was a terrible annoyance to have nobodies pushing about them, but they always stopped for the camera.

"Here, let us get you, won't you, Miss Percival?"

"All right, but hurry up, will you?"

And the beautiful young thing, with her scalloped metallic hair, her picked brows, her smooth skin and insolent eyes, her slim body wrapped about in sables or chinchilla, would look smilingly toward the flashlight until the picture was taken, hurry upon her enchanted way. Diana wanted to be in it all, right in the very center, or else never see it, never think of it, again. It was not real living, real success, real happiness, but oh, it sometimes looked maddeningly like all three.

Neal, she told herself, was only a sort of hanger-on in the great whirlpool; she herself was nothing. Restlessness, dissatisfaction possessed her. She wanted more—more, somehow, than life was giving her. Other women were happy,— sometimes such stupid, plain, elderly women were happy, —but she was continually fretted and harassed by this sense of missing something,—of being cheated.

Perhaps all men were like Neal, and all marriages like this one. Diana remembered Margaret, trying to explain that after marriage one was different, that in the general change of name, position, estate there was no memory of what the long-ago girl thought.

She had moods when she resolutely pulled herself above

these vapors and doubts, cleaned her little house thoroughly, made herself look her best,—pressing and freshening her gowns, brushing her hair one hundred times, two hundred times, coöperating cheerfully with everything Neal suggested. If he wanted to stay at home and sing all the songs he knew, hammering away with his clever big hands on the tinkly little upright piano that had chanced to be left in the apartment, then she wanted to stay at home, too. If he felt like wandering, she wandered; and although the restaurant, the movie he suggested was rarely the one she would have chosen, still she went along with him all the way.

In November he was ill with a heavy cold that interrupted one of his few engagements. It seemed odd to have a big man at home in bed sick; it made Diana feel, she told him, "wifely." Uncomfortable, unshaven, in his crumpled big pajamas, he proved a bad invalid. "God, I believe you like to have me sick, you certainly act that way! God, I hate to see you eating that sandwich,—it makes my throat hurt even to see it!"

She laughed at him maternally. She was his mother now and must be his mother to the end. There was no other way.

His own mother, frantic with fright at the first word of his being ill, came flying down to stay with them. She bought a couch for three dollars in a second-hand store, a comforter for two. The little house was equipped with six rather thin sheets, two bedspreads; Diana could make her mother-in-law comfortable at one end of the one main room. It was good to have another woman there to share the work of trays and nursing and cleaning.

She was a rather common little person, Diana discovered, but she was affectionate and helpful. Her idolatry of Neal was unchanged, but she was not quite what she had been with Diana. There was an element of kindly criticism, of exaction, that was new.

"Come, you bad girl, you don't just flap his covers back every morning!"

"Well, I didn't want him to catch more 'flu."

"Oh, what an excuse!" Mrs. Tressady laughed merrily. "We all have good excuses for what we don't want to do," she said, good-humoredly. "I think we'll just turn you out, young man, and make you all up fresh!"

She tore off sheets and pillowslips; Neal, rolled in a blanket, watched her with the invalid's meek satisfaction.

"Here,—he's wrapped in his blanket,—give me that other from the couch. It's all made up,—too bad. But never mind, we can make it up again! Gather all those things up, Di,— we'll find a laundry later."

Later, when the two women were in the tiny kitchen, she said:

"Quite a lot of your old friends at Bayhead think that you and Neal got a little too fond of each other while we were down at Carmel."

"Too fond of each other? Why, we got engaged there!"

"Oh, I know, my dear! Look at the innocent eyes!" Mrs. Tressady laughed lightly. "But I mean that they said— someone saw you and Neal out on the breakfast porch down there, in pajamas, or whatever it was——"

She stopped, and Diana, with a rather red face, said scornfully:

"Well, they must have been hard up for gossip."

"That's what I thought. But it shows you how disagreeable people can be. I was there all the time, of course!"

Diana made no further comment. But more than the unkindly gossip, she resented her mother-in-law's repeating it. It was idle, it was vulgar. Back in those pleasant afternoons of tea and talk in Mrs. Tressady's room she somehow had never noticed these qualities in her hostess.

Neal was the world, in his mother's eyes. She waited on him, she adored him, she quoted him. Before she had been with them for twenty-four hours she implied that it was Diana's ignorance of good housekeeping that had brought on his illness.

"You've not been sleeping with the wind blowing straight across your bed! . . . You've not been wearing that light overcoat, now that it's almost winter! . . . Di, darling, you don't think ham and doughnuts and coffee are really a meal for a big man, do you? No *wonder* the poor boy came down ill!"

He had tonsillitis, 'flu, laryngitis, bronchitis, just as his own mood decided. He would not have a doctor, and as the hard hot fever had only lasted a day or two, Diana did not call one. Neal wallowed restlessly about in his bed, bemoaning his fate.

"Wait until you have a couple of kids to complicate," said Jean Le Roy. Jean was Diana's nearest neighbor; a hardworking, thin, crisply bobbed and rouged young woman with two infants; she had come to Los Angeles to work her way up to movie stardom; she had ended in La Doradoita with Bunny and Junior. "What a sap I turned out to be!" Jean frequently said, with a significant accent on the pronoun. When Jean's big handsome Illyan was sick, things were indeed in frightful case at Jean's house; the invalid shouting, babies whining and stumbling about, milk souring, small cribs wet, dripping laundry strung across the microscopic kitchen, tradesmen at the door suggesting payments. Illyan Le Roy had been almost a star once; he could not forget his big rôle in *Why Don't You Kiss Her, Mister?*

"Whatever you do, don't let yourself in for a kid, Diana!" was Jean's constant warning. Diana shriveled away from this advice. No one would ever give Joan Rowley, Connie, Elinor,—no one would ever give Bruce Palmer's wife, when he had one,—advice like this. Babies ought to be precious, welcome,—at least there might be a pretense that they were. Jean Le Roy's attitude made her feel a little sick.

She fought her way on, laughed, cooked, accepted Neal's kisses, returned her own warmly affectionate kisses to his brown hard cheek. This was marriage; it was different from what one had fancied it would be, but then Margaret had warned her of that. There must be no such word as "fail."

CHAPTER XV

NEAL GOT WELL and went the rounds of the studios again; it was November now, and in the balmy hot sunshine everyone was working hard. This was the film world's best season. Diana would put her little domain into order when he left every day; deliberate upon his probable occupations as compared to hers. He was in all the excitement of stages and sets and locations; even if he was not actually engaged, he could often drift along in the wake of those who were. She was at home, washing the cups and spoons, rinsing out the milk bottle,—well, that was all right. She could—she could walk down to the library later and maybe see a picture at one of the smaller houses.

Sometimes a fierce ache of resentment would seize her: it was not quite fair in him to leave her like this all day. It would have been fair enough if he had been in the real estate business, in some big office or factory, but it was different when he was just drifting. Of course he had to hunt for work, and of course it did not help to have a woman anxiously accompanying him, but——

She would take a trolley downtown, buy a book in a second-hand bookstore, go home to lay the table, to hull the big late strawberries, to lay the cookies in a neat circle on a blue plate. It was lonely work.

He was often late for dinner now and often indifferent to it when it was served. That meant that he had had sandwiches and cocktails somewhere; well, that was all right. Diana could go on smiling, go on working and serving, go on sleeping contentedly in his big arms. You could not have everything perfect; it was silly to fret over anything that was happening now, when they had been married only five months; presently everything would straighten out, and Neal get a good start——

Their first real quarrel came just before Christmas, when Neal was talking of their money anxieties. He wished he could borrow a thousand somewhere, then they could pay up everything they owed and he could get some clothes.

"A thousand! Neal, we only owe a few bills,—your doctor, and the grocery about sixty——"

"I know. But we need clothes."

"But we don't need seven hundred dollars' worth of clothes!"

"Deirdre Dean pays that for one fur scarf."

"Oh, well, Deirdre Dean!"

"Hammer knows we're hard up, and he came round with a contract today."

"A contract for *you!*"

"*Sure* for me."

"Oh, Neal, aren't you delighted?"

He caught her as she passed him on her busy way from stove to table and pulled her to his knee. Diana clung to him, resting her cheek against his, locking her arms about his neck. At such moments she told herself sternly that she loved him, loved to be close to him and feel that he loved her.

"You're cute," he said, kissing her neck, where the bright hair lay in loose rings.

"But tell me about the contract."

"Oh, he wants me to sign up for three years."

"For three years! Oh, Neal, we're *made!*"

"This is old Hammer, see? Not the young one you met."

"And what did you say?"

"I said I didn't want to tie up for any hundred a week. He saw me do the little part in *Bee's Knees*. The old man has been talking about it ever since, Vince says. He keeps saying that they want a character man for all sorts of parts."

"A hundred a week, Neal! But, good heavens, that means five thousand a year!"

"And what's *that!*"

"What's that? But good heavens—good *heavens,* it means that we're started,—we're fixed here,—we're safe!"

"Started to what? I'd be tied up for three years, doing butlers and older brothers and family servants and doctors and all that. I couldn't get away from it."

"Yes, but—but you may not ever get another offer as good!"

"Don't you worry about my not getting another offer as good."

"But Neal, the alternative is nothing!"

"Never you mind about the alternative."

Diana pondered a moment, more puzzled as to how she could present the subject without annoying him than by any indecision as to what she thought.

"I think you would be a great *fool* to turn that down."

She was back at the table now, serving the jelly roll.

"Well," he drawled comfortably, "I don't."

"But Neal, we need the money."

"Not that bad!"

"You won't refuse it?" Diana's voice had a note of pleading in it. She could not make him do anything he did not want to do; the only possible course was to win him with good nature and flattery. "You might make a tremendous hit in some small part, Neal."

"What good would it do me, tied up for three years? I expect to do my best work in the next three years."

"But it means comfort, and—and security for me!" she burst out, losing her temper at last. "It means that we could have a baby, and save some money——"

She stopped. Neal was angered, she could see; his elaborate air of boredom brought the hot color to her face.

"What's the big idea?" he asked lazily.

"That you're not fair to me, Neal! I'm here day after day alone, while you're having all sorts of experiences, going all sorts of places! And then when the chance *does* come to give me a little more comfort, save me the *eternal* anxiety about bills,—you turn it down, because you think you can make more money! Well, suppose you *can't* make more money,—where am I then?"

"Oh, for God's sake!" the man said in a leisurely whisper, as if he spoke to himself. He got up, unhurriedly, folded his paper and crammed it into a side pocket, took his cap. He was gone.

Diana heard the door slam behind him; she sat on, turned to stone.

The echoes of the loud words she had been using, of the impatient whisper with which Neal had ended the conversation died out of the air. There was a great stillness, through which far-away sounds made themselves vaguely heard: honking of cars in the street, swish and drip of a lawn sprinkler; ecstatic gushes of song from an invisible canary.

After a long while Diana spoke aloud:

"It's my fault. I wanted him to be something he couldn't naturally be. I'm the one that has to change, not Neal. I married him the way he is."

Presently, suddenly, she began to clean her house as if driven by furies. She brushed, dusted, wiped dishes, swept everything before her in the rush of her feeling. Afterward she took a bath, using as a peace offering the bath salts he had given her a week or so earlier, dressing herself prettily. Down in the cool market she bought his favorite dinner, avocado pear, bacon, liver, pineapple, and afterward got herself a book second-hand, Churchill's *World Crisis,* for seventy-five cents. One might as well read up about things; no use to let her mind stagnate.

She was back at home at two, preparing for a long session of rest and reading after the morning's stress, when Neal came in like a whirlwind, crying, breathless, clinging to her.

"Oh, Di, my darling,—my little sweetheart butterfly! Never be mad at me again,—never talk to me that way again! I know I'm selfish, I know I'm a beast—but you love me! Say that you love me! I've been in *hell* all morning!"

Love him? Well, whether or not she was in his arms, crying, too, holding tight to him; their wet cheeks touched. They laughed and sobbed like children in their delight at being friends again.

"And look, I got you a pineapple, and liver, and everything!"

"Oh, you darling!"

"And I fixed your light."

"Well, you're a darling!"

"But are you free the rest of the afternoon? Could we do something?"

"I've got to go out to the Wolfe, but you come along. I think I've got a break at last,—I don't know. Anyway, afterward we'll see a picture at Graumann's; Dave gave me passes. That liver'll keep, won't it?"

Diana laughed. She was happy again. He was the most maddening husband in the world; he was the most satisfying. She put away the meat and fruit, darkened the little kitchen, made herself look her nicest. Ten minutes later she and Neal went out into the hot clear winter world with their hands linked like those of children running home from school.

In February he got a chance to support the exquisite Deirdre Dean in a flaming film called *Girl Mistress*. This was promotion with a vengeance; Diana saw that even Neal himself could hardly believe his good fortune. They had

been in great money difficulties; now back rent and bills
could be paid. Neal must sing in the picture; the theme song
was the lovely old refrain called "Moonlight and Roses,"—
he worked on it day and night.

Diana went to some of the preliminary "rushes," those
sketchy unfinished bits of experimenting that preceded the
serious settling down to hard work; she met Miss Dean, who
leveled half-closed eyes at her, returned to her lipstick and
mirror. After that Neal was very busy; away all day, late in
getting home at night. He was "on location" for almost a
week; a week of fun, it must have been, Diana thought with
a twinge of the familiar jealousy. They had cooks, tents,
camp accommodations of the most luxurious sort when they
were on location. Well, of course she was not in it, and she
did not belong there. But it was terrible to live so close to
Hollywood and have no share in the enchanted kingdom.

There was plenty of money now, and one Sunday she and
Neal gave a late afternoon party, to which Deirdre and one
or two other actual successes came, with some fifty lesser
guests. They ate and drank ravenously; Diana was flushed
and lovely as she flew about getting more glasses, offering
the cheese crackers and the sandwiches and the cake that she
and Neal had prepared with such enthusiasm the day before.
It was a most successful party; it did not end until long
after eight, and then Diana and Neal left Tollie, the big
colored woman, in charge of the ruins and went off with the
last of their guests to Batti's for an Italian dinner.

After that there was a dull time, when the premature
southern spring washed in a wave of green and color over
the flat wide country, and the skies were high, and Diana
felt a great stretching and a vague ache in her soul and
hardly knew what to do with herself. Neal was almost always
away, because a part of any leading man's success with the
great Miss Dean was her affection for him; she was a
common, timid little soul at heart, and the magnificent Neal,

playing the piano, wearing his evening clothes, his golf clothes with such easy grace, tossing off his phrases in French and German, fascinated her as he had fascinated Diana a few months ago. Over the limitations she had inherited from a dull, day-laborer father, and confirmed by a childhood in a Brooklyn slum, Deirdre had imposed a certain arrogance of manner; she used it blindly, stupidly, but it served her well.

"Please let's not have any wives on the party!" she said loudly, and the men about her, and Neal with them, laughed in their delight. This was wit, from Deirdre, whose salary was more than three thousand dollars a week, whose pictures were in every newspaper and movie-theater magazine throughout the world.

Diana accepted the situation with what grace she could. Sometimes she had to walk away the sense of pain and resentment,—block after level block in the spring heat. She must get tired,—get so tired that she need not think. She came to know the various neighborhoods, the drugstore windows, the bakeries,—above all the second-hand bookshops. A respectable line of old books began to form on her bookshelves: *Moby Dick, Main Street, Gentlemen Prefer Blondes, The Story of San Michele, Trader Horn.*

"There was a lot of talk about that," Diana would muse, in the old bookstands, "I believe I'll read it!"

Edna Millay's poetry; Vachel Lindsay's poetry; a new crossword-puzzle book. One day Diana went over somewhat timidly to offer Mrs. Le Roy a free afternoon; she, Diana, would manage the boys. The chance was eagerly seized; Jean Le Roy clapped on her little jockey cap and fled gladly to freedom. Diana had strenuous hours with the little brothers, felt the better for them; presently repeated the experiment. Junior and Buster were always good with Aunt Diana.

Several times she went to movies with La Verne Rohan.

La Verne was a thin-faced young woman with beautiful eyes and a gentle manner. She had come to Hollywood full of hope and courage ten years earlier. She had trailed from studio to studio, had gotten ill; now Mr. Percy Grantville was taking care of her. Mrs. Grantville refused him a divorce; he had sworn to be true to her twenty-one years ago, and she held him to his oath. So he and La Verne had to hide their relationship under the cover of a love nest in La Doradoita.

La Verne was not the type that Diana had ever associated in her mind with irregularity, immorality. She was quiet, reserved, unhappy. She devoted herself to the man she loved when at intervals he could escape to see her, and for the rest she lived a life irreproachably conventional. But Jean Le Roy would not let La Verne Rohan care for her little sons, as Diana did.

It was La Verne who suggested that Diana try seriously to obtain work in the studios and who went the rounds with her. Diana said nothing of this to Neal; indeed, there was nothing encouraging to say. At one or two places she was vouchsafed tests of which she never heard again; at most places her name and address and a solio copy of her best picture were taken, and she was dismissed curtly or kindly, as the mood of the casting director inclined. And on all sides she heard what she had always heard of Hollywood, that just a certain lucky little circle of initiates was in, and everyone else was out, and you could not break the ring.

And if you did break it, what then? Well, then you were in for a few feverish years of this unnatural grandeur and importance,—white furs, jewels, flattery, money,—and then you were out again, and forever.

Far sadder than the girls who never got in were the old stars, girls faded at twenty-five, thirty, thirty-five, who had had their brief intoxicating draughts of success, they knew not why, and had drained the cup, they knew not why. The place was full of them; all the world knew their names, craned its neck to see the one-time favorite. "She used to be good," Hollywood said carelessly. She was not good now. She had lost that momentary charm that had once made her so famous,—that dimpled smile or twist of the head or manner of using her shoulders. It was gone, and her popularity was gone with it,—and she did not know whither or why.

Even Diana, an outsider, had gotten near enough to the glittering world of the films to recognize one of these stars of yesterday when she saw her. The beauty was there, the frocks and mannerisms were there; the star was looking for the "right vehicle," she was planning a great comeback. She had bought this story; had bought that story; she had gone on to New York to discuss the details of her forthcoming picture.

The years, the cruel swift years, rushed on, and somehow the picture never appeared, and the comeback never was accomplished. And the old stars,—old before forty,—were busy with charities, with the entertainment of impecunious European nobilities, with the giving of regretful interviews in which the present state of the movies was gently deplored and the public's vitiated tastes were lamented.

She, Diana Carmichael Tressady, was sick of the whole thing; disenchanted alike with the good of it and the bad of it. She wanted another sort of life, a life that did not depend on her attitude toward casting directors, toward such luckier players and scenario writers as she could attach herself to, toward all the hangers-on of the most coveted profession of them all. She wanted work, clean and hard and straight-forward; work that would help her win to that long-ago ideal. Once again she saw herself a gracious, low-voiced, cultured woman, with her fair hair smooth and her shoulders bare, with a velvet gown sweeping about her feet and a Van Dyck collar of creamy lace outlining her breast. Not a young woman, quite; a woman in the thirties somewhere; the sort of woman everyone admired, loved, followed.

No such women here. The movie atmosphere did not encourage them. Their brief moment, whatever it was worth, was a moment of mummery, of plasterboard walls and tinsel crowns. No time for culture, for character, for all those things that Miss Benchley had preached in her frail, sweet voice, and that the oaks and lawns, the study halls and polished dark corridors of Rutherford seemed to enhance —to encourage.

To be a trained nurse, vigorously washing hospital equipment, vigorously making clean hospital beds; to be a teacher, living in great airy schoolrooms, honestly toiling oneself into discouragement, and into pride over pupils; to be a secretary in some big office, coming and going busily through San Francisco's refreshing fogs,—anything, anything would be better than to live in this strange flat world of heat and sunshine and banked fruit stalls, with the oil wells spiking every horizon, and the fierce battlefield of the movies smoking between one and every normal and simple element in life.

"Neal," she said one Sunday, when they were idling in unusual felicity and comfort over their morning meal, "what about the first of May?"

"We have to get out, you mean?"

"Well, wasn't that the understanding?"

"Sure it was," he said slowly.

"This is April, you know."

"I know. I was thinking," he said, "that we might go up north and see everyone."

"Go north?" She was surprised. This was the first she had heard of the plan. "Neal!" she exclaimed, warming. "I'd love it!"

"I'm sick of this damn' dump," he said moodily.

"Sick of—not sick of Hollywood?"

"I'd like to get out!"

Diana knew that after two quite flattering engagements with Deirdre Dean, Neal was having some trouble in finding fresh work. Deirdre had scored her usual successes, but her director was casting about for a new leading man, on the principle that it was "bad business to let anyone think they couldn't get along without them, and Tressady was getting the big head."

He had not hesitated to express this frankly to Neal, who had left the studio in a rage, determined to make the round of the other companies and show Wilcox just where he got off.

But times were dull; nobody wanted Neal at the moment, though many were interested and sympathetic enough, and Neal consequently had been restless and depressed, and had described himself as "soured" on the whole rotten business.

"I won't get any work here now until the fall," he said to Diana.

"Oh, Neal, you can't say that. You've been so lucky! And we're almost a thousand ahead, aren't we? And all your clothes paid for."

"Well, if we have to give the house up in two weeks, why not go up to Bayhead? We can come back again and find a place for the fall."

"As we did last year!" It reminded her of their honeymoon trip, of her excitement and interest then in the new and fascinating world. But his face did not brighten.

"Yep. As we did then," he said darkly, not looking at her.

"Have another?" She had been making waffles at the breakfast table; the sunshiny spring air that streamed in through the open windows was streaked with the fine blue smoke. Neal shook his head, and Diana snapped off the electric current. On her own last waffle she dripped honey delicately; she reached for the rotogravure section of the enormous bulk of the newspaper and glanced at it carelessly.

"Here's Deirdre."

"Let's see." He looked at it gloomily; it was a "still" of the glorious Deirdre in a gown that spread about her like the petals of a great rose; upon her beautiful little head was a silver wig of puffs, ringlets, ribbons; in a stretched hand she held a great ostrich-plume fan.

"Isn't she beautiful?" Diana said.

Neal started.

"What'd you say?"

"She's lovely." Diana concealed no trace of jealousy in her speculative voice. She had met Deirdre several times and considered her almost repellently stupid. Deirdre was thirty-five, past her bloom, the wife of an unsuccessful theatrical man who spent much of his time in New York; her lovers were many. That Neal could possibly be attracted to Deirdre never had crossed Diana's mind.

"Damn it!" Neal said loudly, suddenly. He crushed the picture with his hand, flung the crumpled paper to the floor. Diana, elevating her fine dark brows, made no comment. She picked up some dishes, carried them to the microscopic sink, began to wash them in a pink enamel dishpan. He was tired, poor Neal, and discouraged as to the outlook, and he had been drinking the night before.

Presently he came behind her and kissed her neck, and she felt his face burning hot.

"Neal, what's the matter with you? Feel sick?"

"No. I just——" He rumpled his hair furiously; tossed his dark handsome head. "No, I feel fine," he said in a gentle quiet voice, sitting down at the table. "Put 'em here, and I'll dry 'em."

And then suddenly, frantically, like a man stung with a sharp prick of pain, "Look here, Di, I feel—I've got to walk! I'll—I'm suffocating. I—I'll be all right. You're darling, and I'm a skunk to leave you the dishes, but I'll be back and we'll go somewhere and swim; I—I can't breathe."

Quickly, jerkily, he was into his clothes; when he was

dressed he seemed much calmer and went to the piano, where he sang for half an hour.

This was better, and the uneasiness of Diana's heart was somewhat assuaged. She finished with her little kitchen and left it orderly and clean, with the sun beating furiously against the drawn shade, and the faucet dripping one crystal drop, and stopping again, and dripping again, in the Sunday peace.

"What would you do if I died, Di?" Neal presently demanded, over a lazy run of soft chords.

"Cheerful thought!" Diana was in an old kimono, creaming her face, brushing her golden mop, getting ready for a bath. "I'd go into a hardware store," she said, after thought.

"You would not!"

"Well, I wouldn't go into the movies,—not if I had the best chance in the world."

"I'll bet," he murmured, "you would."

"Not I! I want to be something more than rich, Neal; I want a home, children, interesting friends."

For a while Neal played on in silence, and Diana took her bath. Later, when she came out in the kimono and began to busy herself with powders and brushes at the mirror, she found him moody again, looking out of the wide-opened front door into the deserted hot Sunday street.

"I believe I'll walk!"

"Wait for me. I'm almost ready."

"No, I'd rather go alone!" he said ungraciously. He went out, leaving Diana to feel snubbed and hurt. Why need he be so rude? She went out presently in a new blue dress all frail ruffles and sat on the top of the three shady brick steps that mounted to the porch. Theirs was the end house of the little court; there had been late breakfasts in all six of the little houses, and now almost all her neighbors were leaving for Sunday outings.

Pretty Paget Pagette went out with her young man; Paget

had injured an elbow in film work six months ago and collected good damages, and now she was going to marry the drugstore clerk. La Verne and her protector went together toward his big car; La Verne was lovely in white; the big white coat over her arm had a white fox collar, her bag was white. But she looked serious and tired, somehow. The Le Roys went away, with the two little boys in white and blue; they would have lunch out near the beach somewhere, and swim, and lie on the sand and read the papers.

The telephone rang; Miss Dean to speak to Mr. Tressady. Mr. Tressady was out, just now. Would he call Miss Dean as soon as possible? Surely. Thank you. Good-bye.

Only a few minutes later Neal came back. Diana hated to give him the message; hated herself for fearing its effect on him. It was worse than her fears. Instantly, at Deirdre's name, he brightened; the color rushed to his face, ebbed away. He attempted a yawn.

"Oh, yes, she said she'd call."

"She may want you in the new picture."

"She isn't going to make another until July."

"Maybe something has come up?"

But Diana knew that it was not their work they would discuss today.

Neal went to the telephone; Diana, ostentatiously busy with the bookshelf, could only hear monosyllables from him. But by some unusual clearness of the telephone connection she heard more than one phrase from Deirdre.

"Listen, Beautiful, you're a fool—well, you're a fool, Nealy—well, that doesn't make any difference, you were a fool to take it that way——"

And then in an undertone, "Listen, is anyone around?"

Diana could have laughed at Neal's clumsy attempt to answer carelessly, in a businesslike way.

"Why, yes, I could do that. . . . Why, no. . . . Well,

yes. . . . Yes. . . . Yes. . . . I can't,—exactly. . . . Yes."

He hung up the receiver; his face bright.

"I have to go out and see a man," he said confusedly, thickly.

"At the studio?"

"Well, no. Yes, at the studio. At least,—it's about a new picture; she's all steamed up about it. She,—it was decent of her,—she said she knew I was keen to get going again. I'll run out and see him and be back; you don't mind? I'll leave you the car——"

She had come to realize that whenever he offered her some little courtesy it meant that his conscience was not quite at ease. She said:

"You take the car. I shan't need it."

"No, I'll leave you the car!"

"I really won't need it, Neal. I'll walk over to the library."

"You keep it and go out to the club and swim. And I'll be there as soon as I can,—Wait a minute, Wilcox may want me to have dinner with him; damn it, you never can tell! You go swim at the club, and if I'm not there by six,—or I'll telephone you——"

He was all excitement, he was completely oblivious of any possible impression he was making on her.

"Here," he said, abstractedly, "have some money,—here's a twenty. My keys, my hanky—good-bye, darling! This is what it means to marry a movie star!"

She caught at him; her face reddened.

"Look, here, Neal! Why shouldn't I go with you? You can have your talk with Wilcox and Deirdre, and then we'll go on somewhere."

"Oh, Lord, no! Good heavens, no!"

Pride paralyzed her; her hands dropped.

"Oh, very well," she said coldly, thickly. He kissed her again, carelessly, his eyes on his wrist watch, and was gone.

After a while Diana found the newspaper picture of Miss Deirdre Dean and sat looking at it for a long time.

That night she was reading in bed when he came in, quite sober, not very late, and fired with a new enthusiasm.

"I've got to be in San Francisco Thursday, Di; so we're packing tomorrow, and we'll move out Wednesday. Too sudden for you?"

It was sudden enough, at least, to drive from her mind all the argument, the protest, the reproach she had been saving for him. She asked coldly:

"Did you have a nice time?"

"Well, we talked business. I went to Wilcox's place and his Jap gave us dinner."

She did not believe him, but it did not matter. To force him to honesty would be only to make him angry.

"See Deirdre?"

"Oh, sure. I went there first."

Innocent, artless, open, nothing was amiss with his manner. He seemed like his old self tonight; perhaps he was over his feeling for Deirdre already; perhaps he would get another good engagement. Anyway, it would be thrilling to go home, see Gram again, see Margaret's baby.

CHAPTER XVI

THREE DAYS LATER they drove down shabby Lincoln Street into shabbier Mason Avenue, and there was the collapsing old house, with its millwork trimmings and peeled and battered paint, and there was Gram with one lean hand crooked against her face to shade her eyes from the sun, and there was Mrs. Tressady all flutter and delight, ready to run into Neal's arms.

They all went laughing and crying into the familiar kitchen and had tomato salad and bakery cookies and rye bread and tea and ham in the old jumbled way, and Diana ate with one hand clinging tight to her grandmother's hand, and her heart bursting with love and gratitude. Oh, it was so good to be home, talking the old language, pouring out the pent-up story that had been seething within her for so long.

Mrs. Tressady, it appeared, was no longer with Gram, but had moved to the rooms back of the tea shop, to be with Kate Witherspoon; but the big room upstairs was rented again. Di could come right back to her old bed, and Neal was going into the city, anyway, and might not be back for two days.

"I'll let you know in plenty of time to make room for me," he said, evidently mad to get away. Afterward Di remembered his careless eagerness, his abstraction, as he kissed her and his mother good-bye.

She was tired, excited, but she could not wait to go see Margaret and Sheila Patricia, could not wait to go uptown and walk along the familiar streets and see the signs and the windows unchanged, and realize that the great change that made her feel so strange, so lost, here at home, was all within herself.

Wandering home, she met Margaret's brother, Robert Hyde. He was a nice big handsome boy of twenty-two, who worked in a local automobile shop.

"Say, I *thought* you'd come home, Diana! I was coming up from Hollister this afternoon, and I saw Neal going lickety-split through Morgan Hill."

"This afternoon? This morning. We came through about ten."

"Nope, this afternoon, after four. I knew it was Neal; we fixed that car last year. He was going hell-bent for election, and he ought to look out, too. Gilroy's a regular speed trap——"

"He couldn't have been going back this afternoon——" Diana said aloud, puzzled. But she was not talking to Bob. Neal was in San Francisco, of course; it was funny,—but she didn't know exactly where. She had no address for him anywhere, although the studio might forward a letter. But they had given up their rooms in La Doradoita, he and she, and they had no foothold anywhere now.

Bob must have mistaken some unknown man in the car for Neal. Neal had not driven through Morgan Hill this afternoon; he had turned north. Funny——

That night Diana regaled the Rogerses and Mrs. Petrie and her grandmother with an account of the movie world that kept them entranced for an hour. She finished the dishes singing; put her young arms about her grandmother more than once with an affection she never had shown before.

"Gram, do you know you're wonderful? You've been awfully kind to me."

But after a few days her grandmother saw a change.

"Your letter was from Neal, dearie?"

"Yes." The tone leaden; the heavy eyes Diana raised, leaden.

"Nothing wrong?"

Diana swallowed with a dry mouth.

"Nothing I didn't expect, I guess."

A silence.

"Neal hasn't left you, Di?"

"For Miss Deirdre Dean."

"He hasn't *left* you?"

Diana shrugged; her apathetic gaze was fixed on space.

"What's he say?" her grandmother asked, stupefied.

"Oh——" The girl sighed deeply, audibly, glanced absently at her letter. "The usual thing," she said.

Mrs. Chamberlain cast about in her distraction for phrases.

"But does he think for one minute—did you know—had you any idea——"

"Yes, I think I knew this was coming," Diana presently offered in a far-away voice, her forehead drawn into a frown, her eyes fixed on the bright faucet in the kitchen sink a dozen feet away. "I knew she wanted him to go to New York with her,—I knew she was in love with him," she said slowly.

She tore the letter into scraps, threw it into the stove. All that day and the next and the next, as her grandmother sputtered and argued, reasoned, protested, threatened, she had little to say. Like her mother, the older woman thought,— taking her medicine, making no complaints.

And ten days later Diana Tressady,—she gave "Miss" before the name,—had a long talk with Albert Roach, one of the managers of Rowley & Palmer's big wholesale hardware house in San Francisco.

"Married woman?"

"Yes. But I'm not living with my husband." It sounded so cheap!

"Experience?"

"Yes. In the Bayhead Hardware Store."

"Know any of those folks down there?"

"The Rowleys and the Palmers,—yes."

"Well, that wouldn't make any difference here. We judge on our own—on our own—er—judgment."

"Of course."

She was to leave her application; they would let her know. A week later she entered the sporting-goods department of Rowley & Palmer at a salary of fifty-five dollars a month.

On the second strange, doubtful day she walked across from the office to the shopping streets of the city at noon and wandered aimlessly past the store windows. At one she stopped for a long time.

There was a woman's figure in the window, dressed in a sweeping gown of black velvet, with a chain of pearls about her plaster-of-Paris throat. The dress was priced one hundred dollars. There was no price on the pearls. Diana went into the shop to ask how much they were. Seven dollars and a half. One hundred and seven dollars and a half for all.

CHAPTER XVII

THE CLERKS in Rowley & Palmer's were so many and were divided into such different departments that Diana had been there a year before she recognized certain of her fellow workers when she met them on the street. There were girls in the offices, girls down on the floor where the sales were made, girls at the telephone board, girls in the mail-order departments; the place was like a dozen stores in one, with all sorts and kinds of workmen employed.

Her own work was in the sporting-goods shops; she had to know about fishing rods, high boots, baskets, flies, pocket torches, tents, camp gear, traps, guns. The list included such trifles as belts and bandanas, rose to the heights of canoes, arctic sledges, sleeping bags.

Rowley & Palmer's establishment occupied two square city blocks, one with the tremendous main building filling it, the other, across the street, only partly built up with sheds and a foundry, storehouses, a clubhouse where the men had their lockers, and a cafeteria. There were almost a thousand men at the place; less than a hundred women. The plant was south of the big city, not far from the railroad tracks and the slaughter houses and tanneries; thick engine smoke, with its acrid hint of open spaces and travel, often blew across the place, and on warm afternoons the sickly sweet smell of the blood of cattle and sheep was heavy in the air. Girls walking up and down in the shade of the big buildings for exercise at noon could smell leather and ashes and the odd thick odor of burning bones.

Off to the east the long tongue of San Francisco Bay ran

up through jumbled docks and piers in a fringe of masts and spars; obscure and humble coming and going of old barges and schooners went on all day long, and on foggy days the air was softly pierced by a hundred hoarse whistles. Between the plant and the waterfront the great trains rushed through, but the factory itself was on a by-street, and little traffic passed its big gates.

Diana's work kept her, she thought, among the nicest women Rowley & Palmer employed. There were about seven women in the department, there were no men, but men came up from the other floors with their customers. Supposedly doing only a wholesale business with the trade, yet there were many retail sales made every day to friends of the firm or the salesmen, or to customers who asked as a favor for the discount on a pair of fishing boots or a camera for some child's birthday.

The newest clerk, Diana, when she first came, had been relegated to the job of stock-checking, filing, hunting for odd bits of merchandise, answering the telephone. She had sat, shy and strange, in her place at the table at the end of the big sales deck for a few days, eagerly doing what they asked her to do, doing more, indeed, than they would have asked.

They all sat at this long table between sales; each woman had some clerical work to do at odd moments during the day. They checked up the traveling salesmen's monthly accounts, they extended bills and worked out the discounts, they entered "day sales" into large ledgers. There appeared to be much bookkeeping; Diana at first had despaired of ever learning what it was all about.

"When you take off thirty and ten you just multiply by sixty-three," Mrs. Baxter had said to her casually on one of the first days. Diana had only looked at her blankly. Why on earth, if you had to take small sums off, should you instead put large sums on? "You mark it off decimally, d'you see?" the other woman had continued encouragingly. But even this had meant nothing to Diana. Miss Benchley had boasted frequently that Rutherford girls, upon graduation, were equipped to meet whatever demands life might make upon them, but Miss Benchley had never advanced so fantastic a theory that, to take thirty and ten per cent off any sum, you multiplied it by so odd—so unexpected—a figure as sixty-three.

Diana had kept her mouth shut, her eyes and ears open, in those confusing old days. She had taken the motorbus from the city to Bayhead every night and gone home to her grandmother completely weary; weary in soul and mind and body, weary in heart. But nothing had been important except that she should hold her new job, and not think. Everything had been swept away,—youth, love, hope, dreams, pride,—but she had her job. She plunged into its complications gladly; the harder it was, the more it would help her just not to think.

To her grandmother she had told everything in one bitter burst of shame and need. Someone must listen; someone must care. Mrs. Chamberlain had said little; she had been kinder than ever to the child she had loved for so long, the bird that had been blown home in her life's first storm with a broken wing.

They had breakfast together, at half-past seven every morning, in the kitchen. Then Diana powdered her nose, and put on her coat, and walked two blocks to the omnibus stop. Forty minutes later she was in the city, with three more blocks to walk to the office.

She went in the big side door well before half-past eight with other early-comers and punched the time clock. Eight: sixteen; eight:eleven; eight:twenty-one,—Miss Tressady never was late.

There was something very pleasant about this beginning of the day; she liked this time best of all, when the world

was still dewy or foggy, when everyone was fresh and
friendly. The big freight elevator would be moving up and
down; Torwaldsen, who ran it, was an amiable old fellow,
and spared all the girls the need of climbing stairs. He took
Diana's group up to the fourth floor, and they stepped off
into the big loft of the sports goods.

Here the floor, showing in wide avenues between the
counters, was oiled dark, as the floor had been in the Bayhead Hardware Store years ago, and there were pleasant
shutters at the high windows. Diana liked these shutters
without knowing exactly why; she told herself that they
would remind her of Italy, only she had never seen Italy. In
Italy sunshine must slant in in just such moted golden lines
through just such shutters.

All along the walls, and on the counters that bisected the
wide floor, was the stock: guns and cameras, boots and
leather coats, decoy ducks, fox traps, polo sticks and golf
bags, pocketknives, tents, oars, tennis rackets, footballs. Up
here in this dim wide pleasant space, shut far above the
world, Diana spent all her days.

The customers up here were known as "the trade." They
came in from Eureka and Three Rivers, Sierra Madre and
Moss Beach, to buy stock for little country stores. They
were country merchants, all much alike, simple and honest
and timid in expenditure; they had gone as far as they dared
with rakes and saucepans and clotheslines downstairs, now
they wanted a few fancy touches for the summer trade.
Sometimes a gun was wanted; it was amazing to Diana how
men loved to handle guns, discuss guns.

Usually a salesman came up from the hardware or pipe
departments with "the trade"; it was for Diana, or one of
the other clerks, merely to go along with him as he made
his sales, jotting down the order, adding suggestions, or
running off somewhere to get a special flag, a special trout
fly from stock. But sometimes, when they were busy down-

stairs, the customer would be handed over to one of the girls of the sports department, and then she had to telephone downstairs presently, to ask for Mr. Moore, and say, "What discount do we give Tom Tolliday, of Gerber?" or "Joe Smoot, of Danville?"

"How much did he buy?" Moore might ask in return.

"Oh,—big bill. Two hundred at least."

"Oh, well, give him an extra ten, then. Have a letter go with it. Thanks, Miss Tressady."

"Thank *you*." She was always very polite, but she never said an unnecessary word, Miss Tressady, and although she listened to the other girls' talk, and her eyes sympathized with them, she confided in no one; she was a mystery.

To some extent they were all mysteries to one another, these seven or eight women who spent most of their waking hours together, called one another by affectionate or jocular nicknames, and talked incessantly of everything that made up their business world. Mrs. Baxter, whose husband had been distantly related to the Rowley family, and who held great prestige in consequence, was their head; she had been in the employ of Rowley & Palmer for eighteen years. She had one son, Royal, now twenty, and finishing his course in engineering at the state university; he was not only the perfect son, but he promised to be a great man. Stout, gray, emotional, capable in so far as her limited intelligence permitted, Mrs. Baxter was proud of the position she held without any attempt to improve it or expand it, without any ambition that was not embraced by the walls of this fourth-floor loft and these high shuttered windows.

Forming a sort of old guard about her were May Blunt, Elva Wiss, Mary Torney. These had all been here for years; the rest of the women clerks came and went constantly, sometimes staying for a few weeks or months only, sometimes completing a first or second year. Then they married, or went to other positions, or were discharged; the odious

Albert Roach was superintendent of the department, and he never hesitated over the unpleasant job of telling one of the "young ladies" exactly why she had failed to be of any value to the all-important firm of Rowley & Palmer.

In this weak fair-headed man with his oily smile Diana found another Mr. Morey and was reminded of the resentments and rages of her days in the Bayhead Hardware Store. But Mr. Roach had no such power to stir her as the other manager had had; she was only vaguely conscious of disliking him, disliking his sureness of himself and his relish for authority over the women. He was sufficiently agreeable to her always; not that it mattered.

Nothing mattered. She lived in a dream of routine; it went on and on,—the days were winter, were summer, were winter again, months made no difference, nor seasons.

Almost without discussion she had moved to the third-floor room at Gram's, the big upper front room she had so wanted a year ago; there was no objection from Gram now; she was only anxious to have Diana want to do something, be happy somewhere. There was no light in the room, but Diana had had it brought up the one flight simply enough, —you could do anything, if you did not care much about it; not that it mattered much, either, when you were through.

Her narrow bed, her second-hand books, her floor lamp, an old chair or two, and she was established.

"I'll get you some fresh curtains up here, Diana," her grandmother said, panting from the stairs, sitting in the comfortable old armchair.

"Oh, thanks." But it was evident that she did not care.

The alarm clock went off punctually every morning in a flight of chimes. Diana descended the stairs, had her bath, came back with her towels and soap, finished her dressing and made her bed. A plain little hat on the bright damp waves of her brushed hair, her office suit trim and neat, she went down to the kitchen, perhaps to find fog pressing against the windows, or summer sunshine slanting against the trunk of the oak outside, or a February rain dripping and splashing from the gutters.

Always she found her grandmother up, coffee boiling, bread cut to toast, newspaper airing. The two talked together over their meal; Diana was gone immediately after it.

In the omnibus, for the forty-minute trip, she had a book. It was changed frequently; Diana read rapidly, voraciously, to keep herself from thinking. At first only novels; presently she graduated to plays, poetry, books of travel and adventure, biographies. While the flat peninsula country slipped past the omnibus windows, and her fellow commuters got on at the little stations,—San Carlos, Belmont, San Bruno,—Diana turned pages, buried herself in the stories of other worlds and other lives.

Then came the office hours in the sporting-goods department of Rowley & Palmer's fourth floor. It had become immediately evident that Miss Tressady was in serious earnest about her position, was determined to make herself useful, and the old guard had accepted her at once as one of themselves. There was no rivalry or competition among them; old-fashioned methods and an old-fashioned atmosphere prevailed; there was much good nature and constant laughter between May Blunt and Mary Torney, who were neighbors in the quiet old-fashioned part of San Francisco known as the Mission, and whose brothers, cousins, beaus were the cause of endless conversations. Why these girls did not marry was something of a puzzle to Diana; they were both in the twenties, but they seemed to feel no interest in matrimony.

"Ix-nay on the iddies-kay and the eye-dees-day!" May would decree hardily, and both girls would go off into spasms of silent mirth.

"You get married, Diana," May advised her one day,

"and Mary and I'll come see you and the babies on Sunday afternoons."

Diana smiled cryptically in answer. She was not yet twenty-one, but she felt herself ages older than Mary or May. Didn't they know that she had been married; didn't the fact scream itself at everyone who saw her?

Apparently not. The office girls were as incurious as wild animals. She was "Miss Tressady" in fact as well as name, as far as they were concerned. She was their new member, silent, but not unsympathetic, beautiful in her quiet way, always studying something, always "nice." "She's terribly nice," they told one another before she had been there a month, and terribly nice they found her straight through the years.

In the empty first hour of the morning they all worked at the long table. It had once served some other purpose; perhaps it had had its part to play in the first directors' meetings of the firm, long ago. It was heavy, old-fashioned, faced with green leather, bound in brass nails.

Down its center ran a row of old inkwells, with trays for pens, rocking blotters, scratch pads. Each girl had a revolving chair; Mary Torney had a typewriter. In an informal, almost social manner they compared invoices, went to the files, brought out ledgers and bills; they clipped and stamped and figured busily in complete harmony.

By ten o'clock the elevator began to creak, and the first buyers were brought up; countrified-looking men who drifted uncertainly toward the fresh brightness of Mary or May, who were approaching them confidently and encouragingly.

"Mr. Mayo"—or Mr. Moore, or Mr. Evelyn—"told me I might git me a lancewood rod up here." Or, "My crick boots is wore through, I'd like to see what ye have."

"Cat'tiges" were one old man's need; another wanted a movie camera to photograph incubator chicks; "they sure are leetle balls of fluff," he told the almost hysterical May.

Sometimes women came up with their men, or with overgrown country boys who wanted leather coats or bright scarlet hunting shirts. At Christmas time there was quite a sale of skates, cameras, B.B. rifles, school knapsacks, and rubber boots. All over the big floor there would be quiet groups of consulting parents, murmuring as they dubiously eyed the packets and sweaters, the big gloves and caps.

When whistles screamed noon there was a lull. Few customers penetrated to the fourth floor between twelve and one o'clock; they were eating their own "dinners" somewhere in the unwonted noise and excitement of the city, and the girls were free to enjoy their own meal.

They usually summoned Pat, at about eleven o'clock, and confided to him a small sum of money and voluminous directions. Pat was a lean, disillusioned messenger boy whose function it was to buy such items as were not on Rowley & Palmer's lists and had been requested by mail-order patrons. Pat bought schoolbooks, drugs, soaps, dolls, and every day he also bought whatever the girls on the fourth floor wanted for their lunch.

Most of the other girls in the big plant went to the cafeteria, but the sports-goods girls rather disdained that; it was noisy, crowded, patronized by the men as well as the women; altogether not restful or attractive.

On the other hand the big closet, back of their department and wedged in between it and the little roof across which was the lavatory, made a delightful lunchroom. It had shelves where they hung their hats and coats, and lockers where each woman supposedly kept her purse and any personal possessions, but which generally were open and empty. There was a sunny window, a gas plate, a table, chairs, teapot, cups, sugar tin, even a small washboard for occasional laundry work, and a medicine shelf with bottles of soda, pills, headache powders, iodine. Mrs. Baxter kept some motherly looking sewing in here and often sat down at noon and composed a long chatty letter to some woman friend in Detroit or Phoenix.

When Pat returned from his morning round with the tinned tomatoes, Saratoga chips, rye bread, cream cheese, cookies, or whatever else the order of the day demanded, one of the girls disappeared quietly in the direction of the lunch-room. They took turns in "starting lunch," which meant slicing bread, getting out butter and sugar from their stores, lighting the gas jet under a freshly filled kettle, and setting out on plates the sliced sausage, cake, cheese. Canned soups were popular, but the daily staple was canned tomatoes, thickened with yesterday's odds and ends of bread, seasoned with butter and pepper and salt, and served boiling hot in deep saucers. Often this was the only hot dish, but there was always tea, and it was over the teacups that Diana came to know her companions.

Day after day she listened to their chatter; her blue eyes moved thoughtfully from face to face. But she never returned their confidences.

"Diana, have you a young man?"

"I have not."

"Oh, you have, too!"

"No, seriously, I haven't."

"You're deep!" said Mary.

"Is it deep not to have a young man?"

"Oh, hush!" May murmured, overcome with enjoyment, laying her black head down on the table, the better to laugh.

"How do you pronounce it?" one of them might ask abruptly.

"Amateur."

"Where do you get that?"

"Well,—I had three years French."

"I took French. Lundi, Mardi, Mercredi,—I remember that. Lundi, Mardi, Mercredi,—that's Monday, Tuesday, Wednesday, ain't it?"

"I'm surprised at you, Miss Blunt, saying 'ain't it.' "

This would be Mary in high feather. May would laugh in equal pleasure.

"I get that from my brothers; it makes Ma wild."

"I love the way Diana says things. Diana, I love the way you say things."

"Thank you."

"Don't thank me. Did you ever hear of the little boy who was asked where he got his pretty eyes?"

"No. And something tells me," Diana said, "that I'm not going to like it when I do hear it."

There was more laughter.

"May, you're so vulgar you shock her. She shocks you, doesn't she, Diana?"

"Things don't shock me," Diana said, "but sometimes they disgust me."

"You hear that, May? You disgust her."

"Lissen, this man asked him where he got his pretty eyes, see? And he said, 'From my father, thank you, sir!' There's nothing disgusting about that, I hope! I must say, Miss Blunt, I think you have an evil mind. Didn't you ever make a retreat? Didn't you ever hear of custody of the senses?"

"I don't see anything disgusting in that story," Diana said innocently, laughing in spite of herself because they were laughing so heartily. "But I must say that I don't see the point, either."

"Oh, well, you haven't heard it all, darling."

"I was afraid so!"

"So then the man says politely, 'Don't thank me, dear.' Now then, Diana, is that so bad? I think that's a nice little story. I told my mother that. She thought it was darling."

"I'll bet she thought it was darling!"

There was a fourth girl who had been long with the firm: Elva Wiss. She was hard, bitter, scornful. From the first there had been something friendly and human and willing in Diana's attitude; she had elbowed May out of the way when dishes were to be washed, she had laughed appreciatively, if somewhat reluctantly, at their nonsense. They had liked Diana instantly, and shortly they came actually to love her.

But with Elva it was different. She was a blonde with hard red peasant cheeks, yellow hay-like hair, stumping feet, a gruff voice. She worked well, was perhaps the best bookkeeper of them all; she was scrupulous as to details and never cut short her morning's work by one minute to get lunch started. Lunch was always late on Elva's day.

But some scarifying experience had caused her to despise herself, her work, her associates, the world, and life in general. Elva went to socialist meetings, she talked communism, rebellion, anarchy. Mrs. Baxter once confided to Diana her suspicions that most of those names were merely synonyms of free love. "Her mother was cracked on the subject, and their house wasn't much more than a—well, house," Mrs. Baxter said darkly. "I'll bet that girl could tell you things about herself if she ever got started."

Elva never got started about herself. But her talk of other things than herself, of politics, social conditions, of the stupidity of mankind and the cruelty of the rich, never failed her.

"Look, there's tons of food stored away,—wheat, corn, beef. And yet people starve to death."

"They do *not* starve to death, Elva."

"They do. If you say they don't, you don't know anything about it."

"Well, rich people usually are people with sense,—that's the difference. They save, and they—they invest, and they make money. They're industrious."

"Industrious your foot! When was Duncan Rowley or Bruce Palmer industrious? With their golf bags and their polo ponies and their trips to Europe!"

"Well, their fathers made the money for them."

It went on indefinitely. Diana found herself rather surprisingly the defender of the social order. There had to be rich people, and lots of times they were decenter than the poor people, and you couldn't expect them to make money and then hand it away——

"Oh, all right, I don't care!" she would say, half angrily, when Elva's relentless logic bore her down, "have it your own way. Only I know there'll always be rich people in the world, and poor people, and hunger, and starvation and low wages and no work, and that's the way it *is,* and you can't change it!"

"And you mean you don't want to do anything to change it?"

"I mean you *can't.*"

"Well, if everyone said that——"

"Oh, good gracious, Elva, have it your own way! I don't care."

But she did care, personally, specifically. Deep down in her being there was a hurt sense that somehow the Newbegins and the Rowleys and the Palmers were mixed into these theories of Elva's; it wouldn't do to admit that life was really as unfair as it seemed sometimes when she was thinking of Joan's life, Connie's life, Patsy's life, as compared to her own.

To let that thought in would be like taking a brick out of a dam that shut back the rushing of released waters. No, she had to work on, hard, and be glad if the rye bread at lunch happened to be especially dark and spicy, and the omnibus not too crowded when she got into it in the morning.

These were the important elements in her life. It was for Joan and Patsy and Connie to have all the prettiness and all the fun. Joan had been among the girls who carried the daisy chain at college; Patsy and Connie had had their year in Europe. They had been entertained in Berne by the members of the American diplomatic staff.

Better not to think of all that. She never saw the old Rutherford crowd now; they went their ways and she hers. Diana would open her book with a gesture almost fierce; she must read, must plunge into the story of Charles the Second, of Pompilia, of Sentimental Tommy or Lorelei Lee. No thinking.

In the evenings, especially in the winter evenings, she and her grandmother often sat long at the kitchen table, discussing the afternoon paper, gossiping comfortably. Their few dishes were quickly handled; when she had cleared the table Diana laid a soft thick red cotton cloth there, and Mrs. Chamberlain got out her cards for solitaire.

Diana would move about the kitchen, wipe the sinkboards dry, turn off both faucets with a jerk, snap off the gas under the kettle. Her grandmother was always tired at night. She was only, after all, a year or two older than the grandmother of Diana's happy last school days, but Diana was wiser now, she realized what a burden the lodging house was to the elderly woman; how tiring it was at sixty-five to mount stairs, make beds, show rooms to prospective tenants. They both hated the miserable business; it was a point of honor never to say so.

Her grandmother asked her no questions. She did not lament the wreckage of Diana's youth and happiness; she never suggested that Diana accept any of the friendships, the invitations, that men were eager from time to time to offer her. Sometimes they two walked to College Avenue and saw a picture, or went up to the college grounds to listen to a lecture. But most often they remained at home, Mrs. Chamberlain musing over the eternal turn of the king, the four spot, the knave, the ace, Diana working at her French, or perhaps reading *The Taming of the Shrew* or some travel or adventure book aloud.

"Six months, Gram, since I saw Neal."

"I don't understand it."

"No, and I don't understand it."

"I saw Kate Witherspoon the other day. I told you."

"She said his mother didn't know where he was, either."

"Is his mother back here again?"

"No. I believe she's still down south."

"Queer, isn't it, Gram?"

"Well, women affect a man like that sometimes."

"She is seven years older than Neal, Deirdre Dean. She looks it, too."

"That wouldn't make any difference."

"No husband's worth while," Diana said one night, "if you have to keep fighting for him with other women. No friendship would be worth while that way. Even if Neal came back, and was sorry——"

"He will!"

"I don't know. Sometimes I think he will, and sometimes that he won't. I'm not sure," Di said slowly, "that I care very much."

"It seems to me queer that he had you, Diana, and let you go."

"It does seem queer." The sore spot was still at her heart; it would always be there. Sometimes she remembered her little domain at La Doradoita, the waffle iron and the upright piano, the hot southern sunlight slanting into her diminutive kitchen; banana palms waving great leaves in the court that scratched against the plaster walls. Hot winds blowing across the oil wells, and banks of fruit, and the sense of excitement and adventure that one always felt on entering the big studios——

It was all like a dream now. It was like a dream that she had been a man's wife, slept in his arms, cooked his breakfasts, nursed him when he was ill.

But the dream bore fruit in her waking hours. Diana was

no longer interested in men. She nodded to them in the omnibus; they were about her all day long; often some man followed up a casual acquaintance and wanted her telephone number, wanted her to come to dinner and a show. She refused it all absently, unemotionally. No more of that for her.

Work was her salvation. She could not drink deep enough of its healing and anesthetizing waters. When she was not actually in the office she thought about it a good deal; thought that they must remember to order plenty of the Christmas flashlights this year, and that the defective football game must be exchanged for a whole one.

CHAPTER XVIII

ABOUT a year and a half after her return home she and her grandmother bought a motorcar. It was a second-hand article warmly recommended by Bob Hyde, who came down one evening especially to tell Diana that she could have this two-year-old model, in perfect shape, its meter marking only twelve thousand miles, for one hundred dollars.

At first the two women merely laughed at him indifferently; then suddenly the odd little transition from "of course not" to "why not?" took place in Diana's heart, and she began to study Bob with dancing eyes.

"Gram, let's do it!"

"You do it, and you'll be glad the rest of your life!" Bob burst out fervently.

"Let's do it, Gram. Other people do, and get away with it. Think of the fun we could have."

Three days later she drove her own car in to work. It was a breathtaking experience; it seemed to give her wings. No more waiting for the bus; she could choose her own time now for starting. At noon she drove up to the big library at the Civic Center, changed her library book, and got back into her car again with the first laugh of excited happiness she had known in months.

That week-end, a soft September week-end wrapped in golden haze, they went down to Carmel, the old woman and the young one, and had a night and a day in the little ocean village. Diana remembered the Carmel of a few years ago, —herself convalescent, weak, spoiled and praised and loved by fluttering little Mrs. Tressady and the magnificent Neal.

He had sung "Son of Mine," he had jabbered French with
the withered little woman at the laundry, he had made
sponge cake, explaining to her every time that you must
whip the egg whites until the bowl could be turned upside
down. And he had adored "Butterfly," his white butterfly,
the girl who was reveling in sunshine and soft salty air and
the return of color and health and appetite. Oh, those had
been happy days!

But she would not remember them now. She and her
grandmother sat on the sand, and stared out at a hazy
autumn sea, and went back to their little hotel to exclaim
appreciatively over white towels, ocean views, delicious bread
—delicious everything.

"We can go anywhere we like now, Gram. Sacramento,—
have you ever seen Sacramento? We could go to Canada
next year."

Slowly—slowly the tides of youth and hope and courage
flowed back to fill the empty spaces in her soul. She had
been one year with Rowley & Palmer,—two years. She
knew the stock now, knew the customers; the men downstairs,—Billy Moore, Billy Mayo, Irving Evelyn, even the
detested Roach, often sent their own customers upstairs with
special directions to be handled by Miss Tressady. "I was
to ask for Miss Tressady," the country storekeepers said,
and not infrequently they followed their business trans-
actions with offers of a more personal nature.

"Ever get up as far as Huntington Lake?"

"No, I never did."

"You'd like it up there, and you and my wife would hit
it off real well."

"You come down to the Big Sur," the kindly voices said.
"You come up to the Klamath and we'll give you a real
good time."

She pored over summer catalogues; steel-head fishing in
the steep swift rocky rivers, golf played on a headland that

ran straight out to sea; camping under great redwoods. People did have fun, sometimes——

Her own summers went on monotonously. Bayhead got very hot in July and August; all the tree-shaded dooryards echoed with voices in the moonlight. Families moved out to their garden steps; the wailing of babies and the hum of insects mingled in the hot nights.

Diana was twenty-one, twenty-two, twenty-three. She was one of the great army of office women who moved through the world monotonously, steadily, filling omnibuses and cafeterias and streets, obeying telephone calls, office bells, noon whistles; always neat and responsive and unobtrusive; machines.

Her heart ached; she was tired, depressed, her feet were damp. It did not matter; nobody cared. The girls in the sports department had colds in their head, headaches, back-aches,—what of it? It was for them to sniffle as little as possible, wipe their noses without ostentation, sell the tennis nets and fishing rods and camping boots that luckier girls would presently use in the deep sweet woods, at the country clubs. Life was like that. For a few happy years,—the Rutherford years of white middy blouses and French verbs and dramatics and gym,—it had all seemed different; for a few wonderful weeks, in the first days of her work in the Bayhead Hardware Store, it had seemed fun enough. There had been the feverish time of meeting Bruce again, of believing that the doors of life were going to open wide; she had seen herself, for that little happy time, his wife; young Mrs. Palmer, of Bayhead, coming and going in the big Palmer house, beloved and admired and envied——

Well, that was over, too, and the brief strange dream of her marriage to Neal was over, and she was one of the clerks at Rowley & Palmer's. Perhaps there would never be any more adventure in her life; certainly many women, at fifty, did not seem to have had as much as she had had, at twenty-three. Perhaps from now on it would be just dull plodding, dull effort just to earn enough to eat and to wear, so that one might go on with the dull effort.

But it was not all unpleasant. There was something rather agreeable about arriving at the office in the dull soft foggy mornings, smelling the spicy oily odor of the floor dressing and the good clean leathery and rubbery breath of the new ponchos and saddles, hip boots and gauntlets. The girls would come drifting in, pulling off their gloves; exchanging the news of the hours during which they had been parted; there was a constant movement, rustling of papers, jerking open of table drawers.

Young boys,—a shock-headed pair of them were eternally in process of education and graduation through the department,—would take the long white canvas covers from the stock, fill the inkwells, stop to gossip with May Blunt and Mary Torney. The house telephone would ring sharply. Was Mrs. Baxter there? No? Then Miss Tressady, please. Had the Hallowe'en masks been included in the Gunney order? Salinas, was it, Mr. Moore? Yes, Salinas. Yes, the masks had been sent along with the other things.

And Diana would turn back to a traveler's monthly statement; she would make clean entries in ink, frown faintly, shift pages.

"What'je do yesterday, Diana?"

"Yesterday? Oh, washed my hair and had breakfast with Gram,—and let's see,—went over to see the O'Connor babies, and then Gram and I went down and had supper with an old friend of hers in San José."

"You sound too good to be true, Diana."

"The way we acted yesterday," May might muse, staring away over the pencil that rested on her lower lip, "was a caution! Out in the park,—I will never forget!—my mother would have skinned me——"

"We picked up two sailors, Di."

"You did not!"

"I give you my word we did."

"But good heavens, Mary, you don't know one thing about them."

"We know they're sailors," May might suggest, with her usual burst of silent laughter.

"No, but Diana, seriously, you've got a beau?"

"Seriously, I have not."

"But aren't you ever going to *marry?*"

"I don't think so. Anyway, what about you, Mary? You're older than I am. Aren't *you?*"

"Well, I may not be married," Mary would assert, in high feather, "but I know I'm going to be. I feel it."

"Diana's young man threw her out," May one day suggested.

"That was it," Diana agreed composedly.

She knew the very day that they discovered that she had been married, although no word was said. Somehow, through some queer indirect channel, the office staff found it out, and instantly she knew it. She knew it because of their changed attitudes, the sudden cessation of teasing on the subject of beaus and marriage, and because of their odd respect—their odd consideration for this junior member of theirs who was yet more experienced than they.

Nobody told her whence the rumor—the story—had come, or how, or how much or little they knew. She only felt that somehow she was different in their eyes now and, strangely enough, was more important. A girl of twenty-three who had had one disillusioning experience in marriage had a perfect right to avoid the subject if she chose.

"Miss Tressady?"

"Mr. Cates."

"I've come up here about something kinder funny,—good morning, Miss Torney. I've come up here about something rather funny, I don't know whether you'll want to do it or not."

"All of us, Mr. Cates, or just me?"

"Just you."

"It sounds like an offer of marriage," Diana said, smiling her own serious smile at the fat, middle-aged salesman.

"Well, you could have that, too, if it wasn't for my wife and my two boys. But here's what I want to ask you to do, and if you don't want to do it, all you've got to do is say so. We're demonstrating the Kozikitch Kabinet this month, and what I want you to do is pose for a photograph, showing it off, see?"

"With a lot of spices and jams and flours in it?" Diana encouraged him.

"Exactly. Only—and here's the catch. We want you to be the Kozikitch Girl, see? And we want to advertise that once every day, for an hour, you'll be there, in the window, yourself, to sort of flourish about with it."

"Oh, wait——" Diana said smiling, a finger to her cheek.

"Go ahead!" May encouraged her. "It'll be piles of fun."

"Look, there'd be that in it for you," the salesman said. He penciled something on a piece of paper, displayed it, crumpled up the paper and threw it into the waste basket.

Diana looked thoughtful. Finances at home never were easy; this would mean the new coat; the camel's-hair coat with the dark fur collar. It would mean a brown hat with the new curled brim. She hesitated.

"I in a smart little gingham home dress with puffs?" she suggested.

"Something like that."

"Well, why not?"

It was not much of an adventure; it was a change, anyway. The taking of the photographs, up in the advertising department, was rather fun, and it was amusing to see what the enlargements made of them; such a pretty, smiling young wife Diana looked, in her striped pink gingham, pointing happily to her new Kozikitch Kabinet.

The occasion, ridiculous as it was, took on the color of a little personal success. The retired president of the firm, old Mr. Rowley, Joan's grandfather, a tiny wizened man with a pink skull showing under a neat curled wig, was known to have liked the advertisement. Various trade magazines wanted it to reproduce, and on the much-heralded day when Diana stepped into the window to display herself as well as the cabinet, there was quite a gathering on the sidewalk outside. Every day, at eleven and at three, she seriously and silently repeated the process; opening the cabinet drawers to show flour and sugar bins, shifting the spice boxes and egg beaters to and fro, turning sometimes to smile at her audience.

"If I had a little gas stove here I could actually demonstrate biscuits or stew or something."

"Say, that's an idea for next Christmas. But could you do it?"

"Could I make biscuits!"

It had rather shaken her up, this experience, and she felt younger and happier for it. She had met men in the other departments; they had made her feel that she was young and pretty and likable. One day a spectacled, capable woman of forty was introduced into the sports department; the renowned Betty Budget of the *Morning Star*. Betty wanted the "Kozikitch Girl" to come to her big Friday morning forum and demonstrate the cabinet for San Francisco's housewives.

This was Diana's first experience with the typical clubwoman. Betty Budget's crisp rush of speech, the handful of papers that she constantly shifted and to which she casually referred, her phrases, amused the girl.

"I gather that the housekeeping forum on the *Star* is an

outstanding department, and that Friday's meeting is an outstanding event, and that Rowley & Palmer are among their outstanding advertisers," Diana observed mildly, when her vigorous caller had gone.

"You slay me!" May said faintly, laying down her head on her ledger. "I thought she'd be the finish of me, telling you how many women came every Friday and what she taught them!"

"Did you *ever* hear such a stream of talk!"

" 'We have made this the outstanding department among all the newspaper departments,' " Diana quoted firmly and forcefully. " 'We feel that we have an outstanding group of women here, and we are trying to interest an outstanding element among the business men——' "

"Why do you suppose clubwomen always use that queer tone, Diana?"

"Do they?"

"Always."

"I don't know many clubwomen."

"My sister goes to clubs,—does she kill me!" May murmured in an ecstasy of appreciation.

Diana retailed these adventures to Margaret, and Margaret, whirling through housework as she listened, beamed with satisfaction.

"Diana, *you're* the outstanding one!"

"Demonstrating a kitchen cabinet."

Margaret always looked anxious when Diana assumed that quiet, disillusioned tone.

"You're having wonderful experiences, Di."

"I don't know." Diana would rub her cheek against the straight fuzzy fluff of the head of one of the O'Connor babies. "These are the adventure, Mag."

"Children? Oh," Margaret would say, easily, "anyone can have children."

Poor Margaret could, at all events. Leonard, Jim, Mary Eleanor had followed one another with startling promptitude. Margaret's days were filled to the brim with the washing of small garments, the sweetening of small cribs, the filling of bottles. Small wet broken things littered her floors; Margaret herself was thinner now, always pale, her hair strained off her face, her hands never still. She could catch a baby up, sit down to nurse it, employ her free arm to feed a small tearful creature in a high chair, direct a third little staggerer to robing or disrobing.

"You're exhausted," Di would say, sitting by the table with a baby quiet in her lap on a Sunday morning.

"I thought I was going to have a good night last night, and then this Jimmiboy got croupy."

"Jimmiboy, do you want a good slap?"

"I think he knows you now, Di. He seemed so fretty when you went away the other night; Len thought so. Len thought he was looking for you."

"He's my boy, aren't you, James? Are you Aunt Di's boy? Where's Len, Mag?"

"He took little Len over to see his mother. I didn't want Jimmiboy to go out; it's sort of foggy, and he was barking all night. So I suppose," Margaret said, sweeping a pyramid of white wet undergarments into a tub that steamed beside her sink,—"I suppose I shall hear from my mother-in-law. She gets as mad as a snake if the boys don't go over with Len."

"Hasn't she got any sense?"

"Not much."

"Doesn't she know what croup is?"

"Oh, well——"

Dishes washed, baby clothes pinned on lines, cribs torn apart. Sweat would stand in beads on Margaret's forehead as she poured the clear hot kettle water into the waiting cold water in the rubber bathtub, snatched sodden Mary Eleanor

from slumber, lowered the little speckled wailing body into
the bath. Guarding the child with a crooked arm, she would
test the bath water with her bare elbow; in another second
be wiping the baby's eyes and ears tenderly with cotton
twisted on matches; presently have the little thing snugly
rolled, presently with a warm white bottle, set down in the
middle of the spare-room bed. Then it would be little Jim's
turn with the same bath water, the same big crash apron
on his mother's lap, and the celluloid duck added for good
measure.

"Yook at him fim!" Margaret would encourage her
second-born. Little Leonard, now three, was a heavy-headed
ash-blond boy; Diana thought the sprightly little Irish Jim
the most attractive of the three.

"Imagine you, married less than four years, with three
of them!"

"I know. And if only—if *only* there aren't any more."

Margaret laughed, but Diana was serious.

"You're crazy, Mag, if you take any chances."

"I know. And we determine not to. And then—I don't
know. We love each other!"

"But that's nonsense. Everyone—everyone, nowadays, has
sense about it."

"Well, maybe. But I haven't that kind of sense."

"But why not?"

"Because I happen to think it's wrong, for one thing."

"But listen. You're thirty, and Len's thirty-two. What
are you going to do if you have ten more?"

"Nobody does have ten, nowadays."

"But you *could.*"

"But you don't."

Margaret would look quite ruffled and rosy, and Diana,
sorry to have disturbed her, would soothe her by artful
praise of whatever baby happened to have the floor. The

two women loved each other dearly, but in Diana's love there was a protective element, and in Margaret's one of simple idolatry. Everything the glittering, golden Diana did was wonderful in Margaret's eyes; if anyone was unkind to Diana, Margaret flashed anger, and when things went right for the younger woman the older was happy.

There was complete confidence between them; Diana could say to Margaret what she could say to no other human being, and Margaret, in return, would comment even upon Len for Diana's benefit.

"He likes to have me alone here when he gets home at night."

"Even doesn't want me here?"

"Well, you know how men are."

"But listen, darling, his mother and the babies and Pauline were all here yesterday."

"I know. And that's why he was mad."

"Aren't men," Diana might muse aloud, biting little kisses from a tow-head as she did so, "aren't men funny?"

"Oh, *funny!*"

"I suppose they'll never get over centuries of harem ideals. The sultan,—or Brigham Young,—that's their ideal."

"Diana, you'll never marry again?"

"I'm barely divorced now. My interlocutory year isn't up."

"I know," Margaret sighed. "It seems a pity," she said, "for you to go all your life this way."

"I don't know why not. Lots of women do."

"But not——" Margaret laughed. "Not outstanding women like you."

"I thought you thought remarriage was awful, Mag."

"It would be, for me. But—maybe it wouldn't be for you."

"I have no religious scruples, if you mean that," Diana said. "I have no religion. I wish I had."

"Oh, I *wish* you had, Di!"

"I've nothing I ought to have,—I'm nothing I ought to be," Diana summarized it bitterly. "I'm twenty-three and a flop. There's something broken inside me. It's all like a dream,—loving Bruce,—oh, *loving* him so, Mag!—and then marrying Neal, and loving him, too, in a different way, really being terribly fond of him, and his songs, and being down there with him, where everything was so new and queer. Our little house, and waffles on Sunday, and pressing his ties for him—I thought it might go on forever. And it only lasted a few months."

"He may be breaking his neck to make good, Di, and get you back."

"I'd never go back."

"You don't know that he's with Deirdre What's-her-name."

"I know he was. About two months after he left me I saw a picture in a movie magazine,—one of the girls in the office had it. And—I showed you that?"

"I remember. Something—they were taking some pic-ture——"

"They were on location. And standing right beside her, holding a coffee pot, was Neal."

"And he's never written?"

"No."

Margaret would wrinkle her white forehead.

"How do you account for it?"

"I don't."

"Well, we know this," the young wife and mother would say with her own earnestness,—"we know that it will come out right, somehow. That was what an old nun I used to know used always to say to us, 'Everything shall be well, and everything shall be well, and everything in all ways shall be well.' Don't you think that's wonderful?"

"I think you are." Diana smiled. She thought that Margaret, with her fine white Irish skin, the transparent circles under her sad blue eyes, her black, black hair and quick, heartbreaking voice, was too fine, too frail for the overwhelming demands life was making upon her mind, her heart, her body in these days. But she was all the sweeter, the dearer, for that.

CHAPTER XIX

ONE EVENING when Diana had come across the Gully in her office clothes to help Margaret put the babies to bed, Margaret said:

"I saw an old friend of yours yesterday."

"Of mine?"

"Yes. Peter Platt."

"Peter Platt! No, did you? I haven't seen him for—oh, years. How does he look and what's he doing?"

"He's going to New York."

"Peter Platt is? How on earth is he going to get there?"

"He's studying law, you know."

"He has been studying law, as far as I can remember, since I was in my sophomore year at Rutherford."

"Yes, well—anyway, you wouldn't know him."

"Fat and red-headed?"

"Fat? No. But square, you know, and—but I always liked him and you didn't," Margaret said, busily pinning and folding above the flattened little form of the baby, on a table. She took a safety pin from her mouth.

"I didn't *dislike* him," Diana protested slowly.

"I thought you did. And I always thought," Margaret said, now with the powdered sweet white sausage that was the baby in her arms, "I always thought that he liked you more than was comfortable for him, poor kid, and that if he'd ever had a break of any kind he would have told you so."

"As a matter of fact——" Diana began, in her slow, sweet childish voice. "—Ah, don't smear it all over your face,

Jimmy!" she interrupted herself to reproach the child on her knee, "it's a teething cracker, darling, it isn't a skin lotion! Please, *please* let me mop you off, you disgusting, filthy, worthless child!" She was kissing the freshened little wiped face as she spoke, and laughing in complete forgetfulness of what she had started to say. Margaret prompted her.

"Oh, I was going to say that as a matter of fact he *did*."

"Did what?"

"Peter. Told me he liked me."

"Peter Platt did? And on what did he propose to marry?"

"I don't know that he proposed to marry. He just—intimated that he was fond of me."

"Di, and you didn't like him?"

"I was mad about Bruce at the moment, or just about to marry Neal,—I've forgotten which. Maybe both. No," Diana concluded, brushing Jimmy's stiff straight fair hair into an awkward aureole, and laughing again at his affronted and puzzled little face, "I somehow didn't see Peter in that light. Maybe I might have if—— But anyway, I didn't. What's he doing?"

"He's with that Frank Cope."

"Senator Cope. The man who ran for governor or something?"

"Ran for lieutenant governor. Mrs. Brock's cousin."

"And what is Peter to him,—secretary?"

"Something like that. Politics, you know."

"And is he happy?"

"Peter? You know he always was happy. The same old grinning boy that used to give us our malted milks. Only much older. His father died, you know, and I guess he has to help them out at home. He sort of suggested it."

"He was always *nice*," Diana said in an almost apologetic tone. "I'd like to see Peter."

The next day he telephoned her at the office. Could she

and would she dine with him that night? He was going
away the next day.

He sounded stiff, almost unfriendly, but Diana, following
a sudden impulse, said that she would be delighted.

"If you don't mind my office clothes, Peter?"

"Why, no, not at all, of course." He was taking himself
a little seriously, she thought. "Where—where would you
like to go,—the St. Francis, or the Fairmont?" he asked.

The St. Francis or the Fairmont! Little Peter Platt!
Diana begged off either, she wanted to go to some quiet
place like New Frank's. Suppose Peter met her at New
Frank's at half-past six?

She looked interestedly for him when she had parked her
car outside of the famous little French restaurant on Pine
Street. The street was dark and deserted, but the windows
of New Frank's gushed light across the sidewalk. A squarely
built man was waiting; Diana looked at him in surprise.
Peter *had* changed.

He was heavier; he looked much older than his twenty-
eight years, and he was nicely dressed and groomed. But
the grin was the same.

"I would have called for you," he said, guiding her in.

"A girl at the office lives up on Bush Street near here,
and I went home with her to brush up."

"Well, you certainly did it!" the man commented.

Diana laughed.

"I would have dressed up, Peter, but I didn't have any
warning."

"I know. It was just on the spur of the moment. I didn't
know I would be free."

They were seated at one of the little white tables that
were ranged starkly up and down the long room. There was
no decoration at New Frank's, no attempts at artistic effect.
The walls were plain brown, set here and there with mirrors;
the table linen and china, white.

"I've never been here before," Peter said.

"You get the best food in the city here."

He smiled at her, amused.

"I didn't know you were such a city person, Diana."

"Oh, I stay in now and then, and some of us from the office go to a show."

"You look awfully well," he said.

"I keep well."

There was a pause. Diana had laid aside her gloves and was studying the menu; her long lashes lowered, a faint characteristic frown wrinkling her forehead.

"You'll have to tell me what's good."

"It's all good."

"Diana," he asked, after a while, "you're happy, aren't you?"

Diana looked down; looked up.

"Are you?"

"Yes," he said, "I'm awfully happy. I mean, I like what I'm doing,—I like the Senator. It's politics, you know, and it's darned exciting. You—you like it all the time,—the men you meet, and everything. We're going on to New York now; he's been put on the national board; it's what I like to do. You aren't happy, you know, until you're doing what you like to do."

"Then I'm not happy," Diana decided, after thought.

"At Rowley & Palmer's?"

"It isn't exactly calculated to make a woman happy,— hardware," she submitted.

"No, but Margaret said that you were working into advertising, and you gave lectures———"

"Margaret!" Diana laid significance on the name, and Peter smiled. "You know Margaret."

"*She's* happy, isn't she?"

"If it doesn't kill her,—yes."

"Why should it kill her?"

"She's had three babies in less than four years."

"That won't hurt her!" Peter stated carelessly. "That never hurt any woman who was happy and had a good husband."

"A good income is important, too." Diana attacked her sand dabs; there was a hint of hostility in her tone.

"That'll all come. Len's a fine kid."

Peter was eating his dinner with great enjoyment; he began to recount some of the experiences he had had in the state legislature at Sacramento, in the cause of the admired Senator Cope. Did Diana know where the Senator had gotten his training? In Chicago, with Paul Porter Wayne, who was darned likely to be the next governor of Illinois.

Her companion seemed to Diana to be an odd mixture of awkward humbleness and odd bravado. She liked him, somehow, when he was simple and friendly. When he was showing off,—impressing the waiter, and talking about this everlasting Cope, whoever he was,—then she didn't like him at all. On the whole the experience was rather disappointing; not that she had had much expectation, at that.

"Where you staying tonight?"

"Oh, I'm going back to Bayhead."

"Alone!"

"Certainly. I'll be home by ten. I often do it."

"Drive down to Bayhead at night?"

"Certainly. The Bayshore road is as straight as a string and lighted all the way. Why not?"

"I can't let you do that. I'll go down with you, and come back on the bus."

"Oh, nonsense!"

He was not listening. They had reached their dessert now; Peter had rather impressed her with his casual "I'll have some cheese, please." Diana was idly stirring the smoking richness of the famous baked "fruits Marie Jardin." The man said suddenly:

"Margaret gave me some idea—I only want to say that I hope everything turns out all right."

"All right?" Diana echoed, looking up. Color rose in her face.

"Yep. About you and Neal Tressady."

"We're divorced, you know."

"Well," the man apologized hastily, "I didn't—I didn't know just how it was. She didn't tell me much about it. She just said—that he was kind of down on his luck—something like that."

"He went off with another woman," Diana explained simply. She saw from his face that he knew.

"That's queer," Peter said lamely. There was a silence.

"Oh, it's all queer!" Diana presently conceded, with a weary sigh. She looked at him apologetically. "I don't say very much about it," she added.

"No, I suppose not. But what—what was the big idea?"

"You'd have to ask him, I suppose."

"He's still down there?"

"As far as I know. He may have been fifty places. He may be dead."

"Did ever two persons talk together as stiffly, as dryly, as this?" Diana thought.

"So you're divorced!"

"Suppose we don't talk any more about me," she wanted to say. Instead she answered merely, "Last year," and went on with her dessert.

After dinner they went out to her car, and Peter suggested a "flicker," or a "show." But Diana explained that she must be early at the office tomorrow, and had nearly an hour's run tonight. Then he would drive down with her,—he'd like to.

"Please—*please* don't!" she pleaded, tired by his stupid, gentle persistence. But in the end he went, and they talked of Bayhead families, and mutual friends, all the way down,

and when they reached Bayhead, Diana drove him around
for a few minutes, to show him the new Waxman apartments, and the post office, and the development at South-
gate.

"You're still in the old place?"

"In the disgraceful old place. Gram holds on to it, because
the new highway may go right through there, if they fill the
Gully. The Pawsey place is going to be torn down,—remember that horrible 'Arbor Villa'? Mrs. Pawsey has rented
the corner for a gas station, someone told Gram, and she's
going to get three hundred a month for it."

"Too bad your grandmother couldn't have fallen into
that."

"We never do, somehow. We always seem just to miss the
bus. She has the corner, anyway. But then they're in terrible trouble, the Pawseys. Emma's brother is that man who
—you read of it?—the 'movie murderer,' you know?"

"Good Lord!"

"Yes, his name is Benny Jung,—Emma's mother married
twice."

"I didn't realize that."

"It seems to me *everything* happens in Bayhead, and that
there are more freaks here, and more crimes here,—maybe
everyone feels that way.—I am making talk with Peter
Platt," Diana thought, "of all ridiculous things in the
world!"

"Where's your father now?"

"Oh, home. Part of the time, anyway. He was working
for a while down in Watsonville, but now he's coming back."

She left her guest at the omnibus.

"Good-bye, Peter, and I hope you love New York!"

"Good-bye, Diana, and good luck!"

"And you didn't get any thrill out of it at all?" Margaret
asked disappointedly, when Diana went over to see her a

night or two later. Len always did night work, at the telephone office, and the two women could fuss over the babies
and the little house, and talk comfortably, without any fear
of disturbance.

"Not the faintest."

"I thought Peter was so nice."

"He is nice. And he feels a little important, too. Evidently
he's getting on."

"They say he's terribly smart. Mrs. Brock told me that
Senator Cope thinks the world and all of him."

"Maybe," Diana conceded indifferently. She at least could
return to the routine at the office without wasting another
thought upon him. The only value his attention had was to
remind her of the paucity of change and amusement in her
life; to go to dinner with a red-headed old friend from soda-
fountain days was an event. "One part of me's dead," she
said to Margaret.

"It'll come alive again."

"I hope not."

CHAPTER XX

THERE was a certain not disagreeable stir in the sporting-goods department on a certain Saturday morning in June, when Mrs. Baxter returned from a trip downstairs with news. She had gone down with a customer who had supposed that garden hose was listed among the articles on the fourth floor,—"With the golf stockings, maybe," Diana had suggested after he left.

Diana had been making out the luncheon lists.

"Let's have oodles of cherries; they're only three cents a pound," May Blunt had suggested.

"And they're good for you, too,—my mother always tells us that," Mary Torney had added.

"Mary, please try to be more delicate in your conversation,—my *goodness*," May protested.

Both girls had been laughing silently but deeply when Mrs. Baxter returned. Lewis, the messenger boy of the moment, stood dully waiting for the list, and staring from girl to girl, with an open mouth, while she imparted a choice bit of information.

"Lissen, girls, the old man is sick."

"Old Rowley? Oh, well, isn't he ninety? He's been home for weeks anyway, hasn't he?"

"No. I mean 'C. C.',—Chase Palmer himself."

"Oh, is he? Sick? Is that so?"

"A stroke, Billy Moore said."

"A *stroke!*"

They were all serious now, their heads together. Lewis stared on, impressed.

"What do you know?"

"He isn't more than sixty, is he, Bax?"

"Sixty! He's only fifty-six, Billy Moore said."

"No more polo and golf," Diana said thoughtfully. "Doesn't it seem short!"

No one paid any attention.

"That means he won't come back?"

"Well, not for weeks, if he ever does."

"Oh, won't that seem queer? Will **they** promote Mr. Mayo?"

"I suppose so. For a while anyway."

Diana told her grandmother at dinner time.

"Chase Palmer is awfully sick, Gram."

"Well, I heard uptown that he wasn't so well."

"He went to Porters' to dinner last Thursday, and he seemed all right——"

They debated the details.

"Doesn't it seem odd to have Mr. Palmer ill? He was always so well and so handsome, playing golf and everything."

"You suppose Bruce'll come home?"

"No, I don't think so," Diana mused. "It isn't as if he had had anything to do with the business."

"How old's that boy now, Di?"

"Bruce? Let's see. I'm twenty-four,—he's thirty, I guess."

Minna Porter was married; she was Mrs. John Towne now. Elinor Palmer had married right after graduation; she and William Truro Wade lived in Paterson, New Jersey. And Joan was going to be married; it had been announced. Joan would only marry a superman, of course. This particular superman was named Francis Clute McAdie; Joan talked as if there never had been quite so dazzling a match made in the world before.

Francis McAdie was in the bond business in San Francisco; he belonged to *the* most distinguished family in

Baltimore, which—as everyone knew, was *the* most distinguished city in America——

Joan had visited his sister, Clara, one college vacation, and Francis had been home, and the mischief had been done. And they had all been so lovely to Joan, promising her old silver and portraits and giving her parties——!

Joan had told Diana about it, on one of the rare occasions when they met. Diana had been lunching at the Turn O' the Road Tea Shoppe on the day Margaret's third baby was being born, waiting anxiously about the hospital corridors for news, eating her lunch absently, without appetite. And Joan had flashed happily in to lunch after a golf game, and had seen Diana and come to her table. It was so nice to see her, and what was she doing?

"I'm with Rowley & Palmer, you know. Only today happens to be the fourth of July."

"I know." Joan had had an air of patronage, of graciousness. "And it's so *nice* to have you in the firm," she had said, smiling.

"And you're going to be married, Joan?"

"Oh——!" Joan had shrugged, flushed prettily. "It seems so," she had conceded, making a little grimace.

"And is he nice, Joan?"

"Nice! You don't think I'd marry him if he wasn't the nicest person alive!"

"And shall you live there, in the East?"

"Not for a while. Mother felt so terribly about my going away,—the only girl, you know,—that Mr. McAdie arranged to be here, for a few years at least. They're like that,—not showy, you know, but *splendid*. They do things solidly,—I've never known anyone like them. And the old silver,—and the adorable old brick house outside of Baltimore,—you'd love it all."

Diana had a vision of the graceful, charming Joan meeting these great folk, charming them. "Francis's girl—my daughter-in-law,—Mrs. Francis McAdie." She listened, smiled, was admiring and sympathetic, but her heart was sore. No mention was made of her own unfortunate marriage; Joan knew of it, of course, and of course she tactfully ignored it.

Being with Joan was like taking a light dose of poison. It took Diana days to get over it. For days jealousy took from her own life all its savor. For days she thought of the atmosphere of admiration, laughter, luxury, furs, great rooms, perfect service, in which Joan moved, and her own life seemed by contrast dull and hard.

And now, just before Joan's marriage, old Mr. Palmer was ill. Diana wondered if it would change Joan's plans; the Rowleys and the Palmers were related,—Mrs. Rowley was Bruce's "Aunt Emily," Joan called Bruce's father "Uncle Chase."

The girls in the office discussed inexhaustibly the change that Mr. Palmer's absence and possible death would cause. He had been the mainstay and backbone of the business; everything had been referred to him. Mr. Will Rowley was all very well, but he was dreamy, unpractical; he liked books and travel; he often brought a rare rose or a rare orchid to the office, and talked about it to his stenographer, Miss Bracey. He was not really a hardware man.

Three weeks after their first knowledge of the president's illness Diana, happening to be left alone in the office one noontime, looked up from a moment's delayed work to see a tall man on the other side of the long desk-table smiling at her. She had not heard him come in, or the elevator stop, she had been thinking only of getting an invoice ready to mail, and of flying out to the cherries and stewed tomatoes that were waiting for her in the lunchroom.

Her heart stood still. It was Bruce.

"Hello, Diana!"

"Hello, *Bruce!*" Her eyes were shining with pleasure and

excitement as she stood up and held out a hand across the littered table.

"Well, how nice *this* is!" he said, in the voice she had not heard for more than three years. He came about the table, and they walked to one of the high shuttered windows and stood there, talking.

"Bruce, when'd you get here?"

"Last night."

"And you found——" Diana was casting about for words —any words. "You found your father pretty sick?"

"Yes. It's bad. And it won't get better."

"Won't?"

"They say not. Isn't it a rotten break?"

"Oh, too bad! But that means you'll be here—how long?"

"Indefinitely."

"No, really?"

"Yes, really."

"No more Berne?"

"I've not been there for two years, you know."

"Bruce! Where have you been?"

"Paris. Vienna. I was studying international law,—certain phases of international law."

It sounded impressive.

"But then where's Mr. Cooper?"

"Back in Washington. He's going to run for senator."

"So you're out of diplomacy?"

"Well, I wasn't ever really in."

Early-summer sunshine was slanting down through the high shutters; the sporting-goods department was suddenly a pleasant place in which to be. The world was a pleasant place in which to be. And to be Diana Tressady, slender and tall, and with a crown of brushed fair hair, and an office dress of checked brown and white silk, and long eyelashes and white teeth, was satisfying—was good.

She stood beside Bruce, looking down through the shutter slits at the street, glancing up, lowering her lashes again.

"You look *awfully* well, Diana."

"I *am* well."

"Where's—I suppose I may ask you?—where's Neal Tressady?"

He got a candid look from her blue eyes.

"I don't know, Bruce."

"You're not——?"

"Divorced, yes. We haven't seen each other for more than three years."

"You little thing, and you've been in here all that time?"

"I like it here."

"I saw the refrigerator ad, downstairs. Keats has it, in his department, you know. I asked him if that wasn't Miss Carmichael and he said no, one of our own young ladies, 'Miss Tressady.' But you're——" He bowed, smiling, the phrase stopped midway. But she knew what it might have been. "You're prettier than the picture."

Bruce went away, and Diana went to her delayed lunch. Her color was high, her eyes shining.

"Bruce Palmer's back," she said, over her tomatoes and tea.

"Oh, is zat so?"

"Who's back?"

"Bruce Palmer."

"I thought he was in Zenagambia or somewhere."

"Switzerland."

"That was it," Mary agreed contentedly, and May giggled.

"Bruce Palmer is not only back," Mrs. Baxter told them a day later, "but he's going to be in his father's office with Mr. Mayo. Roach just told me that at the next board meeting they'd probably make him a vice-president."

"What do you know——?"

Diana contributed nothing to their information concerning Bruce. But she glowed, shone, sparkled with shy new beauty in these days; the world was transfigured for her. Even to her grandmother she rarely mentioned Bruce; at the office she said nothing.

But Bruce kept his feelings no secret. Every day, sometimes two or three times a day, he stopped the elevator at the fourth floor and came into the sporting-goods department to speak to her.

Sometimes it was only a word.

"I'll be delayed at lunchtime today. But I'll be up at about one. Matter?"

"Not a bit."

At other times he lingered, talking with all the girls.

"What on earth is it?"

"It's a camp seat, Mr. Palmer,—you hang it on a bough, or anything, and put a baby in it."

"How d'you mean I hang it on a bough and put a baby in it? What are you trying to do, Miss Blunt, get me into trouble?"

Gales of giggles from the ecstatic Mary and May, and a smile from Diana. Everyone up here adored Bruce: it amused her to see how her companions' respect for her was enhanced by his admiration. Mrs. Baxter decided suddenly that there must be paper napkins for lunch, in future, and went down to the houseware department to get a length of oilcloth with which to cover the table.

"Why all this elegance?" Diana asked.

"It's not *elegance*," Mrs. Baxter said, briskly tacking down the oilcloth. "It just means that we ought to do things *decently*."

Diana laughed, but she flushed, too. It was hard not to be self-conscious under these watching eyes.

When Bruce came to the Mason Avenue house to call for her, she let him wait in the kitchen. It was a prettier kitchen

than it had been years ago, but it was still high-ceiled and
old-fashioned and shabby despite the checked curtains and
the blue pottery. There was to be no agony of pretense this
time, with Bruce, such as she had indulged four years ago.
She would not fool herself again.

"Just why we go on living in this dreadful place is a
secret between my father and grandmother," she told him.
"Did I tell you they've grown quite companionable? Isn't
that funny? They putter about together and talk of old days.
He was terribly sick last winter, poor Dad, and we fixed him
up quite grandly in the back parlor, and he was so grateful,
and so meek——"

She would welcome her derelict, vague old parent home,
perhaps, as she spoke, get him into a chair, put a glass of
lemonade down before him.

"Here, Dad, drink that, it's nice and cold. Isn't this the
blazingest day ever! Do you know what Mr. Palmer and I
are doing? We're taking our supper over to Halfmoon Bay.
Isn't that a grand plot?"

"We could go down to Santa Cruz and swim, Di."

"Oh, but let's do Halfmoon Bay today, it's so much
quieter! And let's save Santa Cruz. I—I don't want to meet
people."

Shy and happy and sunburned, she would get into the
front seat of his roadster after a careful disposition of
picnic box and broiler and thermos bottle in the rumble box.

"What now?"

"Chops. Four double chops. And cream. That's all."

"Diana, do you know I think you're the most wonderful
sport in the world?"

"No! Do you?" The color would rush to her face.

"I *know* you are!"

"When you have snarled and kicked and cried and raged
and dodged as much as I have, Bruce, it's so nice to be called
a good sport. But I'm a completely rotten sport. I've hated it

all for ten years,—I've hated it ever since I left high school. I've hated Mason Avenue, and dish-washing, and dirt, and the smell of our front hall, and my father, too, sometimes, —not lately, since he's been ill. But he used to make me awfully mad. And now you call me a sport!"

"Because you *are*. D'you suppose my sister Elinor would stand for it?"

"What would she do? I tried to break loose, you know. I married, and then—then I guess I found out what *real* trouble was."

"You were so unhappy?"

"Not that so much.—Smell it, Bruce, do you smell the sea?"

"Stop dodging the question, my dear. Were you horribly unhappy?"

"If I was, it was my own fault—mostly."

"Your own fault for marrying him?"

"I suppose so."

"Di, did I have anything to do with your doing it?"

A silence. After a while he asked her again.

"Oh, I suppose you did, Bruce. It's hard to say."

"But you liked me all the while?"

"I thought of you all the while. I'll always think of you," Diana admitted simply.

"Have you thought," he asked her one day, when they were lying on the sands at Santa Cruz, watching the summer sun go slowly down the western sky,—"have you thought what all this means?"

"What all this means?"

"I mean our being together,—our spending most of our evenings and Sundays together?"

"That it's summer, I suppose," she said slowly. "And that your family is up at the Lake——"

"Dad isn't up at the Lake. And Mother only goes up now and then."

"Well——" She evaded the issue again. "What do *you* think it means?"

"Mightn't it mean——" Bruce drew a furrow in the sand, evened it with little blows of the side of his palm. "Mightn't it mean that we were beginning to care for each other, Di?"

"Not *beginning*," she said, under her breath.

The man's head was close to hers; they were lying on their faces, with their elbows sunk in sand.

"You mean," Bruce began very low, "that you've always liked me?"

"In a way," Diana answered, in the same tone, and with a sideways glance.

"You felt badly when I went away, Di?"

"Oh, well——" she said.

"You didn't feel any worse than I did. There's never been anyone else, Di. Only—only now we're in an awful jam!"

"In an awful jam?" Her color faded; her eyes met his again.

"Well, you see it!"

"Oh, yes—yes, I see it, Bruce." All the life, the youth was gone from her tone.

"I mean—my mother, you know. And—damn it! My father, too. They'd both have fits."

"I know."

"How the *deuce* could we be married now?"

She could not believe the words, even when they lingered in the enchanted summer air, with the crying of gulls and the gentle swish and fall of the sea. Bruce—Bruce Palmer, saying the word "married" to her!

"Oh, no, I know that," she said quickly, sensitively. "We couldn't."

"Damn it!" the man said, thinking.

Her smooth fingers touched his.

"This is enough happiness for now, Bruce. Just to be friends."

"Not for me!"

His glance thrilled her to the tips of her toes; Diana could not speak. It was all so tremendous, so overpowering, so much more than her wildest dream!

"You're such a cool little thing, Di. Why don't you get excited?"

"But I am. I'm all turning around inside, all the time. Only,—only I can't believe it."

"Di, we couldn't marry now. It would break both their hearts. We couldn't have a wedding, with my father so ill and my mother feeling as she does about my marrying at all."

"She wouldn't want you to marry?"

"Well,—no."

"And not me, especially." Diana mused upon it. "On account of Neal, I suppose," she said. "I can see how she'd feel."

"She and my father feel that they need me now, for a while anyway."

"I can see that."

"Yes, I can see that, too. But meanwhile I can't think of anything but you."

"She would want you," Diana said, thinking aloud, "to marry a different sort of girl. A girl with a big home—all that."

"I'll never love any other woman."

"You don't *know* that. Connie—Connie Newbegin, for instance. Isn't she very beautiful, Bruce?"

"What on earth made you hit on Connie?"

"Just thinking. Why? Why are you smiling?"

"I was smiling because my mother has always meant to make a match of it between me and Connie."

"You saw her in Paris?"

"Every day."

"And is she beautiful, Bruce? She was striking when she was younger,—when we were at Rutherford. But someone told me she is perfectly beautiful now."

"Yes, she is, sensationally so."

"Sensationally beautiful?"

"Absolutely. And what of it?"

Diana laughed.

"What of it? Don't you admire her?"

"As it happens, I dislike her."

Diana laughed, quite shamelessly pleased.

"Only tell me this, Di, before we plan: you do love me, don't you?" he said one day, when she was in her happiest and most daring mood. They had dined together in the city, not for the first time, but this time Bruce had engaged a suite of rooms in the Fairmont Hotel, high up on the hills above the bay, and they had had a perfect meal on a green iron balcony, watching the slow summer evening die away in purple and mauve over the water, and the first stars come out over Berkeley. The hilly streets sloped down below them to Chinatown and the fringe of masts and spars that was the waterfront; the east-bay cities glittered like ropes of diamonds in the dusk, and toward the north the splendid outline of Tamalpais stood up against a sky still faintly flushed with sunset.

"Love you? Oh, Bruce, only God knows how dearly!"

"Then I have a real plan, Di. Why should we tell them?"

"Tell them what?"

"About us."

Her beautiful eyes were alarmed.

"But we mustn't tell anyone!"

"About being engaged?"

Diana's face was lovely in confusion. They were standing on the balcony, looking down; Bruce's arm was about her.

"But of course we mustn't!"

"Well, why not get married, and keep that a secret, too?"

"You mean now—any day?"

"Now, any day."

He felt her shrink against him; her tumbled bare head against his shoulder.

"Oh, no, we couldn't do that!" she whispered.

"Why not, darling?"

"Oh, because there seems to be something—something dishonorable about that sort of thing!"

"Not when there's such good reason, Di. Why, what could stop us? You're free, you said?"

"Of Neal, you mean? I have been since March. It was a year, you know, and then three months before that when they were trying to find him. Oh, yes, I'm free."

"Don't you see, Di, the difficulties we'd get into if we announced it? Mother calling on your grandmother—receptions and engagement cups——"

"Oh no, Bruce, I couldn't bear all that! I'd hate it. It makes me—creep to think of it. I only want—you. I don't need anyone else!"

"And I don't want anyone but you."

"It would be——" She was pondering. "It would be a shock to your father?"

"Terrible, yes. He's like that. He's a nervous, excitable man anyway, you know."

"And he's conscious? He talks and understands and all that?"

"Oh, absolutely. He's only a little childish and weak. And that might end tomorrow,—he might go out in his sleep, the doctor says. In that case, Di, I'm president of the company, I can do as I like. We don't have to ask anybody,—we tell them, and if they don't like it they can get out. Elinor's going to have a baby anyway, and Pats and Mother are going to Paterson for that,—if Dad isn't too sick to leave. There'll be nobody to care what I do or where I go. Marry me, and we'll have wonderful times,—little trips, parties up here at the Fairmont. There can't be any talk, then,—nobody'll know. If Dad gets better, we'll tell him, and you'll come up to the house as Mrs. Bruce, and if he *doesn't*—why, it won't be anybody's business what I do!"

"They'd talk so much——" she said in a whisper, shrinking.

"They can't talk if they don't know."

"Would I——" She turned to him the trusting eyes of a child. "Would I go on at the office, Bruce?"

"For a while. Until we could taper the whole thing off gradually. Give yourself to me, Di. Be my wife! We'd be so happy, sweetheart. We'd have a little time of heaven, while you're coming and going quietly at the office, and I'm learning the business, and looking out for Dad."

"We don't seem," she whispered, "to have the right."

"Would you do it if I hadn't a penny, Di?"

"I don't know. I don't know."

"I know a man who'd marry us like a shot," Bruce said. "He was on the train coming west with me, and a darned nice fellow. He's Harvard. Shall we go up and see him one of these days, Di? He's a clergyman whose family knows old Dr. Graham, at St. Jerome's."

"Suppose—suppose Neal turned up?"

"My darling, the world is full of divorced husbands, and the one thing they *don't* do is turn up."

"Your—your father would be furious."

"My father's a dying man. Di, you and I were sweethearts years ago; we're made for each other. Will you come up to the City Hall with me tomorrow and get a license? And will you go with me to see Robin Purcell afterward?"

"Well——" Diana said faintly.

CHAPTER XXI

SHE had always done everything he ever asked her to; it was natural to do this too. Diana never thought of questioning his decision; indeed Bruce's plans were dazzling beyond anything she had ever dreamed.

They were to say nothing to anyone; not to his parents, not to her grandmother. He and she were to go on with their respective duties in the store just as before. It was only after a long while that they would break to the world their exciting secret; not until his father was either better, or—well, not until he was better, and not until Patsy and his mother had started east to be with Elinor when the baby came; not until Joan Rowley was married, and until no one was especially interested in the affairs of Bruce Palmer and Diana Carmichael Tressady.

She had two days of excitement almost beyond bearing, when she could hardly speak to her grandmother, to the girls in the office, because of the current of enchanted airs that bore her along, away from all her old moorings. She did not think of Joan, of Patsy, or what a strange thing it would be to be Mrs. Bruce Palmer; she thought only of Bruce, how handsome and big and kind and fascinating he was; how his smooth cheek smelled of shaving cream, and his big topcoat of tobacco and homespun; and how the touch of his big hand thrilled her, and the light in his dark eyes seemed to wrap her from head to foot in a very mantle of devotion and protection and happiness.

The Reverend Robin Purcell married them, out in his pleasant study; it was funny to find him quite as much a man

of the world in appearance as Bruce, for all his imposing
"D.D." and the background of the handsome old church.
They were married at noon, and Diana went back to the
office, not knowing whether she walked on her own stunning
new patent leathers or on her head.

It was a serene September day; the whole world was
beautiful in a soft haze; whistles sounded dully along the
waterfront; there was a smell of roasting coffee, and hides,
and idly slapping salt water along the busy piers. Bruce
walked back with Diana to the office, and passing the long
wall of the great ironworks they linked hands.

"Well, feel any different?"

Her blue eyes were luminous as she turned them toward
him.

"Not—so very."

"You're Mrs. Bruce Palmer now. And wouldn't they
buzz?"

"Your father and mother?"

"Everyone. Scare you?"

"Well, it would. We won't have to tell them for ever so
long, will we, Bruce?"

"But what scares you about it?"

"Oh,—thinking what they'd say, and about Neal and his
mother, and everything. Bruce, we won't have to tell them
for ever so long, will we?"

"Never, if you like."

"Oh, I don't mean *never*——"

They separated at the big side door, and Diana went in to
the elevator and mounted to the fourth floor in a dream. It
was all a dream. All afternoon she sat absent, lost in exquisite
abstraction. The girls laughed at her; she laughed at herself.
At five o'clock she went downstairs, walked to a certain corner, found a smart roadster parked there, and got into her
favorite seat beside the driver. Bruce grinned down at her.

"If you could know what I felt, when I saw you coming along in your brown coat!"

Her face was flushed with exquisite color.

"If you could know what *I* felt."

They sat there smiling at each other for a full minute.

"Di, we're married!"

"I've kept saying it—and saying it—but it doesn't seem real."

They started on the drive to Bayhead, and Bruce said:

"Shall we go to my house and have dinner? No reason why I shouldn't take a friend home to dinner."

"Your house! Oh, no!"

"You mean I'm to drop you at your house?"

"There's only my father there. My grandmother is down with Mrs. Disney Smith, at Pacific Grove."

"Oh-h-h. Why didn't you tell me this before, woman?"

"She only went this morning."

"Went this morning! Why, Di, that's perfect. Who's home with you, then?"

"Dad."

"And what would Dad think if you told him you were going to spend the night with Miss Torney?"

"With Mary? But Mary's—oh! Oh, I see what you mean, Bruce!"

"Today's Friday. We'll go down to Santa Barbara to-morrow,—we'll not show up until Monday. We can take a little apartment there,—there are thousands of them. How's that?"

"That's wonderful," Diana said.

It was as simple as that. It was heaven. The September sea washed idly on the long strand at Santa Barbara, and the sun shone, and Diana and Bruce lay in the white sand, and talked, and smiled at each other, and sometimes linked hands, under cover of their big striped umbrella.

Only a two-day honeymoon, but it was perfect. They re-

peated it the next week-end, and the one after that. They
rented a charming little apartment close to the strand, with
an electric stove and a great open fireplace. There were
awnings and a patio; there was a green-tiled bath, and there
was even a little maid in silver-gray, to appear every morning ready to wash the breakfast dishes, and to go to market
for "Madame."

And these days were the happiest Diana ever had known;
the miracle never lost its thrill. She had a new blue bathing
suit, a blue cap, a blue wrap for the beach; she had a white
coat and white shoes. Her beauty glowed and deepened every
hour, and she knew it did.

Bruce played golf one Sunday with some men he knew;
they were all delightful to Diana, and she lunched with them
at the club, and later they came over to the cottage, and there
were cocktails and little crackers loaded with caviar. Afterward they all went, and Diana and Bruce too, to some wonderful place for dinner; they called Diana "Miss Tressady,"
and Diana,—excited and happy, and enjoying the dramatic
values of the situation,—had never been more lovely. She
wore an ivory satin that left her round throat and her brown
shoulders bare; Bruce had bought her the gown only a few
days before, her slim straightness had fitted into it as if it
had been made for her.

"What do you suppose they think I am, Bruce?"

"Just an especially grand friend of mine, staying here."

"Would they treat me that way if we weren't married,
Bruce?"

"They don't know we're married."

"They must suspect it."

"No, I don't think so, Di. It's a quiet time of year, there's
almost nobody here. I might easily have run into some nice
girl I knew."

"But, darling—darling, they came over to our house for
cocktails and things."

"They'd think of it as your house."

"Well," she said gayly, "I don't care what they think. Do you?"

"I care about exactly one thing," Bruce said. "And that's you. I care about you so much that I'm sick! I'm raving insane about you."

"Ah, you do love me!" Her goldenness, her slimness, her sweetness were in his arms; she loved to come out to the patio in the golden September afternoons and find him in a big basket chair, and establish herself on his knees.

"You bet your life I love you, honey girl. I love you so much I kind of wish we hadn't done this quite this way."

"Done what quite what way, Bruce?"

"Married on the sly, as it were. I wish you'd had your engagement ring, and your announcements, and all the rest of the excitement girls love."

"Bruce, it was more for my sake than yours that we kept it so quiet."

"Oh, no, it wasn't. It was my father."

"It was everything. Your father, and Neal—everything. And then how could I have had a marriage at our house, Bruce, with everything so horrible? It's much, much better this way, and it's so much more fun!" Diana's cheek was against his, her arm about his neck. "The main thing is that we love each other!" she said contentedly.

"Di, if you knew how I love you!"

"I—kind of—think you do."

"But now, about Joan's marriage next week," he burst out one noonday, when they were lunching together between office hours. "What'll we do? I'm supposed to ush. She told me she sent you a card for the church, but not for the house."

"It's Thursday, Bruce. I'd be at the office anyway."

"It's five o'clock. You could get away early."

"I don't care one bit about it. I have a perfectly good

excuse for not going. And then she didn't ask me to the house, anyway."

But even as she spoke, Diana was surprised to feel within herself a sudden longing to be at Joan's wedding with all the others, for the excitement and beauty and the sound of the organ music.

"I could get away Thursday——" she said slowly.

"Of course you could. I'll tell you—I have it!" Bruce said, after thought. "I'll tell Joan that I met you and that you got an invitation to the house by some mistake."

"Oh, perfect!" Diana exclaimed, her eyes dancing.

"No, it's not perfect. But it's good enough. It makes me kind of mad to do it left-handed, that way, but it'll do. But—— Darn it!" Bruce broke off, in his impatient way. "It's going to be always like this. We'll be always getting into these fixes."

"This isn't a very serious fix, dearest."

"Well, if it isn't, it's only because you're such a darling, then."

"It'll be fun to be at Joan's wedding and not to have anyone know!" Diana said.

She wore her new gown to the wedding; it was a simple enough frock of dark green velvet, with a yoke of creamy lace. But the single sable skin, slim and brown, that had been a recent present from Bruce, set off Diana's fair skin and blue eyes exquisitely, and on the very morning of the wedding she found at a bargain a green velvet hat with a curled feather about it.

So that it was with perfect confidence in her appearance at least that she could present herself at St. Luke's, and to have Bruce, stunning in wedding regalia of cutaway coat and gray striped trousers with a gardenia in his buttonhole, take her up to a good seat was unspeakably exciting. Joan was an exquisite bride, and Diana thought the groom distinguished-looking, if not handsome.

But somewhere during the ceremony she began to feel dissatisfied with herself and with life. It was not amusing to have done secretly what fortunate Joan could do so beautifully, so openly. Joan's father, serious and dignified, her mother, smiling through tears, the clergyman, the flowers, the solemn wedding march, the bridesmaids,—all these things passed in review before Diana's senses and stirred up some feeling she had not known herself capable of experiencing.

The best man was Trevelyan McAdie, Joan's new brother-in-law. The senior McAdies were there, a little formal and constrained, but gracious and friendly enough. Marcia McAdie was one of the bridesmaids, and Patsy Palmer, Grace Vanderventer Green from New York, and Caroline Dinsmore Pettigrew, of Washington, were the others.

Afterward, at the house, Diana felt out of things, somehow, and wished she had not come. She had thought to carry all this off with great spirit; a little joke on all the folk who did not know about herself and Bruce. But it was not funny.

Instead the pain at her heart deepened and strengthened as the pageant went on. The house was filled with music and flowers, as the church had been, only there was merriment added here.

Joan and her Francis stood at the end of the long library, under a bower of white blooms, between tall lighted candles. The candles were roped together with chains of fragrant stocks and violets and roses, all white, and the glow of lights and flowers fell on Joan's lovely serious face and her white veil, as she was kissed and teased and congratulated by the slowly moving throng. When Diana came up with Bruce, Joan had kisses for them both, too. But she caught at Bruce with a detaining hand, her laughing glance significant.

"You villain,—you and your mistaken invitations! I'm onto you!"

"Onto what? What did she mean, Bruce?" Diana asked, moving on in the crowd.

"That—what?" He was elated, excited. He stooped his handsome head to reach her voice.

"What did she mean about the invitation?"

"Oh,—I guess she knew that I managed that." Bruce was being interrupted, dragged about on all sides; Diana met old friends too. She smiled at his mother; Mrs. Palmer appeared not to remember her, and Diana quickly turned away and began to talk to old Mrs. Kress, who had made Joan's baby clothes, it seemed, and had come to help with Joan's trousseau; everybody seemed to know this, and the admiring voices echoed, "Isn't that just like Joan?"

Bruce's mother had not known her. Joan knew that Bruce had put up an innocent little deception in the matter of the invitation. Somehow it hurt Diana, humiliated her.

"Mother, you know Diana Carmichael?" Bruce said suddenly, catching her by the hand, turning her about.

"Oh, how d'ye do?" Mrs. Palmer said coldly.

"I used to know Patsy and Elinor at school," Diana said, clearing her throat.

"If I can leave Mr. Palmer, I am going on to Elinor next month," Mrs. Palmer said lifelessly but firmly. "Patsy was one of Joan's bridesmaids."

"I know. And didn't they look lovely! She must think I'm bright," Diana thought, "not to know that Patsy was one of the bridesmaids."

Already Mrs. Palmer had completely lost interest in her. Without further word or glance she walked away. Bruce, momentarily absent, had returned with a tray.

"Where'd Mother go? Here, sit down here,—let's eat. I'm starving. Champagne? Do you like it?"

"I've only had it once." They had had it on their wedding

night. She tasted the fizzy cold stuff gingerly, wrinkled her nose like a sneezing cat. "Duncan says you're going to be here for dinner, Bruce."

"Dunk is wrong, as usual. This is all the dinner they're going to have. What do you think of Dunk, by the way? He's your cousin-in-law, you know."

"He's darling. But sh-sh-sh!"

"No," Bruce said comfortably, demolishing a sandwich with one snap of his firm white teeth. "No, somebody didn't show up for the bride's table, and Joan wanted to put me in. But I said all along that I couldn't, because I had to get away early. It seems we're having to rush into town to entertain a very important customer tonight."

"Who?" Her innocent eyes were round with surprise. Suddenly she laughed. "Why, Bruce, you are a complete *liar!*" she said, on a note of admiration.

"I love the new clothes."

"Aren't they beautiful?"

"I'll tell you what, Di. Slip out,—say in about ten minutes, —and get into my car. I'll beat it, too, and we'll go up to town and have dinner."

"You'll have to change."

"Well, why not? It won't take me ten minutes. You can take the car while I change, and get your heavy coat."

"Oh, Bruce, I'd love it."

So that occasion developed more pleasantly than it had at first promised, and they went off together in complete harmony. That same night, Joan's wedding night, driving home comfortably at midnight, under an autumn moon, Diana called Bruce's attention to the strange glow against the southern sky.

"It's a fire, and down our way too. Well, you and I are safe, anyway."

"My father's down in Watsonville, checking in an apple orchard. But Gram's probably home. She was to get home tonight. Mr. Willis was driving up, and she wrote me to go to the wedding, and not to worry, she'd slip in some time late."

"Well, I think the fire's nearer than Bayhead, anyway; looks more like Redwood City."

They drove on, and Diana said:

"It *is* Bayhead. Margaret—that Mrs. O'Connor, my friend, you know? She was one of the Hydes, and she worked for the hardware store when I did,—when you did, too."

"I remember her. Dark. Pretty."

"They've moved to Hollister now. Margaret told me once that every time she saw a fire anywhere, no matter if it was miles and miles away, she thought of her babies.—That's right near us, Bruce. It's—look, it's *right* near us!"

After that there was a space of blackness, completely confused at the time, always terrible to remember. The old Chamberlain house was blazing like a giant torch against the soft autumn darkness of the night; fire engines were steaming and belching flame into Mason Avenue; the Eureka Garage was already smoking ruins.

"It went up like tinder!" eager voices kept saying, from the fringe of black figures that came and went in the eerie lights and shadows that framed the scene of the tragedy. To Diana it was all a nightmare; pools of grimy water in the familiar yard and garden, trampling firemen, curtains blazing at the windows that had framed her world for all the years she could remember. The lower floor was one pit of flame, but strangely, frighteningly, there were firemen on the kitchen roof, climbing in and out of the back windows, through the angry tongues of fire. And always there were voices, shouts, bells, and the roaring of the fire.

"My grandmother—my grandmother——!" Diana kept saying, anxiously catching at one big arm after another. "She might have been upstairs—'way upstairs, in front. She

sleeps there when it's hot. You've got to get my grandmother out—she came down—where is she?"

There was a flurry up on the roof—something long, limp,
handed down between the men's stooped figures. Diana
heard a groan that pierced her like a knife; she ran forward, pushing hands aside, stumbling, sobbing. When she
reached the center of the ring of wet, crowded, talking men,
it was to see them moving the stretcher into the waiting
ambulance. There was a young doctor there, a nurse.

"We'll follow them," Bruce said, at her ear. "Come on,
dear. We'll be at the hospital before they are!"

"Oh, Bruce, Bruce, was she dying?" Diana faltered,
clinging to his arm as they drove through the dark streets.
The ambulance, with a wild jangle of bell and siren, came
behind them; at the hospital Diana, like a woman in a dream,
her velvet gown stained with soot and splashed with dirty
water, her face dirty and very pale, followed the stretcher
down the hall.

After a while she came back to Bruce, in the waiting
room, and when he saw her he knew. Diana looked bewildered; she clung to his arm.

"I think she'd better go home and have a rest," a nurse
said in a concerned undertone. "She's had a shock."

"Yes," Diana said quickly, obediently. "I'll go." She
turned her faint frown to Bruce. "I can't go home!" she
said, blankly.

"No, you come with me, dear," Bruce said gently.

CHAPTER XXII

A WEEK LATER, sober and pale in new black, she took possession of a little house in St. Francis Wood, above the ocean. Bruce had found it, and had been so pleased with it that he had rented it, sure of her approval.

Approval? Diana had never seen any place that she thought quite so delightful. Sad as she felt, changed as the world was, still there was a thrill in finding herself mistress of this perfect little place; there was infinite comfort in hiding herself away, here, from all the noise,—the voices and eyes, the questions and curiosity of the world.

There were five rooms, all on different levels. The one big room, with a fireplace in the corner, had three great floor windows, facing toward the near-by ocean across golf links and the trees of the park. Diana thought this room the loveliest she had ever seen in her life anywhere; on the pale polished wood of its floor there were dim old rugs; fine thin curtains hung at its windows; there were books in long low shelves.

"It's home!" she said to Bruce, turning back toward him with tears in her eyes. But it was not like any home she had ever known.

A shallow step from the big room mounted to a small glassed circular corner described by the agent as a "diningle."

"A dining ingle!" Diana translated it smiling, eyeing with great satisfaction the blue pottery and the glittering goblets. "Oh, Bruce, it's a fairy-tale house, outside and in!" she said. "It can't be true."

Halfway up a twisted little stairway there was an irregularly shaped big bedroom, with poster beds, patchwork quilts, spindle-legged chairs. It had dormer windows on one side, and a long floor window on a balcony facing the sunset. And besides innumerable closets and book niches and little odd corners for sewing machines or telephone table, there was another bedroom, further up, a big bath and a little bath.

"And I am Goldilocks," said Diana, "and you are the largest of the three bears!"

Bruce, watching her, saw the old light come back into her eyes that had cried so often in the past week, and knew that she was happy again.

"Look here, Di. We've got a vacuum cleaner."

"And look at our silver!"

"You'll have real silver some day."

"No hurry. This is enough."

"You're so *sweet*," he said, kissing her.

"I'm going to love this so, Bruce! It's so *exciting*. It's so wonderful to think that nearly every night you'll be stopping the car outside there."

The big handsome man, as eager as she, was beside her. She came and went happily through the charming rooms and up and down the stairs. This first night they were going down to the hotel for dinner; the next night he helped her set the table, kissing her every time they passed each other, and Diana cooked chicken and made a salad. After dinner they sat together in the great leather armchair, Diana in Bruce's arms, their eyes lazily following the course of a ship along the horizon line and the pricking of autumn stars in the deep blue sky.

"Married, Di. Isn't it gorgeous?"

"It's heaven."

"It's everything beginning."

"And ending, too. It's a new world. I'm your *wife*."

"Perhaps you think I don't know it!"

"It's all like a dream," she said. "Gram gone, and all that life gone, and myself here—your wife, going to stay here, belonging here! And the strangest part of it all is," she added, clinging to him suddenly as he tightened his arm about her and rubbed his brown cheek gently against her temple,—"the strangest part of it is going to the office every day, and having the girls talk just as they have been, for three years, and sending out for crackers and tomatoes and cream."

"Would you like to stop, darling?"

"No, I don't think so. Not until everyone knows about us, anyway. Because what would I do, Bruce?"

"I was thinking. I was thinking that you can't see beforehand how doing a thing like this is going to make you feel."

"Our being married?"

"That, yes."

"But whose business is it except ours, Bruce?"

"Well, that's just it. It seemed as if it were only our business. But now—darn it!"

He ended with his characteristic ejaculation, rumpling his hair boyishly with his free hand.

"Now what?"

"Now I wish we'd let 'em know from the start, and like it or lump it!"

"And make your father frantic?"

"Well, what of it? He'd get over it, and by this time everyone would have stopped talking."

"Oh, I don't know, Bruce. People talk longer than you think. On account of my having been divorced, and being poor——"

"Just the same, I believe we kind of messed it up, Baby."

He kissed the top of her hair. Diana said dreamily:

"When I'm as happy as this I don't feel as if I'd messed things up especially."

"Yes, but later on there'll be complications."

"You mean Christabel and Lorenzo?"

"Great Allah, no! Can't you forget those children for half a minute?"

Diana laughed guiltily. "What did you mean by 'complications,' then?"

"Oh,—things like this. I'm asked to be on the committee of the Bachelors' Ball. We've given it every year, you know, as a sort of return to the girls for all their parties."

"Well, go ahead."

"Yes, but there'll be a lot of pretty girls there, and not one as pretty as my wife. And I don't want to go, anyway."

"You couldn't say that your father's ill?"

"Well, I could. But then there's the big lunch Sunday, down at the Country Club, for the polo team. I knew Yerkes in England, he's a darned nice fellow, and I can't throw him down very well. Hang it, Di, we'll have to announce it!"

"What would your father do, Bruce?"

"That's just it. I've got a good start in the firm now, but he could fire me tomorrow if he wanted to."

"Why, Mrs. Baxter said you were going to be vice-president!"

"Mrs. Baxter was talking through her transformation. I'm not. Besides, I get an allowance from my mother,—she's the one that's got the real *dough,* you know,—and I'd be in a deuce of a fix if the old man pulled some Bible stuff on me and kicked me out."

"I don't seem to remember anyone in the Bible kicking his son out."

"How about the Prodigal Son?"

"He left home of his own accord, darling."

"All right, be a smarty. You see, Di,—darn it, I spend a deuce of a lot of money. That is—I'm supposed to get a salary at the office; I never stay inside it. If my mother,—I don't say she would,—but she's kind of hysterical, you know, and she has gotten herself all worked up about Dad,—if she *did* shut down, it'd be darned awkward! It'll work out all right, but it may take a little time. Darn it, I wish we'd faced the music right from the first."

"Your mother would hate me," Diana said thoughtfully.

"She's the kind of woman who'd hate any daughter-in-law,—in fact, any relative, except her own. She's always been terribly catty to my father's brothers, and she acted simply rottenly to Elinor's outfit,—Bill Wade's father and mother. She'll go on there now and high hat the whole crowd of them when the baby comes. She's like that."

Diana mused on this. It presented a problem. She had other problems; it made her feel serious and grown up to solve them by herself, without any help from Gram or her father. Her father was still in Watsonville, but he might drift homeward at any time, and she must be ready with a story for him. Her position at the office was becoming increasingly difficult.

That she was changed, of course the girls knew. Her new black clothing was simple enough, but there was a difference now in her stockings, her coats, the amount of money in her purse. Perhaps they thought she had collected insurance on Gram; she never could explain. She did not even tell them she no longer lived in Bayhead.

Bruce insisted that she get help with the housework of the little establishment in Santa Monica Way.

"Unless you'd rather stay home and do it yourself, Di."

"No, I'll get Alomel. She's that black giantess who was doing the windows the other day. I'd rather. I'd rather go on with the office,—it keeps me busy, Bruce, and I've someone to talk to."

"Well, I think you're right."

While his mother was away he dined with her four nights a week; was with her all Saturday afternoon and stayed with her for dinner; went home late, had Sunday breakfast with his father, and was back in St. Francis

Wood to take her out on Sunday afternoon. And for a while the sense of novelty and adventure made everything easy; but after Christmas Bruce began to get very tired, and Diana saw it.

"To get to you makes it all right, sweetheart, but in the rain and everything there's an awful lot of highway!"

"I could move down to Bayhead; then I'd be nearer."

"No, then everyone would notice it."

"Where do you suppose everyone thinks I am as it is?"

"Didn't we tell everyone that you were going down to Watsonville?"

"That'll do for a while, I suppose. When does your mother get back, Bruce?"

"Saturday. She meant to get home for Christmas, you know, but Elinor's being so ill delayed her."

"Oh, dear! I wish she'd always stay away."

"I wish she would. Then we could take a chance with Dad. But never mind," Bruce said, ending the conversation with cheerful philosophy, as he usually did. "It'll all turn out right,—patience is all we need! Only you know, Di," he said once, when they were loitering over a Sunday supper of his favorite broiled chicken and avocado pear, "I love you so much that I hate to have to be away from you; I hate bluffing and lying about my wife! I want to come out with the whole thing and have you down there in the old house——"

She had a momentary vision of herself as young Mrs. Palmer, in the lovely Palmer home into whose garden fortunate Patsy and Elinor had disappeared after school every afternoon. Her forehead knitted thoughtfully.

"If your father was dead, how would it be easier, Bruce?"

"Oh, because I'd be the natural person to be president of the company, and that'd mean a big salary, and that my mother'd have to—simply *have* to forgive me. But you see —you see, here's the difficulty, Di. Dad's paralyzed; he'll never be quite well. But he can see the men from the office and all that,—he keeps his hand in things.—And God knows," Bruce broke off to say honestly, "I don't want anything to happen to him! That isn't the point. It's just that it's damn' hard not to know what's ahead."

"It's harder for you than for me."

"Oh, no, it's not. You going down to that dumb department every day and talking with those dumb women! No, it's just that you're a better sport than I am, Di."

"The office is my salvation," Diana said more than once. "I get tired, and I'm glad to get home. If you're coming, Alomel has everything ready, and if you're not, I have milk toast, and a book,—I like it. I like making my own money, even if it's only enough to pay Alomel."

One rainy January day she said to him shyly:

"Bruce, there's something awful that you ought to know."

He had brought her home from the office; he had later to go to the ferry to meet his mother and sister on their return home. Diana had make him a cup of coffee and was buttering toast busily as she spoke.

"Something awful?" His eyes quickened. "Great Scott——?" he began apprehensively. Diana laughed.

"No, no, no, it's not that. But, Bruce—what would you do if we *were* to have a baby?"

"It isn't that!"

"Oh, no, no,—something quite different. But Bruce, what would you do if it *was?*"

"Oh, help, darling, I don't know! We have trouble enough. We'd do something, I guess. But for heaven's sake, unless you want me to drop dead of heart failure——"

"This is the awful thing," Diana said suddenly. She got on his knees, locked her hands about his neck. "My father's home, and I've told him," she said.

Bruce raised surprised eyebrows. He was not angry. He bumped her face against his gently and gathered kisses from her eyes, her lean soft young cheek, the bridge of her straight nose.

"I adore you, Beautiful," he said. "Nothing else matters. Everything else, when a man loves a woman like you, is unimportant. Let the deluge deluge us! Did you tell Papa to put it in the paper?"

"I made him swear—and you can trust him, Bruce, really you can. But he looked so poor, and so quiet and old, and he's living in a dreadful place over on Geary Street. So I cooked him dinner,—I had liver and bacon in the house, because I thought you were coming,—and Alomel was here, and she made hot biscuits, and he loved it so. But he was worried, I could see it. He kept asking me if my grandmother had left any money; he couldn't understand. So I told him."

"Well, that was all right, honey."

"Oh, no, it wasn't. For I'd promised not to tell anyone."

"Funny—I was just thinking," Bruce said. "Remember the night of the fire you were worrying because you said your grandmother would be onto us like a shot?"

She nodded. The memory made her color fade a little.

"Well, I was thinking. Now here my mother gets home just as your father does."

"You aren't suggesting that they were away together, Bruce?" She rubbed her cheek against his temple. Bruce tightened his arms.

"It may be, Di," he said, ignoring her suggestion, "that your father's our way out."

"Our way out?"

"Yes. Why shouldn't you live here in St. Francis Wood with your father? His living here helps a lot. You can have the girls from the office out for dinner if you get lonely, and I can tell my mother honestly, if anyone sees us together, that you are living here with your father——"

"You mean have Dad come live with me?"

"Why not?"

"Oh, Bruce, I'd like that!" Diana said, her eyes bright.

It meant she saw less of him; there was no help for that. Not only were his mother and sister home again, conscious of all his comings and goings, but he knew that Diana had company now, and was less anxious about her. Their cozy evenings, their lazy late Sunday lunches were fewer; it only meant that she rushed into his arms with a hungrier devotion when he came in big and blown and tired for dinner, and that her father's happiness made her happy herself.

While Bruce did his duty at home, Diana and her father drifted about the city in search of amusements. They went to movies, to concerts; now and then on Sunday Bruce could not be with them, and then they drove to the park, or took their luncheon to the ocean cliffs south of the city, and spent the afternoon watching the sun go down over the shining water, and the gulls circling and crying on the rocks.

Money matters were worrying Bruce; Diana knew it. But he would never tell her exactly what they were. She knew that the rent of their Paradise was an enormous hundred a month; her own bills she could keep small, but in his eager devotion Bruce was always making her extravagant presents, keeping her purse full of five- and ten-dollar bills, buying her orchids and gardenias.

"Darn it, I owe so much money!" he would say, rumpling his hair restlessly.

"Do we owe so much, Bruce?"

"We? *You* don't owe any. It's things since before we were married,—fool things, like my big radio and the car,—everything. Well, I've got a birthday coming, and sometimes Mother gives me a thousand on my birthday. But she's kind of hard up herself, she says. However——!"

"Do you owe a *thousand*, Bruce?"

"And then some, Beautiful. But I have you. Diana, why did we do this?"

"Do what? Get married?"

"Get married secretly."

"It seemed so simple," Diana said dreamily.

"It's never simple. It's mixed everything up for me, and it's damned unjust to you."

"Does Connie complicate, Bruce?" Diana had to ask, after much heroic decision never to ask it.

"Connie? What made you think of her?" He considered a moment; spoke hesitantly. "Yes, she complicates."

Oh, it was worse than she had feared—it was worse than she had feared! Diana had a second in which to wish fervently that she never had mentioned Connie.

"How does she, Bruce?"

"But tell me what made you ask, darling. It's like mind-reading. What put Connie into your head?"

"Well, I knew she was back, and I knew she was staying with Pat."

"Yep. She's staying at our house. Mrs. Newbegin's away, you know."

"So you see her every day?"

"Yep." Bruce apparently fell into deep thought.

"Is she beautiful, Bruce?"

"Yep. She's gorgeous. White skin and black hair. She plays the harp a lot. She's written things for the harp."

"Composed them?"

"And they say they're darned good. And she's written a book,—*Europe and Little Constance.*"

"She hasn't!"

"It's going to be published this spring. She doesn't make much of it. She says it's just a kid book; she wants to write one about Charlemagne."

"Charlemagne?"

"She's been digging around in old French books. Yes," Bruce said, thoughtfully, "Connie's quite a person; you have to hand it to her."

"Does she like you, Bruce?" The knife had to be turned in the wound; Diana caught her breath with pain.

"That, my darling, is the complication," Bruce admitted frankly. "I think I can thank my mamma for it. Mother's been talking me up to Con until she naturally thinks I'm the Big Idea. She came at me with a rush, you know,—she was all over me. 'We kiss each other, don't we, Bruce.'"

"The nerve!" Diana said disgustedly. "What did you do?"

"Well, naturally I said, 'Well, let's do it, and we can look up the authorities later.' She's got more darned Paris dresses than you could shake a stick at."

"I hate her!" Diana stated calmly. Bruce laughed.

"Probably some handsome young man boarding in your house could shake your feeling for me, Di, but I don't happen to be made that way."

"You make me ashamed!" she said, putting her fingers over his lips.

"I should think I might. Di, I never loved anyone before I loved you; I'll never love anyone else this way. I want to give it all up,—the family, and running around with the fellows, everything, and just be out here with you in this little place,—just the two of us, talking and going out to buy steak, and doing the dishes. I never thought I'd feel this way; I never saw it coming."

"Ah, Bruce, you're such a *dear!*" She was in his arms, laughing, clinging; she was happy again. They were always happy when they were together; it was only when the world outside intruded upon their privacy that the little frown formed on Diana's forehead, and that Bruce fell into scowling meditations.

"I'm different," he told her. "I'm darned if I want to do anything else except just come out here to you."

And one day he said to her, "Suppose they do find out, and my father raises the roof, and my mother makes a scene. We've got a right to get married, haven't we? We're not kids. I can take care of you, if they hold out on me. That's what other men do."

Diana could say nothing to this. But her eyes glowed and her color deepened, and she tightened the arm he held about her, and dug her head still deeper into the big shoulder where it loved to rest.

CHAPTER XXIII

ONE soft foggy Friday in February she and her father went out to the aquarium. They took their lunch, hoping that the weather would clear, but the day remained bleak and unfriendly; cold airs blew along the bare park walks, and Diana decided that they had better take their sandwiches home again and have a cup of hot tea with their meal.

But for an hour or two they might as well drift along looking at the crabs and the seals, and the fish that swept down toward the gray glass of the tanks, swept effortlessly away again.

Staring at them abstractedly, Diana said some word aloud, and her father turned his grizzled head toward her in interrogation.

"Did you say something, my dear?"

"I was thinking aloud." She smiled, seemed to shake herself together. "I don't know what I said!" she apologized.

But in another moment she had fallen into a brown study again.

Slowly, sickeningly, the conviction forced itself on her. *That* was it, was it? She had thought of this possibility in the first weeks of her first marriage; had thought of it in the first weeks of her second. Then she had dismissed it from her mind.

Now it was back again, in the forefront of her thoughts, insistent, unanswerable fact.

"That's it," she said, again audibly. She went out with her father into the fog-shrouded world and heard dim whistles far away, warning, warning. Figures went by her only half seen; men with children, filling in the holiday morning; little boys with flags. School teachers were marshaling tiny kindergarten children in ranks about some statue; George Washington, of course. "Yes, that's it," Diana said. *"Now* what'll I do? *Now* what'll I do?"

No mother, no Gram to stand by her, and poor Bruce at the end of his resources as it was. The leaves were wet on the little bushes of the park; bunting dripped mist.

"After a while the jolly old sun will come out, and then we'll sing our song to the sun!" one of the teachers said brightly. "We couldn't sing our song to the sun when there *wasn't* any sun, could we?"

All the very small children laughed ecstatically at this and echoed long-drawn "No-o-os!"

February. Diana's shoes squeaked on the wet gravel as she and her father turned toward the parked car. They crossed a wide road and a bridle trail.

"Think we'd better get home, Di?"

"I think so. It's a quarter to twelve now. I don't believe this is going to break. Much better to get something hot to drink!"

While she was driving home through the foggy streets with their subdued air of leisure and holiday, the noon whistles sounded loud and strong. Usually someone would be making tea and stewing tomatoes, in the little lunchroom at the office, now. Diana stopped her car at a market and bought Bruce a fat steak with asparagus. Apricots in a can; she would make her upside-down cake.

Poor Bruce! What would he say?

Oh, maybe it wasn't true—maybe it wasn't true! Maybe a few days more would remove the frightening suspicion forever. She couldn't—she simply *couldn't* face all that now!

She and her father had their luncheon in the little dining ingle, with hot cocoa to embellish the cold food; then Diana, feeling suddenly limp and broken, lay down for a while, making herself work with her French verbs; making herself read *Coriolanus*. The day remained veiled and dull; Bruce telephoned at about three to ask her if she loved him, and to say that he would be with her for dinner. "Oh, Bruce, Bruce," Diana whimpered, getting back on the bed and pulling the satin quilt over her knees, "how I need you! Be good to me!"

In the dreamy afternoon there were strange crickles and creakings through the little house; every window looked into solid mist today. Diana smelled her father's pipe; saw him standing in her doorway smiling some explanation to her; heard the front door close after him. He was going down to the Alhambra Club to play checkers. A lot of quiet old fellows gathered there, every afternoon, to discuss the paper, remember old times, and quarrel shrewdly over halma, checkers, dominoes.

It was a relief to awaken suddenly from an uneasy doze and find that she must instantly set about dinner preparations. Diana, putting sweet potatoes into the oven to bake, carefully opening a round flat cheese in silver foil, setting a dainty table, thought that she would not share her suspicions with Bruce tonight. Time enough later.

Activity helped her to feel better; the lights helped her. She splashed her face bracingly with cold water and brushed her hair into damp order. But there was suddenly a bad moment when the coffee began to scent the air, and Diana stopped short and with a paling face said once again, "That's what it *is,* all right!"

Her father returned with the evening paper, and shortly afterward Bruce was there, taking off his big overcoat, laughing, snipping a raisin from the bunch and a little cracker from the pan, kissing her eyes and hair and the tip of her ear, shocking the breath out of her.

While she went to and fro he glanced at the paper.

"Di, want to see me play polo Sunday?"

"Oh, are you going to?"

"Have to. Harris has wrenched his arm; he's no good."

"I'd love to, Bruce. Who's going?"

"Mother isn't, but the girls are,—Patsy and Con. Listen, I've *got* to be home Sunday night, and I've got to go to a dinner tomorrow night."

"Oh, how rotten!"

"But here's what I'm going to do: I'll dress here for tomorrow's dinner, and be here all night, and Sunday we can have breakfast together."

"Bother for you?"

"Bother? What do you think I *want* to do! Will it be all right for you? Listen, Di, can your father hear me?"

"No, he's taking a bath. He always chooses the ten minutes right before dinner to take a bath. What is it?"

"Old Newbegin came over this morning, and we went off and played golf together."

"Connie's father?"

"Yep. And d'you know the proposition the old man put up to me?"

"What?" She had paused, in her brown kitchen apron; the thick red steak, ready for the broiler, in her hands.

"He as good as said that if Con and I made a go of it he'd put one hundred grand of her money into the firm."

A pause.

"What firm?" Diana asked then.

"Rowley & Palmer."

She came in to stand nearer him.

"Does the firm need money, Bruce?"

"You bet your life it needs money."

"Ha!" Diana said. She went back to the kitchen.

"No, but what do you think of the old man?"

"I imagine that Con gave him a pretty strong hint she'd fall in with the plan."

"That's what I thought."

"Did your mother say anything about it?" Diana asked, coming in with the pitcher to fill the glasses.

"Yep, she was talking to me about it at lunch."

"Well, what do they think you *are*, Bruce, to be bossed about that way!"

"My mother pulled a lot about my father being ill,—all that."

"I suppose so." Diana could return to the kitchen quite composedly; they didn't make any impression on Bruce with all this. But it was humiliating somehow, too——

Presently she heard him laughing, and her annoyance lessened. Nothing much worrying him!

"What's funny?"

"An article in this paper. It's about some clergyman— one of those modern lads who are always advertising themselves. It seems he preached a sermon on the text: 'Who am I? What am I doing? Where am I going?' and the paper says that the Alameda county police answered it by saying, 'You are So-and-so. You are pretending to be a minister of the Associated Church. And you are going to jail.'"

"Oh, Bruce, that's delicious!"

"I thought the smartness of the reporter was good, handling it that way."

"I wonder if Papa saw it. He loves silly little odds and ends like that." Diana put the smoking steak on the table, and Bruce stood up to attack it as she groped about for the scattered sheets of the newspaper. "Papa, did you happen to see that article about some clergyman, in the *News?*"

"I don't know's I did," her father said, falling upon his meal with gusto.

"I didn't have soup tonight, Bruce, because I hate the steak to wait."

"This is grand. Look at the asparagus! It's right there, Di," Bruce said, of the newspaper article, gesturing with his big carving knife, "on that page there."

"Here it is! Listen to this, Papa."

But she did not read it immediately. Instead she said in an odd, bewildered voice:

"Bruce! Did—did you notice? He's got,—this clergyman,—he's got the same name as *our* clergyman!"

"How d'you mean?" Bruce demanded.

"Robin Purcell. Don't you remember your clergyman friend on the train, Robin Purcell?"

"Let's see." He had the paper in his hands; Diana watched his face.

"That's a funny note!" Bruce said, as if to himself.

"You don't think it's the *same?*"

"Well—I don't see how it could be. It's a—it's a funny note!" Bruce muttered.

"But Bruce,—you knew him?"

"I'd met him on the train."

"Is *that* all you knew him?"

"We played bridge together——" Bruce said absently, his eyes on the printed lines. "And he was a seminary man, and all that. He told me he was going to be assistant rector at St. Jerome's."

"Yes,—that's sure! He *was* there, wasn't he?" Diana exclaimed eagerly. "You could telephone there, couldn't you? He can't be the same!"

"Don't worry. We were married all right," Bruce said. "If there was any funny business about it, we can do it right over."

"Oh, I know—I know," Diana agreed, laughing uneasily. "But let's—let's find out!"

"We could walk over there tomorrow,—it'd be just a good walk,—if you liked. I don't have to be home until lunch."

"I have to be at the office in the morning. You go to St. Jerome's. They couldn't—they couldn't have a man there, Bruce, who was that sort!"

"Well, don't get so mad about it, darling. You and I are as much married as if the Archbishop of Canterbury had ridden out of Canterbury on his old dapple-gray to do it!"

"Well, I know!" Her expression was half laughing, half rueful. "But what a *wicked* man!" she burst out.

"He was on the train, coming up from New York," Bruce explained between pauses when he studied the newspaper as if to wrench further information from it. "He asked me if I was going on to California, from Chicago, you know, and I said yes, to San Francisco. Then he said he was going to San Francisco, too, to take a guest pulpit at St. Jerome's, and I said that I knew St. Jerome's and would look him up. He *seemed* a funny feller to be a minister," Bruce admitted, ruefully. "But I never thought that it wasn't all straight."

They presently abandoned the topic, returned to it with fresh interest. Suddenly, on an impulse, Bruce telephoned the rector at St. Jerome's. Dr. Graham? This was Mr. Palmer speaking. Could Dr. Graham give Mr. Palmer any information about the Reverend Robin Purcell?

A pause. A dignified yet embarrassed shred of a cough. Hem! Dr. Graham would be glad to see Mr.—Mr. Palmer in reference to—to the gentleman he mentioned. A very unfortunate affair,—hem! The gentleman had been at St. Jerome's for a very short while,—hem! Could Mr. Palmer find it convenient to stop in,—say tomorrow——

Bruce restored the telephone to its hook and faced Diana with a half-alarmed, half-mischievous smile.

"Well, what do you know about that?"

"Very little!" Diana said, her expression between laughter and tears.

"I'll see him in the morning. And if there's anything cuckoo I'll see Pete Reynolds,—that's Dad's lawyer. We'll fix it all up."

They resumed their meal; Diana with a flagging appetite and languid interest. Everything was horrid. The wretched suspicions of the morning rushed back upon her, and she remembered the foggy park, and herself dawdling along, bored and patient, with her mild old broken father, looking at the blandly swimming fish. She thought of old Newbegin making his tentative overtures toward Bruce——

"Diana," Bruce said later, determinedly, when her father had gone to bed, and when they two were sharing the last of a wood fire, "I think this Purcell thing is an omen. I think we ought to come out in the open. Whether this fellow was a crook or not, the marriage was probably valid, —but it doesn't matter. We'll fix it all up, we'll tell my father and mother and then just take the consequences."

"But suppose it kills your father?"

"It won't kill him."

"And suppose they refuse to have anything to do with us, and stop giving you money, and we owe all that money——?"

"They won't. I'll ask 'em to help us out that much. They'll be mad, and then they'll get over it, and everyone will begin to talk about something else. And you and I'll keep this place,—only I'll be here every night——"

"Oh, Bruce, it would be fun!" She rubbed her cheek against his. "Only—only you know you have always been accustomed to going with all those important people, darling, the Peninsula crowd,—the 'Bachelors' and the 'Spinsters' and all that. And I'll never count, with them,—they'll never like me. And your mother'll never like me. She'll always think I'm the—the divorced adventuress who kidnapped you——"

"Shut up your face!" Bruce advised her drowsily, as she paused. Diana laughed softly. It was good to be here in his arms, in the firelight, with his hard cheek against her own, and her hair tumbled on his shoulder. There were no real dangers, there were no real worries while they loved each other.

The next morning, as fresh and radiant as a fresh pink rose, she cooked his breakfast, and they shared the grapefruit, the coffee, the toast and eggs. Her father always slept late; Diana could leave the kitchen in disorder for him to clean; he would put away the last spoon scrupulously after he had had his own solitary breakfast at ten o'clock. She and Bruce were always away at a quarter past eight, Bruce to drop her two blocks away from the store, or she to leave him there, so that their arrival in the same motorcar would not awaken any suspicions in their fellow workers.

"I'll telephone you what old Graham says," Bruce said. As the president's son he was free to go uptown in the morning hours, whereas Diana must always ask the odious Roach for liberty.

"All right. Don't see your father's lawyer unless you have to. The more people who know, the more danger we're in."

"I'll only see him if we have to make this thing legal."

"Legal! I'll be nervous until I know. And especially nervous," Diana added in her thoughts, "since I already know what I'll do."

Saturday morning in the office, and the girls all rather yawny and bored on the half-day between two holidays. Fog pressed against the shuttered windows; they could hear constant foghorns and whistles from the piers a few blocks away. The smell of branded rubber floated up as usual from the rubber department on the floor below and mingled with the sickeningly sweet aromatic smell of the floor polish and the nutty odor of pencil lead. Diana noticed all these smells keenly this morning; shuddered.

Black silesia aprons. Yawns. Gossip. Alice Lamb, a new girl, asking what was good for an offud code id de doze. May Blunt displaying a modest engagement ring.

"I told him I thought it was a sample and I'd like to see the whole diamond," May said, suffocated with laughter. "I thought he'd kill me."

"Lissen, girls——" This was Baxter. "Roach wants some of us to work stock-taking this afternoon. He says half of us this afternoon and half of us next Saturday afternoon, and we can take our pick. I can't possibly be here this afternoon,—Diana, how about you?"

"I could," Diana said reluctantly. Bruce was going home this afternoon,—home to Bayhead, that was. She put her head down on her hands; was conscious of a deep interior groan.

"Feel sick?" Baxter asked concernedly.

"Feel rotten." She looked up; smiled.

"What'je do yesterday?" This was Mary, with her air of always being ready to laugh.

"I took my father out to see the aquarium."

"Maybe the fish upset your stomach," May suggested, and she and Mary went into their characteristic spasms of silent mirth.

"Girls, get started!" Mrs. Baxter warned them, as the elevator clicked. But it was only idiot Albert, wavering out to inquire if he had "lef' his parkit noife up dere yisday."

"Gimme a kiss, Albert!" Mary said.

"Aw, I will nod."

"Aw, go on!"

"For goodness' sake, Mary," Mrs. Baxter said, "behave yourself! Go on downstairs, Albert,—you probably left your knife at home. Get to work, girls, it's ten of nine."

The dreamy hours began to go by. At eleven there was a telephone call for Diana, but it was only her father, desirous of knowing whether her blue coat was to go to the cleaners. At noon Bruce came up for a moment, and they stood together, talking in the deserted office. This rarely happened now; since September the girls in the sporting-goods department had had every reason to believe that young Mr. Palmer's fancy for Diana Tressady had cooled.

"Old Graham was awfully nice, Di. He said this fellow Purcell comes from a decent family and did well in college, —only kind of excitable and hysterical. He had some letters from friends of the Grahams. Graham suggested that he go down and visit his family at Carmel, after he first got here, and they liked him. They all thought he was a young clergyman, and after they came back Graham suggested that he stay on at the clergy house and take some of the curate work. And then the whole thing blew up suddenly."

"You mean he's not a clergyman?"

"He only had one year at the seminary. He's a kind of a musical poetical freak,—always dramatizing everything. They kicked him out of St. Jerome's. So he went over to Alameda and told some sort of a story, and they let him preach there——"

"Then, darling, we're not married?" It was a pale face she turned to him; her smile was strained.

"I don't know. It may be absolutely valid, Dr. Graham says. We had a license and we had a witness, you know. I'm going to see Pete Reynolds, anyway. Don't worry. Everything's going to be all right. Only you can imagine the ass I feel, letting you into it. It never occurred to me there could be anything crooked about it."

"I'd like to see the credentials he showed Dr. Graham."

"Oh, the old boy talked about that, too. He knew Purcell's father, it seems, and his sister's daughter was in college with him,—that sort of thing. He's wild about it all."

"I should think he might be! How many persons do you suppose Purcell married?"

"Graham said only us, at St. Jerome's. He was surprised to hear that he'd married anyone. They could jail him for it."

"That wouldn't do *us* any good."

"No, but we're all right. Nothing will ever make any difference to us, will it, Di?"

"Not to me." Her lovely face was so troubled, her blue eyes so clouded that Bruce risked a quick kiss on her soft fair hair before saying hurriedly, in departure:

"Your gang will be wondering where you are. I've got to beat it, too, I'm seeing Pete at half-past; he wants to play golf. Listen, darling, I come out to dress at the house to-night, but I can't stay for dinner, see? And you come down on the eleven train tomorrow, or drive down, if you like, and I'll meet you at Burlingame station at noon and we'll eat. Then I've got to play polo, and I'll get you a good seat— bringing your father?"

"I don't think so. He gets tired. I'll have breakfast late with him and be back for dinner."

"Well—and meanwhile I'll talk it all over with Pete, and then we can plan."

"It's an argument for big weddings, isn't it? With flowers and bridesmaids and lots of newspaper talk."

"This kind of thing? Listen, Di, do you love me?"

"With all my heart."

"You don't mean that. You're just saying it!"

But he believed her just the same, and went smiling away, and Di smiled, too, going back to the lunchroom. There was comfort, there was infinite reassurance where Bruce was. She had loved him as an inexperienced girl, loved him even more dearly when he had come back into her life a few months ago. But the married Bruce, the man who was substituting love of her company, of their little home of books and fires and talk together, for all the more showy and expensive amusements his life had always known, was most lovable of all. He had changed, and she had changed, too. There was a different look in his eyes now, when he tipped her face up, and smiled down at her, and kissed her between her own eyes; there were new tones in his voice when he came out to their sunshiny morning kitchen and found her, in crisp blue gingham, busy with toast and oranges, and put his arm about her to say, "How's my wife?"

The next day, Sunday, she dressed herself in her best and drove the twenty miles to the Burlingame polo field alone. The February day was radiantly sunshiny and green, the sky high and clear, and there was hot sunshine. Diana wore her white coat, a small white hat, and the new rough white sports frock with the knotted scarf of French red and blue. She expected a look of pleasure in Bruce's eyes when he met her, and he did not disappoint her.

"Darling, you look simply stunning!"

"Do you like the dress?"

"It's stunning." But it was not so much the dress as the slim golden girl, with the fair hair curving about her heart-shaped face, and the sapphire lights coming and going in her blue eyes.

"Listen, the whole gang's here, Di,—Joan and McAdie, and Minna Towne and Jack, and Con and everyone! They're lunching at the club. I wish to goodness I could take you there. I said my car was out of order, and I wanted to talk to the pony man."

"And what did the lawyer—Reynolds, is it?—what did he say yesterday?"

"Oh, it's a mix-up. Of course," Bruce said, driving to a popular roadside restaurant now,—"of course, *being* a lawyer, he had to haw and hem a lot."

"Was he surprised about our being married?"

"Stunned. He said it would *crush* my father."

"Oh-h-h," Di said dolefully.

"What does it matter what he thinks? He's all for the family, of course. He tried to persuade me to put the whole thing off,—kept referring to you as 'the young lady to whom you are engaged.' I said to him, 'My dear Pete, let me remind you that this lady and I have been living as married persons for six months.' So now he's going to see Graham and Purcell and look everything up."

"And how long will that take, Bruce?"

"He said he'd let me know immediately. Thursday at latest, he said."

"Did you happen to ask him,—did you *happen* to,—if he thought the marriage was all right?"

"Yep, I did. I asked if getting the license wasn't a sort of guarantee of good faith and all that.—Here, Di, this is a swell place,—Bandini's. We'll get spaghetti here.—Yep, I asked him what he thought would happen, and he said that it was his impression that it wasn't a marriage.—Here we are."

They went into the crowded place of sparkling windows, red-checked tables, smoke from grease and cigarettes. The food smelled suddenly welcome to Diana, and she fell upon it with a relish that was a secret delight to her. There could not be anything wrong with a woman who was so hungry for minestrone, and spaghetti, and salad with a hint of garlic in it.

CHAPTER XXIV

BUT LATER, sitting alone in the grandstand and watching the polo in the crisp winter sunlight, she did not feel so well. Her head ached faintly, and her hands and feet felt cold. She began to be very much afraid that she would be sick. Diana tried to distract herself with a resolute study of her surroundings.

Under the high blue sky the beautifully shaven turf of the field stretched as smooth as a band of pale green velvet. Across it the ponies careered and capered, dragged upon short reins, wheeling sharply, their flanks widening as their forequarters rose in air. The sticks flashed, the riders bent close to their little mounts; there were tangles of men and horses, then they would suddenly all be free and off to the other end of the field again. Diana looked at her program, looked at the game; she felt that she did not understand it all very well.

In the boxes, a few rows of seats below her, were the Bayhead groups. The Newbegins and the Porters and the Stuarts, and Bruce's sister. Diana was not more than ten feet from Joan, very pretty and dignified in lovely sports wear that still smacked of the trousseau. Beside her was her husband, with his lean, nice, aristocratic face; their heads were close together as he leaned over the back of her chair and they discussed the game together.

Three other players were dark, like Bruce, and dressed all in white, like Bruce. But when they were near enough for her to identify him positively, Diana watched him all the time. She liked to see him change horses, between the chukkers;

once he looked up at her and waved, quite openly, and she waved back.

Presently Joan turned and looked searchingly along the rows of spectators seated immediately behind her. Did she see Diana? Diana thought she did, and smiled as she said aloud, "Hello, Joan!" but Joan did not smile in return. Her color rose a little, and she raised her chin and turned back without any sign of recognition.

For a moment Diana was sure Joan had not seen her. Then there came a miserable suspicion that she had,—that for some reason Joan was cutting her. Joan had perhaps seen Bruce wave in that direction,—although indeed it might have been supposed to be directed immediately at the box party, —and had suspected that Diana was behind her. Did the girls know that she and Bruce were spending a good deal of time in each other's company?

No, of course not, why should they? But there was no question that Minna and Patsy, and then Con, all managed to glance carelessly backward, during the next ten minutes, pretending to look for someone much higher up in the grandstand, bringing their eyes down carelessly, giving Diana an instant's glance.

Her face burned. They knew. Or if they did not know that she and Bruce were actual lovers, they knew something; knew that the reason that he so often had evening engagements "at the club," or had to "see a man on business tomorrow," was really because he wanted to be with Diana Tressady. Diana Tressady, who had been so smart at school, but who then had married that queer actor person, and had lived in Hollywood and gotten a divorce, and all that, and who now had intrigued poor Bruce——

Everything was wrong today, the ebbing and surging sense of physical discomfort underscoring it all. Diana wished herself home, comfortably ensconced in her bed, with the fat satin comforter drawn over her feet.

She would go home, she thought, right in the middle of the polo game, but for the hope that she might see Bruce for a moment afterward. He had to dine with the Rowleys tonight; it was Mr. and Mrs. Rowley's silver wedding anniversary, a very important occasion, and there would be fifty dinner guests. There were to be toasts, and Bruce, in young Duncan's absence at Yale, would be toastmaster.

"I wanted to toast the third generation," Bruce had said to Diana, "but Joan got shy. She doesn't want anyone to know."

"Oh, are there expectations?" And once again the old pang of deep jealousy of Joan, who did everything with such dignity and beauty and was always so admired for it.

"I believe so. They say the McAdies are wild with joy. Patsy gave me a pretty strong hint of it, anyway. But Joan thinks it's too soon to talk."

Thinking of this, Diana studied Joan with especial interest today. She was not jealous of the coming of a baby; Diana had never thought of herself as noticeably fond of babies. But she did long for some of the praise, the order, that seemed to be Joan's by divine right. The McAdies were wild with joy; Joan's whole circle would be waiting to welcome the newcomer, to make him presents of silver mugs and white coaches and delicately colored knitted baby wear. Whereas, if any one prospect could throw consternation into her life and Bruce's at this particular moment, it would be that same event.

After a while the sun went suddenly behind a black spring cloud, and a cold wind blew across the grandstand, died away again. The polo sticks clicked; the riders shouted as the battle surged to and fro. Now they were down at the far goal, now swaying without change of position close to the side lines; now whirling madly up the field.

"Palmer's doing wonderfully today,—he's riding Preston Harris's horses. He's a wonder. He played at Harvard," a voice said close behind her, and Diana felt proud. She did not know how well he played polo, but he was by far the handsomest and the nicest-looking of all the men.

She tried not to look too often at Connie, sitting in the box below her, but her eyes would stray toward her. Con was beautiful; there was no doubt about it. The men about her were paying her the tribute that men pay only to the extraordinarily attractive girl. Con was dark, vivacious, glowing, very different from the rather lethargic heavy girl of Rutherford days. She was all in saffron yellow, an exquisite ensemble of big loose soft coat, hat, scarf, shoes. She was laughing, happy,—oh, well, why shouldn't she be?

Diana decided suddenly to go home. She could leave a little note in Bruce's car; he'd understand. The day had turned bleak, and the game was almost over. She did not understand it anyway; of course she knew what they were trying to do, but the fine points, and why people clapped or did not clap, escaped her. No doubt Con knew exactly what it was all about, and Joan, too,—they could be very knowing about clapping with their soft white gloves that did not make any noise anyway. But Diana was weary, cramped, cold, and she felt sick. It would be sensible to get away before the crowd and be halfway home before they began to swarm down from the grandstand.

She made her way slowly across the neighboring knees; turned at the rail and walked slowly across the grass toward the gates. A stir among the spectators,—the great gasp of a crowd shocked and fearful,—arrested her, and Diana stopped, looking back.

The ponies were all in a knot; she saw a man jump down, drive his mount away from him with a blow on its flank; plunge into the struggling confusion of men and horses. Another horse limped free, galloped a hundred feet away, stood still, his bridle dragging. There was gasping and muttering from the spectators now: "He's hurt! Oh, he's hurt!

Who is it? The horse kicked him and rolled on him! Poor fellow—he's hurt!" The sound of frightened voices went through the air like a wave.

Still the knot of men and horses, clotted together there on the green grass, under the darkening spring sky, moved little. A man ran from it toward the sheds and the clubroom where the polo players gathered before and after the game; after a moment another man ran, too. A youth leaped along in front of the grandstand, cupping his hands to shout up at the banked audience: "Doctor! Doctor! It's Palmer! He's badly hurt!"

Diana heard it, but heard it like another woman, of some man she barely knew. The name said something to her,—not much. Palmer was badly hurt. She went toward a gate in the white railed fence; started to walk across the field, to where the ponies were, and the jumble of men, talking and bending over. Other men and women were streaming down from the seats now, and there were policemen.

A policeman stopped her.

"You can't go over there, lady. They're taking him to the hospital."

"Was he badly hurt?"

"You can phone the hospital, lady."

Patsy and Joan and some men went by her; talked urgently to the policeman. Then they were through the line,—Joan and her husband, and Patsy, and Connie,—and were running full speed toward the place where Bruce had gone down. The policeman did not stop them.

"He's dead, he was instantly killed," voices were saying all about her. Diana thought for one moment that if Bruce were dead she would like to kneel down beside him and kiss just once the brown firm cheek she had so loved to kiss. Connie could do that, and he had not even liked Connie!

But she felt weak and sick; she was afraid of policemen and their positive voices. She would not dare get into that crowd; it would do no good anyway to kiss him, with all of them staring at her.

She went to her car and got into it and sat idly for a moment, wondering why her head felt so queer and woodeny, as if it had been struck. Her head was all right. It was Bruce's beautiful head that had been crushed against the ground, struck by a horse's ironshod flying heel.

Some persons, men and women, were settling themselves in the next car.

"Wasn't that frightful, that man getting killed?" one of the women said. "Poor fellow,—everything to live for!"

"A sad ending to *that* polo game!" the man who was in the driver's seat agreed. "Flo," he asked, "what'je do with the cigarettes?"

"Pass Papa the cigarettes, Royal," the woman said. They drove away. Other cars were swarming toward the highway. Presently Diana started hers, turned toward home. Heavy fog was rolling in over the western hills now, twilight was gray and cold. Diana thought that her father would be home; perhaps he would have lighted the fire.

Bruce—Bruce would not come to the little house in St. Francis Wood any more. In September she would bear Bruce's child. And Pete Reynolds, who was the Palmers' lawyer, thought that she and Bruce had never been legally married.

When she got to Daly City the mist was so thick that she had to drive slowly and watch the safety line in the center of the highway. She reached home, put the car in the garage, went into the house. Newspaper boys were calling an extra along the quiet avenues of St. Francis Wood at seven o'clock. Headlines were telling the mothers of sons everywhere, and the wives of men, that that afternoon, before the eyes of ten thousand horrified spectators, the young scion of a wealthy Peninsula family had been killed while playing polo.

CHAPTER XXV

DIANA came up the open stairs, paused halfway. She had forgotten the bread. She stood with her other bundles dangling from her ungloved hands, considering, looking downward at the steps below her. The nearest bread was at the delicatessen store, a block away.

There had been a knob of bread left this morning, but probably Papa had eaten it for his breakfast. If there were no bread at all she would feel obliged to make biscuits or cornbread for dinner, and the effort involved was more than that necessary to go back.

Summer daylight still flooded the streets at six o'clock, but it was waning, and the tired men and women who were turning homeward were followed by long hot shadows. Diana, in the moment's pause, heard all the late-afternoon noises echoing through the house: children's fretful, tired voices, the hissing of pork or fish in frying pans, the running of water in sinks. Doors slammed, and radios and phonographs were active on all sides.

A flight and a half more, and she might deposit her bundles and go back for the bread with free hands, at least. But the flight and a half loomed formidable; better to go as she was and have the whole thing over at once. She started down the open stairway.

There were thirty-two apartments in the building; eight on a floor. It was not a large building; the apartments were of but two rooms each; the agent, referring to the open wooden stairway that bisected the whole, had spoken of them as "desirable Juliets." Often, when Diana looked down

at the shabby street from the shabby flights of open balconies, she thought of the term, and her face twisted in a
smile.

Cheap. That was the word that described the desirable
Juliets, the street in which they stood, and the persons who
inhabited them. Cheap clothing, cheap food, cheap jokes and
ambitions and expressions; the very babies looked cheap,
in their cheap buggies. Children skated and screeched along
the sidewalks after school hours; street cars clanged by;
butcher shops did a quick business in cheap cuts. Everything
for blocks all about was dirty, grimy, needed paint, and
perhaps Diana's particular neighborhood more than most.

When she had added a loaf of rye bread to the other
things she carried, she went back to the open wooden stairway between the now dusky apartments and mounted three
weary flights. At the top she was breathless, almost spent.
But she had foreseen this, in the shop, and had her door
key between her fingers.

The door was bunted open by the bundles she carried;
Diana staggered in and sank into a chair in the thick odorous
gloom of the kitchen. And for perhaps two minutes she sat
without moving, letting her packages slide to the table at
their own pleasure, her eyes staring vaguely at the dim
opaque square that was the window, her back bowed because
she had neither thought nor energy to straighten it.

The sun had gone down now; summer twilight still
lingered, and would linger for an hour over the city. But
the kitchen looked into an air well, and dusk was already
here. After a while Diana reached out an arm, pressed a
switch. A single dismal light glared in the room that was
more like a narrow passage, with a small, dingy gas stove
and a sink obstructing it. The table was a flap some two
feet wide and could be lowered against the wall.

Beyond was a slightly larger apartment with another
window on the street, a bureau, a bed. There was a closet

some nine inches deep. Diana did not open the door of it;
that would be to encourage every garment within to burst
forth. She put her coat on the back of a chair, laid her hat
on top of the bureau, brushed her hair from her forehead
with a gesture of both hands. Then she snapped off the light
and went back to the kitchen.

Tea, and rye bread, and half a pound of sole. The man in
the market had shouted cheerfully, "You don't mean half
a pound, lady, it's two pounds for a quarter!" But Di,
scarlet-faced, had stuck to her order: half a pound, please.
She and Dad only wanted a small piece each, to flavor the
boiled potatoes and the rye bread. "And I have some of
that Youngberry jam left," she thought. She had made it
herself on a Sunday a week ago.

Her father, thin and gray and subdued, came in. He had
his paper and two silver dollars. It hurt Di a little to see him
meekly proud over having found a morning's work on the
waterfront.

"Checking cargo?"

"The *Noanoa*."

"Good work, Dad. Did you see Larry?"

They sat down; the tea smelled delicious to her famished
senses, and the rye bread was spicy and fresh. Diana felt
the child stir within her; the soft little boneless elbow struck
and struck at her side.

"I don't know as I'll go south with Larry."

"I wish you would." Oh, she thought wearily, how she
wished he would! How she wanted to be alone!

"I brought you some peaches, Di."

"Oh, Dad, thank you! That's just what I want. It's been
so sticky today. I wanted something cool."

But she ate the fish and potatoes ravenously just the same.
She had had coffee and toast in this same dismal strip of a
kitchen that morning at half-past seven; she had taken with

her the cheese sandwich that had been her only lunch. And her confinement was but a few weeks away.

"Larry gets back by October," the old man said wistfully.

"Now Dad, listen. If you don't go it's your own fault. It really is. I'll be in the hospital two weeks—maybe more. It's perfect nonsense for you to hang around just for fear something'll go wrong."

"Well, your mother was real nervous at the end, Di."

"Well, I won't be. I arranged with Mr. Pally today that I'm to lay off on the first; I've got money enough; I've got thirty dollars. That'll take care of me here for three weeks, if necessary, and the hospital——"

She paused. Her father caught her up suspiciously.

"You're going to a private hospital, Diana?"

"Certainly I am. You don't think I'd go to the City?" she lied.

"You going to borrow the money?"

"I'll have to. And then Mr. Pally says my job'll be ready for me again."

"I don't know what you'll do, with a young baby to manage."

"I'll do something!"

She sat, when the meal was finished, in the litter of soiled dishes, staring ahead of her. The hot food, after the long hot day, had had the effect of making her feel almost stupefied. Her father went downstairs, as he often did on a warm evening, to look in at the tobacco shop, chat with the newsdealer, perhaps drift into a game of checkers, or at least watch one, at Moran's. Diana remained motionless, moment after moment, the bare kitchen light dangling above her head.

Finally she bestirred herself, lamely moving from table to sink, from sink to table; it was but a step either way. She put the peaches on the fire escape outside the window; there was no icebox.

The desirable Juliets were not furnished with bathrooms, but there was a small lavatory off the kitchen, and in the square hallway that connected the bedroom with flights of narrow, angled back stairs that descended to a shabby area door marked "Tradesmen's Entrance," there was a wall bed. This was her father's accommodation; Diana made the bed comfortable and smooth for him every night, for in the mornings he merely jammed it up with all its blankets and sheets in a tumble. It was a sickening job on a hot night like this, but she went through it steadily, faithfully; perhaps Papa would actually drive to San Diego with old Larry Usher, and perhaps she would die in the hospital anyway.

It would be nice to be out in the park tonight, lying on the grass. But then it would probably turn cold and foggy toward morning, and one would be glad enough of walls and blankets. It did not matter. Nothing mattered.

A few years ago Neal had been getting free seats for big movie openings in Hollywood, and they two had been racing along under the night lights, young and lithe and light-hearted. A few years later she had had Bruce,—generous, loving, fast turning from boy to man in his tenderness for her. Taxis, and reserved tables, and gardenias,—and, on a night like this, less than a year ago, Santa Barbara glittering with stars and moonshine, and the cool salt waters of the Pacific kissing their eager bodies as they rushed to meet them.

Oh, deliciousness of cold ocean water and youth and love! Deliciousness of going back to their little patio apartment with its tiles and its doves and its shadowing oaks, and taking possession of a great basket chair, out in the silvery dripping moonlight, and murmuring to each other with laughter and kisses for punctuation.

And now she was alone, and poor, and frightened of the ordeal ahead of her. Bruce's baby would be born in the City and County Hospital, in a great antiseptic-smelling ward.

The nurse had showed it to her, and Diana had smelled illness and yellow soap and drugs as she looked down its spot-
less length.

Well, what of it—what of it—what of it? The City and
County Hospital was ten times more sanitary and comfortable than the conditions actual queens had known a few
generations ago. Only—only Diana wished she did not always feel so tired and so alone and that the whole thing
was over.

When she got into bed she cried herself to sleep; her
father had come in an hour earlier and was lustily snoring.
But Diana had had much to do: socks to wash, breakfast
preparations to commence, last kitchen duties; and even when
she did get into bed the street lights seemed unusually
bright and garish, the house noises unusually loud and shrill.
For a long time she tried to lose herself in her library book;
it was no use. The fearful, the bitter thoughts would come,
and finally she threw the book aside, put out her light, and
was crying into her pillow, as she had cried so many weary
nights before.

The days went on. Presently her father was gone, and
the unwonted hot weather was over, and the street was grim
with fog and wind again. Mornings were bright and pleasant
enough, usually, but by the time she came home at night
the summer wind was moving like a wall along the grimy
sidewalks, blowing chaff and papers ahead of it, and the
two rooms at the top of the third flight were unspeakably
depressing.

Diana missed her father, but the rest and relief from his
companionship—from any companionship—was infinitely
greater than the loss. The blessedness of being alone, even
with grief and despair, was like a healing river washing
over her weariness and pain.

She was working with the Atgeld Mechanical Novelty
Company now. They worked her hard; their methods were

not the fine old-fashioned courteous methods of Rowley & Palmer. But she was making more money than she had ever made before, and she had to have money now.

So Diana demonstrated the toys, the kitchen conveniences, the automobile accessories as long as she could, and, when her changing figure made it impossible to go on, went heroically into the mail-order department and exhausted herself in handling catalogs and games and premiums. The firm worked up all sorts of competitions for its customers and sent out thousands of radio sets and little steam engines and boats and boilers every year to ambitious boys from Eureka to Calexico, and Miss Tressady was their most reliable saleswoman. If it had not been for the baby, she knew that she might have expected to be sent on to New York to buy toys for the firm, sooner or later.

If it had not been for the baby! She rarely thought of her child; she made herself not think of it. It was too utterly daunting,—this thought of another life inexorably, mercilessly approaching, to be forever connected with her own,— a part of her, her responsibility. Poor little chap, he would never have a break! Born to life in the Juliets, fatherless, nameless, unwanted, destined to be the last insufferable straw in the burden his mother was already carrying,—no, Diana could not think of him with any composure, any philosophy. He should not ever have been in existence at all; he seemed to have nothing to do with those brief happy days when she had loved Bruce, and Bruce had loved her, and when they had found the house in St. Francis Wood, and had been so mad, and so young, and so happy together!

She would get through with what was ahead of her, because she must. Perhaps she would not live; perhaps the baby would not. If they both did, then she would have to manage it somehow,—hire some woman in the neighborhood, perhaps, to care for him by day,—very little babies were not much trouble——

But now, before he even came, she was tired all the time, and it was impossible to imagine that with the added worry of his care, his laundry and bottles and crib and croup, she would be able to face the thing at all.

"I go on living," Diana thought, "simply because I don't die, that's all."

There came a time in early September when she had to stop work. Then followed slow days of late sleeping, languid solitary breakfasts, apathetic walks, always alone, in the autumn sunlight. Aimlessly she wandered into the big library at the Civic Center; looked at biographies, at illustrated English weeklies.

Her hour arrived. On a certain night she went to bed feeling restless, conscious of odd twinges and pangs that were unusual even after the long months of such discomforts; she awakened at a cold, sharp, starry three o'clock to know that she could put off the dreaded and unwelcome time no longer. Shuddering, all alone in the drab, garishly lighted place, Diana placed last necessities in her packed bag with hands that trembled, dressed herself for the last time in the misshapen garments she had come to hate.

Then she was down in the deserted street. She spoke to a yawning policeman.

"What—what car goes nearest to the City and County?"

"Harspital, is it? But don't ye want a taxi?"

"No-o-o. I think I'd rather take a street car."

"Thin you walk the two blocks, see? And that'll be Potrero."

"Thank you." Carrying her bag, stopping now and then because she must writhe, and press her hand to her side, and struggle for breath, Diana went on her way. The surface car, incredibly slow in coming to the appointed corner, presently jolted away down the deserted night street. Then the great clean brightly lighted hospital, with its wide hallways and immense elevators, its clean-aproned nurses wide awake and moving to and fro briskly in the night, its strange frightening smells of disinfectants and rubber flooring and strong soaps, swallowed her. Old women were washing the tiled floors; behind closed doors somebody screamed; Diana, in her shabby bulging coat, followed a guide through corridors, entered a white-doored room marked "Reception." Nobody was in the least unkind; nobody was in the least interested. Diana was no longer Diana; she was a storm-battered gull that finds a window in a lighthouse and flutters in too spent to know or care what lies inside.

CHAPTER XXVI

RAIN WAS FALLING—falling over dingy Potrero Street, and over the shabby hills toward the southeast, where scattered shanties were formed into irregular streets, and over St. Winifred's Home. St. Winifred's was a great square iron-barred building, set in a square of iron-barred dim sooty garden and fences; it had been a "Magdalen Asylum" once; girls had been incarcerated there. Diana thought it was empty now, of girls at least; perhaps there were no more Magdalens in a day when girls managed for themselves all the delicate and moral questions that once had caused the city fathers such concern.

Poor girls! she thought, sitting up for the first time in her straight clean hospital bed. Flirting with boys, making themselves pretty for boys, happy in street lights and excitement and flattery, and then shut into places like St. Winifred's, or following a nurse slowly, in complete terror, down the halls to the maternity wards of the "City and County."

But when she was a little stronger, when the nurses began to remind her brightly that she was going home on Sunday, she forgot her concern for other women, to think of herself —and Michael.

Diana's body was weak; her voice was weak. But the passion of love and pity and protectiveness that encompassed Michael was stronger than any feeling she had ever known before. Thinner, older, resting breathless in these few blessed days of peace and care, after the dark descent into the furnace of struggle and pain, she lay quiet, with her arm, when they would let her have him, encircling her son, and her eyes dark and serious with thought. What would she do with him, what could she do with him, the little busily sleeping, busily eating baby who had taken so resolute a grip upon life?

On his tenth day she was dismissed. The stupendous experience of the last fortnight had been the "normal" experience, after all, they told her; other women, their faces twisting with pain and fear, were waiting to fill the wards. Diana had the kindly help of Herbie, one of the orderlies, with her baby and her suitcase, down the big hospital steps and to the street. She panted, sitting in the rattling car, and the sweat stood in beads on her forehead. She was ridiculously weak.

Reaching the Juliets, she enlisted the help of a casual schoolboy who was thundering down the stairs, with his skates banging, mad for escape into the September afternoon sunshine. A strong wind was blowing; Diana, walking the two blocks from the car line, in the teeth of it, had had serious misgivings as to whether or not she could make the little trip at all. But to faint in the street would be to endanger Michael, and that was the unthinkable thing.

The boy took her suitcase, and she, following him slowly, breathing hard above the bundled baby, up to the familiar dark doorway, stumbled inside, gave the boy his dime. Would he—wait a minute—would he bring her a—yes, a quart of milk and a loaf of bread, some time later? Any time?

She sat spent, panting. The baby, unrolling himself on the bed by a series of desperate kicks, wailed desolately. Diana wiped her forehead, gulped, looked at him apathetically. It was a quarter to four, and he would probably cry like this all night, all tomorrow. He would have to be bathed, changed, fed, aired—it was impossible. A baby took all one woman's time, he never could be left alone, and she had no money and no way of earning any.

After a while she took off her coat, loosened her clothing,

and in the cold, empty, dusty place sat down with the child in her arms. He drank ravenously, and Diana's slow tears slid down her smiling face as she looked at his little eager one, confident, bold, preoccupied. The thought that he might ever be cold or hungry or kept waiting for his food made her heart stand still. She must eat something, she must somehow live.

Later she heated milk, cut rounds from fresh bread. There was no butter, but there was salt; she found herself hungry. The little flat was incredibly desolate; it was not believable that human beings had been housed there so short a time ago,—ten days ago. Dust lay thick over everything; the air was stale and flat; the little stove seemed all rust and sooty grease and shreds of caked food.

Michael, still rolled in his hospital wrappings,—the head nurse had charitably found an abandoned blue blanket for him, to top his plain little outfit,—had fallen asleep upon the bed. Diana stood watching him, afraid almost to move, for fear that he would awaken. She dared not quite undress him; suppose she could not dress him again? She gingerly touched his small curled feet; they were reassuringly warm, —*that* was all right, anyway. But he was sopping, of course, and the prospect of the brisk assured folding-and-pinning process that Margaret handled with such ease terrified her.

Somehow she managed it without waking him; went to get the covers from her father's bed, arranged them gently about the baby. The world outside was dark now; she could hear the usual dinnertime banging and chatter, the radios and phonographs of the various surrounding flats, but nobody came near her, nobody knew or cared that she was facing despair, all alone, in the dirty and disordered rooms on the top floor.

She could do nothing more tonight; she was trembling with exhaustion over what she had already done. Partially undressing, slipping off her shoes, she lay down beside the baby and pulled the extra bedcovering over her. Her last thought was that if he cried in the night she would not know what to do for him, and if he did not cry in the night she would not know what to do for him tomorrow. She had two dollars and sixty-five cents in the world.

Michael did cry in the night, piteously, heartbrokenly, and Diana, shaking with cold and fright, took him to her breast again, murmuring, "Hush, sweetheart—hush, my darling——"

He was comforted, slept. But before Diana, shuddering beside him, could get to sleep, he was awake again, wailing. And this time he cried for an hour.

The days, the nights proceeded like a dreadful dream. Diana was always alone, her eyes haggard from want of sleep, her hands chapped from washing, her mind and soul poisoned with fear. She would die, or the baby would die, or the authorities would step in and take him away from her, or Bruce's parents would claim him. Her days were a strange pattern of fatigue and fear; her nights, when it was cold and dark, and when he cried so bitterly, were hideous.

A letter came from her father; Diana tore it open eagerly. Ah, if there had been a ten-dollar bill inside,—even a five-dollar bill. But there was no money. There was instead the news that her father was not coming back for a while; he had met some old friends, men called Kirk and Phil, and a woman called Babe, and they were going to drive to New Mexico.

Perhaps a woman with a child of three or four might find work, Diana mused, but no mother of an infant ever could, unless she turned him over to some other woman and paid that woman. Mrs. Foy, downstairs, told her about the Chatterton Home. Sure, she could leave him there; sure, they took wonderful care of the babies. Diana left Michael in the kitchen downstairs, with the Foy baby, and walked slowly to the Chatterton Home, and talked to Miss Priest.

Miss Priest let her look at the babies there; warm and safe and contented enough, they seemed. Their mothers could see them on Sunday afternoons, after they were a year old.

"After they are a year old?" Her soft, sweet, round little scrap of a Michael was just three weeks toward his first birthday.

"It wouldn't be safe, before that, Mrs. Palmer. They're *so* sensitive to infection, we couldn't let the mothers in."

"I suppose not. But then——" She had been crying from the very first word; it was maddening to feel herself crying bitterly now, trying to smile through her tears. "But then—wouldn't I see Michael—at all—in all that time?"

"You could see him, and see for yourself that he is *splendid!*" Miss Priest said with enthusiasm. "Just as we peeped at Miss Kent's babies just then, through the glass door."

"And when—when could I bring him?"

"I'd have to let you know. We're full up now, and I've two babies waiting. But we think our adorable Tony is going home. He's a little Italian boy,—we all just adore him. I'd have to let you know. But you might fill out a card."

Father's name, Bruce Palmer, deceased. Nationality of grandparents. Age in years, months, days. Her darling—her *darling* was being written down; "age, twenty-one days."

"Oh, the grandparents are living?"

"Yes." A pause.

"They couldn't help out a little?"

"They're rich," Diana said simply. "But they won't recognize my marriage."

"Oh-h-h."

"Old Mr. Palmer—he's paralyzed now. But he was the president of Rowley & Palmer."

"Oh-h-h." Another pause. "But you were married, Mrs. Palmer?"

Like a dream, to be asked the old question by another

woman, to have this ridiculous sensation toward tears in answering.

"It was a runaway marriage. We got our license, we were married by a young clergyman at St. Jerome's."

"At St. Jerome's? I know dear Dr. Graham, of course."

"This man—his name was Purcell. Afterward he—there was some question of his right to marry us."

"But I should think," Miss Priest suggested, in her bright, helpful, sympathetic way,—"I should think we could persuade them,—the baby's grandparents,—that the dignified —the fair thing to do——"

She paused.

"They don't question the paternity, I suppose?"

The blood came into Diana's pale face, an odd glint into her eye.

"No. They knew that Bruce and I were—were man and wife."

"Were living as man and wife," the social worker substituted dispassionately. "Then they know that the baby is their grandchild, and there's some question of the marriage. It seems to me I'd see them, Mrs. Palmer, and see if their hearts wouldn't soften. Sometimes baby hands——"

"Oh, they'd take the baby," Diana said, in the silence.

"They'd take him? Oh, well, then,—my dear——"

"At least, I think that's what their lawyer said. He said something about their providing for the child,—it was long before he was born,—but that they didn't want me to see him."

For the first time a spark of something like real feeling animated the older woman's voice.

"How could they make such hard conditions,—tut-tut-tut-tut-tut!" she murmured.

Presently she added, "What did your lawyer say?"

"I only saw theirs."

Miss Priest considered it for a minute in silence.

"You have a real claim there."

"How can I fight? I have nothing."

"But there are lawyers——"

"I know. But meanwhile Michael and I have to eat."

Miss Priest made a penciled note.

"Will you come back and see me tomorrow?"

Diana, rising, nodded toward the filled blank.

"You'll not—— I'm afraid of them, the Palmers. You won't get in touch with them without talking to me?"

"Oh, no, my dear. All our records are strictly confidential."

Diana went away. She knew that she would never go back. Not to see Michael, not to touch Michael, for eleven long months, and to have to dry out of her breast this miracle of milk that kept him warm and fat and satisfied,—oh, no, no, no, she couldn't do that! God help the poor girls who had to do it, who had to kiss the warm sweet little cheeks good-bye, and surrender the delicious soft little blanketed burdens to the kind, impassive hands of Miss Priest and her associates.

Michael, as if he knew what shadows were drifting above his shabby coverings, his drabby little unironed garments, his downy head, was good that night. He slept for nine straight hours, and Diana awakened refreshed and hopeful beside him, hardly able to believe that the clock said seven, and autumn dawn was over the city.

She lay looking at him, as he snuffled and fussed himself into whimpering, and so violent was the rush of love for him in her heart that she might never have loved him before.

"Mike, what now?" she asked. Mike bit a fist, found it unsatisfactory no matter how he turned it, emitted a shred of a wail, and was silent again, except for the eternal snuffling and fussing.

"Nobody gets you away from me, little boy," Diana told him.

She got up stiffly, stiffly set about her morning offices; the kettle was filled, bread was sliced, Diana finally sat down to her breakfast with a sigh,—she was always tired nowadays.

"I wish we had a hundred a month between us, Michael."

Instead of a hundred she had seventeen dollars; she had borrowed twenty-five from her old firm; they wanted her back; they had lent it readily. But she could not do that again, and there was no use writing to her father; he never had answered, he was cruising about in Arizona or New Mexico somewhere, with Kirk and Phil and Babe, he would not have any money to send her, he never had had.

Michael was getting organized; he was becoming a human being. He cried much less and frightened his mother much less when he cried. If he was fed and dry and warm and had been aired and exercised, she did not mind his crying. And sometimes, when he stopped, with his lashes wet, and his shapeless little mouth vaguely smiling, she thought the tears made him somehow dearer than ever.

His bath still made her uneasy; she finished it and sat nursing him, with her breath shallow and quick, her apron spattered, her forehead wet with perspiration. It always went well enough, it went better and better, but Diana was always glad when it was over. One day she knew he saw her; stopped his alarmed wail when the familiar maternal face came into his view. Only two months old, but he had seen her and known her.

"Baby dear, if you and I could get away with this, and I could somehow take care of you!"

What fun, she would think, seeing other young mothers in the street, what fun to have a baby, and time and money to enjoy him! Michael took his airings in Patricia Foy's outgrown coach; the new Foy baby would need it at Christmas time,—meanwhile Michael might as well enjoy it. Jim Foy had a job with a contractor, and made good money. It must,—Diana would sigh,—it must be wonderful to have enough money.

She thought of Bruce, the beautiful dark head down on the bright green grass, Joan and Patsy free to rush to him, —his wife, the mother of his son, having no place beside him. She had never seen him again. She had seen none of them. But Reynolds, the lawyer, had come to see her.

Sometimes in the fierce ache for Bruce, dimmed in the first hard months of fear and struggle, she would remember, with slow tears of pain in her eyes, how happy he had been in the little place in St. Francis Wood, with the blazing fire and the big steaks; those evenings when Diana, slim and silent, had been utterly content on his knee. He would have been so proud of this scrap of babyhood; it would all have been so different if Bruce had lived!

Reynolds, the lawyer, had had little to say; Diana had rather wondered why he had come to see her. He had said, with an air of regret, that there had been no legal marriage; there had been unquestioned "intent to marry." And Mr. Palmer's parents, who were prostrated by his tragic death, while they had no desire to see Miss Tressady, wished her to know that in case of any financial need——

Diana had protested hotly. She had indeed been married to their son, whether they liked it or not. And she did not need any financial help from Mr. Palmer's family.

To all this Mr. Reynolds had listened respectfully, nodding his head from time to time, as if impressed. But she had known that he was not impressed. He was playing his part, controlling the conversation to suit himself.

She had not told him of the expected baby; the baby was hers, not theirs. But she had learned later that somehow Bruce's people had discovered that there was to be a baby, and her informant,—a Bayhead girl Diana sometimes saw in "The City of Paris," at the book counter,—had assured her that they were frantic. A letter from the obnoxious

Reynolds had concluded the affair; Reynolds had written guardedly that his clients, the parents of the late Mr. Bruce Palmer, would gladly assume entire responsibility for the child, on the condition that the mother agreed never to see him.

To this Diana had returned no answer. She had seen in the paper,—or rather her father had discovered for her,—that the supposedly ordained Mr. Purcell had been completely discredited; that finished it, the marriage had not been valid, and she and Michael must make their own way, unhelped by Bruce's people.

Now, in their extremity, she would not appeal to them. They might have softened, they might be glad to help her, but she could run no risk, in her weakened, anxious, burdened state, of propositions that might shake her resolution.

Her money dwindled; she seemed to be in an apathy. She saw the dollars turn to half-dollars, to quarters, to dimes, and still, while there was enough left for milk, for bread, she drifted on in a sort of dream, alone with the child in the dark little rooms upstairs in the back of a Mission Juliet.

In November she tried to wean Michael, but it was not a success and the baby was ill. Frantic with love and fear, Diana abandoned all thought of leaving him, and clinging to him desperately she sat on the edge of her bed through one whole dull, cold, silent winter afternoon, thinking.

The next morning, carrying him, she went to an intelligence office. She could do general housework, but she must have the baby with her.

Mrs. Pollet was not encouraging. Diana, to her, did not look strong enough for general housework, and no matter what she took or tried, she must place the baby somewhere. To take a two-months-old baby into a position was not thinkable for an instant.

"I'd have to wean him," Diana said, tears running down her face.

"They get along just as well."

"They *can't!*" She looked down at Michael's placid features despairingly. Who would fix his bottles for him, attend to him, love him, if his mother did not? Diana went out into a bright winter street dazedly; she did not know what to do.

In the drugstore, the child balanced on her arm, she turned the pages of the telephone book. Associated Charities——

The office was downtown; not far. Not three blocks. She could go to see them, pretend it was some other woman's baby, find out what they could do and would do. If they would allow her five or six dollars a week she would manage to live on it; she would rent two thirds of the apartment, live in the other room. She was desperate now; there was less than fifty cents in her purse.

Her arm ached, she was getting tired, and presently Michael must be fed, in some odorous department-store dressing room, and she must get some hot food herself. Fifty cents, and lunch would cost something, and there was a five-cent fare home. Diana went into the offices of the Associated Charities.

She remembered, after she got inside of the big, desk-lined rooms, that Edna Horne, of Bayhead, worked here. Blood rushed to her face when Edna, busy with a typewriter, looked up to nod at her as they went through. But Edna, some desks away, did not speak, and Diana went on into the adjoining office.

The same questions. She had no relatives who could help? They had to ask that, of course.

"The father is dead. How was that?"

"He was killed."

"Ah? And how did it happen that you didn't appeal at once?"

"I was working. I didn't need help."

"What was the accident?"

"He was thrown from a horse."

"And are the parents living?"

"His parents. Yes. But they—they won't help me."

"Not for their own grandson?"

"I can't take help from them," Diana said, in a low voice. "I won't need it long. I'll pay it back."

"But they could help, if they would?"

Diana was silent.

"I think," Miss Wood said firmly, concluding the interview, "I think I'd see them, write to them. If they *would* help,—and of course they ought to,—then it wouldn't be strictly a case for us at all. We can only help when no one else will, or can. That's—" she was speaking firmly, pleasantly,—"that's one of our rules."

"I see," Diana said heavily. She saw Edna looking at her brightly, curiously, as she went out. All Bayhead knew about herself and Bruce, of course, and the marriage that some persons said was of course a marriage, and other persons said was no marriage at all. "There was something queer about the marriage,—not her fault, and not his,"— Diana's friend in the book department told her that that was really the worst that anyone said.

Her face burned with bitter color as she left the offices, but she was pale enough when she reached the street, and shifted Michael on her arm, and started toward the Valencia Street car.

CHAPTER XXVII

SHE WAS standing on the mid-street safety station, waiting for it to come along, in the long string of cars, when someone touched her arm. Diana looked up and saw Neal Tressady beside her.

"For God's sake!" he said simply, with a blank stare that took in her pallor, her thinness and weariness and shabbiness, and the strange burden on her arm. "Diana!"

"Diana!" she half laughed and half sobbed. She leaned against him. And "Hold him!" she managed to mutter thickly, with the last of her breath. Then Market Street lurched sickeningly, and the gray pavement rose up like a windowshade rising smoothly—shutting everything else out——

She would not fall; she clung to him resolutely; she must not faint. Diana, in the shadows, could hear Michael's surprised cry.

"Taxi," she said, with effort. They were in one, jogging along slowly; Neal was holding the baby, she herself resting against Neal's shoulder. But she could not see him or the baby; she could not open her eyes.

"Diana, darling—you're fainting! When did you eat?"

"I'm all right." It was merely a whisper. "Just—just give me a minute——"

"Where'll I take you? Where's home?"

Her heavy eyes opened.

"I can't go there."

"We'll go to my place, then. That'll be all right, won't it?"

"Anywhere——"

At the door she roused; they were on a block of Stockton that, starting steeply at Clay, rose to a little plateau of its own before reaching California Street and hung like a balcony above the lower city. There was an ornate door flanked with little mailboxes, and an attendant Japanese hallboy.

The Oriental respectfully took Michael's wrappings and Michael, and Neal put his arm about Diana. It was good for her to feel his strength underneath her weakness, his forceful decisiveness behind her wavering and doubt.

They went upstairs in an elevator and into the brightest and most compact apartment Diana had seen for a long while. The rooms were blessedly warm; sunshine streamed through high windows; there was a deep couch upon which Neal instantly established her. When she opened the eyes that she had closed in sheer felicity, in exhausted relief, he was holding a glass of water.

"Want it?"

She looked about. Michael, bare feet waving free, had been bundled on his back in a chair. Diana laughed feebly, drained the glass, reached for the baby.

"Give him to me." She began to straighten his layers; she put aside his blanket. "You dirty-looking baby!" she said, tenderly.

"Feel all right?"

"I'm all right now." One hand went to her disordered hat, her straggling hair. "Neal, I must look a disgrace."

"Who's the kid?"

"Mine."

"The hell!" Neal observed simply.

"He's starving. If I could mop him up a little I'd feed him——" Diana began, looking vaguely about.

"Take him in the bathroom. Lissen, Di——" It was the old phrase; the old eager Neal. "I was going to a rehearsal when I met you. I'm opening in *Ysobel* next week. Lissen,

will you stay here? I'll be back—it's just noon—I'll be back
at two. Stay here, will you? I'll only be an hour. It's just
one part of one act,—they had to put a new maid in. We've
had seventeen weeks in L.A.,—broke the record. Lissen,
will you wait?"

He was handsome, brown, hard, wearing a big overcoat,
well-groomed, sympathetic. And the rooms were warm and
comfortable, and she had Michael. Diana's eyes were fixed
on him with the faithful trust of one just saved from
drowning.

"Get yourself some lunch. I had breakfast only about an
hour ago—I've got to fly. But swear you'll wait for me?"

"I'll wait, Neal."

He was gone. She could feed her child, lay him down,
banked with pillows, on a wide clean bed, move about peace-
fully. She was saved. Diana drank deep of the exquisite
relief of it all.

While the kettle was boiling she looked at the fat bath
towels, suddenly turned on the generous clean hot water,
stepped into the tiled luxury of the bathtub, reached for the
scented soap. She was clean again, her hair brushed, her
face freshened. There was everything to eat in the icebox:
cold chicken, tea, cream, early strawberries. Diana feasted.

Afterward she made everything clean, bathed the baby,
who was good-natured. When Neal returned, Michael was
asleep, and Diana in a deep chair looking out at the panorama
that was spread beneath the windows; looking at the bay,
and the boats traversing the cold blue water, the glitter of
Berkeley to the east, and the great Gate at the harbor's
mouth, on the north. Between lay the jumbled roofs and
spires of the city, and the tasseled pagodas of Chinatown.

They sat close together, and sometimes Neal took her
hands, and sometimes reached for his big pocket handkerchief and wiped his eyes.

"My God, what you've been through!"

"Only this last few weeks that were really bad."

"And they don't admit that you and Bruce were married?"

"The Palmers? I believe not."

"What a crust!" Neal commented, musing. "You're so *lovely,*" he mumbled, in the remembered way, his lips against her hand.

He was very handsome, handsomer than she remembered him; thinner, older, more definite. His skin was clean and smooth, and his hair more picturesque than ever. And he was as always eager, emotional, appreciative.

A somber fog had come in from the ocean; the city below their windows was wrapped in heavy mist. Diana and Neal sat on talking, talking, a strange excitement and pleasure between them. The years in which they had not seen each other had made them strangers, and yet they were not strangers; they knew each other's every expression, every intonation. There were no mysteries, but on both sides there was a certain shyness; Diana's quick blushes, her lowered eyelashes, her hesitant syllables had in them something virginal.

"You look so much better, Di."

"I think I would have died if I had had to go back to my own place tonight, Neal."

"It was luck. I was wondering about you. I've been— horribly lonely."

"Have you really?"

"Oh, sick with it."

"Where's your mother?"

"She went to her sister in Eureka. She's been there a year."

"You're not married again?"

"Married? I'll say I'm not! No, but she and I scrapped."

"You and your mother?" Diana laughed joyously. Companionship was delicious, after her long loneliness, and Neal was the same old sixpence,—half genius, half idiot, half wiseacre, half child.

"Yep. She thought I was drinking and booming too much."

Diana widened reproachful eyes.

"And *were* you, Neal?"

He got up and walked to the window and looked out. When he spoke, it was out of a deep study that had nothing to do with her question.

"I shall never love—I never have loved—any other woman but you."

Diana sat staring, a shadow on her face. When he turned around, she had covered her eyes with her hand.

She spent that night, many nights, in the comfortable little apartment; there seemed, indeed, to be no alternative. She had no money, and no resources, and she was exhausted, almost ill.

Neal was rehearsing at night, and sometimes in the afternoon. He slept at his club, but came to her for breakfast at noon, and for dinner at six, and they scrambled eggs and toasted rolls in the old way. Whatever she cooked for him he thought delicious, and her company seemed once again to mean to him what it had meant so many years ago, in the very beginning of things, when in the old house in Mason Avenue he had hung breathless on her words, shouted his delight in her beauty, and sat adoringly at her feet while his mother fussed with her tea table.

He brought things home for dinner: a broiled crab, tomato juice, a Persian melon. He set the table nicely, as he had done long ago; on the first Sunday he made sponge cake, turning the whipped whites of eggs upside down, to show how they clung to the bowl, before he would mix them into the batter. Often, at some phrase of Diana's, some glance, he crowed in the old way, "You're marvelous!"

"But you're not living in my house, darling," he would say when she protested against continuing the arrangement, "you're living in Larry Trelawney's house,—his real name is Ed Piper,—he's down in Hollywood. He begged me to take it, just to keep it open."

"That's worse, then. I'm living in the house of a man I never saw."

"Don't be an idiot. You might easily rent a house from a man you never saw. There's no moral law that I know of that says you have to see your landlord. Many and many a time I've wished I never had seen mine,—they're often quite ugly——"

"Oh, shut up, you imbecile!" And they would both be laughing again.

Michael was behaving magnificently. Diana added to her passionate love a passionate gratitude toward the little soft sleepy fellow whose vague eyes moved up to hers, as his little lips were busy at her breast, whose small fingers would grip hers trustfully as she lowered him into his bath.

He had been bathed, and taken out for an airing, and was ready for sleep, when Neal came in, at noon; they could shut the bedroom door upon him and hear him buzzing like a bee as he went off. And when Neal came back for dinner, Michael had always been sponged, fed, made comfortable, settled down for the night.

It would have been a perfect time for Diana, rested, secure, well again, if it had not been for Neal. He wanted to marry,—to remarry,—her. He took it for granted that her feelings were like his own,—of course they were! He and she belonged together; Deirdre had not signified, Bruce had not really counted.

"It's ridiculous to think we aren't married, Di. The Catholics are right, we really are. We belong to each other. It's too wonderful that I'm in love with you,—madly in love with you,—and that I know every beautiful inch of you,—you've been mine, and you'll be mine again,—only more—more marvelously mine than you ever were before! There's no mystery—there's no surprise—and yet—to have you again——"

She listened to him quietly, her beautiful eyes fixed on space.

"Neal, let's not talk of it for a while,—it isn't a year since Bruce—since Bruce! He and I were living out in St. Francis Wood only a year ago,—Michael wasn't thought of—— It's too soon——"

"But what's the difference, if we love each other?"

"Well, that's just it, Neal," she explained, with some little difficulty, one day. "I don't love you,—not that way."

"Nonsense! You're just a scared little girl, you don't know a thing about it."

"A scared little girl?" She was smiling, but her eyes were troubled.

"Neal, I've been through deep waters since you and I left each other, since—since Deirdre came into the picture."

"To begin with, Deirdre never *did* come into the picture! I was never anything but a leading man to Deirdre."

She knew it was not true, but it did not matter. Neal had never been particularly truthful.

"I've been through such—cyclones, Neal. Grandma's death, and marrying Bruce,—his being killed,—and those awful weeks before Micky was born,—and those awful weeks afterward!"

"Well, what of it? Ah, darling, those things don't touch you and me. Be a sport! Suppose—suppose I do love you more than you do me, what of it? That satisfies me.

"But as a matter of fact," he added, as she was silent, "you love me a lot more than you think. I know you!"

"I could marry you, of course," she said thoughtfully. "It'd mean a home for Micky and me,—it'd mean companionship,—and I've been so horribly lonely!"

Hard tears came into her eyes, and her lip trembled. It was a moment or two before she could go on.

"I could go to your first nights, and cook your dinners, and dress the way you like, and—and mother you——"

"Mother me nothing!" Neal interpolated with his confident laugh.

"But that isn't marriage, Neal. It isn't what I felt for Bruce——"

Her voice fell; she looked into space.

"All right, what *did* you feel for Bruce?"

"Oh,—everything. He gave everything," Diana thought, formulating the thought in her mind, "and you take everything." But aloud she said only the first two words.

"Admit," Neal urged, in great spirits, "that he was a good deal of a—of a rich man's son. I hate the type. He was a—a poser——"

"No, he wasn't a poser."

"Well, now listen. When he and I were in prep school together, years ago, he was no such ball of fire."

"No, no, I didn't say he was,—that is, intellectually," Diana admitted honestly. "He didn't read much, Bruce; he liked sports,—bridge and polo,—and talking about his friends. He didn't—he didn't ever pretend to be—deep, erudite. I didn't mean that."

"You would have outgrown him, Di."

"Perhaps," she conceded dreamily. She felt, with a little interior twist of humor, that no one would ever outgrow Neal's intellect, at all events; there was no classifying it. One accepted him on his own terms,—his odds and ends from the classics, his ready quotations from this play or that, his songs, the vague jumble of misconceptions and mistakes he had culled from a superficial glance at books whose reading is a lifework, and that he called his philosophy; a little theosophy, a little Kant remembered from college days, a little dash of Rosicrucianism, and a great loyalty to Ouspenski,—whom, she presently realized, he had never read at all. These satisfied him. His conversation was sparkling with the chips he had gathered up from talks or lectures he had heard about them; he needed no more. Persons in whom their very names inspired awe were impressed by his ready reference to Dante, Goethe, Mills, Shaw, James. And Neal did not often move in circles clever enough to discover that indeed he knew no more than the names.

He laughed, sang, worked, slept, ate prodigiously, talked all the time. And he was handsome, and surprisingly successful in his profession, and generous and amusing——

It would be the marriage of a woman who perfectly understood the sacrifice she must make, with a man who would demand its payment to the last drop; Diana had no illusions about that. But at the same time it would not be quite a calculating step; it would be taken only because she was alone, burdened with Michael, at the end of her money and resources.

Neal would be "nice" most of the time; he always had been. He would be companionable, eager, adoring, he would help with kitchen meals, share his money generously, keep their domicile, wherever and whatever it might be, in a continual cheerful uproar. He would only be "bad" occasionally, like a selfish, pettish child, grumbling and scolding, and expecting to be spoiled back into good humor.

She would be his wife and his mother, too. She could remember the old tone: "Ah, darling, you're imagining that. Forgive me, dear, if I seemed to be having too good a time! I wasn't, really. I was waiting for the moment when you and I could get away——"

And so on, ad infinitum. One rarely talked quite honestly to Neal. One felt one's way cautiously to his mood, tried this cure, tried that. Sometimes abasement, sometimes bullying, sometimes tears, no two quarrels ever pursued quite the same course.

But then they were both older now than they had been four years ago; there was that to consider. Neal really did seem more balanced, more stable, and perhaps, with resolute mothering, with determined attention to his comfort, anticipation of his whims——

He did love her,—as much as he could love anyone. Neal never could have loved a woman objectively; it was only what she gave to him that was significant.

"I'll be anything you like, Di. I'll make myself whatever you like!"

"Can it be done?" Gray twilight was in the sitting room of the Stockton Street apartment, and Di in the big chair, and Neal at her feet.

"You mean I'm too much of a Peter Pan?"

"I don't know." She pushed his thick hair back. "You've been so angel-kind to me for three weeks, Neal——" she said slowly.

"All right, then you be good to me."

"But our marriage might last more than three weeks."

"It would last forever. The moment I am living for, Di, is the night when you let me stay on, after dinner, and my suitcase goes into your room, and we sit on, you and I, here by the fire, talking——"

"And will you sing me 'Son of Mine'?"

"Ah, darling!"

"Love's different," she persisted, troubled. She disengaged her hand, got to her feet, and went into the kitchen. It was almost dark there. Grocery packages were heaped on the neat little tiled sink, the toneless winter light was dull at the window. Up and down the airshaft upon which all the kitchen windows opened there were sounds of dinner activities: hissing, the running of water, voices. A colored woman was singing a hymn, powerfully; the pleasant smell of freshly frying butter came up the shaft.

"Neal, liver and bacon tonight, and mocha tarts."

"I don't believe I'll stay."

Her heart sank; she knew that tone.

"Ah, please, Neal! Why, listen, silly, would you want me to marry you if I honestly didn't love you? Of course you wouldn't!"

"You don't want to marry anyone else?"

"I don't want to marry at all, anyone—ever."

"Di, you know what it is with me," he argued, youthfully eager, and she laughed suddenly at the absurdity of it all.

She tried to escape. She went to her old firm, was offered the old salary; they wanted her back at twenty-five dollars a week. She could put Micky in a home somewhere; there were such places. But somehow it was horribly tiring to go from one to the other; the Guerrero Street place looked dirty; the California Street place was full; the Lyons Street place didn't take the children until they were four years old; "or well past three and a half," Miss Bruce explained prettily to the mother of Michael, aged three months.

The Cutler Baby Garden was sweet, with "two acres of roses and sun for the kingdom of your Little One," but it cost fifteen dollars a week, and was across the bay, up in the hills beyond Sausalito,—too far for a tired mother to come very often.

What *did* women do with their babies when they had no homes and no money?

Larry Trelawney was coming back for his apartment; she had to move. Rent had to be paid somewhere, somehow, from the first of February. The easy heavenly weeks of rest and freedom from care had gone by. Diana must arm herself for the buffeting of fresh adventures. Her mind revolved it incessantly; so much for rent, so much for her food and clothes, so much for Michael. It would not work out.

"Neal, if I could only be your sister, and keep house for you in some darling old studio over on North Beach!"

"My sister,—hah!"

"It would be such fun! We'd roam about everywhere,—· along the waterfront and through Chinatown when you weren't rehearsing, and we'd have people in Sundays for frankfurters and cheese and things. Isn't it a pity?"

"Lissen, Di, there's no use promising you that it'd be that sort of a marriage."

Her quick bright color; her quick laugh.

"I wasn't under any misapprehensions."

"You need me and I need you, honey. I can take care of you in some ways, and you of me in others. Why, hell, Di," Neal pleaded, very simply, very much in earnest, "suppose we *do* get scrapping sometimes, the way we used to,—we won't, but suppose we do,—what of it? Isn't it happier than going along separately, both lonely, with no parties and no fun?"

Her fair head had begun to shake ominously.

"It can't be done like that,—it isn't honest."

And then, quite suddenly, at the last moment, when her anxious search for a new lodging, her uneasy investigations regarding a possible solution for Michael were accentuated by the wretched knowledge that the unknown Trelawney would be back at any moment now, ready to occupy his apartment—then Diana was ill.

It was only influenza, but it was a sharp attack, and there must be a doctor, a nurse, another nurse for Michael, weaning at last, with no question about it.

Diana had come home one afternoon trembling with cold, her bones sore, her head aching; she had gotten into bed feebly, inevitably, Michael at her breast even while she turned down sheets, flattened pillows. She had been curled shuddering wretchedly over a hot-water bag when Neal had come in for his dinner; there had been no dinner.

Instead, a cool wet thermometer in her dry hot mouth, and a doctor writing prescriptions. Diana, laughing hoarsely,

sat up in bed, swept her pajama jacket forward over her
face, felt the round mouth of the stethoscope between her
shoulders.

"Have I a temperature?"

"Yes," the doctor answered briefly, unemotionally.

The doctor came four times and lost his heart to her.
The nurse stayed four days and lost hers to Michael, who
took his bottles like a man. The lamp was shaded, the house
quiet; poor defrauded Trelawney disappeared into the background. Diana went into a place of vague headache, pain,
dreaminess; she slept feverishly, briefly, wakened, looked
with all a baby's empty content at the nurse's white apron.
She was too sick to worry about Michael or anything else;
they did not let her see the baby.

When she was getting well, weakened, broken, pale, Neal
sat beside her bed, on a low hassock, and kissed her cool
hand, and they talked it over. He wouldn't—he wouldn't
ever blame her that it wasn't a girl's wild love. She'd been
through—so much. Tears came to her eyes, the tears of
weakness and uncertainty, as she talked, and Neal wiped
them away. She did love him, as his mother did; she knew
that she could make him happy. They were older now; more
reasonable. She owed him so much. But he—he wasn't grown
up, of course—he would just be her—her oldest little boy,
as Micky was her baby——

"No sensible person could really fall in love with you,
Neal, because you're such a jealous, crazy, unbalanced
imbecile!"

"But you love me!"

"But you're such an *imbecile!*"

She ought to think about it,—she couldn't think. On the
first day that she was well enough to leave the house, a
shaky spring day with a smell of lilac and wet sidewalks in
the air, she and he went up to the City Hall and were
married.

CHAPTER XXVIII

DIANA carried the situation off with a dash, perhaps as much to impress—to convince—herself as Neal, and Trelawney, and the doctor and the nurse that everything was quite as it should be. She was suddenly gay, efficient, cured; she was equal to anything. At a Sunday lunch in the new studio that was really for San Francisco a rather old studio, over the market in Sacramento Street, she told the doctor and Trelawney and one or two other men the whole story.

It was afternoon; they were loitering over their meal, the table was disorderly with glasses, cheese plate, cuts of spongy French bread toasted black. Michael was out in the unsteady March sunshine, with Lottie, his colored slave; he was a mere blue cocoon, smooth and motionless under his covers, but Diana, keeping the conversation moving, had an interior qualm every other minute: was he warm enough?

"You and Neal were married before?" Larry Trelawney demanded with his favorite air of having forgotten that he was a moving-picture idol.

"Six years ago, and divorced——"

"*You* did that," Neal interpolated, as he always did, at this point. "I didn't know anything about it."

"Well,—anyway. And then we met, quite by accident, on a safety station in Market Street of all places——"

The pleasant meal loitered on; cold afternoon light poured through the high studio windows. Diana had cooked the two main dishes for the meal, the fried chicken, the Spanish macaroni; Neal had set the table, inasmuch as it was set at all; someone else had filled the coffee pot, sliced and toasted the French bread, set out cheese and checkered napkins, walnuts and crackers and honey and fat black olives.

Four o'clock. Lottie ought to be bringing him in. Please heaven he wouldn't shriek, with these men here.

Diana smiled, talked on lazily. Her eyes moved from one face to another, and the four men watched her, a slim woman, with a sweep of shining fair hair brushed from her face, and shadowy blue eyes deep set in delicate rings of pallor. An exquisite woman, whose ivory breast showed a little where the blue Chinese silk of her blouse fell away at the throat, and whose fine thin wrists were ivory veined in lapis. Neal was frantic in his delight in her, his possession of her, and her look was always kind,—always understanding,—when it was fixed on Neal.

She had been married a month. But the words, the dates, meant nothing. Diana was in a strange dream; instead of awakening her to a simpler, a relieved and rested, mood, her marriage had only plunged her deeper into bewilderment and unreality. She seemed unable now to look either forward or back. There was only the day to be lived through with philosophy and courage, and love's night to follow the day.

"Isn't my wife beautiful?" Neal demanded, now and then. He was in wild spirits. He had rented this picturesque place for two months; they would never be anywhere much longer than two months, he and she, Diana suspected. He loved the big room with its north light, its canvases that he had not painted and curios that he had not collected. Crooning the words of "Son of Mine," he gazed about, over the flat top of the grand piano, with infinite satisfaction, while Diana went about in the soft, foggy spring afternoons, dusting, straightening, arranging the room. And on such an occasion as today, when his friends were lunching with him, and there was red wine, he was raised to a pitch of high emotional excitement.

Sometimes, during this past month, and during that long-ago time that was coming back to her recollection so clearly now, Diana had tried to restrain this mood, had pleaded that surely this intimate fact—and this—and this—need not be aired for the delectation of their casual friends. But when Neal felt expansive he knew no reservations: "Go ahead, tell 'em, Di! Tell 'em how cute you were that night when you were just getting over the 'flu, and we talked about getting married again!"

Fortunately, she would think with her face blazing with proud, shamed color, no one of her hearers was apt to remember much of anything that went on. They were fed, warm, relaxed, in a mood to find life amusing, touching, exciting almost to the crying point, but not especially clear in detail. They would dawdle about here, now, until perhaps seven o'clock, strumming on the piano, playing cards, thickening the air with heavy blue tobacco smoke, mixing themselves long drinks in long glasses. And always, as they ate and drank and idled and sang, they would profess adoration of her as she came and went.

Michael came home, cold, rosy, ravenous, demanding instant attention. Diana carried him off to the big bathroom that with a narrow strip of kitchen completed the apartment. The bathroom had once been a small bedroom, the plumbing was set about casually, the walls were thin wooden partitioning, and there was always an odor of soap, ammonia, pipes, rotting plaster, in the place.

Still, Michael had to sleep here, some of the time at least, for there was not room even for a baby in the kitchen, much less the basket that held the baby, and the studio was noisy, smoky,—out of the question.

Lottie was off "like a fire horse," as Neal expressed it; Sunday night was her night. Diana undressed the child rapidly, hardly stopping for the brief snatched kisses that his sweetness and brownness and smallness exacted, swept him into dry, warm night wear, put him in his basket while she heated his bottle.

She worked with feverish speed, but not fast enough. Above the piano chords that he was lazily fingering she could hear Neal's shout of "Diana!" A pause; then he recommenced more loudly:

"Diana, what you doing?"

"Fixing him up," she called back from the doorway.

"Fix him up out here!"

She appeared, Michael hung like a round cushion on her hip.

"I can't. All that smoke would choke him."

"Here!" Larry said in concern. "Want us to stop? Shall I open a window?"

"No, no, no, go right ahead." Neal had pulled the rope that opened a high window, and a gush of cold March air came into the room. "Shut that, Neal," Diana begged, shielding Michael, as she brought him and his blanket and his bottle to a low chair, "it's much too cold."

"You imagine all that," Neal said good-naturedly. He went back to the piano, burst into "Danny Deever" with such violence that Michael, startled, stopped his meal and turned alarmed and suddenly tearful eyes toward the frightening noise. "What's the matter, Danny Deever, they are marchin' of 'im 'round——" Neal sang, annoyed.

"It scared him, for a minute," Diana explained, smiling, the child safe and reassured again on her arm.

"How old is he?" one of the men murmured.

"Six months."

"He's a corker, isn't he?"

She looked down at him proudly. When Michael was in sight there was no need to answer.

Presently they all wanted to go to Tony's for dinner. Diana had foreseen this, met the suggestion equably.

"Dinner! Haven't we just stopped eating?"

"Oh, well, but there's music, and the rest of the gang."

"But Neal, just a minute——" She drew him aside. "I've let Lottie go—you know how she is——"

His face—the others could not see it—was black.

"Oh, *hell.*"

"I know, it's too bad."

He frowned, spoke impatiently:

"You could leave him, you know!"

"Not alone, in this fire trap."

She had remembered Neal's temper as a problem in her life years ago. But she remembered nothing as dark, as furious as his expression could become now, at an instant's notice, when he was balked.

"Lissen," he whispered, "are you going to let that kid keep you home, instead of going downtown with me?"

"I'm trying to get someone to stay with him Sunday nights, Neal, you know I am. I've told Lottie that that's the *one* night we need her, and that unless——"

"Oh, talk—talk!" he interrupted her. "You're my wife,—I want my *wife!*"

"I know, Neal. And you know how I love Sunday nights at Tony's. But I couldn't——"

"You could, and any other woman would. But you're so cracked about that kid—and I'm playing every other night, this is my one night——"

"Next Sunday night I'll have someone,—truly, Neal. I would have had Emma tonight, but she was sneezing, so I didn't dare——"

"Why don't you say that you'd rather be here, imagining things about him, and fussing over him," Neal demanded civilly, with a rather ominous smile, "than going anywhere with me?"

A moment later he joined the others; the smoking, talking, card-playing went on. At seven Diana brought Michael, awakened and sociable and dewy, from the bathroom, and all the men went in there to brush up for dinner; it was all uncomfortably constricted and inconvenient for her, but then she never would have taken the apartment anyway. Everything in reason was against it. The rent was high, the neighborhood noisy, Bohemian, inaccessible, and the period of tenancy limited to two months. Neal had rented the place without any reference to her; he had fallen in love with the big studio room, and that had ended it.

Tonight he went away sulky, feeling injured; she stood still, in the center of the big room, when he had gone. Michael, his sleeping hours disturbed and interrupted, had had a hard crying time; he had burst out suddenly, apparently without cause, distracting Diana and hastening the men's departure. But the instant he was alone with his mother he had stopped as mysteriously as he had commenced, and now sat on the broad couch propped in pillows, still occasionally heaving with sobs, still with a tear-streaked face, but contentedly chewing on a teething cracker.

Now she must air the room, and clean it as thoroughly as it had been cleaned by Lottie yesterday, and gather all the sticky glasses and dirty plates in the kitchen. Then a long session there, for Lottie did not come until twelve in the mornings,—Neal, who never breakfasted until noon, even on matinée days, had made that arrangement, too. It had not occurred to him that Michael would take no note of changed hours, and that Diana might be glad of the maid's services earlier.

And then the baby must be settled in his basket in the warm corner beside the ineffectual old hot-air grating, and the big couch made comfortable as a bed. And perhaps, if Neal drank a little too much at Tony's, he would be angry at finding the child's basket in the big room, and carry it into the cold bathroom.

Well, they had only a few more weeks of this; then they would move again. Diana was already searching San Francisco for something sunshiny, old-fashioned, spacious, not too expensive, with a backyard for Michael.

Neal was making good money in stock, but he did not like it, and in any case actors' salaries never lasted long. He had a chance at a good "racket" on the air; Diana was praying he might get it. Two hundred a week, and a two years' contract,—they could have a real home then perhaps in— no, never again in St. Francis Wood.

This was the first year after Bruce's death. She had been thinking about it all day.

CHAPTER XXIX

THE PROBLEM of Michael ramified, grew worse as time went on. Or no, it was not really the problem of little Michael, so gallantly adaptable and good-natured, but the problem of Neal's attitude toward Michael. Neal, from the beginning, was frankly and openly jealous of the baby.

He had never wanted a baby of his own; he had an actual dislike for Bruce Palmer's baby. He thought Diana made too much fuss about Michael. His own life had no room for Michael; he wanted to have her with him, when he breakfasted late, when he walked downtown for rehearsals, when he was at the theater, and for late supper afterward.

Diana often found herself wondering by what insanity she had ever come to believe that she could fit Michael and Neal into one scheme of things. Neal had not changed, she had not changed, in the long years that had passed since their unhappy times long ago. Now here they were together again, with all the old problems still unsolved, and with Michael to add a fresh note.

"Is there any reason why he shouldn't be with his grandparents for a while?" he demanded flatly one day. He had hinted it more than once.

"Why——?" She looked up from the delight, the absorption of Michael's bath, her face paling. Neal, awakened long before his time, was in the doorway, in his tasseled dressing gown. "Darling," said Diana, "I didn't know you were awake."

"Nobody could sleep with this racket going on. What about leaving him with the Palmers for a while, Di?"

Her back was inexpressive; her hands were busy with the splashing child.

"You know they don't like me, Neal."

"What's *that* got to do with it?"

"Well—and they don't think it was a marriage."

"I thought you told me they'd take the child if you'd give him up?"

"They did say something like that." She gathered Michael into the big towel, carried him into the bedroom. She and Neal had a flat of four rooms now; not a pleasant flat, stuffy and dark and down in the theatrical district, but Micky had his own room at last.

"Something like that? They said *that*, didn't they?"

"I don't know." Diana spoke mildly. Michael was just a year old; there was nothing like him in the world, nothing so soft, so brown, so loving, so eager. His mother dried his little feet, her cheek almost touching his dark silky hair.

"Will you do this, Di? Will you get in touch with them? Because, lissen,—this really isn't fair! To have a kid squalling and yelling——"

She knew all this; she had heard it a hundred times. Michael did not yell and squall, but that did not matter. What mattered was that Neal did not want him about.

Everything else she could face, had faced, in the hard year. There had not been many weeks of honeymoon, not much time of illusion. Immediately the old scenes had started, the old sensitiveness, jealousy, suspicion. Long before summer had come Diana had been exhausted, trying to balance the claims of husband and son, to keep the nursery and the studio going, to snatch hours with Michael despite the cunning with which Neal attempted, perhaps not quite consciously, to keep them apart.

If Michael was a little upset, a little croupy, then that

was the exact time that Neal had a plan. After the theater
he and Di were going down to Bob's place at Los Altos;
how about it? Tell Carrie—Alma—Mamie to keep an eye
on the kid.

She did her best. She made herself be amiable, adaptable,
sympathetic. She left Michael, sometimes, when it seemed
as if turning her back on the patient, uncomfortable little
fellow in the crib would break her heart. She kept him in
the background,—and he was well and good, he slept, he
ate, he sat placidly in his pen among his toys,—there was
no *reason* why Neal shouldn't like him.

The summer had been a long horror to her. They had
looked at little places in Mill Valley, in Carmel,—she and
Neal,—any little place would do, where Michael could be
out in the sunshine, and Neal master three new parts. In
the end, quite suddenly one night, when he had been drinking, and without consulting her, he had rented at an ex-
orbitant rent a small houseboat at Belvedere. A houseboat
—when all she had wanted was the good earth and seclusion!

That had meant that they were all cramped together
again, and that Michael could not cry without disturbing
all the men who came out to eat and drink and smoke and
play cards.

Afterward there had been a pretense of looking for rooms
for the winter; it had been only a pretense. For Neal, after
a few impatient preliminaries, had discovered the Ellis
Street place. "You decide," he had said to her angrily, "but
it's the only place I want, and the only place I can live, and
it's the right rent and neighborhood. If you choose to go
wandering about looking at ridiculous things 'way out at
Seacliff and Ingleside, that's entirely up to you. Is it 'yes'
or 'no'?"

"But, Neal, it's so dark. I only thought we might find
something—say on Hyde, or up near Larry on Stockton——"

"Yes. Well, you *can't*. And I'm sick of this thinking always of the kid and never of me. I want to live downtown, near my work——"

There had been a great deal of it. But as the months went on, Diana had argued with him much less often, quarreled not at all. It was no use. It only made him more violent. She grew quieter, more patient. She forgave him quickly; it was the only way. If he left for his matinée in a fury, she would often slip downtown, to be in his dressing room when he came sweating and powdered and tired from the last curtain, and to smile forgiveness at him. And he would clasp her in his arms, sobbing, kissing her, his girl—oh, she couldn't get along without him, and she knew damn' well she couldn't!

And perhaps the next night he would be gone without explanation, unless the casual remark, presently dropped, that some girl,—some Ethel or Joan or "Baby" or "Billee," —was a little damn' fool, was one. Diana endured even this; she did not raise issues. Her one need was for peace in her own soul, and time for Michael, time to bind up the wounds that life had given her, and to regain strength and courage and breath.

But he shook the very foundations of her hard-won citadel when he talked of sending her child away, of his feeling that her happiness and his was jeopardized by the presence of the baby. Michael should be with the senior Palmers, that's where he should be, and Neal could not be happy until something was done about it.

And one day, when they had been married for more than a year, and Christmas was upon them again, he told her he had talked to a lawyer about it, a man he had known for years.

"He says that the getting a license to get married was in effect a contract, Di. Not a legal marriage, but enough to force the Palmers to recognize the kid."

She held herself resolutely quiet; the arm against which Michael was luxuriously sprawled did not tremble. But dark red color crept in her face.

"They *do* recognize him, Neal."

"Ye-ah?" His favorite air of having triumphed in an argument. "Then let 'em come through!"

Diana said nothing. She held the child against her heart. Her face was infinitely tired.

"Why—why—why did I do it?" her thoughts reiterated. "It was my fate, I suppose,—my fate to pay for that mad first marriage with this second mad one. Meeting him a month earlier than I did, he wouldn't have wanted me. Meeting him a month later, I would have had it all solved somehow. I would have had a job, someone to take care of Michael. So many other women have solved it, and I am as capable of it as they are. Why did it have to be that we met in the one hour when I could not go on without help, and why must it have been only Neal who could give me that help—food and a room and a hot bath and nights of rest?"

Three nights later, between matinée and evening performance, Neal brought his lawyer friend home for dinner "to talk about this Palmer business." Diana awaited them with her heart steeled, her mind firm. They might say, they might do, what they would, but she could not part from Michael.

Neal came in hot and rumpled, as he always did from the theater. The squarely built man who followed him was lost in the gloom of the little foyer for a moment, while they disposed of their coats and hats; then he came smilingly in his host's wake into the sitting room, and Diana stood up with her child in her arms and looked at him in the lamplight. And immediately her expression changed, and her eyes shone.

"Peter Platt!"

"Hello, Di." His two big hands were over hers; the fine

white teeth she remembered showed in a smile, but his keen
eyes were not smiling.

"Peter! I didn't know *you* were Neal's lawyer!"

"Didn't he tell you?"

"I'd forgotten you knew each other," Neal explained, in
the doorway, with his hair wet and a towel at his dripping
face.

The once very red hair was darker now, smooth and thick.
The eyes were the same kind gray eyes. But Peter was
changed; thinner, built lean and square, his voice had new
notes, and his mouth was not the mouth she remembered
in the old days of the soda fountain at Sticky's. There was
something about its chiseled fineness, its quick smile, its
quick seriousness that stirred Diana oddly, that made her
sit silent, watching this old companion with half-puzzled,
half-fascinated eyes, listening to him as if he were speaking a language, as indeed he was, for which her ears and
mind and soul had been hungry.

He had been in Washington with Senator Cope, he knew
New York; he had just been offered a junior membership
in the firm of Bauer & Martin. Bauer & Martin? Diana
raised impressed eyebrows. This was recognition indeed.

Neal came out, impatient for his dinner, and they talked
of Neal. But Diana knew now that she could bide her time;
that Neal would go to the theater at eight, and that then
she and Peter could talk. She saw the look he gave Michael
when Lottie carried him off to bed, she heard the surprised
note in his voice as he asked her, in an aside, "But why on
earth do you want to get rid of a little fellow like that, Di?"
and she knew that capricious fate,—that fate against which
she had been railing only that very day,—had brought a
new current into her life, a new hope,—even a friend. And
she had so longed for a friend!

After dinner, when Neal was gone, she drew his chair
near to her own, under the lamp, and sat facing him, her

eyes traveling over him wistfully, the right words somehow hard to find.

"I'd forgotten what you looked like, Di," Peter said, without smiling.

"Shame! I'd not forgotten you."

"Perhaps I mean," he altered it, considering, "I'd forgotten that you were so—so *extremely*—well, let it go at that."

"So extremely," she agreed, and they both smiled.

"Your heart," the man presently began again, "isn't in this business of approaching the Palmers, is it? I can see that it isn't."

"What made you," Diana asked slowly,—"what made you think it was?"

He hesitated.

"Neal," he said simply, and Diana answered as simply, "I see."

"You don't want to give him up," Peter stated rather than asked, after a moment. Diana looked at him, looked quickly away, and he saw her blue eyes brim suddenly with tears, and the thick lashes lowered.

She had not cried for many months; she had learned not to cry. Even now she regained immediate control of herself, and the tears did not fall. After a while she said in a voice she kept low to keep steady, and without looking at him:

"You're *infinitely* restful, Peter. I'm so glad you're here."

He did not answer for a little while. Then he said simply:

"I think I've been hoping, all my life, that some day I'd be of some use to you, Di."

CHAPTER XXX

PETER came up again to talk to Diana about the Palmers' offer to take little Michael; they sat in Diana's dreary little parlor, Peter staring for the most part at the coal fire, as he talked, but now and then glancing up to smile at her his remembered smile.

After his second call he took her to lunch at the St. Francis. They walked the half-dozen sunshiny blocks together, and Peter bought her gardenias. It was in the flower shop, while he was pinning them on her shoulder, his big brown hands moving expertly on the long pin, his brown cheek close to hers, that Diana was conscious of a feeling that swept through her whole body from her heels to her temples like a chill, and that made her heart begin to beat slowly in suffocating strokes.

Luncheon, in the social buzzing atmosphere of the smartest restaurant, was all a haze, and after it Diana walked home, stopping to buy socks for Michael, stopping to buy a magazine, not conscious of what she was doing.

Alone in her own rooms she stood still for a long while, staring down at the carpet with narrowed eyes, her forehead knitted. Presently she put her head back, as if to breathe.

"Peter!" she said, in a whisper.

When he came to report a day or two later the same icy wave went over her again; as Diana met him she was trembling so that she had to put out a hand to the stairway rail to balance herself. She was conscious only of feeling that he must see nothing—he mustn't guess——

The fine brown hands again, and the fine voice, and that

sidewise smiling glance as he sat by the fire,—life leaped suddenly into significance and beauty; once again Diana lost all consciousness of what she was saying. She was a woman in a fever.

It blazed in her; it possessed her; it devoured her. Diana moved about in a daze; her one thought was that Peter was within reach; her one need was to see him, hear him.

During the strange, unnatural days when Neal slept late, rushed through shaving and dressing, and was gone, she would look at her telephone restlessly, feeling every fiber of her being dragged toward it. She could not call him; on what possible pretext could she decently call him? But just to dial the numbers meant to have her heart begin to sing and her spirits soar into that state of unearthly ecstasy that was robbing her food of taste in these days, and her nights of sleep, that was lending a sapphire beauty to her eyes.

She would hear the office operator's cheerful soprano; "Bauer and *Mar*-tin!" hear the cadences in her own voice as she said, "Mr. Platt, please."

Then, if the answer was "Mr. Platt isn't here just now. Is there any *mes*-sage?" the whole world would go dark, and Diana's mouth fill with salt water, and her heart turn sick.

But perhaps fate would be kinder. Perhaps the next sound would be Peter's voice, vibrant and friendly and expectant: "Hello, this is Peter Platt!" And then, with a changing, a lowering of tone: "Ah, hello, Di! What's up, my dear?"

If she could only have found excuses for daily telephone messages! But Michael's little affair was only too simply arranged. His grandparents wanted him, "for a long visit"; his Lottie was to go with him. Neal, in his ugliest, most sullen mood, was counting the moments until the child left the house.

Diana had no choice. The soft foggy January morning came when Michael was dressed in his square short sailor coat and his turned-up white bluejacket's cap, and when Diana knelt down on the rug and put her arms about him and kissed the small beaming face good-bye. Peter, raising the child to his shoulder, gave a concerned look at her white face; he said nothing.

A day or two later, in the dark rooms that had grown so much darker, and the silence that even the hum of the city could not break, Diana, from forcedly quiet reading, stretched on her bed, quite suddenly sprang to her feet, and was at the telephone, and was dialing the number of Bauer & Martin.

She sat back dully, staring. Mr. Platt had left the office an hour ago. The world was all a waste; empty, tiresome. Somewhere downtown among the clubs and shops and offices Peter was busy; perhaps he was with some client, driving slowly in the park, talking. And Diana—Diana was starving for him!

When her bell rang, a few minutes later, she could feel the blood leave her heart; feel it rush back again with a violence that made her experience almost a vertigo. She was holding to the back of a chair when Peter came upstairs. Peter, in his dark blue coat, with his good brown face and his own kindly smile; Peter, whose voice she hadn't heard for forty-eight hours——

They went for a walk, and he told her everything he could of Michael; the royal welcome, the royal preparations for the Palmer grandchild. And Diana, keeping step beside him through the romantic jumble of the piers and the waterfront, her color whipped high, her bright hair flying, was happy again. Peter's gloved hand at her elbow on the crossings; Peter's dark eyes smiling at her across the tea table—the world was right once more!

"How is Neal?" Peter asked.

"Very difficult," Diana said simply. "He doesn't like his part, he's—*going* too much——"

Peter was watching her intently, as he lighted a cigarette. "Of course there's a way out, Di."

"I know——" she said briefly, shaking her head.

"I mean—when you say '*going*,'" he began, "I know what you mean."

To this Diana made no immediate answer. After a while she said, "He doesn't make any secret of his—his affairs, and as for the other,—well, he has to come home to me, and I help him straighten out."

"Very heroic in you to endure it," Peter said dryly. "But *why?*"

"Every reason. It's my job. You know how impossible divorce—I suppose we're talking of divorce—would be."

There was a silence. Then Peter said:

"I suppose I do."

"No, not that way for me, again," she said slowly.

"You punish yourself, Di."

"I punish myself whatever I do. I seem to have been born to punish myself. But I must—I must walk this way, now—now while Neal is so—so strange about it——"

"Not sane," he put in as she paused.

"Not sane, no. But I married him—I married him twice, as he is," Diana said. "He is my problem now. He loves me—in his way——"

"His way," Peter reminded her strongly, as she hesitated again, "is a way that leaves you plenty of loopholes if you want one, Di. He has driven you almost into nervous breakdown,—he wants to separate you from your child,—he is not, you know it,—you *know* he is not——"

"Faithful," she supplied absently. "Yes, I know. But this —this is what I have to do now: I have to keep Neal happy, give him no excuse to say that I didn't do what I could to save our marriage this second time——"

She turned, looking away from him up the foggy street, and he saw that she was crying.

"I thought," she said, with difficulty, trying to smile, to speak lightly,—"I thought, when I was a little girl, that I was such a—such a nice person! I thought I was going straight ahead, a credit to Miss Benchley and Rutherford, an honor student at college. It's all been so different—so commonplace and stupid and blind. And now—now I've lost Michael——"

"I suppose Neal gets some satisfaction out of that?"

"He doesn't express it."

"I suppose not. That," Peter said after a pause,—"that isn't marriage, is it?"

"Lots of married people aren't married, Pete."

There was another silence. Then the man said:

"I've borrowed Stephen's little place in Sausalito, just for a while. I told you that? I can work on this Teazell case over there."

"Oh?" Her eyebrows met. "Does that mean that you come to town less—that I see you less?"

Peter looked at her, and she saw the dark color come up under his brown skin.

"No, that doesn't," he answered, with a little stressing of the second word.

For a long while Diana looked at him in silence.

"Something does?" she asked, very low.

"Yep," said Peter briefly.

"I see——" Diana said, half aloud. Much later, when they had walked slowly through the darkening streets to her door, delaying their steps, dawdling, prolonging the exquisite twilight hour as long as they might, she asked, "When do I see you again?"

"I don't know," said Peter, looking up the street.

"You'll see Micky?"

"Oh, yes,—I'll report! I'll—I'll telephone."

Silence lay like a wall of darkness between them.

"What—what are you doing tonight, Peter?"

"I've a dinner date. I'm dressing at the club."

"Interesting?" Her voice was thick.

"I beg your pardon, Di. I didn't hear you."

"Who's the date with?"

"The Willy Pomeroys,—she was Gertrude Bauer,— they're nice people."

"And then you go back to Sausalito?" They were talking stiffly, like strangers, who had been chattering so thirstily, so insatiably a few minutes before.

"I——? Oh, yes."

"Good-night, Peter, and thanks so much for coming for me. It saved my life! I was just—just missing him so horribly——"

"Good-night, Di. See you very soon!"

He turned, walked away; Diana went slowly upstairs, her joy in ashes, her heart lead, life suddenly dark beyond bearing. Peter was going away—away—away from her. Other women would hear that voice tonight, watch that smile, and the clever quick movements of his hands.

She locked her arms across her breast, catching her elbows in pressed nervous fingers.

"Oh, my God, I love him, I love him! And I can't bear it."

Sometimes she found herself watching Neal with a sort of static wonder, even a species of reluctant admiration. He was so completely, so magnificently self-centered that his very selfishness could not fail to be impressive. He never thought of anyone else at all, and tossed off the possibility of doing so with a lofty disdain.

To say, "Neal, Carrie has a frightful toothache," or "The man is in trouble," to plead, "Neal, I'd rather not. Please let me off. I don't feel well,—I forgot,—I wonder if you'd let me suggest——" was merely to waste breath. He neither heard nor cared. He made his plans, took his comfort, went his unperturbed way. If Neal wanted to bring friends home to dinner, he brought them; if Diana ever had had the temerity to ask guests to the house in the early weeks of their marriage, to make arrangements of her own, he had calmly canceled them. "I'll telephone them and tell them it's all off, that you're extremely sick," he would say, without passion.

When he wanted her to be at home, to superintend his dinner, sleep in his arms, she must be there. When he chose to absent himself from her side for several days and nights at a time, he did so without explanation or apology, and apparently without scruple.

"Don't act like Henderson's wife, she's always ragging the poor devil," he would say, if Diana protested. And to her serious reproaches, in their early married days, he submitted the invariable airy argument: "My dear, you married an actor!"

Girls waited for him at the stage door after the matinées and solicited his autograph; women telephoned him at the theater and asked him to dine. He was only a handsome leading man in a stock company, but he had plenty of flattery, plenty of reason to feel himself a god among men. Neal would come home and toss Diana a sheaf of letters,— simple, common, self-revealing letters from simple, common women.

"What can you say to them?" he would demand, stooping to generous pity of the poor deluded creatures. One day, glancing with distaste at a batch of them, she said quietly, "There's one here from Deirdre."

"I didn't see it!" He made a snatch for it; she saw the quick blood in his face. Was he afraid of Deirdre? Evidently the little screen star was furious at him.

"I saw only the beginning," she said, in good-natured scorn. "I saw 'I love you, you beast, and I shall always hate you!'"

"She talks like that," Neal stammered embarrassed.

"Movie talk!" Diana knew that even in his confusion and fear he was pleased; that insatiable vanity of his was flattered. That was the trouble with their marriage, she mused; she couldn't go on flattering him,—he demanded too much; and to satisfy him she had to make too artificial an effort, say too many things that were completely false. After all, to the wife who saw him unshaven, cross, sleepy, vain, the wife who heard him prevaricating at the telephone, who saw his simple attempts to make himself important, to enhance his own personal glory, he could not be a hero.

She might indeed cook his meals, attend to his comfort, listen to his long meandering talk of himself. But flattery and admiration,—the widened eyes and caught breath of awed idolatry,—must come from other women now. For very self-respect Diana could not render them to him.

One day, ten endless days and nights since the departure of Micky, Peter telephoned and asked her to come for a walk. He gave no explanation; Diana demanded none. It was a windy day, with spatters of rain,—Diana buttoned herself snugly into a dark blue rain coat, pulled a dark blue rubber cap down against her bright hair.

They said very little as they went together down the shining wet streets and along the waterfront. There were pools everywhere; the smoke from the little kitchens where crabs and shrimps were boiled blew fitfully against an iron sky; the bay was lashed with whitecaps.

Taking the exposed way toward the Marina, Peter caught her arm; drew her tightly to him.

"What I wanted to ask you, Di," he said, walking on, "was whether you ever consider a divorce."

"I think I'm the one person who can't."

"Think you can't?"

"Not after—everything." And after a silence she added:

"I've been divorced—and from this man. I can't explain it all—what different moods made me do. I never thought of myself as—as having this kind of a history. But—no, I can't divorce him again!"

Peter did not speak for a while. The sun had come uncertainly to view in the yellow gray of the west, the streets glittered, and roofs everywhere had begun to smoke, when he said:

"What people think makes a difference, does it?"

"What I think," amended Diana.

"It would be the last change," Peter offered.

"Remarrying Neal was the last change," Diana said. "He wants me—he loves me in his fashion," she went on, slowly, seeking the right words, "not to make me happy, but to give me a chance to make him happy!"

"I know——" Peter said, in an odd tone. "Here's the thing," he presently recommenced. "You—matter to me, horribly. I'm not telling you I love you,—I've no right to, for one thing, and for another you've always known it. But— you've come to matter to me more than anything else. I can't work, thinking of you. I keep thinking how easily I could telephone—get in touch with you——"

"I know!" Diana said quickly, nervously. She was at her own doorway now, and as she turned to look down at him from the step, he saw the flush of the setting sun full in her face.

"And that can't be, Di," Peter stated simply.

"We can't be friends?" she asked.

"No."

"I suppose not."

"So I'm going away," Peter said. "Cope wants me, back in Washington. I'm giving up the Sausalito place on the first. I'm clearing out."

Diana had paled a little; her lips were shut, and she was

breathing through her nostrils; he saw the delicate flanges dilate, narrow, dilate again. She did not speak.

"That's the best way, my dear," Peter said. "We can't cheat."

"No," she said thoughtfully, "I suppose we can't cheat."

"You're pretty sure he wants you here?"

"Sure. I think if I left Neal, and went to you," Diana thought it out slowly, "he'd follow me and kill me."

"He'd threaten it, maybe. They never do it."

"He would do it,—it would be his idea of not being a piker."

Peter mused on this, looking away.

"And yet—what a life for you!" he said, half to himself, glancing at the dingy street and the dreary apartment doorway.

"But it is my life. I have to work it out. Marriage, divorce, baby, widowhood, remarriage,—it's a bad pattern," Diana said. "I couldn't—I couldn't—go on indefinitely—tearing up the past behind me!"

"I suppose not. Well, then, this is good-bye!"

"Good-bye," she said, her color fading again.

"I'll telephone you when I go." Peter lifted his hat, wheeled about, and went away down the street. The last of the sunset was gone now; fine cold rain was beginning to fall again. Diana stood looking after him until he was lost to sight.

Then again the strange hours began; nights were long wakeful times without end or beginning, food was plaster and sawdust, telephone and doorbell and the postman's whistle had but one meaning.

Driven by the breathless, thirsty need of it, she telephoned him,—waited a day, telephoned again. Mr. Platt was busy—was not there—was busy. Would he please call her?

He did not call her. She told herself that he had been sent out of town,—he had missed the message, he would be back late. And all the time she knew that his secretary was efficiency's self; that Peter knew she needed him, and that he would not come.

CHAPTER XXXI

ON A CERTAIN Sunday she pocketed her pride once more; telephoned him in Sausalito.

"Peter,—this is Diana."

"Yes, I know." She heard him clear his throat.

"The reason I called you—Peter, are you going away tomorrow?"

A pause. Then briefly:

"Yes—I'm flying all the way to Washington."

"Tomorrow?"

"Yes. They—they think I ought to get there. I'm handling a case for our own firm there, too."

"Oh." Another pause. Then Diana said, with a little artificial animation: "I have company this morning. Who do you think's here?"

"Not Micky?"

"Peter, how'd you guess?"

"I knew they were softening. I told you so."

"Yes, and Friday, when I was alone,—Neal's gone until Monday night,—I just took a chance and went down to Bayhead."

"And they were nice to you?"

"They were adorable! And Micky came running out shouting 'Mom-Mom-Mom!' and, Pete, I've had him overnight, and he doesn't go home until tomorrow! He's eating his cereal now,—aren't you, Beautiful? He says 'desh.' That's one reason I telephoned," Diana said in a voice whose bright naturalness did not hide its nervous excitement. "It's such a divine day, and we could get on the car that goes down to the ferry right here at the door, and bring our lunch over to Sausalito if you think it's going to be clear over there!"

There was a moment of silence; she could hear her heart beat.

"You'll come over to lunch of course," Peter said then in a tone she had never heard from him before.

"Oh, Peter, no—that's trouble for you! And you have guests there; we'd only be in the way."

"No, that's what you'll do, of course," Peter repeated definitely. He was compromising—he had surrendered—there was iron in his tone; it was hard and flat. "It's eleven now," he said. "Could you be on the twelve-o'clock? I'll meet it."

Diana turned from the telephone, sank on her knees beside Micky's position high in pillows in an armchair. Laughing for sheer ecstasy, she buried her flushed face in his firm little brown neck; kissing him, holding him off at arm's length, jerking him to her again.

"He goes tomorrow, Micky! But we'll have our day!" There was no breathing, no thinking, there was just a golden blur of springtime and blue skies and white clouds, and the smoothly welling waters of the blue bay, and the flash of white gulls, until she was going off with the crowd on the Sausalito side, and saw Peter standing square and brown and unsmiling at the ferry place. Their eyes met; there was no other greeting. Then Micky was on Peter's shoulder, and they were walking toward the car.

Later he and she and the child went up to the quiet hills, and heard the larks start up in the grass with their heart-piercing cry, and saw the white ships crossing and recrossing the bay, and the white galleons of the clouds slowly sailing across the blue of heaven.

Diana was all in white; her slender legs and white-shod feet stretched out among the poppies and the tasseled oats, her frock white cotton, her small hat white. And the child who sat murmuring and pulling buttercup heads at her knee was briefly clad in white, too. But the effect of Michael was brown; brown bare knees, brown bare arms, brown little earnest face and mop of dark brown hair.

Peter lay in the grass beside her, sometimes raising his face to look at her, sometimes dropping his head deep into the sweet greenness. They talked, were silent, talked again.

"This is one of the days to mark with a white stone, Pete."

He was silent awhile. The sweet-scented air trembled between them; the man's dark rich hair was down on his arms. Neither spoke again for a long space.

"Neal gets home tomorrow?"

"Tomorrow afternoon. And Micky and Lottie go back in the morning. I'll take no chances. But oh," Diana said fervently, "to have had him, to know that I can have him again, sometimes is like coming out into the most exquisite sunshine, after a tunnel that I thought would never end. I don't mind anything now! They were so kind to me,—the Palmers,—they talked of Bruce, and we all cried,—the poor old man, and Patsy; she's going to be married, and she seemed so gentle, so changed. Elinor died, you know, when her baby came; I think they've all been softened, somehow. And Joan came over; she has two little girls, and she was so sweet, just like old times! They kept me overnight, and then,—when I thought my heart couldn't bear any more joy, —Mrs. Palmer said, in that snorting way of hers,—only even she was terribly kind!—'Why not take this little boy home for a night, if you like, as long as you'll surely let us have him again?'

"And best of all was to have him come flying to me— when I got there, I mean, just frantic with excitement at seeing me again, and shouting 'Mom-Mom-Mom!'"

Michael twisted about to eye her.

"M'now-now?" he asked hopefully.

"Yes, the m'now-now was there, the big white kitty! Peter," Diana went on, "today is one of those days when all the mistakes and stupidities of life seem smoothed out, somehow, and life—happiness—is all the sweeter for the darkness."

"And you have to go back to Ellis Street?"

"After all the sunshine down at the Palmers',—and this," she said. "But my heart—my heart won't go back there!"

"How'd the play go, down south?" he asked, after a while.

"Neal's play? Very well, I gather. He must have seen Deirdre,—I had one telegram in which he said that everything was hopelessly dull, and he hadn't seen anyone, so that means he's up to some mischief. Oh, yes, and the Coggleses, Peter," Di interrupted herself to say suddenly, with her face brightening, "you remember them, at Gram's? My dear, they're the 'Blonde Beresfords' of the movies,—six blonde sisters all together, and Neal says they're going to be simply the rage. Isn't that delicious?"

"It's good to hear a thing like that. It seems to me they were always hungry."

"They *were*. And their father whipped them."

"That always used to get you, when you were a kid."

The last phrase set her to dreaming, and there was a long silence. Then suddenly Diana stirred.

"We ought to go back to the house, Pete. I've to get this little gent home for his supper."

"Shame to have to go in." The exquisite spring afternoon was mellowing toward its close; it was only four o'clock, but long shadows stretched ahead of them as they crossed the high hill meadows on their way home, and the poppies and buttercups were closing their satiny cups. The warm air hummed with the sweetness and the languor of spring; the bay, far below them, was blue; the distant city twinkled with mica points of light against the opal of sunset. All about them the gracious folds of the hills descended to the piers; great oaks clothed their shoulders in plumy green; taller eucalyptus rose like sentinels above the sloping red roofs among the trees of the hillside town.

Peter's bungalow sprawled on the very top of a hill, with wide floor windows in a low long study looking, between oak boles, down to the water. It was a simple shingled place, bedded in riotous, half-pruned garden; every one of the six or seven rooms opened informally into the world of flowers and pepper trees and steep paths fringed with roses and stock and marigolds all ready to bloom. A plum tree, gnarled and bent almost to earth, caught the last of the sunlight in its dazzling blossoms.

" 'Beauty haunts me till I die, Beauty, mercy have on me,' " Diana quoted, standing still, with the wistful longing of a child in her blue dreaming eyes.

"I'm so glad you like it, Di."

She was at the old desk presently, looking at his mother's picture; at a snapshot of a smiling girl in white, with an armful of roses.

"Why, it's myself!"

"On your graduation day, don't you remember?"

"I do—now. You and your camera. Ten years ago!"

"It can't be."

"It is. I was seventeen."

The man made no further comment.

"How long have you had this here?"

"I don't know," he said briefly. And again the air was trembling, so rarefied that she could not breathe it; her breath must come shallow, uneven, like that of a bird held gently in a great hand.

She stood, with something of the spring day's sweet, softened, wilted quality in her loosened hair and white cotton gown, watching from the window. About her his familiar room, the blackened fireplace, the rows of much-handled books, the great jar of frail cream and lavender iris, dimming into early twilight, made a setting.

"When—when do I see you, Pete?"

"Oh, I'll—I'll telephone you."

"But—but you go East?"

"Oh, yes. I go East. That's true."

"Tomorrow." She said it very quietly, without expression.

Silence. Silence. He had come to stand behind her; she could feel the touch of a tweed shoulder against her own shoulder. If he just wouldn't touch her—wouldn't be so near——

It gave her head a strange light feeling,—as if nothing mattered,—nothing mattered,—except not to spoil the wonderful dizzying joy of this moment——

"Do you own this place?"

"I—no, I borrowed it from Gates," he roused himself to say absently.

She sent him an oblique look over her shoulder, looked out again.

"It's lovely, isn't it?" the man asked.

"Perfect. The perfect view,—downhill, and through trees at the water," Diana said. "The fruit blossoms down there —against so much blue and green,—I don't know what I'm saying!" she thought.

"You'll miss the freedom of this," she presently added, to say something,—"if you go to Washington, I mean. There's a kind of simpleness about all this,—these little houses, scattered down the hill, with their smoke going up into the air, and children playing in the backyards——"

"Oh, yes, I'll miss everything."

There was a silence; then Diana said without turning: "What a day this has been!"

"Hasn't it?"

"It was just—just what I needed. I was so sick of the city, sick of winter, sick of being alone! And this has been like a bath, a great plunge into beauty again,—into feeling like a little girl back at Gram's house, when the buttercups and the poppies were in bloom. Peter——" Diana said, her nervous rush of words suddenly falling flat, her voice dropping to a lower note.

"Shoot."

"If I hadn't telephoned you, would you have seen me again?"

His manner stiffened; he was remote again.

"Oh, surely!"

Diana spoke over her shoulder, in a tone with a note of amusement in it.

"You have perfect control, Peter, haven't you?"

A pause. "And lucky for you if I have, my dear," he said.

She wandered away from the window, looked at his books, peeped into his bedroom, told him presently that he had grown to be a person.

"Thank you, Di."

"Would you like to know, before you go East, what I've come to think of you, Pete?"

"I—I think not. I hate to hurry you," Peter said, "but what about getting this infant home?"

Diana's eyes were fixed on him; she said nothing.

"I mean," Peter began again inflexibly, hardly conscious of what he said, "oughtn't the kid get home?"

"He should indeed," Diana agreed, sighing.

She looked at the child, sprawled in a light doze on a couch, with the dark hair in damp rings on his forehead, and wilted flowers still gripped in his small hand.

"Yes, I ought to be getting him home," Diana said lifelessly. "The minute the sun goes down it gets very cold."

"I'll drive you," Peter said, suddenly.

"To what boat? I don't know about boats."

"Every twenty minutes. I'll take you all the way."

"To the city, you mean? Haven't you——" She smiled,

raising her blue eyes. "You haven't anything else you want
to do?"

"It happens—not," Peter said, briefly, and Diana laughed.

Michael's small sleepy face was sponged into wakefulness
in the bathroom; Diana put on his blue coat and his round
sailor cap. Then Peter shouldered him, and Michael, amiable,
but still somewhat sleepy, lopped against the man's cheek
like a heavy-headed flower. They all went out to the car,
and Diana got into the front seat, with the child in her lap.

And so down the green hill, and through the crooked
streets of the little seaport town to the pier, and onto the
boat. Michael drowsed again; Peter and Diana were very
quiet on the front seat. The man sat, squared slightly about
to face her, with one big overcoat arm laid along the back
of the seat behind her.

CHAPTER XXXII

THEY SEEMED to leave the spring behind them, for the bay was rough and gray, when they got opposite the Gate, and a fine thick fog was blowing in across the Presidio hills, and smothering the city. The air was cold and raw now, and the foghorns and whistles began to pierce the mist and the dusk. Peter drove east through the railway tracks, and through the Italian quarter and Chinatown, and the deserted, dingy back streets began to go by—Geary, O'Farrell, Ellis. They were at home.

The car was parked in the empty Sunday street, and Peter took the sleeping child and went with him and Diana into the dim close odors of the house. She led the way, unlocked the apartment, found lights.

"Lay him right there on the bed,—my beautiful, you're so sleepy!" crooned Diana. Then, throwing aside her own coat and hat, she turned to Peter, still with the air of the wind-blown, sun-browned child exhaustedly happy after a country day. "Stay and have scrambled eggs and cocoa?"

"It'd bother you."

"Bother me! But Micky and I have to eat. We'd do it for ourselves, anyway. Cocoa and toast and applesauce—it's all here." Diana's bright hair had been somewhat crushed by her hat; it was all the lovelier for its dishevelment; her blue eyes were the lovelier for the country glory still lingering in them.

"Sausalito agreed with you, Di," Peter said. "You look ever so much younger and better than you did this morning."

"Happiness agrees with me," Diana substituted, stopping her bread-cutting to look at him. "I think today," she added deliberately, "was the happiest day I ever had in my life."

"Too bad," Peter said levelly, "that we can't do it oftener."

"Perhaps some day we shall, somewhere."

"You'll have to decide that."

"I think—if you knew Neal better, you'd see that I'm deciding right. He thinks——" Diana hesitated. "He thinks he treats me splendidly, that I have profited tremendously by his marrying me," she finally submitted.

"As I say, it's up to you," Peter presently substituted for some more impulsive observation. He looked away through narrowed eyelids.

"I see it this way.—*Neal*——" stammered Diana.

She said the last word heavily, amazedly. Peter turned about to follow the direction of her eyes and saw Neal, flushed, tumbled, suspicious, in the kitchen doorway.

"Neal," Diana repeated, but this time in a dutifully pleased and welcoming tone, "I didn't know you were here! I expected you tomorrow."

"So I see," Neal commented, in a significant tone made top-heavy by the fact that he had been drinking and was slightly unsure of his tongue.

"You know Peter Platt."

"Pete Platt can damn' well get out of here," Neal said slowly and thickly. "How long have you had that kid here?"

"Only since yesterday," Diana answered, unalarmed and motherly. She cut two more slices, stacked what she had cut methodically. Peter watched Neal, as Neal's bloodshot eyes moved from one face to the other with a look he tried to keep menacing. "What did you do last night?" Diana, busy and matter-of-fact, demanded, steering Neal to a chair. "Here, sit down——"

"Oh, I made a fool of myself!" Neal admitted, suddenly collapsing, his head in his hands.

"On the train?"

"No,—drove up with Deirdre and Forrest."

"I rather *thought* she was in the picture! Well, we had a wonderful picnic! You look as if you needed sleep, dear. I suppose you aren't interested in cocoa and scrambled eggs? We're just going to have supper."

"Oh, hell, no," Neal whispered, with a look of distaste. "Pete," he said, forming the words painstakingly, slowly, with dry lips, "I didn't mean to kick you out, ole fellow. I just came in and saw that kid on my bed,—Diana don't tell me these things, she never tole me she was goin' to have him here this week-end——"

"I didn't know it, Neal," Diana put in, from the toaster.

"You din know it?" Neal asked, immensely facetious. "No, I guess you din know it. All right, all right. How long does he stay?"

"I was thinking I could take him back to Bayhead to-night," Peter suggested. "It's only about forty minutes' run, I have the car here. Is Lottie down there, Diana?"

"Oh, yes, she's down there. She was coming in for him tomorrow."

"You could telephone her?"

The blue eyes met the gray ones; Diana was rather pale. But there was no nervousness, no misgiving in her glance. She engineered Neal to the bedroom; Peter could hear her murmuring motherly voice in there; presently she came out with the child, established him in his pillows, resumed her supper preparations.

"You don't want me here, Di."

"Oh, stay, of course. Neal's asleep anyway. Listen!" Diana smiled, tipping her head toward the closed bedroom door, through which indeed came the sound of regular snoring.

"Is he—is he often like this?"

"Not so often." Diana was pouring cocoa; she took Micky on her knee, kissed the top of his head between bites.

"Why don't you let me take Micky back to Bayhead tonight, Di? Wouldn't that make it easier for you?"

"Oh, no—no—no! He'll be all right here. Neal will sleep all night; he's completely all in."

"He looks rotten."

"He is looking badly."

Peter finished his cocoa, finished his cigarette, shook himself into his big coat.

"Anything I can do for you,—get you?"

"Not a thing. Wait a minute," Diana said, harking, "who's that?"

"What?"

"Listen, don't you hear it? Somebody asking for Neal——"

She went to the door of the hall; disappeared for a moment. Peter could hear her say, "He lives here. But I'm not sure he's in."

A woman laughed cheerfully, noisily.

"Well, I'm sure he's in!" she said, panting audibly as she reached the floor level. Diana's puzzled quick glance went to her expectantly. She was stout, but she was a pretty woman —extremely smart in a black-and-white checkered fur effect.

"Tell Neal I'm here!" commanded this person, arrogantly abreast of Diana, staring beyond her from the shadows of the hall.

"He's *been* in Los Angeles——" Diana began warily. The other woman interrupted.

"I know he's here. I'm Deirdre Dean. We drove up together this morning!"

"Oh-h-h. Then of course——" Diana led the way into her stuffy little drawing room, with its lace curtains and cloth plants. "But Neal's all in," she explained simply, in

an undertone, with a glance at the bedroom door. "He feels
—terribly tired——"

"He's been drinking like a fool, if you mean that," Miss
Dean agreed, flatly. "You're his sister?"

"I could wake him."

"You'll *have* to wake him; I *have* to see him!" Miss Dean
for the first time gave her hostess a keen look. "You're terribly good to him, I know *that*," she said. "He's always talking about you. I've got to have a long talk with you some
day about Neal."

"I'm glad he's so appreciative," Diana could only reply
politely.

"He's up to something," the visitor said, with a shrewd
look. "He didn't want me to come up here,—made a terrible
row about it."

"Wait a minute," Diana said. She went to the bedroom
door, found that Neal was awake, scowling suspiciously
toward the voices in the sitting room. "Neal, Miss Dean is
here," she told him.

"Miss *who?*"

"Dean. Deirdre Dean."

Tousled, sleepy, unshaven, his eyes puffed leaden pockets
in his pale face, he stared at her.

"Who said so?"

"She did."

"How the hell did she find out where I lived?"

"I don't know, Neal. But she's here, and she wants to see
you."

"Well, you've just got to get rid of her. Tell her I'm sick!"

"Neal, she'll hear you. Don't—*don't* be so rude. Brush
your hair and come out."

He sat staring bleary-eyed at her in a half-stupor. Suddenly he grew alert.

"All right, I'll come out," he said thickly. Diana went

back to her caller; they both sat down, and Peter stood watching them from the window, his hands in his pockets, his head dropped slightly to one side, his eyes quizzically narrowed.

Miss Dean was still beautiful, in a soft, fat, pouting way; her eyes were aggrieved.

"The way that brother of yours treats me!" she said.

"Brother?" Diana echoed, glancing at Peter.

"Neal," the actress said, with a hint of impatience at their stupidity.

"Neal——" Diana began, and stopped. It seemed such a flat thing to say. "Neal is my husband," she managed to explain. "I'm—but of course, I'm his wife."

There was a silence during which the words died slowly on the air.

"What did you say?" the actress whispered after a while.

Diana's eyes were fixed upon her. Her face was very red, and her voice had an odd, strangled note. Miss Dean had turned a ghastly yellow-green under her rouge. On her pallid face the make-up showed in dark blotches.

"Oh, no, you're not," she exclaimed, in a light, breathless voice.

"Oh, but I am."

"Diana left him, divorced him,—don't deny it," the actress accused her sharply, still in a quick, frightened whisper. "Five—more than five years ago——"

"We met last year. We were remarried," Diana explained.

They stared at each other; Diana's face hot, the other woman's livid.

"He didn't lie to me about his sister Mary?" Deirdre presently asked, in a low, controlled tone. But her hands were shaking like aspens.

Diana faced her, breathing hard.

"He has no sister Mary."

"He wouldn't lie to me like that!" Miss Dean was not

speaking to Diana. Her eyes were fixed on far space; her lower lip bitten. "He wouldn't," she repeated.

Before either spoke again, Neal came from the bedroom. He was in his big brocade dressing gown, but he had shaved, and his dark hair was as slick as it had been when Diana first had met him, in her grandmother's kitchen, so many crowded years before.

"Hello, Deedee," he said heartily. But Diana knew that he was frightened. He was like a big uneasy boy, for all his handsome bigness, as he came out.

"You've been lying to me, Neal," Deirdre began, panting. Suddenly the flanges of her nostrils spread, and there were little white dints about her mouth. "You were going to marry me, you loved me, you were making arrangements——"

She was evidently quoting. Anger choked her.

"You were married all the time," she said, gulping.

"Well——" Neal said, in a snarl. He was taken at a disadvantage, and it humiliated him. "Well, well——"

"You have no sister Mary!" Deirdre said, trembling.

"I had to tell you something, didn't I?"

"You—*what?*"

He had mumbled the phrase; he repeated it.

"Sure, you had to tell me something!" Miss Dean agreed. She began to laugh. "But what," she interrupted herself between gasps to inquire, pointing at Diana,—"what did you tell *her?*"

"I don't seem to count," Diana answered for him, in a cold, emotionless voice.

"We had a quarrel, I and Neal, at lunch at Del Monte today," Miss Dean began rapidly, confidentially, to Diana. But she did not move her eyes from Neal. "Forrest, my manager, was with us; we stayed last night at Del Monte, and everything was just like always between I and Neal. He played golf this morning, and at lunch,—we had it served at our cottage,—he began deliberately to pick a quarrel,—oh, yes, you did!—for no reason at all. I *knew* there was something in it, I *knew* he was putting something over on me. You thought I'd wait at the hotel until you came to make the peace, didn't you? You thought you could get——" Her voice rose hysterically. "You thought you could get away with it——"

Neal had remained standing, looking on wearily, tolerantly, at the squabbling women. He made no move in his own defense, unless a slight shrug might have been so construed. Diana, glancing at him, thought that he was playing very convincingly the rôle of the bored, superior male for whom two women were fighting. But she saw the hand with which he lighted a cigarette shaking.

"You ought to be horsewhipped, you dirty cad!" Deirdre sobbed.

"Neal, I think you ought to take Miss Dean somewhere, talk to her," Diana said sharply. "I don't want to hear about it! Just—just spare me hearing about it——"

"I and he were going to be married next month!" Deirdre said, catching eagerly at her sympathy.

"I'm sorry," Diana said briefly, her face white with anger and distaste. Suddenly she felt herself trembling; she felt that she was going to break.

"Looka here, both of you," Neal broke in roughly, "do you think I'm going to take it like this? Well, I'm not. I'm not going to take it!"

Miss Dean was breathing like a spent racer; her nostrils wide, the white dints showing about her mouth again.

"You looka here yourself," she panted, going up close to him. "I've got you, Neal, and this is the time you're going to pay. I've got the goods on you. I've got the checks you signed,—they're in Bill's safety-deposit box,—don't you worry! I'll have you on breach of promise,—fraud,—I'll

have you dragged through every newspaper in this country——"

"Don't pay any attention to her, Di!" Neal said. "Aw,
hell," he said to the other woman, "what can *you* do? You
give me a great big pain in the neck!"

He went quickly into the bedroom; appeared again.
Deirdre screamed, and Diana turned very pale.

"Don't be a fool, Tressady," Peter said sharply. "Put
down that gun!"

"Stay where you are!" Neal said.

"It's like in a movie——" Diana thought. "Micky here—
he might kill—oh, my God, it's a revolver——"

"I've wanted to end it for a long time," Neal was saying,
in a silky, in what was almost a singsong, voice. "Deedee
knows 'at, don't you, Deedee? But I tole you you were going
too, din I? Less all go, hay? Less *all* quit, 'n' then we can't
quarrel any more——"

"Put it down, Neal, you're frightening us!" Diana commanded. The horrible dream was going on, of Deirdre and
Neal and herself and the bright clean little revolver all shut
into this stuffy room with its cloth plants and lace curtains,
and the dull Sunday afternoon with fog at the windows
outside.

Deirdre, strangling, had stumbled to her knees, and was
dragging herself toward Neal as if in some horrible fascination; her voice was choked, deep.

"All right, kill me, but don't stand there smiling like that!
Kill me, kill me,—oh, my God, he's going to kill me——"

"Stay back!" Neal ordered her, backing himself against
the kitchen door. Deirdre, who had halfway risen, fell upon
him with a shriek; they stumbled down together. Diana
heard the sharp clean voice of the revolver; then there was
silence. Blue smoke mushroomed itself softly against the
ceiling, and nobody stirred and nobody spoke; they were all
transfixed where they stood, and Diana in the silence could

hear the clock ticking, and a little sudden trickle of water under the icebox in the kitchen, and some child far out in the street shouting, "Em'ly! *Em'ly!*"

Then Deirdre rose from the jumble that had been Deirdre and Neal, and Neal, in his quilted dressing gown, toppled slowly from the kneeling position in which her body had held him, slid to the rug, and lay still. In the deathly silence Diana could be heard drawing a sharp breath.

Not moving her eyes from Neal, she knelt by Micky, put her arm about him; the child whimpered, looking from one face to the other, and was silent again. Peter went to Neal, bent over him. Deirdre's voice was presently heard in a monotone, as if she talked to herself:

"There,—you bluffer! You bluffer, that's the time you got it when you didn't expect it! He's bluffing. He hasn't fainted. He's always doing that,—waving a pistol around. I didn't shove it onto him,—I'll swear I didn't,—he was going to kill me anyway,—didn't you hear him say he was going to kill me? He does this all the time——"

"Get a doctor, Di," Peter said in a sharp low voice. "He got himself right through the heart, I think. I think he's gone."

"Gone!" Diana said, in an echo of her own voice.

"I think so. Yep—help me get him on the bed here, you," Peter directed Miss Dean. Deirdre was at the window, her shoulder hunched against the curtains, her frightened eyes on the room.

"He's just fooling!" she said, with white lips.

"No, he's done it, this time!" Peter said. He shifted the heavy weight of Neal's relaxed body against his shoulder; somehow raised him to the couch. "Get a doctor, Di,—telephone downstairs and ask them to send a doctor.'

Diana clung to Michael, staring. She saw the blue smoke spread and rise and settle again; the sharp clean report of the revolver seemed still to be echoing through the Sunday afternoon. It was all a dream. Peter here, and Neal lying limp on the couch, with dreadful blue shadows growing about his closed mouth and sunken eyes, and this strange woman muttering and gibbering at the window.

"He wouldn't kill himself; he's bluffing!" repeated Deirdre, over and over.

"Neal—Neal, old boy," Peter was murmuring. And then, "Yep, he's done for himself all right,—he's done it this time. Di, telephone down and ask for a doctor, ask for somebody, will you?"

Diana stayed by Michael, whose soft little whimper she soothed with a hand on his round little cheek. She seemed unable to move. Her eyes did not shift from Peter and the limp figure that was growing less limp, growing to a hideous rigidity, on the couch. The lace window curtains, the cheap lamps and jars and rugs and colored lithographs, the cheap shiny red furniture she had always despised, were etched upon her consciousness like the setting of some incredible play; and with them the baby's whimper, the smell of powder, the sound of a woman hysterically talking to herself, and the murmur of the city far below and outside, under the spring fog.

THE END